PRAISE FOR *IN HER WAKE*

'Atmospheric and moving ... deserves to be a bestseller' **C.L. Taylor**

'A twisty, clever exploration of identity ... an unsettling read'
Elizabeth Haynes

'Slick, smart storytelling with real heart ... Amanda Jennings uses an
expert hand to propel the reader onwards' **Doug Johnstone**, *Big Issue*

'Hauntingly beautiful' **Clare Mackintosh**

'*In Her Wake* is a beautifully observed portrait of one woman's
quest for identity, family and the truth about her past. Thoughtful,
atmospheric and deeply immersive, it wields an almost mesmeric
power over the reader from the first page to the last. As a story about
the love and hope between sisters, parents and children it's both wise,
sensitive and intelligently drawn. I loved it' **Hannah Beckerman**

'Delicately weaves loss and grief with threads of hope in a very
human story with a strong heart' **Sarah Hilary**

'With haunting prose, perfectly formed characters and a plot that
slots together seamlessly and naturally, *In Her Wake* is the kind of
book you'll want to tell everyone you meet to read, and I've already
shortlisted it as being one of my favourite reads of 2016' **Russel
McLean**, *Herald Scotland*

'A gripping and powerful read ... will keep you turning the pages'
Simon Kernick

'In the crowded field of domestic noir it takes a very special book
to stand out, but *In Her Wake* is such a book. Beautifully written
and emotionally charged, Amanda Jennings has created compelling
exploration of self, memory and the slippery bonds that tie a family
together' **Eva Dolan**

'Amanda Jennings is a writer of rare and exceptional talent' **Steve Cavanagh**

'Amanda Jennings really hits her stride with this one. *In Her Wake* is an assured, evocative, rites of passage tale that will captivate readers of psychological suspense' **Mari Hannah**

'A haunting and compelling read, charged with perfectly observed emotion and a poetic gift for language' **Iona Grey**

'*In Her Wake* is one of those novels that you know is going to stay with you for a very long time after you finish it. Bella is a brilliantly flawed protagonist, but you root for her all the way and travel with her on every step of her journey for answers. This is credit to Amanda Jennings' excellent writing – gripping, moving and mature – everything you want in a good read. Loved it' **Louise Voss**

'Gripping and emotional, with enough twists and turns to give you whiplash, *In Her Wake* is a finely drawn exploration of identity and memory, and one woman's journey through her own shocking past' **Tammy Cohen**

'Captivating and beautifully written, *In Her Wake* explores a truly devastating and disturbing subject, yet somehow manages to leave the reader with hope. This is a subtle type of psychological thriller, a compelling tale of a shattered family interwoven with a spattering of expertly timed twists and turns. I absolutely loved it' **S.J.I. Holliday**

'I have fallen head over heels in love with this compelling and beautiful book. Already one of my favourite authors, Amanda Jennings has created something outstanding. *In Her Wake* is one of my favourite reads of all time' **Louise Douglas**

'*In Her Wake* is a captivating and compelling read. A damaged protagonist, who feels more real than any other character I've read in a while. A gripping tale of grief and rediscovery. Above all, it is beautifully written, with every twist and turn thought provoking and evocative. Amanda Jennings propels herself into my list of favourite writers – I'd read her shopping list' **Luca Veste**

'Mesmerising storytelling – a tale of love, loss and trying to belong that will connect deep within' **Mel Sherratt**

'Moving, compelling, and heartbreaking, Amanda Jennings writes beautifully about the things people do for love and how the villain isn't always the monster outside the door. I read this in a couple of sittings and was furious when real life pulled me away from the pages. Simply exquisite' **Jenny Blackhurst**

'Beautiful, seamless writing, Jennings has a magic warmth and addictive quality that keeps you reading on and on' **Lucy Atkins**

'*In Her Wake* is a moving, perceptive and beautifully written story with a devastating conclusion that will stay with you. Amanda Jennings deserves all the plaudits this book is destined to receive' **Howard Linskey**

'Star quality in Amanda Jennings' books comes from her ability to put her characters' behaviour and motivation under a microscope and magnify the darkest, most unpalatable workings of the human psyche whilst balancing a clever sympathy for the main characters' **Kerry Fisher**

'Gripping and hauntingly beautiful, with a totally unexpected twist in the tail, *In Her Wake* is simply brilliant – I loved it' **Jenny Ashcroft**

'A beautifully written, emotionally charged novel that stays with you long after you read the last page' **Jane Isaac**

'Beautiful, haunting, thought-provoking and page-turning. It will stay with you long after you finish it' **Rebecca Bradley**

'Jennings drops you into a dark, twisted and tortured world and then pulls you out again, page by page, until you find yourself in something completely beautiful and evocative' **Amanda Keats, Novelicious**

'*In Her Wake* does it all: it tells of extremes endured in the name of love in honest, searing, beautiful prose. Amanda Jennings is a consummate storyteller; she unravels layer upon layer of complexity and darkness until you arrive exhausted but enchanted into the light. It's a stunning rollercoaster of a ride' **Claire Dyer**

'*In Her Wake* is one of those rare books that touches not just on your emotions, but your soul. Never one to shy away from difficult subject matter, Jennings really puts her characters through the mill here and steps up her game, taking her prose to the next level. The style of the story is lyrical and melancholy, which suits the story perfectly as it grasps the reader in its dream-like haze, while Bella's world fragments around her. *In Her Wake* draws on strong themes of responsibility, identity and bereavement, so the characters' plights feel authentic and their motivations are believable. The haunting visuals of Cornwall and Morveren's namesake will echo in your mind long after reading. A truly exceptional book that's destined for great things' **Lucy Hay**

'*In Her Wake*, the mesmerising new psychological thriller by Amanda Jennings, shudders with suspense from the opening pages ... Jennings presents the reader with a bag of fat, wriggling worms from the outset. She shows how it is possible to take a popular theme – unearthing family secrets – and put a completely fresh spin on it. A wonderful read, which will drag your head and heart through the wringer, while all the time making you believe in mermaids and human redemption' **Vicky Newham**

'The writing is sublime, just beautiful in its simplicity. With a captivating story, who could ask for more?' **My Reading Corner**

'In Her Wake is psychologically chilling, but it is also a beautifully observed story of a journey of self-discovery. Amanda Jennings' words are alluring, persuasive and so incredibly elegant, the reader is carried along effortlessly into Bella's world. Her characters scream with realism, her settings are well observed and precise and the insight into the human mind and the power of family relationships is both unsettling and convincing ... a powerful page-turner from an author who goes from strength to strength' **Random Things Through My Letterbox**

'In Her Wake is a profoundly moving story of loss, grief, depression, acceptance, forgiveness and renewal that is beautifully written and deeply humane. Jennings dives beneath the surface of her characters to reveal heart-breaking and tragic moments of self-awareness that lead to the decisions they make, characters who have no concept of the waves of physical and emotional devastation that they will leave in their wake at the time. It's one of the most subtle and immersive psychological thrillers I've read in long time' **Pam Reader**

'I'm every so slightly speechless. This is an utterly compelling, completely addictive read that is extremely beautifully written. There are several books that are being heralded as "psychological thriller of the year" and I've read these books ... *In Her Wake* blows all of them out of the water. *This,* people, is the psychological thriller of 2016' **Reading Room with a View**

'Every now and then, I come across a book that is so perfect, and that moved me so deeply, that I doubt I'll ever be able to find the right words to write about ... The depth the author brings to her characters is really exceptional – real people, people you know, people you feel with and hurt for. This was a very special book – one that will stay with me for a long time to come. It's not often I'm lost for words, but this book was absolute perfection...' **Being Anne Reading**

'*In Her Wake* is an outstanding novel, a triumphantly tense and spellbinding story of what makes a family and how those secrets you try so desperately to keep, always find their way out, sometimes with the most tragic of consequences. Full of sharply observed emotions, complex characters and an exquisitely depicted Cornwall setting, this is easily one of the best and most powerful books I've ever had the honour of reading' **Reviewed the Book**

'*In Her Wake* is beautifully written, an emotionally stunning story that envelops you in a kind of reading madness, as you follow Bella down the rabbit hole. Distinctive, descriptive and psychologically chilling, this is bound to be one of the standouts of the year' **Liz Loves Books**

'Amanda Jennings has raised the bar and cleared it effortlessly. A truly captivating, gripping read that touched my heart. The hurt, pain and raw emotions were so vivid I could feel my chest tighten with emotion at every page turn. A book I devoured, but the story still resonating a week later' **Crooks on Books**

'Amanda Jennings is a talented author and has set a high benchmark for others to follow. Her use of powerful language and vivid descriptions results in a highly thought-provoking emotional read. I was tearful in so many places along Bella's journey of discovery and I struggled to put the book down. I know already that *In Her Wake* is going to be one of my top reads of 2016' **Off-the-Shelf Books**

'Hauntingly captivating, *In Her Wake* is a pure example of a book that is powerful in its simplicity ... this is one hell of a psychological thriller and one that once it grabs you, it will never let you go. The overriding emotional pull is quite incredible; it's as if at any moment you can expect to read the book with one eye closed and a sharp intake of breath necessary to continue, just to turn the page ... *In Her Wake* is a beautifully written book, one that is both powerful and disturbing in equal measures, a book that you wish you'd written' **Milo Rambles**

'Exquisitely painful, shockingly beautiful, and absorbing on every single level, *In Her Wake* by Amanda Jennings was stunning. Every page, which then led to every chapter, dragged me deeper and deeper into the story unravelling before me and when I finally finished and turned the last page, feeling as if I'd been thrown into a tumble-dryer and flung about a few times, I was able to exhale' **Becca's Books**

'A gripping, tense and compelling book which I was unable to put down. Covering a multitude of topics and spinning the reader round several times I highly recommend this psychological thriller which should be "huge" this year' **Tracy Fenton, TBConFB**

'This is an amazingly written book, full of "I wasn't expecting that" moments, I cried at certain scenes and laughed in some parts that I maybe shouldn't have. *THAT* is a good book. I shall be recommending it to everyone I come across' **Laura Prime**

'A rare treat – a gripping page-turner that you can't put down, with a hauntingly beautiful sense of place and masterful characterisation. I absolutely loved it' **Rachael Lucas**

'A gripping concept powers this emotional, sinuous thriller in which one woman's life is played out against what might have been' **Fanny Blake**, *Woman & Home*

In Her Wake

ABOUT THE AUTHOR

Amanda Jennings made her literary début with internationally best-selling *Sworn Secret*. Her second book, *The Judas Scar*, was optioned by a film and television production company shortly after release. She is fascinated by how people react to trauma and deal with its long-lasting effects, and also the relationships that exist within a family unit. She used to work at the BBC, but now writes full-time and looks after her three daughters and menagerie of animals. She writes a popular blog and is a regular guest on BBC Berkshire's Book Club. She enjoys running writing workshops, is a judge for the Henley Youth Festival creative writing competition, and is involved with the Womentoring Project, which offers free mentoring by professional literary women to talented up-and-coming female writers who might otherwise not have access to such opportunity. She is a regular speaker at festivals and book events, which combines her childhood love of the stage with her love of writing. She likes to keep active, preferably beside the sea or at the top of a snow-covered mountain, and when she isn't writing she can usually be found walking her dog and enjoying the peace and solitude of the great outdoors.

In Her Wake

Amanda Jennings

**ORENDA
BOOKS**

Orenda Books
16 Carson Road
West Dulwich
London SE21 8HU
www.orendabooks.co.uk

Exclusive hardback edition published by Orenda Books in
association with Goldsboro Books in 2016
B-format paperback edition published by Orenda Books in 2016
Second impression 2016

Third Impression 2016

4 6 8 10 9 7 5 3

HB ISBN: 978-1-910633-45-8
PB ISBN: 978-1-910633-29-8
ePub ISBN: 978-1-910633-30-4

Typeset in Garamond by MacGuru Ltd
Printed and bound by CPI Group (UK) Ltd, Croydon CR0 4YY

SALES & DISTRIBUTION

In the UK and elsewhere in Europe:
Turnaround Publisher Services
Unit 3, Olympia Trading Estate
Coburg Road,
Wood Green
London
N22 6TZ
www.turnaround-uk.com

In USA/Canada:
Trafalgar Square Publishing
Independent Publishers Group
814 North Franklin Street
Chicago, IL 60610
USA
www.ipgbook.com

For details of other territories, please contact *info@orendabooks.co.uk*

To my gran, who sadly passed away while I was writing this book. Cornwall was your home for nearly one hundred years. It was your true love, your passion, and this love lives on in the hearts of your family.

Thank you for inspiring me.

I dreamt vividly the night she died. I've had this dream before. In it I am running. Always running. My heart thumps in my ears. My breath comes in short, painful gasps. It is dark and cold and the trees reach out to grab at me, as if they are alive, as if they are trying to capture me with their long, twiggy fingers. Their roots are thick and hidden and I trip repeatedly. I think my feet must hurt. I look down to see that I am wearing only one slipper.

When did I lose the other?

Fear has taken hold of me now. A rising panic fills me and I begin to struggle for breath. My chest is tight, like a giant's hand is squeezing and squeezing, making each gasp impossible. It is getting darker. I must keep running. And then, just when I think it's all over, there it is, a glorious sunrise appears ahead and forces back the darkness. She is sitting, as she always does, in the pool of light on the forest floor. A little girl in a white nightie, soft, golden curls framing her pale face. I run to her and she lifts her head. When she sees me, she smiles. I wave and she waves back and then I laugh because she is wearing my other slipper. We both have one bare foot and one slipper. How funny! As soon as I laugh, the light begins to fade and so does she. I scream so loudly my lungs feel as if they might split open. I have to reach her before she melts away. But it's always too late. As I stretch my fingers out to touch her, she vanishes. My hand grasps at nothing, like catching smoke.

Then everything turns black and the ground beneath me disappears. I am falling through a void, into a pit with windowless walls that stretch up for miles, walls that are slippery with darkness and impossible to climb. I am lost forever.

This is what I dreamt the night she died.

ONE

'You should stay in the car and let me speak to him first.'

I don't reply; it isn't a question, so requires no response.

I stare out of the half-lowered window at the countryside we're passing through, the sun flickering through the trees, throwing long, dappled shadows across the single-track lane and the unruly hedgerows. I draw in deep breaths of the air I grew up with, air still scented with rain-dampened grass, a hint of the farmyard a few miles beyond, the pungent cow parsley that swamps the verges. A feeling of foreboding gathers inside me as we round the familiar bends in the road and I wait for the *tick tick tick* of the indicator that will mean we've arrived.

The car slows and turns, then draws to a halt. I wait for The Old Vicarage to appear though the parting gates. But seeing the house is too much and I quickly drop my head to focus instead on my wringing hands. David reaches over and pats my knee, a brief and perfunctory gesture designed to remind me to hold myself together. I lean against his shoulder, wondering for a moment if he might take it upon himself to turn the car around and take me away from it all.

'I always forget how beautiful it is,' he says, as he drives slowly through the gates. 'Your mother might have been nuts, but she was bloody good in the garden.'

I want to tell him not to be mean about her, not today, not with tomorrow still to get through. But I don't. Instead I say, 'Yes, she loved the garden.'

He's right, of course. It's a beautiful house. A perfectly proportioned grey stone rectory, thickly clad with ivy the colour of wine bottles, set in the middle of a magnificent garden enclosed by a high brick wall. Wild roses clamber around the front door. A Virginia creeper, now green and vibrant, but which glows a fiery red as autumn takes hold, pushes its tendrils into the eaves and guttering. There's a shabby charm about the peeling paint on the window frames and the weeds that grow between moss-patched pavers on the terrace. Inside are floorboards that have creaked forever and windows that rattle in the mildest of winds. It is a place of heady memories, memories of intense love, of bolted doors and claustrophobic loneliness, and as I reluctantly lift my head to look at it, I'm hit with wave after wave of rolling emotion. The house without her, I can't begin to imagine it.

Gravel crunches beneath the tyres as we pull up on the driveway. The trees around us seem to bow a disconsolate greeting. I see us then, me with my mother, wandering between them, my hand gripped in hers, as she taught me their names. I glance down towards the pond, at the weeping willow, its delicate branches trailing sadly in the murky water as if in mourning. The trees will miss her too.

'You'll be fine,' David says, tucking the hair that has fallen over my face behind my ear and brushing something off my shoulder. 'I'm here for you.'

I nod but don't say anything. My attention is taken by the front door, which has begun to open. My stomach churns as my father walks onto the doorstep. He stands, slightly stooped, arms limp at his sides. As we stare at each other through the windscreen, it strikes me how old he's become. When did this happen, this dramatic ageing? Was it a slow creep over decades, each day a fraction frailer, a fraction more withered? Or has it happened suddenly, in the last ten days, in the time passed since he greeted me in the hospital waiting room with nothing more than a solemn shake of his head.

I notice his maroon cardigan is pulled together on the wrong buttons. It sits skewed on his shoulders and my heart lurches. If I'd needed proof she was gone his badly fastened cardigan was it. Had she been alive, heart beating, it would have been rebuttoned with an impatient tut and a sigh as she neatened him for our arrival.

David climbs out of the car and I watch him approach the front door. He clasps my father's reedy hand between both of his and shakes it. He speaks a few words. My father gives a small, tight smile, nods, says a few words in reply. They both glance back towards me and I look away.

I'm not ready, I silently cry. I'm not ready to bury my mother.

When I look back at them, David beckons me to come, as if coaxing a timid animal from a cage. I take a breath and open the car door.

'Hello, Bella.'

My father sounds beaten. He lifts his arms towards me but then drops them. Maybe he sees my hesitation. Up close he is painfully frail. It shocks me. His eyes are faded, a pale liquid blue, the deep-purple puffiness beneath them like a pair of matching bruises. His face is gaunt and wan. My mother's death has clearly ravaged him. Neither of us speaks and I am aware of David staring at us, aware of him judging our relationship as he always does, our lack of affection, the emotional chasm between us. I force myself a step closer to my father. I should embrace him, that's the right thing to do, so in spite of my reluctance, I reach out and open my arms. For a moment or two he doesn't do anything and a self-conscious awkwardness creeps over me; but then, in one swift movement, he steps forward and grabs at me, pulls me into his body, holds me so tightly I grow rigid with alarm. He hangs on and as he does my anxiety seems to ease and I hold him back, clutch at the soft cashmere of his imperfectly buttoned cardigan, breathe him in, his musty bookish study mixed with Imperial Leather soap, the soap he's used forever. My mother and I use a different brand. Pears Glycerine. I take a kick to my stomach as I remember she's gone and that now it's just me who carries the scent of that soap.

As my father and I hold on to each other, everything else fades to nothing – the desolate willow tree, the house that looms over us, even David's silent judgement – all of it pales as the smell and touch of my father envelop me.

'I'm sorry,' he whispers, his breath warm on my neck. Then his body stiffens and that rare moment of closeness is over. He steps backwards and gives a curt nod. 'Please, both of you, do come in.'

I hesitate for a moment or two, bracing myself for the eerie quiet that pervades the space held by the grey stone walls.

Inside, the house is cool and smells of stale air and furniture polish. I feel her all around me, in the worn flagstone floor, in the reproduction oil paintings that hang on the walls, in the absence of flowers on the console table. There was never a day when there weren't flowers in the house; she'd have hated that he's forgotten to cut some, and her stern disapproval eddies around us.

David and I walk through to the kitchen as my father locks the front door, first the Chubb, then the chain, then the top and bottom bolts, which clunk loud and familiar as he slides them home. I can hear the house whispering, blaming me for her death.

I couldn't have stopped it, I want to shout. Even if I'd stayed, she'd still be dead.

It's not my fault.

The kitchen curtains are open. My stomach clenches. I should like that, I know, but I don't. It feels wrong, as if my father is somehow being disloyal. I resist the urge to close them and sit at the table. I pass the flat of my hand over the grainy wood, pausing to scratch at an ancient mark from a felt-tip pen. This is where I did my schoolwork, every day, in this very spot, moving only for maths and science, the lessons I had with Henry in his fusty, book-filled study. My mother would sit next to me, her face serious, pencil in hand, using it to point at passages in various text books, her voice calm and firm. I loved learning. I never told her I preferred Henry's science lessons, of course. She'd have been terribly hurt. She was a good teacher, I think, and nothing gave me a greater thrill than making her so pleased with my work that she'd stick a shiny gold star to the bottom of the page.

I look over at my father as he comes into the room. There is still a part of me that half expects him to break into a wide smile and say, *Guess what? It's only a little joke of mine. Your mother isn't dead at all, just a bit poorly. Don't worry yourself. She'll be down in a jiffy.* But he doesn't. Instead he takes the kettle over to the tap and I watch as he fills it. I want to tell him he's filling it too full, that it will take an age to boil, but the effort needed to muster the words is too great.

'All set for tomorrow, Henry?' asks David. 'Any last-minute things you need me to help with?'

My father's eyes stay fixed on the kettle. 'Oh, that's kind, David. But I think I'm more or less there. You've been so helpful already. She wouldn't have wanted a large affair. I've kept it simple.'

'Well, I'm here if you need anything. In a way it's good you've managed to sort it all so quickly. I think it's helpful to get these things over with and not let them drag on.'

Get these things over with? Did he mean to say that? I glance nervously at my father, but he doesn't seem to have noticed my husband's tactless choice of words; he merely nods and sets about making the tea.

Watching my father try to perform this simple task is painful. He appears hopeless as he stands in front of the pine dresser. He scans the shelves, then reaches hesitantly for a cup, which he walks to the table and deposits. Then he heads back for another. And again for a third. With three cups on the table in front of him he appears to run out of steam. I watch his confusion grow, hear him mumble that something is missing, that it looks different when she does it. A moment later a flicker of recognition crosses his face and he wanders back to the dresser, returning with a small stack of saucers, which one by one are paired with a cup. There's an extra saucer left in his hand, which apparently throws him. The kettle starts to boil noisily, spluttering steam and water all over the worktop. He turns to look at it in mild shock, then returns his gaze to his hand, perhaps hoping the redundant saucer might offer salvation of some kind.

He needs help, but I don't move. I sit there like a cold, mute statue and I loathe myself for it. It's David who places a hand on Henry's back and guides him to a chair. My father collapses into it as if he's run a marathon, shattered by trying to make three cups of tea. I turn my head away from him; I don't want to think about how difficult his life is going to be.

A few hours later, as David sits in the armchair in the living room and works his way through *The Times* crossword, I force myself to talk to my father. I find him sitting at the leather-topped desk in his study, the room where he's spent most of his time since retiring from general practice, reading medical journals and biographies from the Great War, and preparing my lessons. I try not to look at the portrait of my mother that hangs on the wall behind him. It bears little resemblance to her – far too regal, far too thin – and the look on her face, in her eyes, has always scared me.

'How are you doing?' he asks, as I close the door behind me.

'I miss her,' I say, as I sit down in the sagging armchair in the corner of the room. 'It feels peculiar without her, doesn't it? Like the house has no rudder. Does that sound strange?'

'No, not strange at all.' He leans back and rubs his face, sighing heavily. 'I should ask you, really,' he says. 'If you want to see her.'

'Sorry?'

'Her body. Do you want to – do you need to – see her one last time before the funeral? The undertaker said you could visit in the morning.'

A shot of horror passes through me as I imagine her lying dead and grey in a mortuary drawer next to other dead, grey people.

'No,' I say, barely concealing my shock. 'I don't need to see her.' I pause. 'Thank you, though.'

He nods and a film of tears glazes his eyes. My body tenses; the thought of him crying is almost as dreadful as the thought of seeing my mother's dead body. We fall into an uncomfortable, stilted silence and, in search of distraction, I let my gaze fall on the bookshelf beside me. On the second shelf are a handful of photograph albums, their spines carefully labelled with gold adhesive letters. I trace my fingers over them and select one that reads *Elaine and Henry, Summer 1977*.

I open the album and there she is. The photograph takes my breath. I touch my fingers to her face, then her hair, thick and blonde, the colour of honey. In the picture she wears it piled on top of her head, a few loose curls hanging down to brush against her shoulders. Her hair is so very different to my straggly tangle of mousy strands. I went blonde once. It was when I was twelve, after Henry had insisted I take swimming lessons, telling my mother as firmly as he could that me learning to swim was imperative and that she would have to overcome her fear of large groups. The next day, grumbling and griping, she bundled me into the car and drove to the hairdresser.

'Why aren't you cutting it, Mama?' I asked.

'If you're going to take blasted swimming lessons you'll be meeting other children. You need a good cut and some colour. Children can be so very mean. I've told you that. We want you looking your best.'

And then in we marched.

'We need highlights put in,' she said, too abruptly, to the stylist. 'Chestnut and copper. And you're to be as quick as possible.'

'It takes as long as it takes, I'm afraid,' said the hairdresser.

'Just get it done.'

My mother, who rarely went out of the house, sat nervously tapping her foot with her eyes bolted on the door, unaware of the hairdresser conspiratorially suggesting to me that blonde would be a better choice. She made blonde sound so exotic, so thrilling.

'They have more fun, you know. Apart from that mother of yours. No offence, lovey, but she could do with taking that stick out her arse and getting a bit of fun in her life, couldn't she? Not blonde *enough*, maybe.' The woman laughed and gave me a wink. 'So? Blonde?'

I shrugged slightly and nodded. 'Whatever you think,' I managed to say, through my crippling shyness.

I can still remember the pleasure of looking at my new self in the mirror. Reflected back at me wasn't a timid, quiet girl with mouse-coloured hair, but another girl, a girl with beautiful blonde hair that lifted her features and drew attention to her eyes. I turned to my mother. I expected to see her smile. But she was crying. At first I thought they might be tears of joy, but they weren't. She cried all the way home, guttural sobs that shook her body and made me worry the car would spin off the road and kill us. My mother never told me what had made her so sad, so even though I couldn't be sure it was the highlights – they were her idea, after all – I didn't ever get them again.

I recall for a moment how her hair used to feel as I twirled my fingers into it while she read to me, wishing aloud that mine was as soft.

'Well, I wish I had eyes as beautiful as yours,' she would whisper, before kissing the tip of my nose. 'Pale green, the colour of sea-glass. Just like my grandmother's. So unfair you got them and I didn't.'

Something my mother and I do share, however, is our skin, milk-white and translucent, so translucent you can see the network of blue and purple veins that pump our blood.

Though not hers anymore, I think and my stomach seizes with a fresh bout of missing.

I flick through the rest of the album and there, on the last page, is a photograph I can't remember seeing before. She's on holiday, sitting on a towel on a beach. The yellows and reds of the heat and sand are exaggerated by the seventies' camera film. She wears a white bikini, its thick belt with a black plastic hoop buckle rests on her hip. Her hair is held loosely off her face and is flecked with grains of sand. She leans back on her hands, smiling brightly, her freckled nose ever so slightly wrinkled. I carefully lift the photograph from beneath the protective film and take it over to my father.

'When was this picture taken?' I ask, laying the photo on the desk in front of him. He picks it up and squints and the faintest flash of a smile dances across his face.

'Long before you were born. In Greece.'

'She looks happy.' I trace my fingertips across her face. 'I thought she didn't like to go abroad?'

He hands the photo back to me without a word.

'I'm sorry you have to be without her,' I say, in absence of anything more suitable.

'I'll manage.'

'You'll need help with the garden. Maybe a gardener could come in once or twice a week? It would break her heart to think of it becoming neglected.'

'The garden will be fine,' he says. 'I can look after it perfectly well.'

I shake my head. 'It's not only raking the leaves and mowing the lawn, you know. I mean, you've never pruned a rose and there are hundreds of those.' I wait for him to say something but he doesn't. 'She'd hate the roses to suffer,' I say softly.

I turn my head to look out of the window. An evening haze has settled in. Night is approaching and soon it will be tomorrow.

Tomorrow we bury her.

'Bella?'

I draw the curtains closed and look back at my father. 'Yes?'

'There's something I need to say ... to tell you. It's ... important...' His voice is quiet and there's a gravity about it that feels at odds with his grief. 'I ... well...'

'Yes?' I say again, as his hesitation fades to silence.

His face has become wracked with sadness and he shakes his head. 'No ... no, not now ... It can wait.' His words, each syllable, are as heavy as lead, and his head collapses into his hands.

For a moment or two I simply sit there, waiting for him to regain himself. But he doesn't. There is no movement.

'Dad?' I ask softly. 'Are you OK?'

He doesn't respond and I stand for a moment wishing I knew what to say to him, what to do, wishing I felt able to help him.

'Would you like anything for supper?' The offer sounds thin and insufficient.

'Thank you, but no,' he says, finally raising his head to look at me. 'I'm not hungry.'

I'm shocked by the raw pain that hangs in his eyes. I don't want to be in his study any longer. I need to get out.

'Goodnight then,' I say.

He doesn't respond and I close the door behind me, feeling relief as I do. I stand outside his study for a while and find my mind wandering back to the photograph of my mother, the one on the beach. I should have pushed him harder about that. She hated the idea of going abroad. I'd always wanted to travel, and I'd been desperate to escape the walls of The Old Vicarage, to experience the world beyond. One day, on her birthday, shortly before I was due to leave for university,

I'd bought her tickets to France. She'd cooked a special meal for us and after we'd finished our apple crumble and custard, I slid the card containing my gift across the table towards her. The tickets had cost nearly all of the money in my savings account, money I'd been given by Henry instead of presents for birthdays and Christmases over the years, money I'd never had the opportunity to spend.

'Happy birthday,' I said. My stomach fizzed with adrenaline.

But when Elaine opened the card I saw her face drain of colour.

'They're for the Eurostar, Mum. We're off to France. To Paris.'

Henry stood to clear the plates without a word.

'I know you're nervous. I am too. But it'll be great. We'll go to the Louvre and visit the 'Mona Lisa'. We can walk down the Champs-Élysées and have a meal in some fancy restaurant where the waiters wear bow ties.'

She didn't speak. The only noise was the sound of Henry scraping food off the plates with a knife.

'I paid for them myself. From my savings. I want to do something together. Just you and me. Before I go to university.'

Elaine's eyes grew wide. Her body shook. I watched as her hand began scratching at her arm, her nails digging into her skin, raking over and over and over, so hard that welts and scratches began to appear.

'Mum. Stop it.' I reached for her hand, trying to still it. 'You're hurting yourself.' But still she scratched. Harder and harder. Blood seeped out of the self-inflicted wounds.

'Mum! Stop it. Please.'

Elaine looked at me as if she didn't know who I was. 'I can't go,' she said. Her voice was flat and gravelly, and shivers cut through me. 'I can't ... go.'

'It's OK,' I said. My heart hammered with growing panic. 'It was a stupid idea. Please don't do that to your arm. It wasn't supposed to upset you. I didn't think. I'm sorry.'

Elaine rounded on me with an anger I wasn't expecting.

'Promise me you won't go. Not *ever*. You can't do that to me. Promise me now.' She grabbed my hand and dug those scratching nails into me. 'Promise me, Bella!'

'Yes, I promise,' I said quickly, as her vice-like grip squeezed harder and harder. 'I promise!'

Then she pushed away from the table. Her chair clattered backwards onto the floor and she ran from the room. I looked over at Henry, who avoided my eyes as he placed the plate he was holding on to the worktop and followed her.

And there I was, left alone at the table, with only the relentless ticking of the clock on the wall to break the oppressive silence. I picked up the tickets and tore them into tiny pieces, while the walls of the kitchen inched slowly inwards as if trying to suffocate me.

TWO

Henry Campbell – 28th July 1977

'You're exquisite,' he said as he kissed her taut brown stomach, his tongue picking up the fine layer of salt left on her skin from their swim.

She laughed and reached down to run her fingers through his hair, her nails lightly raking his scalp and setting his body on fire, overwhelming him with a sudden need to be inside her.

'Mrs Campbell,' he whispered, drawing himself upwards, grazing her body with feathery kisses as he went. 'I must be the luckiest man alive.'

'Yes,' she said, looping her arms around his neck, trailing her fingertips over his shoulder blades. 'You most certainly are. You're the luckiest man who ever lived.'

They kissed again, this time with more urgency, their skin growing damp with sweat where their bodies met. The heat in the room was intense. The air still and heavy. He'd already paid far more than he could afford for the room, and the hotels with air conditioning were out of his budget. She had assured him the room in the quaint, whitewashed guesthouse perched on the cliff top overlooking the harbour was perfect, but he could see by the way her face fell ever so slightly when they arrived that the room was a little disappointing. She had smiled, of course. Told him not to be so silly. That it didn't matter. That it was about the two of them being together, and anyway they didn't need anything more than a bed. But he could tell, and it pained him.

After they'd made love, they lay tangled in the sheets, her legs, tanned and smooth, entwined with his, her honey-coloured hair soft against his shoulder.

'Do you think there's a baby inside me right now?'

Her question took him by surprise. 'What?' he said with a laugh.

She propped herself up, a hand supporting her head, and stared at him intently. 'I'm serious, Henry. Do you think it's possible? Do you think there's a child, our child, growing inside me right now?'

'Gosh, I doubt it, darling. Statistically speaking, it's highly unlikely.'

Her face fell and she snatched at the sheet, pulling it across herself as she rolled over, turning her back to him.

'Lainey?' He reached out to her, but she recoiled from his touch, shimmying herself further away from him, curling an arm over her head as if cowering.

'Hey,' he said gently, rubbing her shoulder. 'What's wrong? What did I say?'

For a moment she didn't move and then, very suddenly, she snapped her head round to face him. Her eyes were narrowed and burning. '*Statistically speaking*?'

'Well, you know, it's ... well, you've just had a period and, these things ... they take time usually.'

She shook her head with contempt and he watched tears forming in the corner of her eyes. 'Always the doctor, aren't you? I wasn't asking for medical *facts*, I was dreaming, enjoying the moment, and you *ruined* it. All you needed to do was dream with me, but you ruined it.'

He hesitated, unsure how she had gone from being consumed with love to being this upset so quickly and without apparent reason. He hadn't seen this before. In fact, this was the first time he'd seen her lose her temper. He watched her face, wondering if she might soon smile and laugh and tell him not to look so serious, that she was playing with him, but instead he saw tears rolling down the sides of her face.

'Hey, shush, shush, my angel,' he soothed. 'I'm sorry. I misread your question.' He moved over to her tentatively, wiped the tears from her cheeks with the tips of his fingers. When she didn't move away, he pulled her into him, cradling her head and stroking her hair. 'I'm sorry,

Lainey. You're right. I was thinking like a doctor, and I can see now you didn't want that. I'm a fool sometimes. And you know what? I can't think of anything more fantastic than the idea of a baby, our baby, inside you right now. What a honeymoon that would be. To arrive as two and go home as three.'

He felt her body relax and she hooked her arm over his chest. 'Oh, yes,' she whispered sweetly. 'That would be wonderful. To arrive as two and go home as three.'

His body flooded with relief and he kissed her forehead.

'It's all I've ever wanted,' she said then, her fingernail tracing a figure eight on his skin. 'A baby to care for. It's what I need, and until I have one, until I'm holding my very own child against my breast, I can never be truly happy.' She kissed his neck. 'You understand that, don't you, my love?'

'Of course,' he said softly. But he didn't and as he held her closely he tried to ignore the unease that pooled in the pit of his stomach.

THREE

The following day I am woken before eight by shafts of sunshine streaming in through the window and across the bed. For a moment or two I don't remember it's the day of her funeral, I don't even remember she's dead, but then the realisation hits and in an instant I'm re-immersed in cloying grief.

David is already up, his side of the bed barely rumpled, just a dent in the pillow where his head has been. He never sleeps past six. It's something I've had to get used to. I don't like it. Not because I care when he gets up, but because it – no, he – makes me feel lazy. He makes no effort to hide his disapproval whenever I sleep late, and by late I mean anything after seven-thirty. *Well, you've missed the best of the day*, he'll say, as he shakes his newspaper with a reproachful tut. My mother was the same. She liked me up bright and early, breakfast eaten, teeth brushed, our first lesson under way by half-past seven. I sometimes wonder what it must be like to lounge around in bed all day, mooching and daydreaming to my heart's content. Even while I was at university, I never did it. Too conditioned, perhaps, to try it. But one day, I will. One day I'll lock the door to keep him out and lie there doing absolutely nothing until it's time to go to sleep again.

I climb out of bed and walk over to the window, tying the belt of my dressing gown as I go. Dread gathers in the pit of my stomach as I look out on the day. It's beautiful. I can hear the birds singing, hidden from view in their treetop shelters. The sky is a deep cobalt blue with not a wisp of cloud in sight, and I can already feel the heat of the sun forcing its way through the single-glazed panes. The weather doesn't make sense. It should be raining. Rain would be better, rain and dark skies, a miserable down-in-the-dumps day. My mother would have liked that. She adored the rain. *Rain rinses the world of its sins, Bella. It wipes the slate clean.* I look down towards the lawn and I can see her, clippers in one hand, cut roses in the other, face turned up to the sky, eyes closed as raindrops wash over her skin.

The sun shines beats down on my back as we walk slowly and silently into the church. I note the painfully sparse congregation as I take my seat and my stomach pitches. What was I expecting? I have no idea. Certainly that there might be a few relatives present. My parents never told me why they'd become estranged from their families, but I'd hoped, naïvely perhaps, that her death might be enough to heal the rifts, if only for one day. I'd got used to not having grandparents, aunts, uncles and cousins a long time ago, but it breaks my heart to look around the church and see these duty-bound acquaintances scattered in pitiful ones and twos checking watches, looking bored. My mother didn't believe in friends. *The three of us*, she would always say, *is all we need*. But looking around the church I know now she was wrong.

I glance at my father. He doesn't cry, which both surprises me and fills me with a strange sense of relief. Instead he stares straight ahead, his hands clasped behind him, upper lip firm, his back as straight as it can be. I wonder at his lack of visible emotion. Perhaps this is due to his mistrust of religion. He never went to church despite Elaine's best efforts to make him. She was very religious, attending church every Sunday, and always leaving clothes outside our gate for the Christian Aid lady. Her visits to church were the only times I remember her willingly leaving the house. I always had to accompany her, however hard I begged to be allowed to stay home.

'God insists,' she used to say. 'He doesn't ask for much, but if you want to avoid the *Other Place* – and let me tell you, you certainly do – high-days and holidays aren't enough.'

As far as Elaine was concerned, if you had Heaven in your sights you had to show due commitment, and she despaired of Henry.

'When you're as old and grumpy as he is,' Elaine would say, buttoning up my smart black coat, 'you can decide if you're a Godless heathen, too. Until then, you're coming with me.' And off I'd go, dragging my specially polished shoes and wrinkling my nose in complaint, her hand clamped around mine as she reminded me to keep my eyes on the ground and not speak to a soul.

I begin to cry when the music starts and once I start I know I'm not going to stop. David leans close and tells me to be quiet. I nod through my tears as I try to stifle the sobs.

After the service David drives us behind the hearse to the crematorium. He advised my father against a funeral car.

'I can take us, Henry. No need to go to the expense of a second car.'

I lean my head against the window, my eyes sore and puffy, and wish I'd been more involved in organising the funeral. The whole thing feels pared down. My father even decided against a wake. Unnecessary, he said, not least because she hated the thought of people in the house, which I suppose is a valid point.

'Can I get you anything?' David asks, loosening his tie as we walk into The Old Vicarage after it's all finished.

'No, thank you.' I stoop to bolt the bottom lock then turn the Chubb as my father walks upstairs without a word. 'I think I'll go for a walk in the garden.'

'Without a sweater?'

'It's not cold—'

'You need a sweater. Wait here. I'll fetch one for you.'

I used to complain about him fussing so much, but he'd tell me it was his way of loving me, that I was lucky to have someone who cared, and in the end it became easier to let him fuss than try to battle him. And anyway, she'd always done everything for me, so really it wasn't so difficult to accept. Sometimes I want to scream at him, to tell him how claustrophobic I feel, but I hate it when he gets angry, when his face closes down and he glares silently, so most of the time I give in.

'Fine,' I say. 'I'll take a sweater.'

'Good,' he says with a smile. 'I'm glad I'm here to look after you. You're no good at it yourself. In fact, I'll grab one too; I'd like a breath of air.'

'Do you mind if I go alone?'

'You need company. I—'

'I'll be OK,' I say quickly. 'I won't be long.'

He looks doubtful.

'Please?'

I breathe a sigh of relief when he grudgingly nods. I let him fetch me the sweater and then I thank him as I put it on, and quickly slip outside before he changes his mind.

Clouds of midges hang in the air and the hollow calls of wood pigeons ring over the stillness. I walk across the lawn and up to the oak tree. This is my father's favourite place. Years ago he made the wooden bench that half-surrounds the trunk. It took him a month of weekends. Such care he took. I watched him from the window of my room, transfixed by his banging, shaping, sanding, and, every now and then, smoothing his hand over the wood, caressing it with love. Once I saw him asleep beneath the tree. I'd heard shouting the night before, angry shouting, crying from my mother, and then the back door slamming shut. In the morning I woke and caught sight of him through my window, curled up, hands wrapped around his body. It was summer, but I still remember thinking it must have been a pretty bad argument for him to want to sleep outside. He didn't even have a pillow.

I sit on the bench. The branches of the oak tree sway in the mottled light above my head, its leaves rustling in gentle, ancient whispers. I scuff a tiny mound of worm casts with the toe of my shoe and turn my face up towards the canopy of the oak. I wish I'd stayed away from the crematorium. The funeral director said we didn't need to be there, but it had seemed wrong to let her go alone. It was by far the worst part of the day, clinical in its coldness, with fluorescent lighting, wooden chairs in uneven rows and a coarse carpet the colour of burnt oranges. I'd had to turn my face into David's shoulder as the red velvet curtains opened up to swallow her in a slow, onerous gulp. I couldn't stop imagining her being spat out the other end, nothing left but a handful of smouldering ash and stubborn slivers of bone that refused to incinerate.

My thoughts are interrupted by a distant cough. I look down in the direction of the noise. My father is making his way across the lawn towards me. I raise a hand in subdued greeting. He doesn't acknowledge me in return, but continues to trudge nearer, the weight of the world on his fragile shoulders. I wish we had a better relationship. It would be nice to be united in our grief, rather than isolated by it. Despite the odd moments when we've been comfortable in each other's company – biology and maths lessons, primarily, when his face would light up and there'd be excitement in his voice – we've never been close. I suppose, looking back on it, my mother never gave us the space to do so. If I needed anything it was she who was there for me. Henry and I circled around her as if she were the sun, orbiting separately, yet both of us drawn to her. That was just how it was. Her family: claustrophobic, reclusive, dependent. I wish I knew what to say to pull us together now, but perhaps that's not possible, perhaps we're too old, too set in my mother's ways. I reassure myself that the fond respect and detached love we have for each other is sufficient, that when our separate grief has ebbed, it will be enough to bring us comfort.

My father sits beside me. I pick up a fallen leaf, brown and skeletal, and crumble it between my fingers in silence. His brow is furrowed with deep, craggy lines and his eyes, clear and rimmed with red from private tears, appear otherworldly.

'Am I disturbing you?' he asks.

'Not at all.'

'Good.' He clears his throat. 'Bella...'

'Yes.'

'I ... I need to talk to you...' But then, like yesterday in his study, he stops himself.

'What is it?'

'Oh.' He seems caught off guard. 'Yes ... I...' His voice trails away and his attention is caught by something unseen and far away. Then he turns back to me. 'How's work?'

'Work?'

'Yes, work,' he repeats. 'Is everything going well at work?'

I know it isn't what he wants to ask me but I answer as if it is. 'Work's fine, thank you. Not too much drama in a university library.'

'Good.' He hesitates. 'That's ... good.'

I wait for a few moments in case he manages to say whatever it is that's on his mind. But he doesn't. I won't push him. I'm sure when the sadness of my mother's death has lessened he'll be able to tell me.

I glance up at the branches above us. A breath of wind blows through them, sending the shadows of the leaves dancing over me. 'It's nice here, isn't it?' I say. 'Under this tree. I can see why you love sitting here. It's very restful.'

The noise that escapes him makes me jump. It's a strange, plaintive mewling, as if he is physically hurting from an unseen wound. His face has crumpled. His eyes are tightly closed, tears escaping them as his head shakes imperceptibly.

'Dad? Oh, Dad.' I take hold of his hand. 'It will get easier, I promise. It doesn't feel like it, but it will. You'll be alright. We'll both be alright.'

He squeezes my hand then pulls away as he tries to hold himself together, tries to contain the outpouring of emotion. He shakes his head again then opens his eyes and turns to me. 'She loved you,' he says, his voice a quiet rasp. 'She loved you very much.'

'I loved her too.'

'And I'm sorry for the terrible mistakes we made.' He grips the edge of the seat with both hands as if he's trying to draw strength from the very wood itself.

'There were no mistakes. I was happy. I promise you. In the most part, I was very happy.'

He seems to shrink further into himself and wearily rubs his face with his hands. 'I wish I was a stronger man,' he whispers.

A sudden gust of wind blows from nowhere and sends the branches above us into an agitated flurry. I wrap my arms around my body as a shiver passes through me.

What is it they say – someone's walked over my grave?

'You know, if you want to come back with us for a few days, you're welcome. If you think you'll be lonely. It's a big house for one person.' I can't imagine wanting to stay here alone. Too many things that would stop me from sleeping. The creaks of cooling timbers, the terrifying staircase that leads up to the attic room, the shadowy corners and damp walls that seem to breathe.

And now the ghost of my mother.

He doesn't appear to have heard me. He sits back and smoothes both hands down the length of his thighs. Then he stands.

'Forgive me.'

At least I think that's what he says. His voice is so thin and quiet, I can't be sure.

I watch him shuffle back down towards the house. If it's possible, he appears even older than he did yesterday, even more withered and frail, as if another unexpected gust of wind might lift him into the sky like a kite.

I sit beneath the oak tree until the chill in the air becomes too much. Back in the kitchen, I scoop up my mother's cat and push my face into his soft fur. There has always been a longhaired grey cat in the house. This one is version number three. I sit down and begin to stroke him, but he refuses to purr and soon jumps off my lap and skitters out of the room.

'You were longer than you said you'd be,' David says, as he appears in the doorway.

'My father joined me. He wants to tell me something but can't seem to get the words out. Has he spoken to you?'

David shakes his head. 'It's going to be hard for him. She was a strong personality.' He touches the backs of his fingers to my cheek. 'I'll heat you a mug of milk while you shower and wash your hair.'

By 'strong personality', my husband means difficult. I often tell him he just has to accept the way we are. He might think my parents are different, peculiar, but isn't that like all families? Doesn't every family appear strange to the outside world? I try not to let David's disdain bother me. He and my mother never saw eye to eye, but then I knew they never would. Although they both forced smiles every time they were together, the mutual distrust was palpable. They were in constant competition over who knew what was 'best' for me. Being in the same room as them, simultaneously trying to be both loving daughter to her and adoring wife to him, was exhausting.

On my way upstairs I pass my father's study. The door is closed, a crack of light visible beneath it. I press my ear to the door and hold my breath as I try to listen, but I can't hear anything.

'Goodnight, Dad,' I say through the door. 'I'm tired. I'll see you in the morning. Sleep well.'

I wait for a reply, but it doesn't come. I should go in, but the thought of having to face his desperate sadness and shackled tongue again stops me, so I turn and walk as quietly as I can upstairs. The house watches each step I take. When I reach the top I turn towards the spare room. I lower my eyes as I pass the staircase that leads to the attic room. My heartbeat quickens. Narrow and dark, the top in blackness, as if the treads are never-ending. I won't look up. It doesn't matter how much I reason with myself, tell myself it's only a staircase to a room that's filled with boxes and broken furniture and unwanted books, that every house has a space for these things, and it's only an attic, it still scares me.

David is already propped up in bed by the time I get out of the shower. My skin tingles from the burn of the hot water and it feels good to have clean hair, to wash away the tightness on my face left over from crying. I climb in beside him, wriggling out of my towel when I'm safely beneath the duvet. Even after eight years, I am self-conscious being naked around him. He has this way of looking at me that unnerves me, like a greedy child staring at a chocolate cake. I should be flattered, I know. I wish I wasn't so uptight, so prudish, that I was the type of girl who could strip off and run through the rain without a care in world. I reach for the mug of milk he's left on the bedside table. He closes his book and rests his hand on my shoulder.

'My beautiful thing,' he says. 'I have to say, I'm glad you've put some weight on. You were getting too skinny. And you know what I say...' He runs his hand down over my chest. I try not to tense, and stare intently at the patch on the ceiling where the paint is discoloured by ancient damp. 'Never trust a skinny woman. There's something wrong about a woman who doesn't like food. No passion.' He bends his head and kisses my breast. His greying hair is soft against my skin, his day's growth of stubble is rough. I put the mug down on the bedside table then shift over on my side, moving myself away from his lips.

'Do you think my funeral will be like hers?' I ask, hoping to divert his attention.

'In what way?' he says, as he presses his body into mine.

'No real friends; just you, my father, and a handful of unmoved others.'

He laughs.

'Is that funny?'

'I'm sorry. No.' He hooks a finger under my hair and exposes my neck, which he kisses. 'It won't be like that.'

'How do you know? I mean, who would come?'

'Jeffrey and Barbara for a start.'

'That's because they're your friends. Not mine.'

'Don't be ridiculous. We're married; they're *our* friends. Anyway, you work in the college library, Jeffrey's your employer. And some of the college staff, they'll come.'

'They'll be the unmoved others.'

He rolls away from me, his face clouded over. 'Bella. You're twenty-eight. Stop worrying about your funeral. You'd be better off worrying about mine. I'm forty-seven in three months.' He makes a groaning sound. 'God, forty-seven. How bloody awful is that? Lucky I've got you to keep me young, isn't it?'

'Why don't I make friends, David? I've never had any. My best friend, no, my *only* friend, was imaginary. How tragic is that?'

'It's not tragic at all. Anyway, you don't need friends. You have me.' He kisses me again. 'And lots of children have imaginary friends.'

'Did you?'

He laughs. 'No, of course I didn't.'

And then his face gets that look and I know he wants sex. He pushes his lips against mine, his tongue prising my mouth open as he moves his hand beneath the duvet and between my legs.

'Do you mind if we don't,' I say, trying to move myself away. 'I don't feel like it, not after today.'

'But I'd like to. And you don't mind, do you?' He rubs it against my thigh. His breath is hot and wet on my neck. 'Don't worry, I'll be quick.' And then he parts my legs and rolls on top of me and I bite down on my lip as he pushes himself into me.

FOUR

Henry Campbell – 12th February 1983

Henry rubbed the sweat off his neck with a towel and leant back against the squash court wall with a happy laugh.

'Good game, Fraser,' he panted. 'Shame you still can't beat me though.'

'Shut up, I nearly had you in the third and if you'd not barged me I'd have taken it.'

'You should have called a let then.'

'What? And have you call me a pansy for the rest of the day? I don't think so.'

Henry laughed. 'You know me too well.' He stood and began packing his things into his squash bag. 'How's Mum?' he asked carefully, without catching Fraser's eye.

'She'd like a call from you. She doesn't know what she's done. Why won't you go and see her?'

Henry didn't answer immediately. He hoisted his bag onto his shoulder and moved towards the court door. 'It's not like that. I'm not avoiding her. We haven't found a date that suits all of us, that's all.'

'She also wants to know what your plans are for Christmas.'

Henry sighed. 'Jesus, Fraser. It's only September.'

'I know, but come on, Hen, you know what I'm talking about. Yes, it's early, but she wants to make plans, and so do I, to be honest. Abby and I will take the children to Pembroke to stay with Abby's folks if you're not going to be with us. They've said Mum and Dad can come too, but Mum won't say yes until she knows what you and Elaine are doing. I know Elaine won't want to come to my in-laws, but you're both welcome, of course. Anyway, if you want to come to Mum and Dad's, we'll say no to Abby's parents. It's been ages since we've spent Christmas with you.'

'Fine. I'll talk to Lainey on the weekend. I'll let you and Mum know on Sunday. Is that OK?'

'Sure. Thanks. Really hope you'll be with us. We miss you.' Fraser patted his brother's shoulder. 'Want to grab a drink?'

'I should get back.'

Fraser laughed and shook his head. 'She really does have that leash tight, doesn't she?'

'Shut up, Fraser.' Henry bristled at his brother's comment.

'Well, she does. Women shouldn't tell their husbands what to do all the time. You've got to stand up to her. Grow some balls, man.'

'Will you leave it? For God's sake, you have absolutely no idea what we're going through.'

'Look, all I'm saying is I'm sure you can have a drink with your brother every now and then without your wife throwing some sort of crazy fit.'

Henry took a breath to steady himself. Getting cross with Fraser wasn't going to solve anything. Truth be told, a drink with his brother was exactly what Henry felt like. But Fraser was right. If they went for a drink, by the time he got home, she'd be raging. 'She's my wife. I love her and I'm going home because I want to, not because she tells me to. I don't want you to speak about her like that again. Do you understand?'

Fraser and Henry stared at each other, both of them tense, both prickling with truths they wanted to tell.

It was Fraser who stepped back first. 'Sure, Hen. No problem. I just thought we could have half an hour for a drink. That's all.'

The tension in Henry's body eased 'I know. Look, things at home are just a bit tough at the moment.' He sighed heavily. 'Lainey had another miscarriage, if you must know. She's not taking it well and she needs me right now.'

'I see. I'm sorry about that. That's bad luck. Is there anything I can do?'

Henry laughed bitterly. 'No, Fraser, unless you can make my wife stop miscarrying, then there's nothing you can do.'

Henry saw his brother's face fall and was stung by guilt. Christ, it wasn't as if it was Fraser's fault. It wasn't anybody's fault. All the specialists they'd seen over the last five years had cleared them both of blame. There was nothing wrong with either of them. Nothing to explain the devastating losses with which she was having to cope.

When Henry got home he found her crumpled in a heap on the kitchen floor. Her head was bowed, her mane of hair falling over face, legs bent at the knee, hands clutching a disintegrating piece of kitchen roll sodden with tears. When she looked up at him, he saw her face was raw from crying, puffy and blotchy, her usually porcelain cheeks streaked with smeared mascara.

'Oh, Lainey, sweetheart. I'm here now. I'm home.'

'Where ... have you ... been?' she asked weakly, her words coming between snatched breaths.

'I told you,' he said, as he sat beside her, putting his arm around her shoulder and pulling her close to him. 'I went to the club for a game. You remember?'

'I tried to call you at work. I wanted you to cancel it and come home, but the receptionist said you'd left already. It was only four-thirty. How come you'd left already? And then I thought you'd be home, but you didn't come. I ... I thought you'd come ... home.'

'My last patient cancelled, sweetheart. Roger said I could go – he said he'd stay on to see anyone who showed up.'

Her eyes narrowed and a chill set in. He braced himself. 'Were you with Fraser?'

The diamond edge to her voice cut through him. He would need to choose his words carefully if he was to avoid one of her turns. He took a breath to steady himself. 'Yes, I was with Fraser. We arranged the game weeks ago. We played squash. But I came straight home.'

'I can't believe you didn't cancel the game! Our baby died seventeen days ago. Our baby *died*, Henry! How could you not cancel? You know how upset I am. You *know* how difficult this is for me. You know ... you ... *know*, Henry.'

'I'm here now, Lainey. I'm here now and everything is going to be alright.'

'You know what, Henry?' She spat the words out as she got to her feet, then she stood looking down on him, arms crossed tightly. 'Everything is actually pretty far from all *right*. Nothing is *right*. I'm going through all this and you can't even cancel a game of squash? I don't even know you. I mean, how can you play a game of squash at this time? Do you have any heart at all?'

'Lainey, I...'

'Shut up, Henry. *Shut up*! You know how much I wanted this baby. I thought you wanted it too.'

'I do.'

'You don't! If you did there'd be no way you'd meet up with your brother for a game of squash when another of our children has died. You'd be too *sad*. You'd be too *sad* to have a fun game of squash with your brother.'

Henry stood and put his hands on her arms. He spoke softly. 'I'm sorry. I really am. I should have realised you were too fragile to leave.' He rubbed her arms, rhythmically, softly, watched her features for signs of softening. Her eyes stayed cold as she considered his words, flicking back and forth, searching his face for God knows what. At last he saw a slight crack in her steeliness, and he breathed out, took hold of her hands. She moved forward and rested her forehead on his shoulder.

'Will you hold me, Henry?' she whispered. 'Just sit on the sofa and hold me in the dark until I fall asleep? I feel desperate. I picked up a knife while you were out. I held it against my wrists and thought how easy it would be to end it. All this pain. Will you hold me?'

'Of course I'll hold you. All night if you need me to.'

She nodded and then stepped back from him. Then she smiled and ran her hands through her hair in an attempt to tidy it up and he saw she was back. Her face had relaxed. The episode was over. 'So how was Fraser?' she asked. 'Was he well? And Abby and the children?'

'He was fine,' he said, trying to make his voice light so nothing could be read into his words. 'It was good to see him. He asked about Christmas.'

'And you told him we're going away? You told him we're going to the Canaries for some sun?'

'It wasn't the right moment. But I will.'

'You must. You need to tell him. I need rest, Henry. A break and some sunshine. Just you and me together; we need to be alone. The last thing I need is to be stuck in your parents' house with those awful, screaming boys. They're a nightmare and you hate them. Remember how much you hate them? So, you'll tell Fraser? And your mother? The last thing I need is more stress. Honestly, Henry, I was so close to hurting myself.'

'I'll tell them tomorrow.'

'You promise?'

'Yes.'

He leant forward and took her in his arms. He felt so helpless. Why couldn't she just stay pregnant? She needed a baby more than anything else. If she had a baby he'd get his wife back. She would return to normal and they would be happy again.

FIVE

I wake feeling disloyal. Restful sleep seems disrespectful to my mother, all ash and bits of unburnt bone in her cold brass urn.

David is at the kitchen table eating toast and marmalade and reading the paper.

'We'll head home this morning,' he says.

'Don't you think we should stay with my father?'

'We're on the end of a telephone if he needs us.' He looks at me. 'We should give him some space, Bella. I'll drive you back here in a week or two.'

'When do you want to leave?'

He glances at his watch. 'Within the hour. I thought I'd pop to the supermarket first and stock up for him. There's no food at all in the house and we don't want him to starve, do we?'

'No,' I answer. 'We don't want him to starve.'

I call for my father, first in the house and then out of the back door in the direction of the oak tree, but there's no answer. I knock on his bedroom door, wait for a moment then peep in. He isn't there, he's up already, bed made. I hover on the threshold. The room smells of her and is filled with her belongings – her slippers at the foot of the bed, her makeup and perfumes lined up on the mantelpiece, her book and reading glasses waiting patiently on the bedside table – all of them trying to create the illusion she's alive. I look at the chair in the corner of the room, a small tartan armchair that Henry used to carry through to my bedroom when I was ill. My mother would sit beside me all night, stroking my head with cool flannels if I had a temperature, holding my hair back if I was sick, soothing me with lullabies and rocking me. I remember waking from fitful sleeps, hot with fever, and she'd be there, right beside me, soft whispers of reassurance.

I back out of the room and walk along the corridor. I pause at the foot of the attic staircase.

'Dad?' I call up tentatively. I listen hard but can't hear anything. He could be up there. Maybe sorting out some stuff. I put my foot on the first step but hesitate. My heart thumps. I remember her screaming at me when she found me sitting outside the locked room. She screamed so loud I thought my ears would burst. She ran up the stairs, two at a time, and grabbed my arm. She pulled it so hard I cried out in pain.

'Don't you ever go up there, do you hear me?' she said after she pulled me down and we were sitting together in the kitchen. 'It's dangerous up there. It's full of furniture that would fall on top of you and crush you, you silly girl.'

Later I remember Henry moving my shoulder in circles. It hurt so much I fainted and when I woke up he gave me chocolate.

I tell myself not to be so pathetic and I walk up the staircase. I pause at the door. There is no handle. Just a square hole where the handle should thread. I hold my breath and listen. No sound.

'Dad?' I say again. 'Are you in there?'

But there's no reply.

'No sign?' David asks, as I come down the stairs.

'I suppose he might be out walking.'

'Yes, more than likely.'

'Though I've never known him go out for a walk before.'

David stands and stretches his back. 'Well, you go and pack our bag while I do this shop. I might be a couple of hours. The seal's degraded on the shower head, that's why it was dripping. I'll fix it but I need a few bits from the DIY store.' He walks over and takes hold of my shoulders. 'And don't look so worried; I bet you he's back before I am.'

I wait until David leaves and then shout for my father again, unable to keep the panic from my voice. 'Dad! Henry! Where are you!'

I walk down the hallway to his study. The door is closed. He could have fallen asleep in his chair. He sometimes does that, and without my mother to marshal him upstairs to bed, it's possible he's stayed there all night.

I reach for the handle and turn it slowly. I push the door open. It's dark inside. The heavy curtains are pulled shut and there's a strong smell, warm and sweet with alcohol and damp. I walk over to the window and pull the curtains open. The room floods with light.

When I turn around, my heart stops.

'Dad?' I whisper. I want to scream, to run, but I'm frozen.

My father is at his desk. He is slumped back in his chair, mouth gaping as if calling out to someone. His skin is bleached. His eyes are wide and glassy and stare at nothing. Two deep gashes run up his forearms from each withered wrist and beneath his flaccid hands is a large pool of blood as dark as molasses. Beside it, lying bloodied and quiet, is a knife that belongs in the kitchen.

SIX

'Oh my days! Who'd have thought he loved her that much?' says Miss Young, fanning herself as the colour returns to her cheeks.

Miss Young is the first poor soul I run into – quite literally – as I stumble out of the gate and down the lane, screaming David's name over and over as I go.

She does exactly what's required of someone in this type of situation, she takes hold of my hand and listens intently, allowing her look of calm concern to give way to animated horror as I explain what's happened in garbled words that barely make sense.

As I finish telling her, my breathing becomes rapid and shallow. My head spins and my body starts to shake uncontrollably as it succumbs to shock.

'Come on, dear,' Miss Young says. 'You need a little sit down.'

She walks me back towards the house with her arm wrapped tightly around my shoulders. I don't want to go into the house. I want to be a million miles away from it. But she insists, tells me I need to stay warm, that I need to sit down, and once we're inside, she settles me on the sofa in the living room, wrapping a woollen throw around my shoulders.

'You sit here while I check the study.'

She leaves the room and I listen to her footsteps in the hallway, then her smothered gasp of disbelief and some urgent mutterings. When she returns to the living room, she goes straight to the telephone.

'The police, please ... An ambulance? Well, you can send one if you want, dear, but I think it's a bit horse, stable, bolted, because he's definitely dead, no doubt about it and I'm no doctor.'

Then she offers me tea, sweet tea, that great British cure-all, suitable for a range of situations including, as far as Miss Young is concerned at least, the discovery of a father's suicide the day after a mother's funeral.

'I'll make a pot,' she says, wrapping the throw tighter around me. 'I'm sure those nice young boys will fancy a cup when they get here.'

I grip the mug of tea but don't drink it. None of my muscles work. All I can do is stare ahead, concentrating every bit of energy I have on keeping my father's lifeless body out of my thoughts. I become aware of cars pulling up in the driveway. Of muffled voices. People moving to and from the study. The crackle of radios. A woman outside laughing.

Miss Young sits beside me and rhythmically rubs my knee. I resist pulling away from her, though the contact feels uncomfortable.

'What a thing,' she mumbles. 'What a very thing indeed.'

Miss Young is the vicar's housekeeper, has been for years and, in the absence of a vicar's wife, was a regular presence in the church. My mother once mused that there had to be more to the story, though at the time I didn't know what she meant. On the few occasions I'd met Miss Young she insisted I call her Suzie. But I always use Miss Young; Suzie feels too familiar and doesn't suit her at all.

The shadow of a policeman looms over us. I look up at him and in an instant my heart starts to thud and my stomach fills with butterflies, as a deep-rooted fear takes hold.

'I'd like to talk to you now, Mrs Bradford. Would that be OK?'

'David,' I whisper. 'I need David.'

'That's her other half, dear,' Miss Young adds helpfully. 'He nipped out a while back. I'm sure he won't be long. I'll leave you two to talk.'

She stands to leave, but I snatch at her hand. 'Please. Please stay with me,' I say, my voice catching in my constricted throat.

The policeman, a tall, thickset man in his late fifties with a lilting Welsh accent, asks question after question after question. I manage to give a variety of one-word replies and non-committal shrugs, and when we're finished he presses the number of a suicide helpline into my hand. I can't help but feel it's a bit late for that now.

I close my fingers around the card and look out of the window, at the trees standing rigid and tall as if guarding the house.

'Right, I should get going now, really.' The policeman appears reluctant to leave, hovering on the spot. 'Will your husband be home soon?'

'Don't worry about her,' says Miss Young over my head. 'I'll keep the tea flowing until Mr Bradford gets back.' Miss Young pats my knee briskly as if to say with a steady flow of tea and her company I'd be right as rain in no time.

'That's kind of you, Miss—' He pauses, trying to recall her name.

'Suzie,' Miss Young says. 'Everyone calls me Suzie.'

The policeman clears his throat. 'The guys next door will need a while with the...' He stops himself and glances at me. 'With Dr Campbell. If we need to talk to you again, Mrs Bradford, we'll call you.'

I nod but don't speak; I'm starting to feel as if I'm stuck in a television programme, a bizarre reality game show where everyone else is an actor and I'm the unwitting star, like *The Truman Show*, but crueller.

The policeman leaves and I relax a fraction. As soon as he closes the door, Miss Young reaches into the pocket of her skirt, then sits beside me on the sofa. She is holding a letter.

'I found this before the police arrived,' she says. 'It was on Dr Campbell's desk and I slipped it into my pocket. Things like this are best kept private. You read it when you're ready, dear. Maybe another cup of tea first? What do you think?'

Miss Young places the envelope on my lap.

'I'll go and feed that cat of yours to give you some space. Call if you need me. Lord only knows what it says.'

I regard the letter as if it holds anthrax. He's used his Smythson of Bond Street. It's his very best writing paper and was given to him by a well-to-do patient years and years ago. He keeps it on a high shelf in his study, in a special leather writing box, and only uses it for the most important occasions. The last time, as far as I'm aware, was when he wrote a letter of condolence to his mother, my unknown grandmother, following notice of his father's death.

Seeing my name written across the light-blue envelope in his immaculate copperplate handwriting rams the reality of what's happened down my throat. I pick up the letter and try to imagine what it says, what reason he might give to explain what he's done. A part of me agrees with Miss Young, surely he didn't love her *that* much?

I slide my finger along the length of the envelope and tear it open as neatly as I can. Inside is a single sheet of writing paper with a newspaper cutting, brittle and yellowed with age, folded within it. I place the cutting on the sofa beside me and take a deep breath as I unfold the letter.

SEVEN

Henry Campbell – 2nd June 2014

He closed the kitchen door behind him, then walked purposefully to the window. He drew the curtains. Ran his fingers down the length of the material. Arranged the folds to hang evenly, as she liked them. Closed curtains. Bolted doors. The tyranny of his wife's neuroses.

What kind of suffocating fog had he been walking around in? What kind of man had he become? Where and when did it go so very wrong? At what point should he have stopped it all and walked away. But how could he have? There was only her. There was only ever her.

Henry Campbell breathed deeply as he reached for a saucer and then a can of cat food from the cupboard. He fed the cat, who purred happily as he tucked into his supper.

Henry remembered the first time he had seen her. She was sitting at the bar in a pub near the medical school, elegant, out of place, too classy to be there. She was drinking a cocktail of some description, idly playing with the straw while the man she was with spoke words that Henry could tell bored her. She wore a red dress that clung to her body as if it were painted on. Her hair hung to one side, exposing her neck, soft and pale, not a blemish on her skin. Oh, that curve, the line of her, calling to him, begging him to touch his lips to its softness.

Henry and his group were celebrating a birthday. There was a lot of raucous drinking, as was the case whenever they went out, but as his fellow medical students laughed and joked and played ridiculous drinking games, all he could do was watch her. He couldn't tear his eyes away. He saw her check her watch. Saw her push the man's hand off her leg when he had the audacity to touch her. Saw her sigh and twice look over her companion's shoulder. There was only her. Everything else in the pub was a blur.

He stood and excused himself from the table.

'I'm sorry, gentlemen, I've got something I need to do.'

And then he'd walked up to her, bold as brass, and said: 'I don't mean to interrupt you, but there's a woman outside who asked me to say that you need to come immediately. There's been an emergency.'

'Really?' she said, craning her neck to see out of the window.

'What's going on?' asked her companion. 'What emergency?'

'It's for your own good,' Henry said to her. He smiled and bowed his head a little. 'The emergency, I mean. You leaving now. To attend to the emergency. It's for your own good.'

'My own good?'

'Yes. Consider me your rescue service. Would you like me to take you to her?'

'Well, actually, my good man,' said her companion quite genially, 'if anybody's going to take her, it should really be me.'

But the girl was smiling up at Henry.

'You'll come?' he asked and held out his hand.

She stared at it for a moment or two and then nodded. 'Yes,' she said. 'I will.'

That was the beginning. The beginning of it all. That smile, the curve of her neck, the control she had over him from the first moment. Her utter power. All the sirens rolled into one. This was how it all began. What weakness within him allowed her to bewitch him?

And now she was gone.

He had tried to tell Bella what she needed to hear, but he couldn't get the words out. They stuck in his throat with the bile and the shame and the guilt.

Henry opened the drawer and looked down at the neat row of knives. He ran his fingers over their handles and then selected the carving knife. He went to the drinks cupboard and took down the bottle of single malt and a crystal tumbler. He filled the glass to the rim and then returned the bottle to the cupboard. He stroked his hand down the back of the cat, who purred and blinked slowly up at him, then he carried the glass and the knife through to his study and closed the door. He placed the knife and the glass on his desk, went over to the shelves, and reached up for his letter-writing box. He passed his fingers over the leather, aged and cracked. He opened the lid and removed a single sheet of paper and an envelope, then he replaced the box on the shelf.

Henry sat at his desk and wrote the words he hadn't managed to say. And when he'd finished writing, when the letter was sealed in the envelope, he opened his top drawer, took out a packet of painkillers and prised all twelve from the silver foil. Then he knocked back the handful of pills with the glass of whisky and turned off the table lamp. He waited until the pills began to take effect and then he felt around the surface of his desk for the knife.

'Forgive me,' he whispered into the darkness. 'Forgive me.'

EIGHT

My dear child,
Firstly, I must apologise for what you have found. I am a coward. This
has never been in doubt. A coward and also weak. So very weak. Even
yesterday, trying to talk to you, this weakness kept me silent, and now I
have no option. No choice. I cannot keep the truth quiet any longer.
   And I cannot go on.
   I have struggled with this from the start. Questions. So many
questions without answers. So many whys. Because Why? is the only
question that matters. I have no answer to the Why? No answer that
makes any sense. Writing this now, seeing my own hand form the letters,
it's all I can hear.
   Why? Why?
   Why...
   Elaine and I are not your real parents. We didn't adopt you and we
didn't foster you. Your real mother is a woman named Alice Tremayne.
Her address is, or was, at least, 4a, Mount Sinai Road, St Ives,
Cornwall. Whether or not she still lives there, I cannot say.
   I cannot answer your questions. I cannot even begin to try. But please
know that Elaine loved you deeply and in her own twisted mind she
believed she had your best interests at heart.
   Forgive me.
   I wish you peace,

Henry Campbell

The image of Henry Campbell's mutilated body sticks in my mind as my emotions swarm like bees.

I push my fingers into my temples and try to process his words. It makes no sense. I cast my eyes over the newspaper article, dry and brittle, but it doesn't help. None of it makes any sense.

He's lying.

Of course he is. He has to be.

But part of me knows he isn't. Part of me is nodding. Agreeing. Saying, *Ahhhh, this explains so much!* My brain is pounding. It races from recollection to recollection. I feel faint. Debilitated. It's all too much. Elaine's death. The funeral. Finding Henry in that state. And now the contents of this envelope. A single sheet of writing paper and an aged newspaper cutting that – if true – change everything.

He has to be lying.

But why would he?

David runs into the living room and I quickly thrust the letter into my back pocket before he sees it. His face is contorted with shock as he opens his arms and comes towards me.

'My darling thing,' he says. 'My darling, darling thing. Christ. I should never have left you. What was I thinking?'

When he reaches me I step backwards. I shake my head. He blurs as my eyes fill with fresh tears.

'Bella,' he whispers. 'My darling Bella.'

Then I turn and run. I push past him and tear out of the living room, leaving behind me the stench of Henry Campbell's death as I take the stairs two at a time. I run down the corridor and throw open the door to my old room. I stand in the doorway and look around at the slice of time preserved, no different now than it was fourteen years ago, fourteen days ago, fourteen hours ago, yet everything is changed.

I stare at the poster of the kitten with her big blue eyes. At the strings of coloured beads that lie in a wicker bowl on one side of the chest of drawers and the dressing-up box that contains a thousand different fantasies. The single bed with its rosy bedspread. Then the books, shelves and shelves and shelves of them, each and every one of which had at one time swallowed me whole and let me wander the safety of their magical worlds, to feel the hooves of Black Beauty pounding the grass beneath me, to creep through wardrobes into a land locked in ice, to guard rings, to fight pirates and Lilliputians and tigers.

There are footsteps on the stairs. David's. I don't want to see him. I pull the door to my bedroom closed and turn the key. I walk slowly over to the dressing table and stare at my reflection in the oval mirror.

But I don't see me.

I see a woman with tired eyes and unkempt hair, with dirty tear tracks streaking her milky face like a vagrant porcelain doll.

'Bella!' says David through the door. He tries the handle then starts to bang repeatedly. 'Open the door. Please. Let me in.' He rattles the handle again, this time with more force. 'Open the door!'

I reach forward and flip the mirror on its hinges, banishing the woman with the unkempt hair to the wall. I put my fingers in my ears to muffle David's clamouring, but then all I can hear is Henry Campbell. His voice echoes around my head. Those three words over and over. The three words I heard ten days ago that set this all in motion.

Your mother's dead.

I don't recall what else he said during that phone call. It was as if the death facts passed to me by osmosis. A heart attack. Rushed to hospital. Too late. She called my name. Dying in the ambulance, she called my name.

'Bella! Bella!'

A shiver of excitement runs down my spine. I'm a child again. I'm hiding from her. The rising panic in her voice makes me shiver with excitement.

'Bella!'

I turn and look at Tori, lift a finger to my lips. Tori nods and we both grin. My mother's voice rises, that recognisable tinge of distress creeping in around the edges.

'*Bella*! It's time to come in! Don't play games. I mean it!'

We hold our breath and wait, squeezed into the space behind the big green drum that's filled with rainwater and hundreds of tiny mosquito larvae, which wriggle crossly off the sides when I kick their watery incubator.

'*Bella*!' Her tone, the panicked shriek, tells me the game is over. If I stay hidden she'll be angry and her anger isn't worth the fun. I shrug, and Tori smiles then melts away into the shadows.

I sidle out of my hiding place on my bottom.

'Coming, Mummy! Don't worry, I'm coming!'

I take a deep breath and push the memories away. I let my hands fall from my ears and listen to David banging repeatedly. I force myself to move towards the door but my limbs feel frozen.

Move.

You can't stay in here forever. Move your feet, for goodness' sake.

I manage to walk over to the door and reach out to unlock it, unsure whether I'll be able to step out of my old bedroom without crumbling.

TEN

'I need to leave.'

I need to get away from this house. This dark, locked, desolate house, with its unbearable stench of death.

'Yes,' David says.

'Now.'

His face momentarily clouds, as if he might be about to tell me off for barking at him, but then he appears to take hold of himself. I can hear the voice in his head making excuses for me, *Grief. It's the grief talking. She didn't intend to speak to you like that.*

Miss Young is pleased when I ask her to look after the cat, but is clearly put out that I haven't disclosed the contents of Henry Campbell's letter. She makes a few pointed comments, a *Did his letter explain things, dear?* here, and an *I wonder what could have been on his mind when he did it?* there. She hangs expectantly in the background while David and I silently tidy a few things away, empty the bins, wash and dry the dishes. I try to sate her curiosity by saying his letter didn't say much, simply goodbye and he was sorry. When she drops another hint, I say, 'I'm sorry, Miss Young, I really don't want to talk about it.'

This isn't a lie. I'm not ready. Perhaps when I've got my own head around it, made sure I know what's truth and what's lie, I might be in a position to watch other people try. Until then, I'm not telling a soul. Not even David. If I tell David, he'll want to make it better. He'll take over. He'll involve the police and the newspapers. He'll tell me what to do and how to feel, and alongside all of that, there'll be the judgement on his face, the worry and the anger.

He asked to read the letter, of course, up in my old room, before we came down to face Miss Young.

'I burnt it.'

'Burnt it? Already?'

'Yes. Straightaway. I did it outside so the ash wouldn't make a mess.'

'But why?'

'It didn't explain anything. I was cross. Upset. It was a spur of the moment thing.'

'That's rather rash. Did he give any reason at all?'

'No. Just that the thought of life without her was devastating. That it wasn't worth living.'

David had nodded as if he understood how love alone could drive a man to suicide.

Outside on the driveway, the car packed up, I hand the cat to Miss Young and thank her for taking him.

Miss Young lifts him out of my grasp and begins to stroke his back. The cat starts purring immediately, spooning his front paws into her ample chest.

'We'll be fine, won't we sweetheart?' she says in a singsong voice that grates like nails down a blackboard.

'I'll send money for cat food.'

'Please don't worry. There's plenty to go round at ours.' Miss Young ruffles her fingers into the cat's scruff. 'You won't starve will you, lambkin?'

The cat lifts his nose to brush against her jowl. Clearly for him any old mother will do.

I climb into the car and buckle my seatbelt. David checks it's fastened securely and then turns on the ignition. He is about to pull away when Miss Young bounds over, the cat half-strangled in the crook of her arm. She taps frantically on the window.

'What about the roses, dear?' she asks with genuine concern.

Jesus Christ. Fuck the bloody roses.

'They'll be fine, Miss Young. Thank you for helping with the cat. '

'It's Suzie, dear. *Do* remember to call me Suzie.'

ELEVEN

Henry Campbell — 3rd August 1989

Henry Campbell would have liked to have been anywhere else than where he and his wife were now. He followed her through the heaving crowds. It was hot and sticky.

Hundreds, no, thousands of people, lined the walkways, ambling in all directions in a manner that made him want to shout. He was exhausted after yet another dreadful night's sleep. He hadn't slept properly in months, but last night any chance of sleep had been impossible. The hotel room was small and shabby, with paper-thin walls and noisy guests next door, and a shower that dripped like metronomic water torture. He'd tossed and turned in the narrow, lumpy bed, its sheets musty, having been folded and put away damp from the laundry. He was plagued by insistent thoughts, by worry, sadness, helplessness, forced to silence his many protestations, the things he wanted to say to her. Why couldn't she accept their childless future and find a way to move on. Time was the only healer. Time would surely help her bear her grief.

They trudged along wordlessly, drops in the stream of visitors united in their search for divine intervention, for a spiritual connection or an outright miracle. Elaine, of course, wanted the latter. A miracle. For faith to help where nature and science had failed her.

He concentrated on breathing through his mouth not his nose, the stench of sweat and cologne mixed with the occasional flash of unwashed human made a cocktail of smells that caught in the back of his throat. People of all shapes and sizes, able-bodied and disabled, all races and ages, ambled or strode or hobbled. There was a mix of excitable tourists, the occasional bored child dragging weary feet, complaining of the heat or a rumbling tummy. Then there were those who were filled with the same anguish that filled his wife. You could see it in their eyes. Their desperation. The way their hope clung to them by a final thread.

They passed a man lying on a wheeled hospital bed. It reminded him of a medical-school charity event he'd helped organise at university. Students entering in teams of two in fancy dress, one of each pair lying on a bed, the other pushing as they raced through streets lined with cheering, drunken spectators. Back then he'd been full of potential, full of youthful vigour and sexual appetite, no idea of the bleak and hopeless future that lay ahead of him.

He sighed. He was hungry now. His body needed food. There was a small restaurant next door to their dreadful hotel; they were bound to serve a half-decent steak. Maybe the humourless Gallic waiter could bring him a glass of rough red *vin de table* to go with it. Maybe two.

Yes, he thought. Two.

'I don't care if you're hungry. We're not going back until we've seen Her.'

'I don't understand this. You're not even Catholic.'

She stopped walking and turned to face him, her frustration clear. 'Henry, God is God. The assortment of religions in the world are merely versions of the same All Mighty being. If I'd been born to a Catholic family, I'd be Catholic. If I'd been born in India, I'd be Hindu. God is bigger than any mortal construction of Him. He will hear me. He will. I have Faith and He will give us our miracle.' And then she closed her eyes and he saw her lips mutter silent words. Cursing or praying, he wasn't sure.

As they neared the grotto, the number of souvenir shops selling water bottles, candles, ornaments, all fashioned into a likeness of the Virgin Mary, increased. Henry had become numbed to her image, which was repeated again and again and again, her beatific tranquillity a backdrop to this place of mass conviction and agony.

They drew to a halt as they neared the grotto. He stared upwards. The sky was pale blue, the same shade as the Virgin Mary's dress. He tried to take Elaine's hand, but she drew away from him, her gaze fixed on the effigy ahead, her hands clasped in prayer in front of her.

His stomach turned over.

He had never felt so distant from her. So impotent. They were here because he was unable to help her. There was nothing he could do. He had vowed to look after her always. As a young man, when he'd been overflowing with lust and love, when she'd lain in his arms, her soft, honeyed hair brushing his lips, her beautiful scent filling him up as he breathed her into his very soul, he'd vowed he would never let anything hurt her. It was a visceral feeling that had kicked him in the gut. That sudden and overwhelming need to look after her. But he'd had no idea of what pain lay ahead. Pain he was powerless to stop. How naïve he'd been to think he could protect her forever, but he was damned if he'd stop trying. She needed him. He was all she had in the world. Especially now.

Next to him stood a young girl with a delicate gold cross around her neck. Her hair was scraped back so tightly it pulled painfully at her skin. Her face was rapt, tears pooled in her eyes as she stared at the statue perched in the hollow in the rock. The girl had her hands raised, palms facing outwards, tilted a little towards the sky. The divine love that he apparently repelled seemed to soak into her as if she were a sponge, saturating her, so much so he wondered whether she might actually pass out. The people around him murmured as one. Some chanted under their breath. Some whispered prayers and Hail Marys. There was the soft chatter of rosary beads passing through fervent fingers as the crowd swayed like a forest of saplings in a light wind.

So many saplings in search of a miracle.

This was what brought them to this place. This town. This pilgrim's stop. The unending belief that each and every one of them was deserving of a miracle. He wanted to scream at them, shout until there was no breath left in his body.

You are delusional! he wanted to shriek. *There is no God listening to you! Don't you understand that? There is no Virgin. There are no such things as miracles. You are buying a falsehood. Life is a bastard! A godless, barren bastard where cruel things happen that have no meaning, no purpose, happen for no reason at all.*

But instead of screaming Henry Campbell closed his eyes. He lowered his head and then he clasped his hands together and prayed to a god he didn't believe in for the miracle they both so desperately needed.

TWELVE

We pull into a petrol station on the motorway and while David fills the car, I sit with my hands tight in my lap, pressing the side of my head hard against the window. All I can think about is whether I can continue without finding out the truth. I wish I could forget it. Wish I could rewind time and leave Henry's words unread.

David knocks on the glass and makes me jump. 'Do you want anything?' he mouths.

I shake my head, then press it back against the window, this time forcing it harder against the cool glass until it begins to hurt. I wonder how hard I'd have to push to break it.

When David returns he deposits a carrier bag at my feet. 'You must be hungry.'

I don't say anything. How could he think I'd be interested in eating? He buckles his seatbelt and pulls on it twice to check it's fastened. Then he checks mine. A double tug. Just to be on the safe side. I grit my teeth, grind the enamel.

'It's fastened,' I say. 'I heard the click.'

'Better to be on the safe side.'

'I fastened it,' I say, digging my fingernails hard into my palms. 'You don't need to check.'

I close my eyes and lean against the window. I am aware of him reaching into the backseat. Then something falls over me, a cover, it smells of him. His coat, I think.

'There, there, my lovely thing. Try and sleep.'

I pull the coat up to cover my face. Breathe in my breath. The car engine starts. And I breathe deeper as the oxygen level falls and the air trapped inside the coat gets warmer and damper. Then a sudden panic grabs me from nowhere. Hard and real, it overwhelms me. Something in the recess of my memory flares. Darkness. Hot, thin air. And fear. Fear grips me, squeezes harder and harder until its bite becomes unbearable.

I throw off the coat. Sit up and reach forward. I stab frantically at the button to lower the window. As the cool air floods the car, I stick out my head and open my lungs as wide as they will go to draw the fresh air deep into me.

'Bella? Are you OK?' David is worried. His hand is on mine. He indicates and checks his rear-view mirror as if to pull over. 'Bella?'

I turn my head towards him and nod tightly. 'I'm fine. Keep driving. I'm fine,' I manage. Then I lean my head out of the window again. Although the panic has eased, I'm unable to shake off the heavy sense of foreboding that smothers me.

David leans forward and switches on the radio. I try to block him out, focus on the world outside – on the trees and telephone wires of Oxfordshire, which morph into those of Berkshire then Surrey – as the jarring musical discord of JazzFM cuts through me like a knife.

We near Guildford and my anxiety lights up again and spreads like wildfire. What am I supposed to do when we arrive home? Act like everything's OK? That things are unaltered? That I haven't just read a letter that suggests my life as I know it might well be a lie? That I'm simply someone whose mother died of a heart attack and whose father killed himself the day after we burned her to ash and bits of bone?

We walk into the hallway of our neat and tidy mid-terrace house, furnished mostly from the Ikea catalogue. David bends to pick up the post and leafs through it.

'Nothing interesting,' he says, discarding the pile of torn envelopes on the console table. He looks at me. 'God, you're so pale. Please eat.'

'I'm not hungry.'

He strokes my cheek with the backs of his fingers. 'I'll make you a sandwich.'

I should cling to him as if he were a life raft in the sea. David has always been my rock, the person I lean on, the person who protects me. It has been like that since the very first day we met, when I finally ventured out of my room in the noisy, intimidating halls of residence, and crept, heart hammering, into a seat at the back of the lecture theatre. I can still remember how anxious I felt, how exposed, sitting alone amid the rows and rows of other students – each one of them so confident, laughing and joking, at ease in our brave new world.

He walked into the room and his command was instant. The room hushed, only the sounds of papers shuffling and pen lids popping. The way he held himself was mesmerising. It was as if the lecture theatre had been plunged into darkness, leaving this man illuminated by a spotlight. When he spoke it was strong and direct, his voice like a blanket that wrapped me up, and when his eyes caught mine a flush of heat bloomed on the back of my neck and across my cheeks. I looked quickly away, but when I glanced back he was watching me. He later told me he knew right then that I was The One.

'Emerald eyes are my Achilles' heel,' he said. 'Yours called to me from the sea of faces.'

Of course, I'd been too shy to smile back. I dropped my eyes, heart thumping, and fixed them on my paper. I focused on his voice, lilting yet authoritative, not a stutter or hesitation. Looking back I wonder how much of it was sexual attraction and how much of it was needing someone to replace my mother, to take control of me, something subconscious, conditioned within me, that was drawn to him. As I listened to him talk, the tension eased from my muscles. I picked up my pen and watched my hand translate his words into writing, my pen moving up and down and around to form letters, catching his voice and pinning it down. I would reread these notes a dozen times when I returned to my room, my body tingling with each read-through.

At the end of the lecture I gathered my files and waited until the others had bustled out. I was the last to leave the lecture hall and as I walked towards the door, he called to me.

'Young lady?'

I stopped and turned, my heart racing.

'I know this great little café,' he said. 'It's quiet and the coffee is fresh and delicious. And, the cake, well, the cake is to die for. Will you join me?'

And with that simple invitation he took the baton from Elaine. I was safe. But now, back in our home, it feels like a barrier has been thrown up between us. It encircles me completely. Seals me off from him. I should feel lost and vulnerable but I don't. I just feel numb. Detached from everything I know.

Everything you thought you knew.

Yes, everything I thought I knew. I feel detached from everything.

THIRTEEN

For a few days I try to negotiate my life as normal. I move from break-fast to work to supper to bed in what amounts to a catatonic daze. David tries to help. He holds me, runs baths, makes neatly packaged lunches from a balanced range of food groups. He drives me to work and picks me up, breaking the silence in the car with whimsical anec-dotes intended to cheer me. I should talk to him. I know that. None of this is his fault. But it's hard. Inside my head is bedlam, filled with conflicting memories, emotions and questions.

'Jeffrey asked after you,' David says as we eat supper. 'Barbara has offered to help in any way she can. She's really rather nice, you know. The two of you have more in common than you realise. She'd be a good friend to you if you gave her more than half a chance. You mustn't shut...'

As I stare at him the words he is speaking fade away and are replaced by a kind of white noise. And suddenly, as if a blindfold has been removed, I am filled with the utter conviction that Henry Campbell's letter contains the truth. I grip hold of the table, my head swims. I look at David. His face has become indistinct, like it's been covered over with a layer of thin gauze. I squint to help me focus and as I do the gauze falls away, but it's not my husband who's revealed. It's a new person. A person I don't know. His face is contorted with concern. His greying hair is thin on top. His teeth, a little yellowed, are neat and straight. This man is a stranger. Not a stranger to a woman called Bella, a woman who shares his life and his bed, but a stranger to me, the person partially revealed in Henry's final words.

I drop my head.

The man – David – reaches across the table and rubs my arm.

No, not my arm. Bella's arm.

My head pounds.

'I need some time away.'

He frowns. 'Away? Goodness, Bella, I can't take a holiday now. It's the middle of term and I've just had time off for the funeral.' He hesitates, perhaps noticing the rigid set of my mouth, my crossed arms, the tears forming in my eyes. 'It might be possible to take a few days next month. I'm sure Jeffrey will understand. These are exceptional circumstances. He knows how hard you're taking this. I don't blame you, of course, nothing can prepare you for losing both your parents like this.'

Losing both your parents.

No, David, you're right. Nothing could have prepared me for that.

I blink quickly, trying to disperse my pooling tears before they fall. 'I need to be on my own for a while.'

'On your own?'

I nod.

'No,' he says firmly. He closes his fingers around my arm. 'You need me. You know you do; you won't cope alone.'

I pull away from his grip. 'I need some time to sort my head out.'

'No, I can't let you,' he says. 'I won't let you.'

Then from nowhere I feel a sharp stab of anger. Anger at this man who wants to control his wife all the time. Anger at Henry. At Elaine. At all of them.

I look madly around the room and catch sight of them on the mantelpiece.

I walk over and take hold of the photograph. It was taken one Christmas Day a few years ago. Elaine and Henry sit next to each other on the sofa. Her hair frames her face, his hand rests lightly on her knee. I look at her face, her smile; it's just for me. I remember telling her to smile.

'Smile, Mum. Say cheese!'

And she did.

And then the anger overwhelms me. I bring the frame down hard on the edge of the mantelpiece. The glass shatters. My fingers pulls at a shard of glass that is stuck in the photo frame. Tears course my cheeks. David is shouting at me to stop. I pull the jagged piece of glass out and rake it over Elaine's face, tearing at the smile until it begins to disappear.

David grabs my hands. 'Stop it, Bella! For God's sake, what's got into you.'

He squeezes my hand hard. The glass is trapped and begins to cut into me. He presses harder still. I look down and watch a trail of blood run from my closed fist down my wrist. David must see it too because his grip loosens. I open my hand and the blood-smeared piece of glass falls to the ground.

'Oh, Bella,' he says softly. He takes his handkerchief from his back pocket and presses the folded cotton against the cut. Blood soaks the white fabric like an ink blot. 'Look what you've done, you foolish girl.'

'I need some time away,' I say, holding my hand up to my chest.

He sighs heavily, his displeasure clear. He drops my hand with a petulant tut. 'If that's what you want, but you're making a mistake.'

'And you'll talk to Jeffrey?'

'He won't be happy at all.'

I know Jeffrey won't mind. I only got the job in the university library because of how 'terribly fond' of David he is. The two of them arranged everything. I didn't even have to have an interview.

'Great to have you on board,' Jeffrey had said , when he popped in to the library on my first day. 'I'm am terribly fond of David.'

'Where are you even going, for God's sake?' David says, his irritation clear.

The cut on my hand has begun to throb. 'I'm not sure yet.'

I get up and start moving towards the stairs.

'And for how long? A few days?'

I don't answer.

He runs up behind me and grabs my arm, holds on so hard I can't pull away from him. 'Talk to me, Bella. You have to talk to me. I can help if you tell me what's going on inside your head.'

And for a split second I think maybe I *should* tell him. I imagine his arms encircling me, holding me tightly. Imagine him taking charge. He would tell me Henry is lying. He would convince me it was all made up, the work of a madman with an unknown agenda. He would tell me I am still Bella and that Bella's life is my life. And I would pretend to be her. I would live in her house and do her work and live with her husband.

But I know it won't work. There would always be that gnawing suspicion that somewhere out there is the real me, waiting to be found.

I force myself to look at David as he softens in fresh tears.

'I'm sorry,' I whisper. 'I have to go.'

FOURTEEN

The name of the imaginary friend I had growing up was Tori.

In the curious world of my childhood – of locked and bolted doors, of drawn curtains, of reclusive parents and no freedom – she was every one of my absent, wished-for friends rolled into one. I can't remember the time she first came to play. She was just always there, as far back as I can remember, and she was amazing. In many ways she was better than a real friend; well, better than any friend I could have had in real life, that's for sure. Tori was beautiful, with blonde curly hair and perfect features. She was brave and brilliant, fun and adventurous, and it was she who allowed me to be mischievous, she who gave me the guts to climb trees, to hide from my mother, to light the bonfire behind the shed with dry sticks and stolen matches. It was Tori who laughed as the first flames took hold. She who squealed with delight as I panicked and shouted as the fire licked at the timber shed, threatening to burn it to the ground.

'What a *stupid* thing to do, Bella! What on earth possessed you to be so idiotic, so bloody irresponsible?' my mother demanded after she'd managed to put out the fire by shovelling earth on it and stamping the determined sparks out as if she were dancing.

'It was Tori,' I mumbled.

'Don't you dare,' she said. 'Having a friend who doesn't exist is one thing. Blaming this figment of your imagination for lighting fires and eating biscuits between meals is a totally different thing all together. And yes, don't look at me like that; I know it's you eating the biscuits. I'm not stupid.'

When we were alone Tori apologised.

'It's not your fault,' I said. 'It was me who lit the match.'

I haven't spoken to Tori since I left The Old Vicarage to go to university. Leaving her behind was difficult; she was such an integral part of me. But I was determined that my departure from the house should be the start of my new life, my independence, and Tori didn't seem to have a place outside those towering brick walls. But sitting on my bed in my adult home, holding Henry's letter, I am like an alcoholic staring at a bottle of vodka; I need her.

What harm will it do? her voice says then.

I don't say anything.

I mean, things are pretty shit, right? And you can't talk to David, so you might as well talk to me. You can send me away again afterwards. I won't hold it against you.

I smile.

So what's up?

'You don't know?'

Of course I know – I know everything you know – but I thought I'd ask anyway. Give me the newspaper article. I'd like to read it again. It's mad. I can't believe it.

'I know. God, it's weird I'm talking to you, but it's good to have you back.'

Stop being soft and give me the bloody article.

Tori clears her throat and takes hold of the yellowed piece of newspaper with both hands. She gives it a quick shake as if she's a newsreader shuffling notes. The voice that comes out of her is like a proper 1950s television announcer's, regal, a bit nasal, with all the vowels pinched together.

Holiday family is devastated by lost child, she reads, her eyes wide as saucers to convey the drama perfectly as she elongates the word 'devastated'. *A young couple are begging—*

Tori stops and stares hard at me. They are literally begging, she says in her normal voice, then looks back at the article and continues in her staged voice.

—for clues as to the whereabouts of their daughter, who is aged three. Alice and Mark Tremayne—

She stops again, musing. Nice names. Alice and Mark. Nicer than Elaine and Henry, I think.

—*are both from St Ives in Cornwall*—

I've always wanted to go to Cornwall, you know.

'Stop with the asides; it's off-putting.'

God, you're so demanding. And anyway, it's not off-putting, I'm adding colour.

'It's not colourful, it's annoying.'

Fine. Have it your way. You're the boss. So, where were we? Yes. These Tremayne people. Alice and Mark – nice names – from St Ives in Cornwall.

—*were staying on a campsite not far from the French town of Biarritz. Mr Tremayne is calling for anyone who might have seen his daughter on the night she went missing to get in touch. The couple were asleep*—

Asleep? Asleep, I ask you?

—*in their caravan when the child went missing from her bed. A team of local police*—

I do believe the correct word, newspaper writer person, is *gendarmes,* says Tori with a raised eyebrow, which makes me smile.

—*led by senior officer, Jean-Paul Leclerc*—

She says the name in a pantomime French accent that sticks in her throat.

—*have been searching the dunes and beaches near the campsite with dogs. Many concerned locals have turned out to help. Air search and rescue have been scouring the coastline. Leclerc has appealed to anyone with any information that might lead to the safe return of the child to come forward.*

Tori and I look at each other. There's a sadness in her eyes that belies her jocular tone.

'And the letter?' I say. 'Will you read me the letter again?'

You read that one.

My heart picks up pace as I unfold the single sheet of blue paper. I stare at the sentences written in his beautiful handwriting. His body flashes into my mind, the slick of dark blood beneath his chair, his skin as white as freshly fallen snow, his wide, glassy eyes.

'Elaine and I are not your real parents. We didn't adopt you ... Your real mother is Alice Tremayne ... Forgive me.'

Tori is quiet for a moment. I refold the paper, the article inside it, then slip both sheets of paper carefully into the envelope.

I love the way he says *Forgive me*. Like it's as simple as that. Like it's all, *Hey, I kidnapped you and kept you prisoner in my house for twenty years, but you know, no hard feelings. Forgive me, yeah?* What a fucking idiot.

'I wonder what the Tremaynes are like?'

You mean your *parents*.

I rub my face. My brain is tired from grappling with it all.

'They might not be my parents. This missing girl might not be me.'

She is you though, isn't she? I mean, it all makes sense.

I don't reply to her.

You have to find them.

I pause and shake my head. 'I'm not sure. What if he made it all up? What if Henry's some eccentric crackpot and happened to read the story and thought for some insane reason he'd pretend she was me.'

You know it's true in your heart of hearts.

I shrug.

You never believed that stupid green-eyed great-grandmother story, did you? Such a crock of shit.

'It would explain a lot, wouldn't it? Why they never saw their families for starters. They'd have known I wasn't theirs, wouldn't they? They'd have known she hadn't had a baby. You can't turn up at a family get-together out of the blue with a three-year-old and expect people not to ask questions.'

And remember how she freaked out when Henry helped you apply to university? She never wanted you to leave. She wanted to keep you locked away in that spooky old house forever, didn't she?

My fists clench involuntarily.

You know if you really don't want to meet them, the Tremaynes, you could always take the next flight out of Heathrow and leave the whole sorry mess behind you.

Tori laughs and the sound rings in my head.

'This isn't funny.'

Not funny-ha-ha, but definitely funny-peculiar. She was weird though, wasn't she? Your mum, I mean.

'Elaine.'

Sorry, Elaine. She was, though. Definitely weird, but I never had her down as a kidnapper.

'That house gives me the creeps. It's like it was in on it.'

A conspirator, you mean?

'Exactly that.'

Thinking about The Old Vicarage sends a shiver through me. I hear the echo of bolts, smell the stale, imprisoned air, recall how the house seemed to whisper behind my back as I skipped along the lonely corridors.

I fall back on the bed and push the house from my thoughts.

I go over the article again in my head. 'I have so many questions, Tori. How did they get me out of France, for goodness' sake? And why did they take me? How did they manage to hide me?'

Tori shrugs. You're one of those kids, aren't you? The ones you read about in the newspapers. The ones who are snatched and locked up for decades. You're pretty lucky you didn't end up having five of his babies in the basement, you know...

I think back over those years growing up at The Old Vicarage, but as I do my mind slips back into confusion. Yes, there had been moments of extreme loneliness and frustration, but isn't that the case with all childhoods? Even if Henry was telling the truth, and they did take me, there had been no rape, no torture, no cruelty. No starvation or beatings. No terror and no pain. Instead, there had been home-cooked meals, laughter, books and toys, affection, and all-consuming love. Behind those towering walls and drawn curtains and triple-bolted doors, in that gilded prison, there had even been happiness.

FIFTEEN

The still hush of the British Library swaddles me as I sit and read. There are numerous articles relating to the case of the little girl from Cornwall, who went missing from the south west coast of France in the summer of 1989.

As I read each article my chest tightens a fraction more and I have to concentrate on my breathing to keep myself calm. Though the writing style varies from paper to paper – some highbrow, some sensationalist, some judgemental – they all repeat the same basic facts. The girl disappeared from a campsite (a grotty, rubbish-strewn place, one of the reports says snidely) near a village called Vaiches. A teddy bear and a pink Mickey Mouse nightie were found washed up on the shore a few miles north of Biarritz. The Atlantic had been whipped by off-shore winds for over a week, the current was strong, too strong for a small child to battle, and she was suspected drowned. No body was found. The parents were distraught.

I sit back in my chair, which creaks loudly and breaks the quiet. I imagine people reading those articles all those years ago. Some of them tut sadly, others drip cereal milk from their spoons as they turn the page, passing blindly over the wretched facts. I think of this little girl. How she had occupied people's thoughts. How strangers had worried for her safety, if only for a few days, before her story slipped back through the pages to obscurity and concerns for her whereabouts were abandoned.

I gaze around the library at people absorbed in their reading or writing.

Was I this little girl?

I look back down at my notebook and stare at the handful of facts I've jotted down. The father of the lost girl was Mark, an out-of-work trawler-man, aged thirty-one. Her mother was Alice, an office-cleaner, aged twenty-six. The little girl was three years old. The child was missing, presumed drowned. She was called Morveren. I've never heard of this name before. Cornish, I suppose. It's odd and doesn't sound like the type of name you'd give to a baby girl. I close my eyes and repeat the name in my head, concentrating, searching my memories for any sparks of recognition.

I look back at my notebook. The final thing I've written is underlined and ringed with circles.

The little girl, Morveren, had a sister.

There's something about this piece of information that kicks the air from my gut. As a child, all I had ever wanted was a sibling. I'd never been a contented only child. I yearned for company and used to beg Elaine to take me to the playground so I could make friends, but she never did. Perhaps if I'd been allowed to go to school, I'd have had friends. But Elaine said all schools were dreadful, either violent hellholes or sausage machines that churned out children who couldn't even write their own names. She said I was too clever, too precious, to go to one of 'those places', so she home-schooled me herself, sending me to Henry's study for science and maths. There had been no friends, only Tori, and I'd have given anything for a sister.

Was I this little girl?

If I was, how could Elaine Campbell have let me love her? She'd played the part of loving mother without missing a beat. I had to admire her for that. Not like Henry and his rare and awkward interactions, his lack of interest, the hours he spent shut away in his study avoiding me. I think about our 'fond respect', which I'd always tried to pretend was enough, and realise that all along his attitude to me, his distance, was in fact a manifestation of guilt.

My head hurts as I wrestle with it all. Had Henry written the truth or lies? Much of the time I don't believe it. I can't; it's too surreal. Every now and then I even wonder whether his letter actually exists;

perhaps I dreamed it. Crazy thoughts fly in and out of my head. I wonder if Miss Young wrote the letter. Or maybe the policeman. Or had someone snuck in while we slept? Had they murdered my father and planted the letter to mislead me?

Don't be ridiculous, a voice in my head says. *Of course the letter is real. Who on earth would want to murder a retired, country doctor?*

I need to talk to them. These people from the yellowed clippings. The Tremaynes. I need to see them. I need to know if there is any shred of evidence that supports Henry's story. There's no other option; until I know the truth, I can't let this lie.

SIXTEEN

The countryside outside the train flies past in a mush of greens. I watch it racing by and try not to think of David. Of how angry he will be when he gets home from the tennis club to find me gone. Even though he agreed I could have some time away, I don't think he ever really believed I would. I don't think I ever really believed he would let me, so I left him a note saying that I was sorry I'd gone without saying goodbye. I told him it would have been too difficult. That I needed to go. I said I'd be gone for a few weeks. I said I'd call as soon as I could and that I'd put clean sheets on the bed.

On the train, racing away from my home, my heart is beating faster than usual. The confusion and sadness I'm becoming used to is now mixed with an undeniable thrill of anticipation. I listen to the sounds around me, chattering voices, the stationmaster's whistle, the slamming of train doors, the noise of the train itself as it speeds along the tracks, shooting me further and further into the unknown.

I think back to Elaine and her fears of travelling, her twitching and worrying whenever she was on the wrong side of our gates. Agoraphobia, I had assumed. I think back to the Eurostar tickets I'd given her, remembering how desolate I felt as I tore the tickets into tiny pieces. I'd always given myself such a hard time for being so insensitive to her issues. Worrying I had drawn attention to a condition over which she had no control. For weeks I would relive the incident, pretend I'd given her a plant, a beautiful white standard rose in a terracotta pot that would have been perfect for the front doorstep. But, of course, it wasn't my fault. I had done nothing wrong. It was the mention of that place that sent her crazy. The place from which she had taken me.

I lay my head back against the seat, wrap my arms around my body and hold myself tightly.

'Excuse me,' says a voice. 'Is anyone sitting here?'

The voice startles me. I turn my head and see a clean-cut man in a pinstriped suit, his tie loosened at his unbuttoned collar. He smiles when I nod. Then he winks at me. I look quickly away, but he doesn't seem to get the message and starts talking to me as he settles himself down. I ignore him and hunch up my shoulders. I know it's rude, but I don't want to get into conversation with him, and God knows, he won't want to get into conversation with me. I'm a mess and the mess is best left inside me. He eventually takes the hint and mutters something crossly under his breath. Later, when my stomach starts to rumble and I ask if I can get past, he scowls and grumbles.

I lurch through the carriages, alternate hand to alternate headrest, until I reach the buffet car. The boy behind the counter is young and spotty and, judging by the look on his face, isn't working in his dream job. I look at the menu on the wall, at the sandwiches on offer. Tuna and cucumber, plain ham or egg and cress.

'It'll have to be an egg sandwich, please,' I say, doing my best to mask my nerves. I've got better at handling myself in public. I pretend I'm Tori sometimes, when my anxiety levels rise, and it helps. 'I don't like tuna and I'm allergic to ham.'

It's an odd thing to say, but it pops out of my mouth before I've properly thought about it.

Allergic to ham? Tori asks indignantly.

The boy behind the counter looks rightly surprised.

'I didn't know you could get allergic with ham,' he says flatly.

'Oh, yes,' I nod. 'It's rare though.'

'What, like you get a rash or puke up or whatever?'

'Swelling. I just have to smell ham and my throat swells up. I ate a quiche Lorraine by mistake once and turned blue.'

The boy leans backwards and eyes me warily.

'It's OK,' I say. 'You can't catch it.'

He doesn't seem convinced and grabs an egg sandwich from the fridge and chucks it across the counter.

I turn away and walk out of the buffet car. Fibbing to the boy was strangely freeing, as if I'd put on a mask and concealed my shyness. It occurs to me now that this is the perfect opportunity to reinvent myself: I'd lost my parents, my past life was possibly built on a tangle of lies, I'd left my husband (albeit temporarily) and nobody on this train or in Cornwall, or indeed outside of the university library, knows who I am. I could be anybody, even a person with a peculiar allergy to ham.

I sit down in a different seat in a different carriage so I don't have to be near the man in the pinstriped suit and peel back the cellophane of the sandwich. The heavy tang of egg surrounds me and when I feel the sogginess of the bread my stomach heaves. I should have had an allergy to egg not ham. I'm not sure I like egg sandwiches that much. I manage a bite then put the rest back in the box, which I push away from me. As I do, I catch the eye of a woman in a camel-coloured coat in the seat across the aisle from me. She looks up from the crossword she's doing and briefly smiles. I look away. Her pen clicks repeatedly, an absentminded tic as she reads, her thumb tapping against the top of the biro, like she's tapping out code.

Click, click. Click, click, click. Click.

And then the sea comes into view and I can't help but draw in an excited breath. Grey and flat, it laps against the brown, cricket-ball pebbles on the shore a few feet from the track. I love the sea. I remember the first time I saw it. I was with David. He'd booked a cottage in Norfolk for the weekend. It was the weekend I would lose my virginity and the weekend we would get engaged. I remember being so nervous in the car on the way there I actually shook. I think I'd known within a few hours of meeting David that he was the man I'd have sex with for the first time. After we'd had coffee in the café, he wrote his number in the front of my notebook, and while everybody else on my staircase in the hall of residence chattered excitedly, moved in and out of each others rooms, music blaring, I carefully tore around the number in a heart shape and pinned it to my notice board. As I pushed in the pin I knew. But when the time finally came, I was so bewitched by the sea, the actual sex went almost unnoticed.

'This is really the first time you've seen the sea?' he said, as we sat on a bench, nursing watery hot chocolates in paper cups and looking out across the dirty-brown water.

I nodded. 'I've got a scrapbook with pictures torn out of magazines and I've seen it in books, of course.' I shook my head at the beauty of the water rolling in and out in front of me, crashing onto the shore in a mass of spume and noisy, tumbling pebbles. 'But I've never actually seen it. It feels as if it's calling to me. As if it's been waiting for me.'

I press my hand against the train window and gaze in awe at the miles and miles of ocean that stretch out towards the horizon and beyond. I hear the *click, click* to the side of me again and glance back at the woman engrossed in her crossword. As I do I suddenly feel doubt billowing up inside me again.

Click, click.

What are you doing?

Click, click. Click, click.

Am I making a terrible mistake? I go over the newspaper articles in my head yet again. Nowhere does it mention a kidnapping. There was speculation, of course. Fear of the worst. But no concrete leads. Just a lost child. A girl missing. Then a search. She was presumed dead. Drowned in the sea. The sea I am looking out over. And if that child drowned, if her body had been swept out into the ocean, I *couldn't* be her, could I?

I'm sweating now. Panic has hold of me, tossing me like a leaf in a storm. My lungs constrict as if someone has tied a rope around my chest and is pulling it tighter and tighter. Breathing becomes a struggle. The tips of my fingers and toes begin to tingle. They are growing cold. I can't get oxygen into my body.

'Are you OK? Do you need help?'

I jerk my head up and look at the woman with the camel coat. I snatch at her wrist across the aisle. Still I struggle to draw breath. She gets up. Kneels beside me. Puts a hand on my forehead. Looks up and down the carriage for help.

'Do you need your inhaler?' she says loudly, as if I am suddenly deaf.

I shake my head. She takes my hand, squeezes it. Strokes her other hand down the side of my face. Her touch seems to kickstart me, calms me enough that I can draw a desperate breath. Then another. I drag lungfuls of oxygen deep into my body as the woman in the camel coat strokes my forehead.

'It's alright. Take deep breaths. Try and stay calm.'

Her touch is like Elaine's. How she used to stroke me when I was ill. I never went to the doctor. *No need to*, Elaine always said. *The doctor's in the house.* And then she'd smile. I close my eyes and recall the armchair. Henry has carried it up from their bedroom. She will sit with me all night. She will stroke my head and feed me sips of water. She won't leave my side. She will be next to me until I am better.

I miss her so much.

My mind flips to the day before Henry killed himself. When we sat together beneath the oak tree, when he was unable to tell me what he wanted to say. The pain that haunted him. He wasn't lying. He wasn't. They took me. They lied to me. They kept me locked up.

But I miss her so much.

I press my fingers into my temples as the tumbling anxiety begins to subside and my knotted stomach eases.

'I'm fine,' I mumble. 'I'm sorry. I don't know what happened.'

'Had a bit of a turn.' She stands up and reaches into her bag. 'A panic attack. My sister-in-law has them. Maybe some water?'

I drink from the small bottle of mineral water she hands me.

'Thank you.'

'No bother.' She sits back down in her seat. 'You should probably see a doctor when you get where you're going. And get yourself a paper bag. Paper bags help.'

I concentrate on breathing slow and deep and watch her as she goes back to the crossword. She looks nice. Kind. I imagine she has a big family. A kitchen table that holds lots of grown-up children, maybe a few grandchildren. There's joking and laughing. They pass around bowls of buttery vegetables and a jug of gravy, and the lady in the camel coat tells them all to eat up before it gets cold.

Did she read about the girl who went missing in France twenty-five years ago? Did she give it any thought? Did she watch the news then climb the stairs and check on her own sleeping children? Kiss them gently? Tuck their blankets around them? Thank her lucky stars it wasn't them?

SEVENTEEN

The train eases into Penzance station, and as they stand and stretch their cramped bodies the excited murmurings of passengers fills the carriage. I wait until most have got off the train and then walk back to my original seat to fetch my bag. It's a relief to find that the man in the suit has already left. I reach up and pull my bag off the luggage rack. I trace my fingertips over it and my mind drifts. I imagine how lovely it would be if I was arriving for a holiday. If this bag held a few books, a bottle of coconut-scented suncream, a beach towel and a swimming costume, and I could unfurl the towel across a wide, flat rock that's been warmed by the sun, then settle down to read with the heat on my skin.

A loud call from outside the train jolts me out of my daydream, and surreality resettles itself over me like a leaden shawl as I hoist my bag on to my shoulder. I move towards the door reluctantly, unsure what lies beyond, unsure what my first move will be.

But when my foot touches the platform, as the smell in the station envelops me, something extraordinary happens, something I can't explain. Perhaps it's in my mind, but I feel an immediate connection, like an electric charge running up the inside of my legs and through my body. The hairs on my skin prickle. I have a sudden and vivid recollection of being here before, surrounded by the sounds of the station, the murmur of voices, hundreds of footsteps on the concrete platform. A hand holds mine. Pulls me along. Jerking my shoulder. A voice tells me not to cry. I remember crying...

And then it's gone.

Was that fleeting image real or imagined? I search my head for more, stand motionless for a minute, breathing the salt-water air and train fuel deep into my body, in the hope it returns. But there is nothing and I soon become aware of the last remaining passengers jostling around me, arranging luggage on trollies and greeting loved ones. The whole station is filled with the cries of seagulls from somewhere above the enormous arching vault of the roof. It all feels familiar, yet alien at the same time. My mind is playing tricks on me.

I am the last to leave the station; I have plenty of time, unlike the others who hurry home for cups of restorative tea and cake, maybe a scone with jam and cream. As I walk I focus on placing one foot in front of the other. I feel the ground beneath each heel. Beneath each toe.

One, two, three, four, I count. *One, two, three, four.*

Each step takes me closer.

To what?

I don't know.

One, two, three, four.

Outside the sky is dull, the grey of old cotton underwear, with no sign of the sun. It isn't unpleasant, more of a nothing day, as if whoever's in charge of the weather has forgotten to paint it in. Across the road is the taxi rank, where a couple of cars with bored-looking drivers wait. Behind that is a wall that holds the sea at bay. There is a boy on the wall, sitting beside a man I take to be his father. At a guess the boy is nine or ten. He's eating chips from a cone of paper patched with grease. Above their heads wheel a pair of seagulls. I watch as one of the birds takes its chance and dive-bombs the child, screeching as it falls, attempting to grab chips straight from the cone. The boy shouts and his father jumps up, starts flailing his arms as the other gull joins the first, both birds ignoring the man's attempts to shoo them off. Two more join from nowhere and they hover menacingly around the boy, who in panic throws a couple of chips as far as he can. The gulls are on them in seconds, shrieking and fighting for a share of the prize. The man says words I can't hear and the boy nods and stuffs a handful of chips in his mouth before hurrying after his father. I watch the two of them settle themselves in the bus shelter. The father glances warily at the sky and seeing no looming thieves, allows himself a smug smile before leaning in to pinch a chip.

I cross the car park to the wall where the gulls are still scrapping on the pavement. Yet again the sea steals my breath. Here it is different from the gentle brown water lapping the shore by the railway. It is angrier, darker, a gunmetal grey fringed with deep green and white as it crashes over enormous jagged rocks. I am transfixed by it. By the relentless way it pummels the shore and the noise it makes as it strikes the sea wall, sending up a fine mist of water to spritz my face and salt my lips. I used to beg Elaine to take me to the seaside. She had a hundred reasons not to go – sandy picnics, sticky saltwater, gritty toes, uncomfortable pebbles, too hot, too cold, too many people, too unhygienic – so instead our holidays were spent in the Cotswolds. We went for one week every year, setting off on the first Saturday of August and always to the same cottage, thatched with no near neighbours, and with chintzy curtains that were drawn the instant we walked in.

'Why on earth,' Elaine would mutter, as she unpacked the cooler bag of food, 'would anyone want to spend precious holiday time meeting imperfect strangers they'll never see again?'

I'd been so bored the last few years we'd been, it had taken every ounce of effort to muster my excited smile as we pulled up in front of the cottage.

'Well, here we are,' Elaine would say, patting her lap with both hands. 'On holiday.'

Cue my excited smile.

Henry would never say anything. He just parked the car and silently unloaded the cases.

Staring out across the endless expanse of water, knowing what I suspect is true, I wish I'd been more trouble. I wish I'd argued more. Stamped my foot and slammed some doors. I should have told them I hated that stupid Cotswold cottage. I should have crept out after bedtime to drink cider in a nearby graveyard with all the other bored teens. I should have screamed at the top of my voice and smoked out of the bathroom window and played punk music at full volume. They stole me. I should have been a little bitch. I should have made them regret taking me every day of their stinking lives. Instead, I did as I was told, did everything I could to make Elaine happy, because when she was happy she was lovely and I adored her, but when she was upset, her unpredictable behaviour – the black moods, her quick anger, the way she hurt herself, scratching and cutting her arms and face – scared me. So I did everything I could to keep her happy. And Henry did the same. Her emotions were the epicentre of our lives. If Elaine was stable the home was stable. And though Henry and I never openly discussed it, this was the unwritten rule between us. Keep her happy, keep her stable.

I lean against the stone wall and peer down into the heaving swell. I picture the sea floor below, fathoms of cold, murky water between us. I feel it cold on my skin, the way it makes me tingle, a numbness creeping through my body. I bend to pick up a pebble. It lies in the palm of my hand and I run my fingers over it, enjoying its cool smoothness. Then I close my fist around it and throw it as far as I can, watching it break the surface of the roiling sea with a splash and disappear.

I reach into my jeans pocket and pull out the letter that contains the Tremaynes' address. But as I stare at it I know I'm not ready. I need time to prepare. To get my head around what on earth I will do when they open the door. What will I say?

Hello, so you know your daughter? The one who went missing? Well ... surprise!

I think of David. Am I wrong to attempt to do this without him? I remind myself how he hurt my hand, the look in his eye as he told me to calm down. No. I am better without him. But then I imagine his serious eyes looking directly at me. His voice, unwavering and emphatic, speaking words that make sense, like a well-written instruction manual. I root around in the bottom of my bag for my mobile phone. Maybe if I call him, hear his voice for a few seconds, it will give me strength.

I hold the phone and picture him answering my call. He'll be in his office at this time of day, most likely in the middle of a tutorial. I see him sitting at his desk, surrounded by books on floor-to-ceiling shelving, more on his desk, more on the windowsill. I found his love of books reassuring that first day I met him, after I'd walked with him from the lecture theatre to his office, listening to him tell me about the café and the coffee and the cake to die for. In my mind, there's a student with him. He's trying to concentrate on what she is saying. But he can't. He's staring at the framed photograph of me, tapping a pen rhythmically against his desk, his lips tight with worry. Then, as I watch him, he glances up at the student. I see her clearly now. She is a first year, and pretty, no, more than pretty, she is beautiful, with dark, shiny hair and a T-shirt that's a size too tight stretched over her full, rounded bosom. She looks at him through her eyelashes, smiles a lop-sided smile through parted lips that betrays her infatuation. He smiles back at her and then lays my picture face down.

I turn on the phone and I look down at the screen. Thirty-six missed calls and fifteen texts since I turned it off this morning. As I debate whether to read the texts, the phone rings and startles me. David's name flashes up. I hesitate, my finger hovering over the keypad for a moment before I answer the call.

'Bella. My God. Where are you?'

I don't say anything.

'Bella, can you hear me? Please say something, for crying out loud. Where are you? Are you back at home? Christ, I can't believe you've done this. I'm worried. You've made me so desperately worried.'

I bite my knuckle to stop myself from speaking. If I speak, if I connect with him, I know I'll falter. I know I'll sit down, right there beside the sea wall, and wait for him to come and get me. And if he comes for me I will have to tell him and then it will be out in the open, and before long it will be in the newspapers, on the television, on social media. It will be hashtagged, discussed, devoured and spat out before I even know what's fact and what's fiction.

I turn the call off. My heart pumps blood around my body. I stare at the phone.

I need to do this on my own. For the first time in my life I must take control of myself. So I set my mouth, fix my look straight ahead, and cross the car park in the direction of the taxi rank. As I pass a bin, I drop my phone into it and a burst of exhilaration floods me.

One, two, three, four.

'You're OK,' I whisper. 'Small steps, one after the other.'

One, two, three, four.

'You can do this.'

EIGHTEEN

The taxi driver folds his paper neatly and lays it on the passenger seat as I bend to talk to him through his window.

'St Ives, please?'

He nods and turns the ignition key.

'Got an address?'

'No,' I lie. 'You can drop me anywhere. Somewhere in the centre, maybe. Wherever you think best.'

I rest my head on the back of the seat and close my eyes. My lids meld together and I realise how badly I need to sleep.

'I'll drop you on the front.'

'We're here already?'

I sit up and look out of the window, stifling a yawn as I watch people milling about in the middle of the narrow road, pointing in shop windows, chatting casually. They are relaxed and happy, most of them on holiday, I assume, and all of them seemingly oblivious to the huffing and puffing of my taxi driver as he negotiates a way through them.

He drops me on the corner of the harbour on the edge of a cobbled street that disappears up a hill in another throng of people. I pay him from the stack of notes I'm carrying in a bag hung around my neck and inside my jacket. I emptied our joint account before I caught the train. I'm not proud of it but I need money and David would find me if he was able to see where I was withdrawing money. I was terrified walking into the bank. My palms sweated so much you'd think I was about to rob it at gunpoint.

Nobody else knows anything. Keep pretending everything is normal. This is your account, your signature, your PIN…

'I'd like to make a withdrawal,' I'd said, my voice quivering horribly.

'How much would you like to take out?' asked the softly spoken woman behind the bulletproof glass. She smiled at me and I forced a smile back, convinced that at any moment the doors would lock tight and the lights would flash in time with an ear-splitting alarm.

'What's the balance, please?'

She referred to her screen then wrote something on a piece of paper, which she slid beneath the glass barrier.

Eighteen hundred and thirty-two pounds, fifty-three pence.

'Could I take one thousand eight hundred out? If that's OK?'

She laughed a little. 'It's your money, Mrs Bradford. You can take out what you want.'

I tried to smile back but the corners of my mouth wouldn't move. David would be furious. He had full control of the bank account. My name was only on the account so I could pay for the weekly shop. Other than that, I wasn't allowed anywhere near our finances. My paltry salary from the library went directly into another account from which I assume he paid the bills or mortgage, and he gave me a small sum every Sunday night. My 'pocket money' he called it. But, I reasoned, as the lady counted out the notes and sealed them into a plain white envelope, even though I knew he'd be angry, I also knew he'd want me to be safe, and when things are settled I'll pay it all back, every penny. I haven't stolen it; I'm borrowing it.

The taxi pulls away from me, and despite being surrounded by people, I feel very alone. I stand and watch those around me. A group of girls laughing hysterically, a few people sitting on the wall eating ice creams; there are a couple of families on the harbour beach, and lots of others walk languidly with nothing more on their minds than what souvenirs to take back to those left in grimmer parts of the country.

The salt air is mixed with a thick smell of warm fudge and fried fish that wafts over from the parade of shops and cafés on the seafront. The tide is out and a large number of beached boats lean sideways on the exposed sand, waiting calmly for the water to return. A handful of children, some clad in wetsuits and others, tinged purple, in not very much, poke about together in the sand. I look up and see a large number of gulls patrolling the sky in sweeping circles. They call to each other and I watch as one of them dives, falling like a lead weight on an ice cream held in a middle-aged woman's hand. Unlike the chip thieves outside Penzance station, this bird is gone before the woman even knows what's happened. She turns to her companion, her alarm quickly replaced by laughter, and I allow myself a smile. I like St Ives.

I haul my bag onto my shoulder and head up the cobbled street in front of me. I amble, enjoying the beat of the sun on my back as I window-shop. There are wooden toys next to surf shops, next to bakeries with enormous golden scones on wooden trays, beside galleries selling trite paintings of white-sanded crescent coves and moody photographs of fishermen pulling in nets, next to shops selling mother-of-pearl jewellery displayed on kaleidoscopic sprays of coral. There are baskets lined up along the pavements, filled to the brim with cuttlefish bones, shrivelled seahorse corpses and shells of all sizes, some white, others pink, their insides splayed like blooming orchids. I fit in well with my bag and my curiosity, and quickly become camouflaged, another early-summertime visitor at whom nobody looks twice. To them I am normal. I am anybody and nobody. It doesn't matter where I'm from or with whom I grew up or what dead body I'd recently discovered. I am simply a face in the crowd.

As I walk I allow my thoughts to wander. I think about why I'm here, the people I will soon be meeting, the house where they live. I imagine it's on one of the narrow streets that run off the waterfront. There's a gnarly old fisherman watching as I knock on the door, the scent of mackerel hanging on to his thick woollen sweater, his fingers calloused from years of tying off nets. I will wait for someone to answer the door and I will smile at him. He will remove his pipe and run a hand through his snowy beard.

You're back then, he'll say in an accent so thick it will be hard to decipher his words. *That'll please your parents. They've missed you.*

Later my new parents, beaming from ear to ear, will show me up a creaking staircase to the beamed bedroom I had as a toddler. The room has pink candy-stripe wallpaper and a crowd of soft toys on the bed waiting patiently for my return.

A woman comes out of the shop to which I am nearest and begins tidying away the bits and pieces laid out on the pavement. I look around and see the rest of St Ives is beginning to shut for the day. It dawns on me then I have nowhere to sleep. I walk back down to the harbour where I remember seeing a pub on the corner. I search the front of it for information and, sure enough, they have rooms. I hover outside, intimidated by the hum of voices inside. Despite my nerves pooling, I open the door and force myself in.

The pub is warm and crowded, full of people standing, chatting and drinking and laughing. Near the door there is an older couple sharing a bottle of wine and some crisps. They talk, heads close, faces wrought with mild irritation as they try hard to hear each other over the noise.

I look at the floor and wind through the people to make my way to the bar. When I get there I clear my throat and smile at the barmaid.

'Hello.' I'm too quiet and my greeting is lost in the rumble. I try again. 'Hello?' And again, a little louder. 'Excuse me?'

She looks at me and I flush, heat quickly spreading over my neck and cheeks. 'I wonder if ... um ... do you have any rooms? For tonight?'

'Hang on,' she says, as she scrapes her hair back off her face and takes a ten-pound note from the man she last served. She spins around, flicks open the till and her fingers grab at the change so quickly they blur. She turns back, shoves a glass beneath the Guinness tap and lets it pour while she flips the lid of a slimline tonic and pushes it across the bar with a glass filled with ice, lemon and what I presume is gin. She holds one hand out towards a man further down the bar, stops the Guinness tap with her other, then wipes her brow in the crook of her arm and looks at me.

'Sorry,' she says smiling, and blows upwards against her fringe. 'Manic today. What did you say?'

'I'm looking for a room. For tonight? A single. Or a double would be fine too.'

'No,' she says, nodding for an order over my shoulder. 'We're totally booked. You'll struggle to get a room anywhere in St Ives at this late notice. It's crazy at the moment and it's only June!'

'Oh, yes. OK. Thanks then.' I pick up my bag.

'Do you want a drink?'

'Sorry?'

She waves an empty glass at me and smiles again. 'A drink. Would you like one?'

'I wasn't going to,' I say. 'But, yes, why not?'

'Let me sort this order out and then I'll be back with you.'

She blows her fringe up again and bends for a glass.

'Right,' she says, when she returns. 'What'll it be?'

I automatically think of David again. He always used to order our drinks. I would sit at a table while he went to the bar, keeping my head down to avoid eye contact with anyone until he returned with a pint of bitter, half a lager and a packet of honey-roasted peanuts.

'Half a lager, please.'

There's no space to sit at the bar and I don't fancy standing alone at the wall, so I take my drink and push back outside. The late-evening sun bounces its apricot light over the surface of the sea, which the tide has brought part-way in. A few of the boats have been lifted free of the sand and now bob noiselessly. I sit at one of the tables and sip my drink. A group of teenagers – the girls underdressed and the boys looking hopeful – roll past clutching bottles of beer and cigarettes. There's a chill in the air so I pull a sweater from my bag and wrap it round my shoulders.

'Hey,' says a voice from behind me.

It's the girl from behind the bar. Her forehead is glistening with a film of sweat and she carries an empty tray. She looks out over the sea and breathes in. 'It's lovely, isn't it?' she says, caught for a moment by its beauty. Then she looks back at me and smiles again. 'You looked a bit lost in there. I texted a mate of mine. He runs a bed and breakfast, a hostel. It's just up the road. It's not the smartest, more a surfers' hangout, but he's got a bed for tonight. If you want to stay longer you can chat to him.'

It's all I can do to stop myself crying. I want to thank her for her kindness but I worry that if I try it will come out in a jumble, so I smile at her and nod. I wonder if she might sit and talk to me. If she might listen to my story. Maybe she would understand? Be full of sympathy and gentle words. Or maybe she would stare at me with newly cooled eyes, her compassion sapped by a world where the haunting faces of stolen children fight for column inches with celebrity tittle-tattle every single day.

'It's not far, but if you'd prefer not to go, I can ring him back,' she says, her face now showing signs of uncertainty.

'No,' I manage. 'That's great. Thank you.'

'No problem.' She sidesteps out of the way of a table of people as they get up to leave. 'His name's Greg.' She puts her tray on the table and as she clears the glasses and empty crisp packets she gives me the address and directions to the hostel. 'It's not far. About a ten-minute walk. Maybe fifteen.'

'Thank you again. I appreciate your help.'

She shrugs. 'It was nothing; I hope the room's not too grotty.' She smiles. 'And now back to the fray!' Then she disappears back inside the pub, a wave of noise spilling out of the door as she opens and closes it.

Her directions are perfect and she is right, it's not a long walk and I'm grateful for this; my bag is growing heavier with every step and the straps are digging into my shoulder. The hostel is in a largish residential house on the edge of town. It's quite modern, built in the seventies, I guess, with white, pebbledash walls and large, plain windows that look over the sea, the glass marked with dried salt splashes. I push open the door and find myself in a scruffy lobby that appears to double as both hostel reception and a sitting room for guests. There are two old sofas and a small melamine table in one corner, which holds a selection of teabags, instant coffee and sugar sachets in a faux-wicker basket next to a grubby kettle. There is nobody behind the front desk and though there's a small bell with a sign telling me to ring for attention, I decide against it, happy to wait until whoever is supposed to be there returns of their own accord.

As I wait, I pick though the display of leaflets fanned out beside the bell. They advertise a multitude of distractions for rainy days: tin-mine tours, pirate-themed adventure playgrounds, a seal sanctuary, an aquarium that looks as if it's seen better days and a handful of places to plod nose to tail on shaggy, pot-bellied ponies. Ten minutes later and still nobody has appeared so I tentatively ding the bell. A girl in a tie-dyed smock with purple streaks in her black hair and a nose-ring arrives. Her nails are painted dark green and her eyes are rimmed with thick black kohl.

'Can I help?'

'I'm looking for Greg,' I say, my voice coming out in a strangled mess.

'Join the queue,' she mutters as she slopes off.

She yells for Greg and when she returns she says, 'Wait here. He'll be down in a sec.'

'Thanks,' I say, but she's already disappeared into the back room.

I sit on one of the sofas and occupy myself with the straps on my bag until I hear a door. A man walks into the room. He's about my age, perhaps a little older, though his clothes are those of someone much younger with rips in his jeans and a long-sleeved T-shirt stretched loose around his neck to show the strong line of his shoulders. He has film-star looks with wavy hair that's been bleached by the sun and a knowing glint in his eye that, of course, immediately renders me tongue-tied.

'I hear you want me,' he says, a West Country accent colouring the edges of his nonchalant drawl.

I stand quickly. 'The girl ... she called ... from the pub...' My voice trails to nothing.

'Which one?'

'Which pub?'

'Which girl.'

'Behind the bar,' I say. 'About ... a room.' My face is burning.

'Oh, sure, yeah. You need somewhere to crash for the night.'

I nod.

'St Ives is like Jesus and Jerusalem at the moment. No rooms anywhere.'

'Bethlehem.'

His brow furrows. 'What was that?'

'Nothing,' I mumble.

'Anyway, you're in luck. I had a couple of arseholes cancel this morning. Like I haven't got a business to run or anything.' He stops speaking and smiles. 'You don't need to know all this.' He laughs and holds out his hand, tanned and smooth with a surprisingly delicate wrist encircled by a collection of leather bracelets and faded fabric bands. 'I'm Greg.'

I look blankly up at him. 'I'm...'

My chest begins to constrict. I feel my breath coming in short bursts and a heat spreads up the back of my neck. A name. I need a name. But not Bella. I can't say Bella. I don't want there to be any chance of David finding out where I am.

I need a name...

Be me, silly! says a familiar voice.

Of course.

'I'm Tori,' I say quickly. 'My name is Tori.'

Tori squeals with glee. How exciting, she says. I get to come out and play!

'Tori?' Greg says. 'That's pretty. I like it.'

I smile. And so does Tori.

'Well, Tori, I was about to have a beer. You fancy one?'

I hesitate before nodding.

He disappears into a room behind the front desk and a few moments later reappears with two cans of lager. He hands me one, then sits on the sofa and stretches out his legs in front of him as he opens his can. It fizzes loudly and he puts it to his lips to catch the foam. My heart quickens and I feel ridiculous.

I pull the tab on my own can and we sit in silence. The silence is uncomfortable, but when I glance up at him, he doesn't seem in the least bit worried, just sits there looking handsome and relaxed and drinking his beer. I want to say something. But what? Should I mention books? Or music? No, not music. I know nothing about music. I could talk about my job, but in my experience mentioning I'm a librarian tends to cut a conversation dead rather than start it.

'So what brings you to Cornwall?' he says.

I stare at him, hands gripping the can, which is cold and wet with condensation.

'On holiday?'

Oh God, speak! You look like a fool. A dumbstruck fool.

'I'm a ... a journalist.'

He sits forward, his hands resting on his knees. 'A journalist? That's cool. What are you investigating?'

I laugh, which I think is very brave. 'I'm not investigating anything. I'm writing something. An article. For a magazine.' I hesitate again. 'On missing children.'

'I'm impressed! I knew someone who went missing once. Went on holiday and never came back. She went to the same playgroup I went to—' And then he sits back and laughs as realisation dawns on his face. 'Oh, of course. *That's* why you're here! You're investigating her, the Tremayne girl.'

My heart is thumping nineteen to the dozen. 'You know her?'

He drinks from his can and nods.

'Yup. The family live here. Her sister was at my school. Year above. The whole town went mental after she disappeared. Her dad was a fisherman, used to drink with my dad in the pub. Not sure they were friends, though. I remember my mum cried about it. The girl drowned but her body never washed up.'

I don't know what to say.

'Mum and her mum knew each other a bit. You know, from school? Her mum got depressed, at least that's what Mum said, but I suppose if you lose a kid on holiday you're going to be upset.'

I stare at him, unable to speak. He regards me oddly and I know he thinks my reaction is strange. He doesn't understand why I'm not excited that he knows the girl, why I'm not jumping at the chance to interview him for my article. I drink from my can in an attempt to look less shell-shocked.

'Would you recognise her now?'

'No. I was only about five or six and she was younger. Not at school yet.' He drinks some of his beer. 'So what's the magazine?'

'Hm?'

'Will I know the magazine you work for?'

'I'm ... freelance. You know ... I write for a few.'

Greg's face loses its frown and he nods again. 'I've never met a journalist before.'

'Do they ... still live in the same house ... do you know?'

He shrugs. 'No idea.'

I try to relax. I hold the can of lager and grip it until my knuckles turn white. He asks me questions and I do my best to let Tori answer, let her pretend to be a confident, successful features writer, while my mind tumbles.

Where do you live?

Central London, near Bloomsbury, like Virginia Woolf.

Who's Virginia Woolf?

A writer.

Television?

No, books, and she's dead.

He doesn't read books, he says. And he doesn't like running the hostel. His passion is surfing, which he also teaches. He says the hostel is owned by his parents, who also own a fishing tackle shop in Hayle.

'They think I should be married and have children and a proper job.' He laughs and tips the lager to his mouth.

I tell him he's lucky to be able to do what he loves every day. He tells me Tori is lucky too. That she has a life that would make lots of people jealous. I agree. Tori has an amazing life. A smart flat in a trendy part of London, a great job, so many friends she can't keep count. All in all, she's a pretty fabulous woman, the kind of woman who would intimidate me if I happened to meet her.

As we sit and talk I notice Greg hangs on every word Tori says. He looks at her in a way that men never look at me, watching her every move, his dark-brown eyes drinking her in and, in spite of everything, I smile.

NINETEEN

I am awake too early. The fluorescent arms of the alarm clock show a little before five. David, of course, would think it virtuous that my mind is alert and ready to tackle the day, but I want to go back to sleep. What little I had last night was fitful, with a racing mind and a stomach that tumbled with nervous energy. Today is going to be hard, and being tired will only make it worse. But as the sun creeps into the sky and a soft-blue hue casts its light across the small, plain bedroom with its narrow bed and battered wooden chair in the corner, I allow insomnia its victory and ease myself out of bed.

It's quiet and everything is still. I dress quickly in yesterday's clothes, grab a clean pair of socks from my bag and put my trainers on, then leave the room, careful not to make a sound as I close the door. There is movement from the room next to mine, then the gentle murmuring of someone talking in their sleep. I stand still and hold my breath until the muttering ceases, then I hurry along the corridor, praying I don't meet anybody.

I boil the kettle and make a coffee, digging at the granules, which have hardened into a crusty mass. I hesitate briefly before stirring in two spoonsful of sugar. I don't usually take sugar, but I tell myself it will help keep up my energy levels. And anyway, maybe Tori takes sugar, part of that devil-may-care attitude she so embraces. Tori enjoys life. Screw the empty calories. Screw the consequences. She's all about the pleasure. I smile as I sip my coffee and head towards the door.

Outside the air is fresh and dewy. The sun has broken free of the hills behind St Ives and a crimson shepherd's warning is reflected across the sea like firelight. The bed and breakfast is at the end of a no-through road and backs onto farmland, areas of grazing separated by dry-stone walling. The fields are punctuated by the occasional slate-grey rock, belligerent and unapologetic, begrudgingly allowing men to farm the land but refusing to make it easy. I walk to the end of the road, lean against the wall and stare out at the sea. It stretches out for miles and miles and miles, and a fine layer of morning mist hovers lightly over its surface. It makes sense, this place. If this is where I am from, it makes sense.

If...

The doubts I have about Henry and his letter still pull at me like a riptide. Yesterday I was so sure, but fresh uncertainty inches in again. I push away from the wall and finish my coffee. My nose wrinkles, the tepid dregs too sweet, even for Tori.

I leave the mug on the table in the reception and return to my room to wash my face and clean my teeth. Then I sit on the end of the bed, hands clasped on my lap, and think about David. I miss him. He has been with me, every day, for so long. He made leaving Elaine and The Old Vicarage possible. Without him I would have scurried back to her, I am sure. The room seems to magnify my solitude, so, like a cat that can't get comfortable, I stand and go outside again. I decide to head down to the beach for a walk, hoping this will ease the churning in my stomach, which I suspect might never stop.

I follow the road down from the hostel and soon arrive at a car park that has a ramp and stone steps giving access to a magnificent beach. It's wide and sandy, and its expanse is dotted with rocks clad in dark seaweed and mussels that huddle together in spiky black colonies. The tide has dragged the water back across the beach and left a maze of hard ridges with tiny pools of water caught within. The sea is flat further out but nearing the shore it breaks from nowhere into rolling, white-crested waves. A solitary surfer is out in the water and I watch him for a while as I breathe in the tang of salty air.

I pause beside a large rock cloaked by a colony of spiky black mussels and seaweed. I balance flamingo-like to pull off each trainer and sock in turn. The sand is cool between my toes and I scrunch them into it as I bend to roll up the legs of my jeans.

And then I have a flash of déjà vu, a vivid picture in my mind that crackles into being. There's a woman. She sits next to this very same rock. She has thick auburn hair, which catches in the breeze. She wears a light summer dress with green-and-white stripes, and has bare legs that stretch out in front of her, crossed at the ankle, with strappy sandals on her feet.

She kisses the arm of a little girl. Her arm is red and swollen. And it stings.

It's my arm.

She's kissing *my* arm.

Then the image vanishes like a sigh.

I drop to my knees. Press the flats of palms against the rock. I've been here before. The woman in the green-and-white dress is real.

My heart quickens as I stand and look around me, greedy for anything more. I begin to walk down towards the sea, searching for anything that will nudge my mind into remembering.

I near the water and a wave breaks and races up the sand in a foamy rush. It runs over my toes and I breathe in sharply as the icy water hits my skin, wrapping my arms around me to block the cold that spreads upwards through my body. I look out over the sea, lifting my face into the onshore wind. I watch the surfer who now sits astride his board beyond the break of the waves. He is looking straight at me. My heart skips a beat as I recognise Greg. He lifts his hand in greeting, but I don't return it, tightening my arms around myself instead. He gestures at me then leans forward on his board, paddling towards the beach, arms windmilling through the water. A wave breaks and carries him in. I look down at my feet and burrow my toes into the sand. When I glance up I see he's approaching, his surfboard tucked under one arm, his face cut in two by a wide-open smile.

You're Tori. You're a journalist from London. You like sweet coffee and drink beer from a can.

'Hi,' he says. He draws to a halt closer than feels comfortable and I take a step backwards. In the morning light he is even more beautiful than I remember. His tanned skin is clear and weathered and I become conscious of my pallor, my unbrushed hair, yesterday's clothes. He rests his board on the sand and shakes his head, sending surf off him like river water from a Labrador.

'So you fancy it?'

'Sorry?'

'Surfing.'

'Oh, no, I don't think so,' I say, stumbling over my words. 'It's not … me. But one day maybe.' I sweep the hair from my face as the wind takes it.

'You should give it a go. I'm an excellent teacher.'

I don't know what to say in reply and focus my eyes on my buried toes.

'You slept OK?'

I have a flash of me wide awake and staring at the bedroom's cracked ceiling, tossing and turning, aching with exhaustion but unable to sleep, as images of Henry's body lying above a sea of blackened blood battered me. 'Fine, thank you. Is the room free … for a few more nights?'

'Sure. I'll need to check the diary to make sure. I've a phone in the office; I'll give Fi a quick call and she can check. Best to get you booked in, the room will go quickly. How many nights?'

'I … don't know. Two? Maybe three.' I pause. 'You need more coffee, by the way. The stuff in reception's gone hard.'

He laughs as I flush with heat. 'Look, let's phone Fi now and find out about the room. I've a lesson starting at eight, a group of beginners, God help me.'

As I follow him up the beach, I am stung by guilt. David would hate me being alone with this man. He has always been jealous. Sometimes his jealousy makes him moody. It doesn't matter how often I tell him I'm not interested in anyone else, and that men aren't interested in me anyway, he is never convinced.

'You're young, beautiful, of course men are going to want you. I did, didn't I?'

I suppose the guilt could also stem from the fact that I'm lying to Greg about who I am and why I'm here. It feels wrong, in a way, to allow him to believe I'm a glamorous journalist and not, in all likelihood, the girl from his town who went missing.

When we reach what I assume is the office he mentioned – a small hut with a bright-orange roof at the top of the beach – he unzips his wetsuit and pulls it off his arms and down to his waist to reveal a torso so toned and muscled it reminds me of a sculpture.

'Give me a sec while I find the phone,' he says. 'God knows where it is.' He smiles at me again. I wish he would stop; it's unnerving now we're together in this enclosed space.

'Are you going to talk to them today?' he asks.

'Sorry?'

'The Tremaynes. The family of the kid.'

'Maybe,' I say, trying to keep my voice light. 'Yes. Probably.'

Greg turns his back to me, and starts rummaging amongst piles of paper on the tiny desk. I gasp. On his back is an incredible tattoo. A tiger prowls across the top half of his back and shoulders. The detail is breathtaking. I have never seen one like it, not that I've seen many, only the Chinese symbols, doves and butterflies that decorate the ankles and wrists of some of the students who come into the library. The animal stares right at me. His mouth gapes wide in a silent roar. Its teeth shine with saliva as it clenches its claws, each one as sharp as Henry's knife. The fur is etched into Greg's skin in a thousand fine lines that quiver as the tiger appears to breathe. I imagine myself climbing onto the creature's back, scrunching my fingers into its softness and laying my cheek against it, allowing it to carry me wherever it's going.

Greg coughs and stands up and I am back in the hut with a jolt.

'I like your tattoo,' I say, somewhat childishly.

'Had it done in Indonesia. By this local guy. A proper artist,' he says as he continues to search for his phone. 'It hurt like a bitch.'

His fingers continue to root around the desk, papers falling unnoticed by him from their precarious piles until he finally finds the phone at the back of an overflowing in-tray. He dials. Then mouths to me, 'Three more nights, yeah?'

I nod and wait while he talks to the girl back at the hostel. I imagine her surly face, kohl-rimmed eyes narrowing as she checks the diary.

'Great,' says Greg. 'Yup, book it as taken. Cheers, Fi.' He throws the phone back on to the desk. 'All done.'

'I'll sort the money out sometime this afternoon if that's OK?'

'Whenever. So, I hope your interview goes well. And to warn you, when I knew her, the sister, well, she's strange. A mate egged her door once and she lost the plot, which was quite funny. But that was years ago.'

'Egged her door?'

He grins. 'It's when you chuck eggs at a door for a laugh.'

I don't say anything.

'Kids' stuff,' he says, as if this helps explain why someone would throw eggs at a door.

'Was it Sinai Road?'

'Don't know, but maybe that rings a bell. Sinai Road is about ten minutes up the hill at the back of town. Head that way,' he says, pointing. 'Then ask at the Co-op. It's near there.'

He pushes his arms back into his wetsuit and zips it up, hiding the tiger, the palpable tension in the cramped hut lessening as he does so. 'And if you want a drink later, give me a shout. A few of us are going to the Queen's Head tonight.'

I feel my face redden with heat.

'It's just a drink,' he says with a laugh.

He walks out of the hut and picks up his board. 'Unless you get lucky.' He raises his eyebrows at me then jogs back down towards the water.

I walk back across the sand, pausing at the rock where I'd remembered the woman in the green-and-white dress. Was it Alice Tremayne? Will she recognise me when she opens the door? Will she burst into tears of joy or back away in shock?

I start to walk, drawn not in the direction Greg pointed or back to the hostel, but across the beach towards a path that climbs up to the cliff top. At the base of the rocks, I tuck my socks into the pocket of my jeans, push my sandy feet into my trainers and start to scramble up it. The wind is strong when I reach the top and I am buffeted left and right as it billows around me. I breathe in and am immediately invigorated by the pulsing vibrancy of the wind and the sea. The kernel of belonging, the feeling – perhaps even concrete knowledge – that I'd been on the beach before mushrooms inside me. I walk onwards, away from St Ives and along the coastal path. I stride out, lift my face into the wind as the beauty of this place fills me up – the incessant sea below, the expansive sky above, the sea birds gliding on invisible thermals, so at home in the vastness of it all.

To my left are clouds of yellow gorse and green fern that unfurl away from me in a thick carpet with wild flowers in purple, blue and pink exploding like fireworks across it. An outcrop of rock looms ahead, coarse tufts of grass at its base, its grey patched white with salt-loving lichen. I stop for a moment or two and stand facing the sea. Out on the horizon the sky is darkening. Towers of distant rain smudge it from cloud to sea. I step off the path and move towards the cliff edge, which falls away with such severity it makes my head spin.

What would it feel like to jump?

People do it, I think. When they are too lost to find their way back. Or too alone to care.

'Yes,' I whisper. 'That too.'

Before I found Henry Campbell I hadn't given much thought to suicide, but since discovering his body it occupies my thoughts more often than it should. I think I understand a little better now about turmoil and devastation. About despair. And hope.

Or the absence of it.

I stare down at the sea and imagine launching myself from the cliff, sinking like a stone into the roiling water that muffles the sounds above it. I would shut my eyes, open my mouth and breathe in deeply, sucking the silken water into my lungs. People say drowning is peaceful. I have no idea how they know, but looking down at the sea right now, it seems a far less brutal way to go than taking a knife to your wrists.

I turn myself away from the heaving swell. I've been walking for hours, but I still don't want to turn back. Each stride feels forceful and strong, and I drive myself onwards. The path eventually turns away from the open sea. It passes a sheltered cove that reaches into the land with turquoise water and gentle waves rolling over time-blackened rocks. The track grows muddier underfoot and I come to a small stone stile with a lane beyond. There are two paths to choose from, one heads over the stile and up a tarmac lane, the other continues back to the coastal path. I choose the lane and climb the stile, and walk past a white house on my right. The noise of children happily playing in the garden behind the house carries on the salted air.

The lane snakes up a shallow hill. On one side it's flanked by hedgerows and moorland beyond, and cows in lush fields chewing languorously on the other. I arrive in a small hamlet with a pub, a few terraced cottages and a church. The houses are immaculate, with clean, white walls and window boxes stuffed full of colourful flowers. Though cars are parked bumper to bumper either side of the narrow road, there isn't a soul in sight. I pause at the bottom of the three granite steps that lead up to the church.

Despite Elaine's best efforts, I never felt much religious conviction. I'm not an atheist as such – that feels too absolute – but I certainly seem to be more sceptical than not. I like churches though. I love the architecture and the reverence they inspire, their pomp and grandeur, the still calmness they all seem to offer. So, without thinking too much, I open the wrought-iron gate at the top of the steps and follow the gravelled path through the gravestones. Some of the stones are neatly tended while others are overgrown, with sad jars of dead flowers in murky water sitting at their bases; others are so weathered by time the names of those lying rotted beneath are long since lost. The wind blows noisily through the trees and I shiver slightly as I walk through the graves.

The door to the church is old and dark, with *fleur de lis* hinges. A sign crudely covered in cling film welcomes me in four different languages, and another beside it reminds me to close the door to stop the birds getting in. The door is heavy and I have to push my shoulder hard against it to open it. Inside is cool and dank with that aged smell you find in all churches, yet perhaps even more concentrated, as if the air is as old as the blocks of granite that contain it. I wait for my eyes to adjust to the darkness then walk across the stone floor to a back pew. I sit and clasp my hands. It is deathly quiet, no wind, no gulls, no people. I lean my forehead against the pew in front like the old people I stared at as a bored child. I breathe deeply. Try to relax every muscle in my body. Open myself up. This would be a good time for God to find me.

But He doesn't come – or if He does I don't recognise Him – and I sit back with a small sigh.

I get up to explore the church. There's a table with printouts on its history but I don't pick one up because my attention is captured by an area to the right-hand side. Despite a stained-glass window high up on the wall, this part of the church is even more shadowed than the rest. In the centre of it is a small wooden pew about a quarter of the size of the others, maybe smaller, and despite the gloom I can see it's a solid, substantial piece of furniture made of highly polished wood. As I get closer I am struck by a magnificent carving that adorns the side of it, a woman, no, a mermaid, with a rounded belly above a fish tail slung low on her ample hips. From nowhere I feel David's hand on my own stomach, his voice muffled against my neck as he voices his hopes that this month will be different.

I kneel beside the pew so I can study the carving. The mermaid's breasts are unclothed and full, bereft of nipples, naked and chaste simultaneously. Her arms are bent upwards at the elbow and she holds an oversized comb in one hand; in the other is a spherical object I assume is a mirror. Her braided hair reaches her waist and frames her face. Her features are somewhat indistinct, worn down, I imagine, by the gentle caresses of ten thousand fingertips. She is serene and grace-ful and for the first time in days my anxiety ebbs.

'It was you who drew me here, wasn't it?' I whisper. My voice echoes against the stillness in the church.

I rest my hand over her. The glossiness of the wood feels wet, as if she's swum straight from the ocean only moments before. I circle my finger around her roundness, touch her cheek, her hair, her tail, and as I do shocks of current ripple though my body from my fingertip. My head becomes clearer. The sediment swirling around my mind settles as her tranquillity fills me.

Not God, but this mermaid.

I sit back on my haunches, my hands resting on my thighs, and as I do I think of the address written on the notepaper in the back pocket of my jeans.

I can feel it. Pulsing. Burning me through the denim.

You should go to them.

Was it my voice or hers?

It doesn't matter. I am finally ready.

TWENTY

I sit rigid in the taxi, knees together, hands on my lap, answering the chirpy driver's questions with monosyllabic directness, hoping he will soon stop talking.

Am I on holiday?

No.

What brings me to Cornwall then?

Work.

Have I been to St Ives before?

No.

Do I know the area used to be famous for tin?

No.

'This is the road,' he says at last, and my stomach immediately seizes. 'What number?'

'Here's fine,' I say.

'Well,' he says, as I hand him his fare, 'been nice talking to you. Have a good rest of your trip; you look like you could do with the break.'

As the red-sky warning had predicted that morning, the weather has begun to close in on St Ives and I stand on the corner of Sinai Road, ominous clouds, glutted to the point of rupture, swiftly driving through the deep-grey sky above me. The cries of the gulls sound sharper now, as if calling a mass-retreat to their cliffy overhangs. I've memorised every digit and letter scrawled onto Henry's sheet of paper, but I pull it from my pocket and stare at it anyway. My nerves shiver. I try to keep my mind off the clammy sweat that creeps over me and concentrate on my breathing, steady and deep, in and out, as I count my steps.

One, two, three, four.

I pull my jacket tightly together, cross my arms and bow my head. It isn't only the weather that is unnerving me. It's the area. I am annoyed with myself for feeling anxious, but I can't help it. I am no more than a mile from the quaint harbour in St Ives but I could not feel further from its fudgy smell and postcard-pretty streets.

One, two, three, four.

I am in the midst of a run-down estate with front yards like dumps and windows rimmed with cracking PVC. A dog barks from inside one of the houses to my right. There's an abandoned red Ford, patches of rust around its wheel-less wheel arches, perched on piles of bricks, its rear window smashed and crudely repaired with a black bin bag and blue tape that flutters in the wind, small squares of shattered glass, vestiges of the broken window, in the road beside it. I try to convince myself there's nothing to worry about, that my fear is irrational, merely the consequence of Elaine's phobias. Even as a teenager, whenever we stepped outside the walls of The Old Vicarage, she would grip my hand so hard that it crushed the bones in my fingers. Grief stings the back of my throat as I remember how I was back then, trotting after her like a faithful puppy, my hand aching, head ducked low to avoid the monsters, just like she told me to do over and over and over.

'Danger is everywhere and everyone's a threat,' she'd say. 'The only place you're safe, my darling, is at home with me. You understand? Outside the house live monsters. Monsters wherever you look.'

Figures are walking towards me.

One, two, three, four.

They are young, I think. Three boys. Their low-slung jeans and tribal tops with hoods pulled over their heads make my heart thump. I keep my eyes on the pavement as they approach.

One, two, three, four.

My hands clench. I ready myself to run. They are a few metres from me. Their footsteps are as loud as thunder.

'Please don't hurt me,' I whisper. 'Please don't hurt me.'

They pass me by without casting me a look, but in my mind they change their minds and turn to follow me. I hear them breathing, inches from me. They wield hammers and murderous snarls. What if they find the stack of twenties buttoned inside my shirt? Do I hand it over? Or do I run? I glance over my shoulder, but they are nowhere near me. They have continued to walk in the opposite direction. One of them laughs. Pats his friend on the back.

They are kids. Just nice kids hurrying back home before the rain starts.

I hate her then. I hate her for my fear. Elaine and her ivy-clad prison. Who were we hiding from, Elaine?

Who were the monsters?

You.

We were hiding from you. You were the monster. You were the evil outside our gates, the child thief, the reason you kept me locked away. You knew empirically that the monsters were everywhere, walking the streets, masquerading as normal people, because you were a monster.

The first drops of rain hit my face. I turn my head upwards and let the droplets fall on me.

Rain rinses the world of its sins. It wipes the slate clean.

I make myself walk on.

One, two, three, four.

I reach number 4a and stand in front of it. My knees threaten to buckle. I rest a hand on the gate post to steady myself. The door is pea-green, paint peeling, wood rotten at the bottom. There's a ramshackle shed with torn felt roofing in the front yard, with a request not to fly tip scrawled in black paint across its doors that looks more like graffiti than somebody's dictate. The yard is littered with weeds so mighty they've torn through the concrete and there's a window next to the door in which hangs a greyed net curtain punctured with moth holes.

I want to run, but I won't let myself.

There's no bell so I lift my shaking hand, picture what's behind the door, a warmly lit hallway, a console table with cut flowers, a rack of coat hooks, shoes lined up beneath.

I knock.

Footsteps approach the door.

My heart is pumping hard and fast. The familiar clamp tightens around my chest. I breathe slowly. Try to keep calm. And when the door opens the air is slammed from my lungs.

A woman stands in front of me. I try to take her in but all I can see are her eyes. Eyes that shine out of her pallid face like beacons. Green eyes the colour of sea glass.

My eyes.

The woman standing in front of me has my eyes. And now I am in no doubt at all that this person, this woman, is my sister.

TWENTY-ONE

I try to talk but no words come out. Everything begins to spin. I'm worried I might be sick.

'Yes?' Her voice cuts through me.

Speak.

'I ... well, it's ... I...' My voice stutters. 'I'm a ... journalist. I'm researching ... the child that went ... missing...'

Her green eyes narrow to thin slits. She crosses her arms. She's thin and her face is so gaunt it gives the impression she's sucking in her cheeks. Her lips are pale and cracked with a small cold sore in one corner. She has lank, mousy hair, almost the same shade as mine. It hangs below her shoulders and is in need of a cut. She wears a clean white T-shirt, a pair of grey tracksuit bottoms, and a blue plastic watch, an ancient digital one, like a child might have.

'Fucking vultures. Go away.' She slams the door in my face.

I don't move. All I can think about are her eyes and her mouse-coloured hair. We are even the same height. Her skin is pale and translucent, like mine, the skin I'd grown up with, the skin I thought I shared with Elaine. My skin isn't the same as Elaine's. It's the same as this woman's.

My sister.

I bang against the door as hard as I can, battering the wood with the flat of my hand. My palm stings with each hit.

The door flies open. Her face is flared with anger. I don't allow her to speak or shout or slam the door again; I come out with it. A tumble of words falls from my lips, my nerves obliterated by my need to tell her everything. I tell her about Elaine's death, about Henry's wrists, the knife, the letter on his best blue writing paper, the crispy, yellowed cutting, worn through along the folds. I tell her everything and I don't stop speaking, not even when she falls backwards into the dim hallway, a hand against her open mouth, her head shaking backwards and forwards, mouthing *No, no, no.*

When I finally run out of words, when I have told her everything, I stop and I wait, panting like an exhausted athlete. Her face is pale, her eyes wide. I search for signs of understanding, of acknowledgement, perhaps even happiness, but there are none. She glances over her shoulder into the darkness behind her, then looks back at me before stepping out of the house and pulling the front door closed behind her.

The lock clicks loudly.

'You can't be her,' she breathes. 'She drowned. She's dead.'

I shrug unsurely.

'You're her? You're *Morveren*?'

My eyes fill with hot tears. 'I don't know,' I whisper. 'But I think so.'

TWENTY-TWO

We don't speak for what feels like forever then she looks up at the rain.

'You'd better come in. You're getting soaked.' Her voice is a mumble, thick with the Cornish accent I am starting to get used to.

A door key hangs on a piece of string around her neck. She fumbles with it, her hands trembling too much to fit the key in the lock. Finally the door opens and she ushers me in, avoiding my eyes as I pass.

The hall is dingy and smells of soup and damp. The carpet is brown and wiry, threadbare along the centre from years of footsteps. I follow her into a tiny but immaculate kitchen. There are no eye-level cupboards, just three shelves stacked with tins, glass jars holding teabags, coffee and sugar, and a spider plant in a plastic pot. Beneath the shelves is a two-ring electric hob. I have never seen a smaller sink, its stainless steel clouded from years of use, but clean, like everything, it's all so clean. To the right of the sink is a small television, switched on but without sound, the black-and-white picture dancing noiselessly.

Even more so in here than in the hallway, the air is stagnant and thick. I want to fling open the back door and fill the place with fresh air and the smell of falling rain. And the curtains are drawn. I feel immeasurably trapped. I never close curtains, not now, not even in the middle of summer. I haven't done since I left The Old Vicarage, where murkiness and claustrophobia and monsters with dark fury, who loomed from the blackness and haunted my dreams, were a permanent presence. Trapped in that house with the shadows and creaks I felt sorry for Elaine, coping with the agoraphobia from which I assumed she suffered. What wasted pity it was.

The woman leans both hands on the work surface and I watch her.

What are you thinking?

A black-and-white cat with one bent ear appears from nowhere and jumps up to rub itself against her. She shoves the animal to the floor, where it curls around her ankles. I think of the longhaired grey cat and wonder briefly if he is missing Elaine.

'I'm sorry,' she says. 'I don't know what to say.'

The cat saunters over to me and I bend to pick it up. I tickle it behind its ear and it begins purring, pushing its face against mine.

'He's sweet.'

'It's a she.'

'How long have you had her?'

'I don't know. A couple of years. Maybe longer. It showed up one day and never left.'

'What's her name?'

'She doesn't have one.'

'Really?'

'I didn't know she was going to stay.'

'And your name?'

She narrows her eyes, her defences instantly up. 'Dawn,' she says flatly. 'My name's Dawn.'

She finds it hard to look me in the eye, seemingly more comfortable looking at her shoes, her hands knotting into her T-shirt.

I rub my chin into the cat's fur, thankful she's there to dilute the atmosphere a fraction. The silence feels wrong. It must be hard for her. I know her head will be a mess of questions, doubts and confusion.

'Would you like me to leave?' I ask.

She doesn't answer.

'I could come back another time?'

Still nothing.

I put the cat on the floor and turn and begin to walk towards the door.

'Would you like a glass of juice?' she says.

I turn back to her. Her eyes are still on her shoes, arms now locked across her wraith-like body.

'You might as well have a drink or something.'

I'm not thirsty but I nod. 'Thank you.'

I pull out a chair from under the small kitchen table and sit. I watch her reach into a doorless cupboard below the worktop and take two glasses from beside a neat pile of mismatched plates. She stands and takes the glasses to the sink. She is moving as if in a trance. Her head rigid, eyes fixed ahead of her.

'Hope you like orange. It's all I've got.'

'I like orange.'

She nods and reaches for a bottle of squash from the shelf and I notice her nails are bitten to the quick.

I look at the television and try to make out what is on, but the lack of sound, the small screen and black-and-white picture make it impossible. I rarely watch television; Elaine hated it and we didn't have one in the house. David hated it too. He says it kills brain cells and numbs the senses to the richer arts of literature, music and art. I realise then I have no idea whether I like television or not. Why did I let them – Elaine and then David – control me like that? It is suddenly baffling.

Dawn fills the glasses with water and then turns and hands me one. I sip the drink; it's a welcome something to do.

'Tell me again what this man said.'

So I tell her again what Henry Campbell had written in his immaculate handwriting on the blue Smythson notepaper. I tell her slowly this time, giving as much detail as I have, and as I talk I see him clearly, as if he was sitting a few feet in front of me. I watch him put the lid on his fountain pen. Then he places it deliberately on the desk. He seals the envelope, knocks back a handful of ibuprofen with a glass of whisky, then picks up the glinting carving knife and draws it firmly and deliberately down the length of each wrist.

When I stop speaking, she lifts her head and for the first time looks directly into my eyes. My skin prickles hot and sweaty and my eyes cloud with tears. I try to stop myself crying but a tear breaks free. I swipe it away with the back of my hand; I don't want to cry. If I start I might never stop.

'Is Alice here?' I ask quietly, when I've got control of myself.

Dawn's gaze flicks to the wall and then back to me. Her lips purse tightly and she nods once.

'Where is she?'

'In her room.' Dawn puts her glass down and walks out of the kitchen. 'Come on then, if you're coming,' she calls from the hall.

My stomach turns over as I follow her. I'm terrified. My knees feel weak. I try to clear my mind but it's impossible. There is too much going on. It's surreal. What will she do, this woman who once wore a green-and-white striped dress and kissed my stinging arm? She's bound to cry. Or laugh? Will she hug me? Will I recognise her? I count my steps as I move down the hallway.

One, two, three, four.

One, two, three.

Dawn reaches out to open a door at the end of the hallway. Her hand moves as if through water, silently and slowly.

'So you know ... she's not ... well...'

Dawn hesitates before entering the room, as if she might say something more, but she doesn't.

The stale smell in the room, which I guess was once the living room of the flat, is even more intense than it is elsewhere. The moth holes that punctuate the gauzy net curtain let in a certain amount of light, but not enough.

A person sits in an armchair facing away from me, in the direction of the wall. I can't see her face, but the back of her head looks old, fine grey hair with greasy streaks of yellow. I walk further into the room so I can see her fully. Her face is even thinner than Dawn's. Her eyes are surrounded by such dark-grey shadows they look like hollows in her skull, and her lips are so pale they vanish into her papery skin. She is dressed in a tired dressing gown that might once have been lilac, with a belt that doesn't match drawn loosely around her skeletal waist. Her hands, one resting on each arm of the armchair, are mottled, her thickened nails curled under ever so slightly. She makes no movement at all, not even a twitch.

This can't be her. This listless, frail person isn't anything like the snatch of memory from the beach, the pretty woman with thick hair in her green-and-white striped dress and strappy sandals.

'She doesn't speak.' Dawn's voice breaks the silence like a stone through a window. 'Hasn't for years. It stopped gradually.' Dawn doesn't look at me as she straightens the blanket that lies across the woman's knees.

'She doesn't speak to anyone? And she just stares at the wall?'

'Not always. She's happiest looking at the wall though. Before she became so ill she spent a long time rearranging her pictures. Now she likes to look at them.'

My hand goes to my mouth and I shake my head.

No, I don't want this.

It's all wrong, this flat, these people, the smell; it belongs to someone else, not me.

I follow the woman's gaze towards the wall where a collage of pictures, postcards and newspaper cuttings paper every centimetre of space. My body stiffens; the display is the artwork of insanity. I glance at the whisper of a woman sitting motionless beside me. My skin crawls with unseen insects and I rub my arms as I lock them protectively around my body. I step closer to the wall, close enough to read the words. The newspaper cuttings are about her child, her disappearance, the thieving. Like so much in this flat they are stained with age. Shocking headlines – some of them the very same articles I'd read in the British Library – shout out of the wall: *Child Goes Missing in France, Police Fear for Campsite Girl, Cornish Girl Presumed Drowned.*

Surrounding the articles are pictures. Mermaids. Mermaids in a myriad of guises stare back at the woman in the armchair. Some are glamorous and graceful, pert bosoms peeping out from flowing golden locks, waves lapping at their silvery tails. There are pictures torn from magazines. A perfume advertisement with a woman lying on the sand holding a cut glass bottle to her chest, her bent arms covering her breasts, her eyes shut, thinking thoughts to which we aren't privy, thoughts that make her back curl off the beach in pleasure.

'She loves mermaids.' Dawn's voice catches in her throat. 'Any picture of a mermaid she found she stuck up. I do it now. If I find one I put it up there.'

I look back at the woman who supposedly gave birth to me and recoil slightly. I am starting to hope Henry was wrong, that he lied, that this place, these people, aren't anything to do with me. I glance at Dawn, but she won't look at me, instead she studies the large patch of damp on the wood-chip ceiling. I drop to my knees in front of the armchair.

'Hello?' I say. Dawn draws in a breath. I ignore it. 'Hello?'

The woman moves her head slightly, her eyes are on me, yet seem to be unfocussed, as if she's aware of my presence, but I am invisible. I look at her hand nearest me. I take in every little mole and mark, irrationally looking for any I might also have, anything that might link us.

'Answer me,' I say loudly, shocking even myself. 'Say something!'

'Get out.'

It was a whisper.

I turn my head to look at Dawn. Her brow is knotted and her lips drawn so thin they've all but disappeared.

'Sorry?'

'Get. *Out.*'

'What do y—'

Dawn rushes forward and grabs at my arm, yanking me upright. 'Who do you think you are? Why are you doing this? I can't believe I fell for it. Christ, you people make me sick.'

'What do you mean *you people*?' I say. The jumbling nerves in my tummy turn to panic as I see how angry she is. 'What have I done?'

'Lies. Fucking lies. You're not her. She's dead! Morveren is *dead*. You're filth, filth to pretend to be her. Get the fuck out of my flat.'

'But—'

'You turn up here with some made-up story about a dead man and a letter, walk into my life and pretend you're her? Why would you do that? Don't you think we've been through enough? You parasite. Get.

Out!' She is screaming now, her face bright red, eyes wide and staring. 'Get. Out. Get out. Get *out*!'

'I'm ... telling the truth. He ... he ... gave me this ... address. H-he said—'

'We buried her! There was a funeral. My sister's dead. Get the fuck out of here, you stupid bitch. There was a *funeral*. We buried her. Get out!'

I have no words. Anxiety mushrooms as I watch this person screaming words at me. She lifts her hands and hits me on my shoulder. I try to breathe, but it's as if all the oxygen in the room is used up. She shoves me backwards into the hallway. Then she does it again, a hard shove to the chest that winds me as I fall against the front door and bang the back of my head. Still she comes at me, like a lion, teeth bared, her fingers fixed into claws. I scrabble blindly for the handle behind me with one hand, while shielding myself from the barrage of blows with the other. She catches me on the mouth and I taste blood. And then her banshee shrieking grows to a distant hum as time slows. My fingers search the door, my nails rasping the paintwork, until at last I find the latch. I turn it and the door opens and a flood of wind and rain engulfs me.

As I stumble out of the house I hear Elaine screaming. The past replays like a horror film before my eyes, as the shadowy figure of a man looms over me. His hand reaches out to grab me. I'm terrified. This man is the monster. He wants to eat me and only Elaine can protect me. I squeeze my eyes shut and bury my face in her neck. I block the monster out of my sight as Elaine screams over and over again.

Get out! Get out! Get out!

TWENTY-THREE

Henry Campbell – 22nd May 1990

Henry Campbell told his wife he was going to a medical conference. He told her the conference was in Bristol and he apologised and said there was no way he could get out of going, even though it was the last thing he wanted to do. He explained that British Medical Association representatives would be detailing new government outlines in medical procedure and his attendance was mandatory. He wouldn't stay the night. He would be back, but late.

As he closed the door behind him, he heard the bolts slide across, top, then bottom, the Chubb, then the chain, and he stood for a moment as his stomach clenched yet again with the pain of this horrendous situation.

He drove to Cornwall in a daze. Questions pummelled his brain. The same questions that had been repeating in his head for months. *What have you done? What were you thinking? Are you insane?*

Nine months had gone by and with each passing hour his disbelief had thickened. He couldn't bear to be in the same room as the little girl. Every time she opened her mouth to speak or laugh or cry he wanted to tear off his ears. He felt physically sick on those occasions he'd been forced to sit through Elaine's happy chatter about the day the two of them had had, making bread dough, planting seedlings, collecting fallen leaves from the garden to make a collage.

Every morning, on his drive to the surgery, he considered whether this was the day he would go to the police station to confess. Yet he never did. He couldn't do that to Elaine. It would destroy her and he couldn't be responsible for that.

He slammed his hand repeatedly against the steering wheel. 'You are contemptible!' he shouted at the top of his voice. 'You are weak and contemptible!'

When he arrived in Zennor, a hamlet on the sea at the very tip of Cornwall, the first thing he noticed was the number of people milling about in the road. There were so many children, so many young parents, so many wracked faces. The search for the little girl, for Morveren Tremayne, had been called off two weeks after she went missing. The French police had scoured the area with dogs, had dredged lakes, checked cellars, appealed to the public for information, but then, when her Mickey Mouse nightie and teddy were found washed up on a beach a few miles north of the campsite, it was announced that she was presumed drowned. Yet, only now were the parents having a funeral. He imagined them holding out in hope all this time. Praying that she would be found alive and well. Then finally having to admit the worst. Their baby wasn't coming home. Their baby was dead.

The worst thing a parent could ever face.

Henry drove slowly past the church where two men stood in cheap, shiny suits at the foot of the steps, ushering people in and handing out service sheets printed on pink paper. There was a policeman directing traffic down the narrow road to a field the farmer had opened up for parking. He held up his hand to stop Henry's car to allow an elderly woman to cross. Henry once heard that police officers could read guilt in the faces of criminals with one glance. He hoped it was true, that the man would see the crime in Henry's eyes and arrest him. Henry held his breath.

'Come on,' he muttered. 'Come *on*.'

But the policeman nodded genially and waved him through.

Henry parked the car, turned off the engine and sat in the quiet for a while. He reached over and took the light-blue envelope that nestled in the flowers he'd bought, and studied the writing on the front: *To the parents of Morveren Tremayne.* He thought of her then. Pictured her sitting on the floor of their kitchen behind drawn curtains, hidden from prying passers-by who might recognise her, who might take her from Elaine. This child they called Bella, so trusting, so loving. She was the only thing in the world his wife cared about.

Losing Bella would kill her.

Henry began to sob. Tears flowed unchecked down his cheeks. When he finally stopped crying, he pushed his sleeve against his eyes to dry them, sat up straight and drew in a deep breath. Then he slipped the envelope into his jacket pocket and got out of the car.

Henry Campbell laid the flowers – a bouquet of lilies and white Lisianthus that the florist said would be ideal for the funeral of a child – beside the others that were collected outside the church entrance, and joined the people filing sombrely into the church. He squeezed himself in at the back. There was a soft rumble of voices around him. Two women in front him were whispering loudly, one wondering to the other whether she really did drown or whether, as she suspected from the start, she was taken by a foreign paedophile ring.

'I've read they do that, you know. Pick up young kids and then make them do all sorts of God-awful things. Disgusting.'

'Don't think those thoughts,' her companion said. 'Poor little mite. It's better she drowned than that.'

He had a sudden overwhelming urge to push his way to the front of the church and face these people wracked with a grief that had long since lost its bite and shout: *You stupid idiots. Why haven't you found her? You gave up too soon. She's alive. If only you'd keep looking. We took her. She's in my house.*

But why was she in his house? How was she? He'd spent so much time trying to work that out. In the end he blamed love. Love had made him do it. The love he had for Elaine. Visceral, powerful, over-whelming. People sometimes questioned the force of love. Not him. He knew full well what love could make men do. Crimes of passion happened all the time. People killed for love. They also stole children. Ironic that this ultimate act of love had destroyed the very love it was designed to protect. He felt nothing. Nothing but grim acceptance of his own innate weakness.

After the vicar finished the service and had reiterated they must all find a way to believe in God's will and trust in His plan, the congregation waited for Alice and Mark Tremayne to walk out of the church. There was no coffin. Henry knew that made it easier for people; nothing was as heartbreaking as a tiny coffin. Mark Tremayne walked in front of his wife. He was a large, swarthy man, with unkempt black hair. His face was reddened by the weather and, by the look of his rheumy eyes and capillaried skin, drink. He and Alice didn't hold hands and he didn't offer his shoulder for her to lean on. When Alice Tremayne walked passed Henry, he felt his heart crack. She was a petite woman, with thick brown hair and delicate features coloured grey with grief. She didn't look at anybody as she moved through the pews. Her dull, blank eyes stared fixedly ahead. People touched her on the arms, patted her, offered their condolences, but she looked straight through them, as if none of them were there. She was the spitting image of her daughter, the little girl they called Bella, who now lived in his house – a house of which none of their estranged friends or family was even aware – and called his wife Mummy. Then Henry noticed the child. Another girl. She gripped her mother's hand. When he caught her eyes, pale green, the colour of sea glass, he had to look away as a wave of bile rose in his throat.

This wasn't right. These people were broken and it was his fault. He put his hand into his pocket and fingered the corner of the envelope, his mind turning over and over. He walked out of the church and into the sunshine, and as he passed the collection of flowers he stooped to tuck the envelope back between the stems of the Lisianthus. And then he walked back down the pathway and out, leaving the others to stand around the brand-new marble headstone, gleaming white, with Morveren Tremayne's name etched into it.

It was done.

It was nearing eleven when he arrived home. He turned off the car engine and looked up at the house. Elaine was peering through a gap between the curtains. The room was lit behind her. She smiled and lifted a hand to him but he didn't respond. Instead he got out of the car and locked it. He slipped the keys into his pocket and walked up the lawn to the oak tree. Then he lay down at its base, his cheek against the earth, his knees drawn up to his chest. He stayed there until morning when he woke stiff and cold. Elaine was in the kitchen when he walked in through the back door, but she made no mention of it at all.

TWENTY-FOUR

I only make it a few houses down the street before I collapse. I press the flats of my hands into the wet pavement on my hands and knees. My lip and head hurt, my ribs, too, are bruised. I want to be at home. At The Old Vicarage. I want the high brick walls and drawn curtains and bolted doors. I want to be safe.

I want Elaine.

I can feel her with me now and it's comforting. She has sent me up to my room, told me she'll be up in a minute, and when she arrives she has two slices of hot buttered toast and a mug of hot chocolate. She peers through my curtains, before checking the window is locked, and pulling them tightly closed again.

'All safe, my angel.'

'Who are you looking for, Mummy?' I ask, as I pull my doll's arm through the little cardigan Elaine knitted her.

'Nobody, sweetheart. Everything's fine. I just like to be on the safe side, that's all.' Elaine sits next to me and takes my hand in hers. She holds it to her lips. 'I don't know what I'd do if anything happened to you. My precious, darling gift.'

There was a funeral. We fucking buried her. My sister's dead!

Dawn's shrieking voice drowns out Elaine. Her sister is dead. That's what she said. They buried her. She should know, shouldn't she? So if Henry told the truth, there must have been two children lost in France, one drowned, one snatched. A coincidence, yes, but possible. Morveren drowned. I don't belong to those people in that stagnant flat. The emerald eyes are a red herring. That family is Morveren's family. Mine is somewhere else, sad and missing me, waiting in the whitewashed cottage with the pink candy-stripe wallpaper and the patient soft toys. I rock back and turn my face up to the sky. Big fat drops of rain patter down on me, running down my neck, soaking my jeans.

I don't know how long I kneel in the rain; long enough to drift away to some far-off corner of my mind, and when there's a touch on my shoulder, I struggle to refocus.

It's her.

'You'll catch your death,' she says gently. She reaches out to me and I flinch. 'Come on, now. Come inside.'

She takes my hand. I don't want to go with her and pull feebly out of her grasp, shuffling away from her as I try to get to my feet.

'Please.' She holds out her hand and beckons me with her finger. I hesitate but then take hold of her and let her lead me back to the musty-smelling flat and into the kitchen with the flickering television.

'You believe him, don't you? This man.'

I shrug and pull at a loose thread on my sleeve.

'You think you're Morveren?'

'You said there was a funeral. How can I be her if you buried her?'

'There was no body. She wasn't found. They said she drowned but maybe that's because they'd had enough of looking.'

'All I know,' I say, trying to keep my voice steady, 'is that I didn't wish any of this on myself. I didn't ask for it and I'm not making anything up.' I chew my lower lip to keep myself from crying. 'This is all I have to go on. The man killed himself. He wrote a letter saying they weren't my parents. He included the newspaper cutting and this address and he said my mother's name was Alice Tremayne. He asked me to forgive him.'

Silence takes hold of us again, but it doesn't matter now. It can be silent for eternity and I'd be happy; the thought of talking is exhausting.

'There's a scar.'

I look at her blankly.

'My sister had a scar on her arm. Round, like a ten-pence coin.'

My heart feels as if it might leap out of my mouth.

'I can't remember which arm.'

Tears begin to pool as I pull up the right-hand sleeve of my top as far as it will go. I turn myself so my arm and the white, indented circular scar is facing her.

Dawn gasps then reaches tentatively out to graze her fingers over it.

'Oh my God,' she breathes.

A look of bewilderment is written over her face. She drops her hand from my skin and looks at me and I pull down my sleeve to cover the scar. I stop myself asking her how she knows about it, because of course it's self-evident.

It was there before I was taken.

Henry Campbell was telling the truth.

TWENTY-FIVE

'She said you weren't dead. When they buried you, she said it was stupid to have a funeral because you weren't dead.' Dawn steps away from me and leans back against the worktop. 'She said she felt it in her heart and that she'd have known if you'd died because part of herself would have died, too. She knew you were somewhere.' Dawn pauses and smoothes the edge of the worktop with the flat of one hand.

'She was right.'

'I can't believe it's you,' she whispers.

I sit down at the kitchen table and rest my forehead on its surface, deflated, as if no longer capable of emotion, as if I've reached saturation point.

'Did they do bad things to you?' she says. 'The people that took you.'

I lift my head slowly. I think of them then, Elaine cooking in her kitchen, Henry reading in his study.

'No, they didn't do anything like that. They had ... issues,' I say. 'Issues that make more sense now. She liked me close to her. She wouldn't leave the house unless she had to. He was distant. Spent a lot of time alone. He was a doctor.'

'I *hate* doctors,' Dawn says, picking at her fingernail. 'They talk so much shit and poke their noses in where they're not welcome. Know-it-alls, the lot of them.' She shakes her head and sniffs. 'And they never did anything to hurt you?'

'No,' I pause. 'They loved me.'

'Loved you?' she spits. 'They didn't love you. People who steal children. They are bastards and they destroyed our lives.'

We fall quiet again, both lost in different thoughts.

'Do you remember anything? From when they took you. From France?' she asks after a while.

'I've tried to remember stuff. I have dreams. About being alone in the woods and being terrified. I don't know if that's a memory. It could just be dreams.'

'And you never suspected a thing all these years?'

'She had my skin.'

'What about baby photos? They can't have had any baby photos. Didn't you think that was odd?'

I want Dawn to stop interrogating me. I want her to take that hardened look off her face. It's like she's challenging me, as if any moment she expects me to throw both hands in the air and admit I was in on it all.

'She said they were destroyed by a burst water main. She cried when she told me. Said she missed looking at them.'

Dawn glances at the clock on the wall and stands. 'It's past Mum's tea-time. I need to get her fed and washed.'

'How did I get the scar?'

She furrows her brow, as if shocked by my question. 'I don't know. Look, I really have to get her fed. She needs her routine.'

'Can I help?'

'Up to you.'

I sit at the table while Dawn puts a pan on the gas hob, then reaches for a can of soup from the shelf above. She opens the tin and tips the contents into the pan; the soup sizzles as it hits the hot metal. She sets a tatty plastic tray with a mug of water, a spoon and a roll of kitchen towel, laying everything out precisely, taking care to line up the spoon so it's parallel with the edge of the tray.

'Shall I bring...' I want to say *Mum* but it doesn't feel right. 'Shall I bring Alice through?'

'She's done in her chair.'

'Dawn,' I say. She turns to look at me. 'Should I tell her?'

'Yes,' she replies. 'Of course you should. She's been quiet for years. Don't be surprised if she doesn't respond.'

'Will you tell her?'

Dawn nods and I follow her into the other room.

'Tea-time, Mum.' She pulls over a low wooden stool, on top of which she rests the tray.

Alice Tremayne slowly turns her head and blinks.

Dawn kneels by the armchair and tears three squares of kitchen towel from the roll and tucks them into the neck of Alice's faded dressing gown. She takes a spoonful of soup and blows on it, and then moves it towards Alice's mouth. Alice opens her mouth like a baby bird. Some of the thick orangey liquid dribbles onto her chin, and Dawn scrapes it up with the spoon and redelivers. Dawn smiles at Alice who gives a slight nod of her head.

Dawn takes another spoonful and blows on it. 'Mum, there's someone here to see you.'

Alice opens her mouth for the soup. Dawn delivers it and dabs her clean with the kitchen roll.

I step forward so I am standing in front of the chair.

I notice Dawn's eyes have glazed with tears. 'It's Morveren, Mum. She's back.'

I kneel beside Alice so my face is near hers, and then I take her hand in mine. I smile at her, unsure what to say, but she doesn't look away from the wall of mermaids and cuttings. I glance at Dawn, who looks at her feet.

'It's OK,' I say. 'There's no hurry.' And then I sit on the bed and watch as Dawn finishes feeding her the soup, methodically scooping, cooling, spooning and wiping until the bowl is empty.

'Now a nice bath, Mum. You'd like that wouldn't you?'

Alice doesn't respond.

Dawn hooks an arm underneath her and Alice stands, then moves with Dawn as if in a trance. They walk slowly out of the bedroom, and I follow them down the hall and into the small bathroom. Dawn sits Alice on the closed loo seat and turns on the bath taps. Then she begins to undress her. Without her dressing gown I see she is more skeleton than living human. Is this shrivelled body the one that carried me?

I look at her breasts, hanging low, empty sacks of skin on her ashen ribcage.

'Did she breastfeed me?'

Dawn recoils from the question, her noise wrinkling as if she's smelt something horrid. 'God knows.'

When I'd asked Elaine if I'd been breastfed she said she hadn't been able to. She's glossed over it. I assumed she was embarrassed. Elaine didn't discuss intimate subjects like sex or boys or pubic hair, preferring instead to pretend none of it existed, but as with so many of these remembered vignettes, I am forced to reassess that torturous conversation; I now understand why she didn't like talking about baby photos, green eyes and breastfeeding.

Dawn puts her arm underneath Alice's, lifts the loo seat, then lowers her back down. Then there's the noise of urine against the water in the bowl and I look away; to watch feels like spying. Dawn pulls off some toilet roll and hands it to Alice who robotically wipes between her legs.

'Can you move?' Dawn asks abruptly. 'I have to get her in the tub.'

Dawn turns the taps off then pours a capful of clear liquid into the bath, which turns the water chalky white.

'What's that for?'

'Helps stop bedsores.'

Dawn holds Alice's hand while she steps into the bath, still in her hypnotic state, then she reaches up for a scratchy looking towel from the rail, which she lays on the floor to kneel on. I watch her take cupfuls of the water and pour them over Alice's skin. She rubs soap between her hands then cleans Alice's front and bony arms. The scene reminds me of a Roman slave bathing her mistress in ass's milk.

'Got any kids?' Dawn's voice takes me by surprise.

I stare at her as I process the question, but she doesn't look at me.

'I just wondered. You're married, so I thought you might have kids.'

'How do you know I'm married?'

Dawn gestured towards my left hand. I look down and see my ring, telling tales with its shining gold. 'No,' I say, my stomach knotting. 'We don't have children.'

'How come?'

'It wasn't the right time.'

'Because of your job?'

'My job?'

'Your career. Not the right time because of that, I guess.'

'Let's say I'm not one of the lucky ones.'

'Lucky?'

'We've been trying. It's just not happened. Children are a gift, aren't they?' David's words echo around my head.

Dawn purses her lips and then pours a cup over Alice's hair, stroking the water away from her eyes. 'How come your husband isn't here with you?'

'I needed some space.'

'He didn't take it too well?'

'I didn't tell him.'

And then I notice Alice is peacefully rocking.

'She loves her baths.' Dawn takes a flannel and carefully wipes around my mother's face then between her legs without a flinch. 'I remember her taking a bath with you, when you were a newborn. She told me warm water was good for relaxing babies. I'd sit like this on the floor and watch her in the water with you. You were tiny.'

As the woman in the bath gently sways back and forth, I can't help but wonder if it's her lost baby she's rocking. If it's me.

'Is she ever ... normal?'

'Well, she doesn't skip around the house looking for her trainers to go for a run, if that's what you mean.'

I lower my eyes.

'She's been ill for years. What you see *is* normal.'

'What's wrong with her?'

'The doctors said her mutism is a form of psychosis, and it happened because of depression, they said. She withdrew slowly, gradually got quieter and quieter. Then one day she stopped talking altogether.'

'Why isn't she in a hospital?'

'What?'

'A hospital. Would she not be better in a hospital?'

'No. Of course she wouldn't. I don't want her anywhere near one of those places. She doesn't need anybody else to look after her.'

'But—'

'But nothing. She doesn't need a hospital because she has me. OK?' Dawn is staring at me, her eyes hard, angry even, her hand clenched into a tight fist around the flannel. 'She has *me*.'

TWENTY-SIX

Alice is back in her dressing gown. I have been sitting with her for a while, not talking to her, just being still, absorbing. But soon my mind is overrun with questions and continuing to sit in silence isn't possible.

Dawn is in the kitchen washing up the saucepan.

I pull out a chair and sit at the table. 'Where is Mark? Will he be back later?'

Dawn stops washing the pan and freezes for a moment or two before starting to scrub, hard and fast, at the pan again.

'Dawn?'

She places the pan in the sink of water and turns to face me. 'He left. Soon after she got ill.'

'Oh.' I wait for her to say something more, but nothing comes. 'I think he should be told I'm alive. Do you have details for him?'

'He didn't leave any.'

'None?'

'No.'

I open my mouth to speak, but she jumps in before I have the chance.

'I don't talk about him.'

She turns back to the sink, takes the pan out of the water and begins to dry it.

'I'm sorry,' she says. 'I didn't mean to snap. I don't ... talk about him, that's all.'

Dawn wipes her hand across her face and furiously continues drying the pan, which must surely be already dry. 'I'm finding this hard. I can't get my head around it at all. I'm sorry.'

'I should have sent a letter first. Explained things. Let you get used to the idea.'

'I wouldn't have read it.'

I briefly think back to Henry Campbell's letter. I see it in my hand and imagine myself not reading it. Instead I hold it by its corner, unopened. In my other hand is a lit match, which I use to light the envelope. I watch the flame burn and then die to a smouldering line, which eats his unread words, leaving nothing but ash, which takes off into the air like spider silk, leaving me in contented ignorance.

'Maybe you should tell me about yourself,' she says softly.

So we sit at the small kitchen table and I tell her the basic facts, how I'd been home-schooled, about the succession of longhaired grey cats, what I'd studied at university, that sort of thing.

'Which university?'

'Surrey.'

'I've not heard of anybody that went to university,' she says. 'You must be clever.'

'I worked hard.' I hadn't even thought of university until I'd overheard Henry and Elaine arguing about it. Elaine was shouting, but it was unusual because normally, when she got into one of her states, Henry would back down, and quickly placate her with calming words. This time his voice was raised too. Intrigued, I laid my book down and crept onto the landing so I could hear better.

'No, absolutely not. I won't hear of it! She. Stays. *Here*!'

'It's not fair on her, Elaine. You can't keep her locked in this house forever. Give the girl a chance. She's bright. She works hard. Her results were exceptional. She deserves to go university.'

'But what if they find her?'

The monsters, I had thought. *She doesn't want the monsters to find me.*

'Then so be it! But, damn it, if I do one thing right in my life it will be this. She needs a future.'

'She *has* a future! Here. With *me*!' Elaine's voice had grown hysterical.

'What kind of bloody future is that? Set her free, Elaine. For God's sake set her free!' He shouted so loudly I jumped. Then the kitchen door slammed and Elaine screamed as if she'd lost her mind, so I quietly crept back into my room, my stomach fluttering with excitement as I thought about what it might be like to pack my bags for somewhere new.

'Is that where you met your husband?' Dawn asks.

I nod.

'In the same lessons?'

'He was my tutor.'

'Your teacher?'

I don't say anything.

'How old is he?' she asks, not making any effort to disguise her shock.

'Forty-six.'

'Forty-six!' The look on her face is similar to the one on Elaine's after I told her about David, who she seemed to think was some sort of child molester, loitering in the bushes like a wolf hunting lambs.

'He wasn't forty-six when we met and, anyway, he looks younger.'

'Why did you marry him?'

'What?'

'He's rich, right?'

I stare at her; how dare she make assumptions like that? She hasn't even met him. 'I loved him. I still love him.'

'Not enough to tell him what was in the letter.'

I open my mouth to reply but stop myself. After all, I hadn't told him, had I? I'd kept it from him, walked out on him, dumped my mobile, and him with it, in the bin. And thinking about him now, I don't ache for him, and I should, shouldn't I? I must have loved him at the beginning, but all I can recall is the moment he took a small box out of his inside jacket pocket and opened it to reveal an emerald ring.

'It matches your eyes,' he said, and then, 'Marry me.'

'I don't want to talk about it,' I say. 'So how about you? Do you work?'

Dawn gives a burst of laughter. 'You mean on top of looking after my helpless mother 24/7?' She sits back in her chair and folds her arms. 'No, I don't work. I just do this.'

'I didn't mean ... what you do ... is incredible. I'm sorry ... if it sounded like ... It really—' I stop myself mid-sentence as I can see she's not interested in hearing what I did or didn't mean. 'You know, I think it's time I got going. We're both ... exhausted.'

'You'll come tomorrow?' she asks.

'If that's OK.'

And then I stand up and leave this girl, my flesh and blood, a stranger, sitting at the table. This place, these people, belong in a parallel universe of which I have no understanding, a world into which I've been unwittingly thrown. And I'm stuck here. This isn't a storybook. There are no ruby slippers, no enchanted wardrobes, no ships to take me home.

I'm stuck and there's no way back.

TWENTY-SEVEN

I walk down the hill into St Ives and pass a supermarket. It's still open and I go inside to get something to eat. I choose a sandwich and a packet of crisps and then pass a display of mobile phones. I hesitate, then pick up a simple, inexpensive pay-as-you-go model. As I queue for the till, Dawn's voice rings in my ears.

And you never suspected a thing?

I think about the bolts, the absence of baby photos, the knocks on the door that sent her loopy...

'Go to your room,' she said. Her voice had that hard edge that told me she was serious.

My heart pounded as I leapt two stairs at a time. But I didn't go to my room. I crouched at the top and peered through the banister. I watched her check the spyhole in the front door and saw her flap one hand while resting the back of the other against her forehead. She stepped away from the door and I caught a glimpse of her panicked face.

'Henry,' she whispered with an urgency that scared me. She took a few steps towards his study. There was another loud knock on the door. Henry's study door opened. 'It's the police, Henry. Oh Christ, the police.'

Henry and Elaine came into sight again. She was walking behind him, her whole body was shaking, small whimpers coming out of her like an injured animal. He turned and grabbed her by the shoulders, shook her so roughly I thought her head might fall off. 'For God's sake, get in the kitchen,' he growled.

She stayed glued to the spot. There was another loud knock at the door.

'Elaine, get in the bloody kitchen!'

I held my breath and gripped the banister as he slid the locks and opened the door. My heart pumped and a cold sweat spread. Two policemen stood on the doorstep, dark uniforms, hats pulled so low that from where I was seated I couldn't see their faces. Terrified, I let go of the banister and ran to my room, leapt into bed and pulled the covers over my head.

A while later I tentatively climbed out and peered down at the front door from the top of the stairs. It was closed and there was nobody in the hall. Elaine and Henry were talking in the kitchen. I crept down to join them. Elaine was clutching a cup of tea, her body rigid.

'—break-in at The Gables. I told you, they were only asking if we'd seen or heard anything. You've *got* to get a grip, Elaine. You've *got* to—' He stopped when he noticed me standing in the doorway.

Elaine turned and as soon as she saw me, a wide smile broke over her anxious face. 'Oh, sweetheart, what can I get you? Milk? A glass of water? How about we open a packet of chocolate biscuits? What a silly thing I am. Don't look so worried. Everything's alright. Come here, baby. Come and give me a hug, will you? Don't worry. It's just monsters stealing from The Gables. We're safe here. Have a biscuit.'

There were signs. How did I miss the signs?

It's around seven-thirty when I get back to the hostel. The girl with the purple streaks is idly flicking through a magazine. She glances up and gives me a muted greeting.

When I get into my room, I plug the mobile in to charge then collapse back on my bed and peel open the sandwich. I take a few bites but very soon my eyelids are too heavy to keep open.

I am standing at the foot of the stairs that lead up to the attic. I listen hard because I am sure I can hear music coming from the other side of the door. It's soft and tinkly and makes me feel a lot less scared. I take a tentative step. I wait and listen for a moment. I can still hear the music. I take another step. One foot after the other, I push myself upwards into the shadow, holding my breath as I climb, drawn by the music. If she finds me on these stairs she will shout and get that crazy-mad look in her eye.

I am not allowed here. It's dangerous. But I climb anyway because I can feel the warmth of the music from behind the sealed door. I reach the top. My heart thumps against my ribs like a caged animal pounding its bars. It's pitch black. So dark I can't see my own hand as I slowly reach out to turn the door handle. The handle is cold and smooth; when I touch it I imagine someone is behind me and I flood with fresh terror. The door creaks as it opens and the music suddenly stops. My legs buckle. Don't go in! I hear a voice shout from somewhere far away. In the room behind the door is a wood. Trees and leaves and moss surround me. Sunlight leaks though the branches, lighting up the carpet of leaves on the floor in patches. I look up. There's no ceiling. No roof. Just towering trees and blue sky and a multitude of seagulls circling miles above.

Are they seagulls?

I squint hard to see better and now I think they might be angels. I look down again and then see a figure up ahead. The person is lying down and doesn't move. When I get close enough I see the figure is a woman. I think she might be dead. I bend to see if she is breathing, but there's no movement, no breath on my face. Then, startling me slightly, she opens her eyes. She smiles and when she does I recognise her immediately and I laugh with joy because I've found her. I've been searching for her all this time and at last I've found her. I've found my sister.

I've found Dawn.

TWENTY-EIGHT

I wake still dressed, lying on top of my bedcovers, with the half-eaten sandwich beside me on the bed. My mind is thick and it takes me a while to remember where I am.

I glance bleary-eyed at my alarm clock. It's a few minutes past eight in the morning. I have been asleep for over twelve hours. I can't believe it; I haven't slept like that in what feels like months, deep and heavy, no stirring. *Like the dead,* Elaine used to say.

I wash and dress in fresh clothes and then head down to a café on the harbour I recall passing yesterday for some breakfast. When I get there, the owner is opening up, taking chairs off tables and wiping each one with a cloth as he does.

'Are you serving yet?'

'Give us a sec, love.' I'm not great at guessing accents, but if I had to, I'd say he was from one of the northern cities, Manchester or possibly Liverpool.

I cross the road to sit on the low stone wall overlooking the harbour.

There is something strangely reassuring about the sight of the same boats stranded on the beach once again. They even seem to be leaning the same way as they did yesterday, their colours reflecting a little in the sand, which shines silver in the morning sunlight. Sea birds hop between them, poking about for buried crabs and worms, while a couple of men fish the open waters beyond the harbour wall, rods cast out as they perch on tiny stools.

'Hello? Miss?' calls the café owner from behind me. I turn around and lift a hand to him then climb off the wall.

'What can I get for you?' he says as I near him.

'A coffee, please.'

'Plain or fancy? I do a pretty special cappuccino.' He lifts his eyebrows and grins.

I smile back at him, liking him instantly, which is unusual for me. 'A cappuccino sounds great.'

He looks out over the sea. 'Today's a beauty, isn't she?' he says. Followed by, 'Holleck ooey.' At least I think that's what he said.

'Sorry?'

'How li eck *hoo* hee. Hoo hee. Though it's spelt why, vee.'

I can't help a small laugh escaping from my lips as I shrug slightly. 'I'm sorry,' I say. 'I don't know...'

'How. Li. Eck. *Hoo* hee,' he says again, slowly, his mouth making exaggerated shapes around the sounds. '*It. Is. Sunny*. It's Cornish. I'm learning.' He lifts his eyebrows and smiles again.

'Oh,' I say. 'I didn't even know they had a language.'

'Aye,' he says, nodding gravely. 'They do. I'm doing bits and bobs and the weather first, but soon I'll start on food.' He nods backwards, towards the café. 'Makes sense with me running this place. Now,' he says as he ties his apron strings behind his back. 'One of my extra special cappuccinos coming up.'

I watch him make my coffee or, more accurately, craft it. Working the stainless-steel coffee machine with care and then pouring the hot milk slowly before shaking down a thick layer of frothy foam and artfully grating some fresh Cadbury's chocolate onto the top of it.

'You here on your holidays?' he says as he slides it across the counter to me.

I shake my head.

'Local? I've not seen you before.'

'Work.'

'How long are you staying?'

I dip a finger into the foam and lick it off as I consider his question. *How long will I be here?* My money won't last forever and it's difficult to know what my next move will be. After all, how long does it take to get to know a sister and a mother?

'I don't know,' I say. 'As long as I need.'

'In that case, I'm Phil.'

'I'm...' I hesitate for a second or two. 'Tori.'

'Well, Tori, marplegged to meet you.' He grins at my blank face. 'Marpleg. It means *please*. Pleased to meet you, marplegged to meet you. I think if you use good grammar it's something else, but it'll be marplegged to meet you until someone tells me better.'

'Marplegged to meet you too.'

'Ah, nice one, love.'

I grab three sachets of sugar from the counter and stir them into my coffee. Then take it outside to one of the silver tables on the narrow terrace at the front of the café.

I take the new mobile phone out of my pocket and check the time. It's not far off nine so I pull out a scrap of paper on which I'd written a number before leaving my home, then sit down and dial.

'Well, I have to say I'm glad you've finally rung,' says the solicitor in a clipped voice, after I've introduced myself and we've run through a few forced niceties and condolences. 'To be honest, I thought I might hear from you a little earlier, but no matter, at least I have you now. As you're aware, I've been dealing with Dr Campbell's will. Most of the inheritance is tied up in the two properties—'

'Two? That must be a mistake. There's only one. The Old Vicarage?'

'And another. In Bristol.'

'Bristol? I don't know about any property in Bristol.'

'I see. Well, I need to do a bit of work on that anyway, as at first glance it appears there's a lodger of some description, but it's not that straightforward. There are no obvious contracts and the house isn't rented out through an estate agency. I'll get back to you on this. The other thing that's a bit out of the ordinary is a clause in the will, referring to the estate being left to *the person I brought up as my daughter, name of Bella Campbell*. The wording is odd.'

My stomach turns over. I look around me, irrationally expecting to see David coming to find me.

'He ... often did things ... strangely,' I say, weakly. 'He was an unusual character. Quite peculiar. They both were, really.'

'It doesn't matter, it affects nothing, and I have certainly seen stranger things written into wills.' She laughs tightly, as if laughing isn't something she is used to doing.

When she tells me how much the girl brought up with the name Bella Campbell has been left, I only just manage to contain my shock. Both houses are worth an awful lot, even after fees, taxes and other associated costs. Plus there are reasonably large savings and three paintings – ones I'd hardly noticed – that are insured for upwards of fifteen thousand pounds.

'There is also a trust fund, which appears dormant. Certainly no payments have gone in or out in years, but it's in your name with Dr Campbell as administrator. It has a little under two thousand pounds in it. There's a protective clause on it, which I need to look into. I'm sure it will be straightforward to release the clause and transfer the money into the bulk of the estate, but again, I'll get back to you when I know a bit more. All of this is going to take some time to get through probate, it always does,' she explains, 'but Dr Campbell was seemingly insistent you have access to immediate funds and set up an instant-access trust fund that will pay out a monthly living sum.' She paused. 'He kept everything in immaculate order, which makes my job very much easier, and as it's only you who is named as beneficiary; providing nobody appears to contest the will, we should be fine.'

I know I should be grateful to Henry for his consideration and generosity, but at the moment I don't feel like touching his money. The idea of it makes me feel grubby.

'Do you need me to do anything?' I say.

'No, as long as I can get hold of you, I'm not concerned. If I can have a forwarding address so I can send you any paperwork that would be helpful.'

I glance at Phil who gives me a cheery smile and turn myself away from him. I give her the address of the hostel. 'And can you address any paperwork you send to Ms,' I hesitate, 'Tori Bradford. I've never used Mrs and Tori is the name I go by sometimes. A childhood thing, really.' I make a face. Annoyed I'm talking too much. 'And you won't give details of my whereabouts to anyone, will you? Even Mr Bradford. I'm trying to have a bit of time to myself to get my head around my...' I hesitate again. 'Loss.'

'Of course not. Client confidentiality,' she says. 'Though your husband is extremely worried; he's called here numerous times.'

'Can I ask what you said to him?'

'I said that as your solicitor I'm unable to give him any information, not that I had any to give at that time, but that if you made contact, I'd pass on the message that you should call him. He's trying to organise Dr Campbell's funeral, but is unsure when to set the date.' The judgement in her voice is plain, which grates. She has no idea what my reasons are, but I'm sure if she did she'd realise I have every right to disappear for a while.

'Please tell him to hold the funeral without me.'

'We are not a messaging service—'

'Of course not. Sorry. Perhaps if he calls again you could tell him I'm fine?'

'Perhaps you should tell him yourself?'

Though she remains professional for the remainder of our conversation, I can tell she now thinks less of me than she did at the beginning of the call.

I put the phone down and look out across the sea. Viscous memories of Bella's life envelop me. Her world still exists, tripping along as it always has. David is there, teaching and lecturing and trying to get hold of her. Miss Young is feeding her mother's cat. The library is there with students writing essays and borrowing books and flirting, and Jeffrey is continuing to be terribly fond of David. Her life exists and it makes me feel lightheaded to think about it.

I pay Phil for the coffee and drop a pound into the tips tin on the counter.

'Thanks, love. You have a great day.'

When I get back to the hostel I speak to the girl with purple streaks about taking my room for another four weeks.

'Can you pay fifty percent now? We tend to take that for longer bookings,' she says.

'Is cash OK?'

'Of course. I'm Fi, by the way. We should probably know each other's names if you're going to be here for that long.'

Blimey, says Tori from out of the blue. That's two friends in the space of an hour? You won't be needing me soon!

And I smile.

TWENTY-NINE

Dawn opens the door only a fraction and her face peers through the gap. I expect her to step back and open it fully when she sees it's me, but she doesn't.

'Hello.' I pause. 'Is everything OK?'

'Do you think you could come back later?'

'Later? But ... is there a problem?'

She hesitates. 'No, no problem. It's not a good time, that's all.'

I look at my feet, deflated. 'But ... I...'

She sighs heavily, muttering under her breath, then she throws open the door and stomps back into the gloom of the hallway.

I don't move.

She comes back into sight at the end of the hall. 'Come on then.'

I step cautiously into the flat and walk towards the kitchen. I know she doesn't want me there, but where else would I go?

Dawn stands near the sink. The curtains are open, which is a great relief, but the television flickers silently like it did yesterday, the picture showing two women on a sofa chatting animatedly with no words, and it lends the room a peculiar atmosphere.

I sit at the small round table and clasp my hands in front of me. Within moments the cat is on my lap, purring loudly, a welcome noise in the dismal quiet. I start to stroke her but Dawn scoops her up, then opens the back door and throws her out.

'I want to help you look after Alice,' I say. 'I want to be a family. I want to share the workload with you.'

She puts her hands on her hips. 'The *workload*?'

'I want to help.'

'I don't need *help* with my mother. I haven't had *help* in twenty-five years. I don't bloody need it now.'

The cat scratches at the back door. She mews feebly and my bravado slips further away. I search Dawn's face. There is so much behind her frozen façade, so many thoughts she isn't sharing with me, tantalising shadows of which flicker across her sad green eyes like the noiseless pictures on the television.

I stand and go to her, take her hand. 'You know,' I say. 'I spent my whole life wishing I had a sister.'

She doesn't answer immediately. When she does her voice is quiet. 'And I spent mine wishing I'd never had one.'

Her whisper rips though me like a forest fire.

I drop her hand and concentrate on trying not to cry. I focus on the spider plant on the shelf behind her, its cloned babies hanging precariously from feeble umbilici. The flat needs a happier plant or, even better, a vase of sweet-smelling roses. They'd need replacing every five or six days, but they'd make such a difference.

She shifts position, which draws my attention back to her, then rubs the tops of her arms as if trying to warm herself. 'Look, I—'

'It's OK.'

She moves towards me but I back away, spin around, and make for the kitchen door.

'Last night I couldn't sleep,' she calls after me.

I stop and turn back to face her. She is looking straight at me. Her hands hang loose at her sides.

'I was picturing you. Trying to feel something. But I was empty. All these years I've wondered what happened to you, whether you were coming back or if they were right and you drowned. Up until yesterday you were a ghost, a memory. The idea of you was stronger than the actual you, if that makes sense. It's like that still, like that now. I'm talking to you and I can see you, but you don't feel real.'

A clot of emotion heaves its way through me as I realise how similarly we feel, how well she has articulated it. Morveren, Dawn, the scar on my arm, the silent woman sitting in front of a wall of pictures and cuttings in the next door room, it's all a hallucination, a dream, real enough that I can feel the pinch, but not real enough to be sure of.

'I shouldn't ... have turned ... up the way I did,' I say, hating the way my voice falters. 'Appearing out of the blue ... it wasn't fair. I didn't think it through. I panicked.'

'What else could you do?'

I don't say anything.

'And I'm glad you didn't tell the papers, though; I'm not ready for all that.'

'Where's my father, Dawn?'

Her body tenses. 'I promise I don't know. He and Mum fell apart after you went. He started drinking more. Lost his job. Got more aggressive and then one night he left and never came back.'

'Just like that?'

She nods once.

'Have you a photograph?'

'I told you I don't want to talk about him.'

'I need to see what he looks like.'

Dawn's stony face seems to soften, then she turns on her heel and goes into her bedroom, a boxroom off the kitchen. She returns holding a photo that she pointedly avoids looking at as she casts it onto the kitchen table in front of me.

There are four people in the photo. The man, my father, is familiar. But rather than comforting, the familiarity makes me uneasy. There's something about him. Something bad, and the fingers on one of my hands move subconsciously to the scar on my opposite arm. Of course it could be suggestive, picked up subconsciously from Dawn and her apparent hatred for him. But something tells me it's not, that this wariness is innate, that it's been hanging about in the unreachable area of my memory since before I was taken. He is a large man, with a round face and curly, unkempt black hair. He sits in an armchair and looks out, unsmiling, at whoever held the camera. It's as if he can see me and I feel scrutinised by his piercing stare. At his feet is a young woman with a toddler on her lap, and she's looking down at her with a smile. In contrast to the brooding presence of my father, the love that pours out of this woman is tangible, it drips out of the photo like honey. The young child must be me because in the background is an older girl who is unmistakably Dawn. I am wearing a blue dress with frilly white pants over a big fat nappy, and my little pudgy fingers are entwined in my mother's hair. I have a silver Christening bracelet and I move my finger from my scar to my wrist to feel for it. Alice's beauty steals my breath. How is this the same person who wastes away in the next-door room? She has smooth, blemish-free skin and shiny brown hair that hangs loose to the middle of her back. And she wears a green-and-white striped dress.

I chew at my lip ferociously but can't keep from crying. It is me as part of a family I have no recollection of. The four of us locked in this moment. However hard I dredge my mind, I have no memory of it, not the sofa, not the bracelet, not even the feel of my mother's soft hair.

'It's the only photograph I kept of him,' says Dawn, her voice shattering my thoughts. 'I burnt the rest. But I like you and Mum in it.'

'What was he like?'

Dawn laughs bitterly. 'The man was a drunk. A violent drunk. I'm glad he left. Mum and I were better off without him.'

I look back at the picture.

'The night you went he hit me across the face.'

'Why?' I say, unable to contain my shock.

'He said it was my fault you went missing.'

'What?'

'It's *your* fault, *you little bitch*,' she mimics. 'Your. Fucking. *Fault*.'

'How can it have been your fault?'

Her eyes well with tears. 'I was supposed to be looking after you.' She visibly winces at whatever recollection she's reliving. 'I let you go.'

'But you were only a child. Seven? I wasn't your responsibility. They shouldn't have left me with you.'

She doesn't say anything.

'Listen to me, Dawn. It was nobody's fault but the Campbells,' I say firmly. 'Do you understand? It was them. They took me. It was not your fault.'

'But I watched you go.' The way she says the words, quiet and distant, a thousand miles away, leaves an eerie resonance that hangs like an aftertaste. 'I watched you walk away.'

I watched you go.

I reach out and touch her shoulder. She looks at me with wide and fearful eyes, reliving whatever it was that happened the night I was taken. I want to push for more, for whatever she remembers, but we're interrupted by a knock on the front door, which makes me jump.

Dawn swears under her breath and dries her eyes on her sleeve. My stomach floods with nerves and Elaine bustles into my head, muttering anxiously.

Don't move. Stay there and be quiet while I see who it is.

'You have to go,' Dawn says then. She pushes me towards the kitchen door.

'Go?'

'Yes.'

There's another knock.

'Who is it?'

'Nobody, but you have to go.'

'I haven't seen Alice—'

'Shit,' she whispers. 'Shit, shit, shit.'

A man's voice calls through the letterbox. 'Dawn? Are you there? You alright?'

'Yes! There in a sec,' she calls. Then she turns to me and with a lowered voice says, 'Look, it's a friend of mine. If you're here—' She stops herself and the look on her face shows a sudden vulnerability. 'I'm not ready to tell anyone.'

'Say I'm a friend.'

'I don't have any friends.'

'You have him. You said he's a friend. Well,' I say. 'I'm another.'

'I don't have any other friends and he knows that.' Her hand shoots up to her mouth and she begins chewing her nail. 'Maybe we should tell him?'

'No.' It's my turn to panic. I think of David reading the newspapers, seeing my picture splashed all over the pages, his shock, his immediate call to the police.

'What shall we say?'

'Say I'm a journalist. I've already said that to a few people.'

She nods, but looks sceptical.

'Follow my lead. It'll be fine.' And then I give her what I hope is a reassuring smile.

She takes a breath and smoothes her hair as she goes to open the door.

'Sorry,' I hear her say. 'I was on the toilet.'

She walks back into the kitchen. Her eyes don't meet mine. The person at the door follows her, chattering all the way until he reaches the kitchen and sees me, then he stops talking abruptly. The surprise on his face is bordering on comical.

'Hello,' I say, forcing my voice to sound confident.

He looks at Dawn, who in turn looks at her feet.

'Tori Bradford.' I hold out my hand.

He stares at my hand, a little confused, and then regains his composure. He's holding carrier bags in both hands, and places one lot of bags on the floor and shakes my hand. 'Craig.'

He is a small man with longish hair, and he wears a battered biker's jacket and tight jeans that hug his skinny legs. The skin on his face is marked by teenage acne scars and creases around his eyes that suggest he laughs a lot. He picks up the bags from the floor and puts them all on the table.

'Your shopping,' he says to Dawn, and looks at her quizzically, clearly after an explanation. When none comes he turns back to me.

'I'm a writer,' I say. 'Well, a journalist, really. I'm doing a magazine article about missing children and I am here talking to Dawn about her sister.'

Dawn takes a sharp inhalation of breath.

The man nods slowly. 'I'm surprised she even let you in; she usually tells anyone asking to sling their hook.' He smiles kindly at Dawn.

'I can be persuasive.'

'I can imagine.'

'And Tori Bradford was just this minute leaving.' Dawn gives me a meaningful stare.

'Yes. That's right. I was. I was just leaving.' I pick up my bag. 'Thank you so much, Dawn. It was good talking to you.' I smile at Craig again. 'Nice to meet you.'

'And you. Maybe we'll see you again?'

'Maybe.' I glance at Dawn but she won't meet my eye. 'I can let myself out, Dawn. Thanks again.'

I walk down the hall and when I get there, I realise Craig has followed me. This annoys me a little as I had hoped to pop in on Alice quickly, but I can't think of a suitable reason why Tori-Bradford-the-journalist would do that.

'Don't mind about Dawn,' Craig says, as we reach the front door. 'She doesn't mean to be like that. She's had it pretty tough. She's a good girl.'

'Yes, she seems lovely.'

'She'd do anything for anyone, you know. Did you meet her mum?'

'Yes,' I say. 'Yes, I did.'

'Dawn's amazing.' He hesitates. 'The magazine will be nice about her, won't it?'

'Sorry?'

'The thing you're writing. About the missing kids? When you talk about Dawn you'll be nice about her.'

'Oh,' I say. 'Definitely. She probably won't be in it much, to be honest. I couldn't get a lot out of her.'

'Like I said, she's had a difficult time. The night her sister went, the days running up to it, and since...' Craig reddens and drops his head.

'Will you tell me about it?' As soon as I ask the question, I feel dishonest; I shouldn't be fishing for information behind her back. Thankfully, Craig shakes his head.

'I've said too much already. It's not my story to tell. If Dawn wants to talk to you, she will.'

THIRTY

Greg is in the reception, leaning on the counter talking to Fi. When I walk through the door he looks up at me and grins.

'Hi,' he says. 'I hear you've become a permanent resident. Might have to get you a special sign for your door saying *Tori's Room*.'

I flush red. 'Not permanent, I've only booked until—'

'I'm joking. You're here until the end of July? That's good; you'll love St Ives.'

'I love it already.'

'I'm heading down the pub for a drink with a few friends in a bit. Do you want to join us?'

I am startled by his invitation; he'd mentioned it before when we met on the beach, but I didn't think he meant it.

He laughs. 'You don't have to.'

'I'm not ... I'm just—' I hesitate, unsure what to say. Part of me wants to, but the other part, the stronger part, is exhausted and uneasy about going out with a group of strangers. 'I'm actually a bit tired today.'

'No problem. Another time.'

'Yes,' I say a little quickly. 'Another time would be good.'

'There's a party on the beach on Thursday night. Come along to that?' He glances at Fi. 'You're coming, aren't you?'

Fi shrugs.

'Well, even if she isn't, I am. Come. It'll be fun. I promise.'

Say yes, says Tori's voice. What harm can it do you? You might *actually* have some fun.

I hesitate but find myself nodding. 'Yes. OK.'

'Great. We'll be leaving here around sevenish for a few drinks in the pub then we'll hit the beach.'

'Sounds good.' I'm lying, of course. It sounds terrifying. I smile and then begin to head out of the reception.

'Did you get what you wanted from the Tremayne girl?' he calls after me.

'Oh,' I say, turning to face him again. 'Yes, thanks.'

'Hope you got a good story.'

I force a smile.

'Is she still a bit of a weirdo? That sister of hers?'

Suddenly I am twelve years old and sitting with my head bowed at the back of the church. My hand is held in Elaine's and she is squeezing too hard. I hear sniggering and glance up. Two girls in the pew across the aisle are looking at me, giggling and whispering behind raised hands. My neck flushes with heat as I stare at the embroidered hassock on the floor in front of me.

'She's so weird,' one of the girls whispers loud enough for me to hear. 'You know she doesn't even go to school. She's basically too weird for school.'

'Her whole family's weird. My mum said so,' whispers the other so loudly that a woman behind taps her crossly on the shoulder and makes a shushing gesture.

The girl gave the woman evils and then the two girls giggled again. I held hot tears back all the way through the service, and when the vicar began The Lord's Prayer, our signal to leave, I couldn't get out of there quick enough, managing to make it to the door before he'd even said 'deliver us from evil'.

'Actually,' I say to Greg. 'She was lovely. And after her sister went, she singlehandedly cared for her mother, who's really ill. She's an amazing person. And not weird at all.'

But Greg just shrugged and turned back to Fi.

THIRTY-ONE

Henry Campbell – October 30th 1984

There was blood everywhere. It soaked her. Matted her hair. Slicked the floor. Her nightdress was saturated with it, the blood coming from between her legs mixing with the blood that ran from the cuts to her wrists. Thankfully she'd cut badly, so the flow had slowed before bleeding her dry. She would live. This time.

She still held the knife, which she flailed around her as she screamed and tore at her hair. There were words amongst the screams but they were mostly unintelligible. He had stumbled into a horror film and for far too long he stood rigid, a hapless idiot unable to help her. The only thing he could do was hold her, restrain her thrashing arms as she continued to claw at herself.

'Elaine, enough,' he begged, incapable of keeping his voice steady as she fought. 'It's OK, please. Don't do this to yourself. *Please.*'

She turned her eyes on him and, as a vague recognition dawned, she began to batter him with her bloodied hands.

'Why?' she screeched as she beat his chest. 'Why do they keep dying? How can He do this? How can He give them to me then rip them out of me like this?'

Henry wrapped his arms tighter around her body, finally able to trap her arms by her sides. He looked down at her, wished he could stroke the hair back from her face, wished he could wipe away the blood that was smeared across her cheeks, through which tears had streaked rivulets.

'Nobody is doing anything. There's no explanation. It's just ... happening.'

'No,' she growled. 'God is doing it. He is taking them away from me.'

As Henry absorbed his wife's anger and despair, he turned his head to hide his tears. After a few moments, when he felt able, he looked back at her and smiled kindly, whispering soft words he didn't believe, 'And God is raising them as angels, Lainey. Angels. He is caring for every single one of your children. He wants them with Him. Where they are safe.'

Her body relaxed a little and he drew her into him, held her head against his chest and hushed her.

'I can't do it,' she said, her voice fallen to a weary murmur. 'I want to give you a child so much. But I can't do this anymore.'

'I know, my love, but I don't need a child. Not now, not ever.'

'You do. Of course you do.' She looked up at him, her madness absent, her face innocent, like a child.

He smiled at her, finally able to tuck her hair behind her ears. He trailed the backs of his fingers down her cheek. Leant forward and kissed her clammy forehead. 'No, my love, I only need you. Only you.'

Then her body heaved into silent wracking sobs.

'It's over,' he said. 'I promise you it's over.'

The guilt Henry felt was immeasurable. He would never forget tonight. The hellish scene into which he had walked would stay with him forever, the impotence he felt, the fear he might lose her. He vowed then and there, sitting on the floor of their bathroom, rocking his blood-drenched, emotionally destroyed wife, that he would never allow this to happen again. He was the only one who could help her, the only person in the world who was there for her, and until he drew his final breath, he'd make sure she never did anything like this to herself again.

THIRTY-TWO

I ask Phil to put my cappuccino in a takeaway mug and as he's making it he tells me it's going to be 'dead *tesa*' today, which, he tells me, means hot.

He's not wrong. As I walk up the street, I can already feel the sun warming my body. I tilt my face upwards and close my eyes, pausing a minute to enjoy the light flickering its orangey dance on the backs of my eyelids. It's odd, and I can't explain it, but I'm looking forward to seeing Alice and this cheers me.

Dawn seems more pleased to see me today. She opens the door at my first knock and smiles as she steps to one side to let me in. We sit at the kitchen table, her with a glass of water, me with the last of my coffee, and I broach the subject of helping her with Alice again. I need a role, something that will give me purpose in this brave new world of mine, and I'm convinced that helping out, being involved, will make it easier to feel anchored.

'But I said already, I don't need help.'

'I'd like to though.'

'It'll take me longer to tell you what to do than if I just do it.'

'You'll only need to tell me the first time.'

'You don't want to do most of the jobs. Trust me. It's not fun.'

'Dawn, I don't want to do it for fun. I want to get to know her.'

'What's there to know? She sits in her chair.'

I reach across the table and rest my hand on hers. 'She's my mother and I want to feel like her daughter.'

'Helping someone in and out of the bath doesn't make you feel like a daughter.'

'No, but it—'

I am interrupted by a sharp bleeping from Dawn's watch. Without saying a word, without even an embarrassed glance or a mumbled excuse, she silences the alarm, then reaches forward to unmute the television and, as crass, tinny music fills the room, she turns her chair to face the screen.

'Dawn, don't you—'

'Sssh,' she says, lifting a finger to her lips.

'But—'

She frowns and reaches forward to turn up the volume.

I stand, baffled, and stare at the television to work out what she is watching. After the opening credits finish, I realise it's a one of those daytime gossip shows with a panel of middle-aged women sitting behind a desk and smiling fixedly as they welcome Dawn back. Dawn stares at the screen and doesn't move a muscle.

'I'm going to go and sit with her. With Alice.' I wait for a moment, but there's no response.

I leave the kitchen and walk down the corridor, unsettled by Dawn's behaviour. How can she switch off like that, right in the middle of talking to me?

I reach Alice's room and open the door carefully, not wanting to startle her. She's in her chair, wearing her ragged dressing gown, and staring at the collage I find too creepy to look at. When I walk in she turns her head. I smile at her and sit on the bed, which is militarily made, the corners tucked in tightly, not a wrinkle in sight.

'Hello, Alice,' I say quietly. 'How are you this morning?'

An ache for our lost years grows inside me like a blackening bruise. I want to hold her face in mine and tell her it's me. Tell her I'm back. That her baby is home, so now she can talk again. She can get better. We can rebuild our shattered lives and finally have the relationship denied us.

'You know, my husband wants children,' I say. It's the type of thing I always wanted to share with my mum. I couldn't talk to Elaine about it; she hated David. 'He told me that the first time we slept together.

We've been trying for about a year, but it's not happened yet. I can't bear seeing how disappointed he is each month when there's no baby. I keep telling him it's early days, that it will happen, but he's so impatient. He got us tested. But the doctors say we're both fine, that it's *unspecific infertility*, whatever that means. They recommended having more sex, which was the last thing I wanted them to tell him.' I sigh and pick at a thread on the bedcover. 'Truth is, I'm not sure I even want a child. I don't think I'd be a very good mother.'

I stand up and stretch my back a little.

'I'm not an impressive person, Alice. You need to know that. I'm not that good at anything. I'm far too shy and I can hardly make my mind up about anything. I work in a library and I don't even enjoy it that much. I'm not sure I'd make you very proud.' I look at her then, hoping for some sort of change, but there is nothing in her face but impassiveness. I shake my head. 'Let's not talk about this anymore.' I look around the room and notice the bookshelf on the wall. 'Hey, how about I read to you? Would you like that? I'd like that. I love reading. Stories are the best places to lose yourself. Better than that horrid wall of clippings, anyway.'

Beside the ancient Argos catalogue with its corners bent and curling, are a few books. I tip my head so I can read their spines. There are two novels – a copy of *The Hitchhiker's Guide to the Galaxy* and a *Moby Dick* with most of its pages missing – and a book of Cornish legends.

'Perfect,' I say, as I slip the book from the shelf.

I sit on the floor, lean against the bed with my legs stretched out in front of me, so my toes rest against the foot of her chair, then look down the list of contents. I fall on a story about halfway down the list, *The Merrymaid of Zennor*. I recognise the name of the village from the pamphlets in the church I visited before I came to this flat that first day, and when I turn to the page, she's there, the mermaid carving from the pew, in a grainy sepia photo.

I look up to check Alice is sitting comfortably and then I begin.

'*The village of Zennor nestles on the harshest coast of Cornwall. The houses turn in against the wind and waves beat at the foot of the cliffs. For hundreds of years the people of Zennor lived by the sea and, many a time, died by it too. When the sea was kind to them, and the fisher-men returned safe and sound with a full catch, the villagers would make their way to the church to pray for more good days to follow and the choir would sing to give thanks. Now, in the choir was a handsome man called Matthew, whose voice was that of an angel. Loud and clear, he could be heard above all of the others. One evening, when the village was gathered in the church, a beautiful mermaid, part girl, part sea creature, with a magnificent silver green tail, climbed out of the sea to sit on a rock. Her name was Morveren—'*

I stop reading.

'Morveren? That's her name? You called me after the mermaid? I love that. I've seen her – her carving – in the church.'

Alice makes no movement.

I'd hated the name Morveren up until now and was convinced I'd never get used to it.

Morveren.

I say the name quietly a few times and smile; it used to sound obscure and clunky, now it's poetic and lyrical, and I smile.

'*Her name was Morveren and she sat and gazed at her reflection in the glassy water, combing her hair as she did. Then she closed her eyes, lis-tening to the whisper of the wind and the gentle caress of the water against the shore. And then, from nowhere, she heard another sound, the like of which she had never heard before. Her heart quickened. It was singing, the voice of a young man; the most beautiful singing she had ever heard.'*

The story continues, telling the tale of how these two became lovers, how Morveren listened to him each evening, until she could bear it no longer, and had to find out who he was. As I read, I fall into the words. I can hear his voice. I can smell the salt in the air. My heart physically lurches as she begs her father, the King, to give her legs so she can walk on land to find her love. I feel pain as she treads on dry land, the pain of a thousand needles that shoots up my legs in fiery shots. When she lays eyes on Matthew for the first time, it's my own heart that soars.

And when the beauty of his song so overwhelms her that she sighs aloud, and he looks up and falls instantly in love, I have to pause to gather myself.

'*Terrified of being seen by a mortal*,' I read on, '*Morveren fled, but Matthew chased after her, begging her not to return to the sea. But she had no choice. "Then I will go with you," Matthew cried and, picking her up, he raced towards the sea. The villagers shouted for Matthew to stop, but their cries only made him run faster. He and Morveren plunged into the sea and the water closed over their heads. Though they were never seen again, sometimes the villagers would hear his songs carried on the breeze, and even today, if you listen well, you can hear him singing his love to Morveren or warning of angry seas.*'

I close the book.

'What a beautiful story,' I say.

I shuffle over to her, then reach out to rest my hand against her forehead and gently sweep the fallen strands of hair from her eyes. She leans her head slightly into my touch. And then, for an instant, a fraction of a second, her eyes seem to fix on me. They unglaze, as if the fine layer of mist has lifted away from them.

'Alice?' I say. 'Mum?'

I take her face in my hands and bring it towards me, but she has sunk away again, the moment has passed. I lean forward and plant a kiss on the tissue-paper skin of her forehead. 'It's me, Mum, I'm back,' I whisper. 'I'm back and I saw you.'

'Everything OK?' Dawn is standing in the doorway.

Do I tell her? Would she believe me? Would she panic and get angry? I decide not to say anything. There's every chance that this type of thing has happened before and that Dawn is aware of it. Even if it hasn't, I don't want to get her hopes up.

'Everything's fine,' I say and get to my feet.

'Hungry?' She asks. She doesn't wait for an answer and disappears back to the kitchen. 'I'll put the soup on.'

I look again at Alice, peer close into her face, smell the warm sourness on her breath. 'I saw you,' I whisper again.

I stand and slowly back out of the room, keeping my eyes riveted to her in case something, anything, happens again.

Dawn is tipping a can of soup into a pan when I come into the kitchen. 'We'll eat first and then I'll feed Mum. It's minestrone today. Do you like it?'

The cloying smell of soup envelops the kitchen and eating a bowl of it is the last thing I want to do, but it seems too rude to say no. We are silent as we take our bowls to the tiny table. I toy with the soup, take spoonful but let it pour right off again. Dawn watches me like a hawk and I wonder whether she might grab the spoon any minute and try feeding me like she does Alice. I manage a couple of mouthfuls and then, when she finishes, I stand to clear our bowls. She runs a sink of water and I reach for a tea towel to dry.

'I was lonely growing up,' I say, as I pick up one of the bowls she has washed.

She is wiping the worktop and stops to stare at the cloth in her hand for a moment. Then she nods and begins to wipe again. 'Yes. Me too.'

Dawn shakes the cloth out and hangs it over the edge of the sink, then she smiles at me. 'I've got something to show you. Come with me.' And she walks into her bedroom. 'I feel bad about being so sharp with you when you wanted to see a photo of our dad. It's understandable that you want to know about your family.'

Her bedroom is sparsely furnished. There's a single bed with a flowery duvet, childlike and faded, and one pillow, neatly straightened. She has a wooden bedside table with a photograph on it, a small desk light, one of those black and shiny ones with a bendy stem, and there's a shelf above her bed with some school exercise books and a shoebox tied with string and decorated with splodges of Tippex outlined in dark felt-tip pen, and stickers and scribbles. There's a picture on the shelf beside the box. It's the same woman I remember from that clear snatch of memory on the beach. In this picture she is dressed in jeans and a T-shirt, but it's unmistakably the woman in the green-and-white dress. Her hair is thick and lustrous, her head thrown back as she laughs, a baby clutched in her smooth, tanned arms.

Dawn hands me the frame from the bedside table. The photograph shows an elderly couple sitting in canvas folding chairs. They sit side by side, arms linked. The man has a shock of white hair, his ears and nose are overgrown with age, his chin lost beneath a loose jowl, and deep laughter lines fan out from the corners of his eyes. The woman, her mouth soft and smiling, leans into him and squints into the sun, her grey hair blown nearly upright by the breeze.

'Your nan and granddad. Mum's mum and dad.'

My heart beats faster as I take in their faces with excited fascination. I remember how it felt to grow up without grandparents, imagining what it must be like to have kindly old people to shower you with presents and unconditional hugs.

'Do they live nearby?'

'They're both dead,' she says sadly.

'Oh. I see ... that's a ... shame,' I say, trying to hide my disappointment. 'They look nice.'

'They were,' Dawn says. 'I loved them more than anything. They always had something good to say. They always told me how lucky it was I was safe and sound, that I was their sunshine, that sort of thing. Nan always hugged me and said, *What would we do without you?* Mum and Dad never said things like that. Dad barely spoke to me after you went, unless it was shouting or calling me names.'

'Was he that bad?'

'Yes,' she says with narrowed eyes. 'He was *that bad*, Morveren.' The name jars and sounds harsh again. 'He was a drunk. A violent, selfish drunk. He—' She shakes her head, and then her hands shoot up to cover her face. 'I'm sorry,' she says. 'This is all so hard. It's...'

I put the picture down and rest my hand on her knee.

'Dawn, it's OK. We need time, that's all. It's hard, but it will get easier. It has to. There isn't a right way or a wrong way to deal with this. It's not like this is a normal situation. We'll find our way. We will.'

She nods. Her hands fall from her face and she takes a deep breath.

'Can I ask you something? If it upsets you, don't answer.'

She doesn't reply, but I take it as a yes.

'When I showed up here, when I knocked on the door that first time and you told me to leave—'

'I'm sorry—'

'No, you don't have to be sorry, it's just, well,' I pause. 'You said they buried me.'

'Yes,' she says. 'There was a funeral in the church at Zennor. Lots of people came. There were so many flowers.' Dawn's voice cracked. 'I hate bunches of flowers now. Absolutely *hate* them.'

How strange to think of people mourning me, singing hymns and saying words to lay me to rest, and all the time I was oblivious, playing alone behind those towering red-brick walls.

'She never wanted the funeral,' Dawn says. 'Never wanted them to stop searching for you. I remember her screaming at my dad on the morning of the funeral, screaming until she went blue in the face that it was wrong, you weren't dead and they should still be looking for you.'

I spend the rest of the day with Dawn, shadowing her as she looks after Alice, watching everything she does intently. I help with lunch. Stroke Alice's hand while Dawn feeds her. When we help her bath, Dawn shuffles over to allow me room to kneel beside her. I hesitate, but rather than difficult or embarrassing, I am surprised to find how calming it is. I dry her carefully with the towel Dawn passes me. It's worn through in places and I make a mental note to buy them some new ones, large and fluffy and white, and maybe some Pears Glycerine soap, which is so much nicer than the cheap pink stuff Dawn seems to favour.

Once we have tucked Alice up for the night, we eat scrambled eggs in the dimly lit kitchen, and then sit on Dawn's bed to chat. I want to ask her about what she can remember from the night I went missing, but I don't know how to bring it up without running the risk of upsetting her, so instead we talk about television, of which I know little, books, of which Dawn knows little, and cinema and sport, of which we both know nothing. We do, however, find common ground in our lonely childhoods. She was saved, she says, by Craig, her only friend, and when she talks about him she opens up in a way I haven't yet seen. Her words are imbued with a tenderness and warmth that's contagious, and as I listen to her talk about him, I find myself smiling. She tells me he has been there for her since they were young and without him she couldn't have coped.

'I'll never be able to thank him enough.'

With Dawn so relaxed, I brave a question. 'How did Alice get so ill?'

'She just got quieter and quieter. After the funeral she sort of ran out of batteries. Then something happened with Dad one night … it wasn't good … and she … switched off.'

'What did the doctors say?'

Dawn grimaced. 'They wanted to give her drugs, anti-depressants, but Nan said no. Nan said Mum was rightly sad about her daughter and that she didn't need drugs, she needed time. She said drugs would make her worse, turn her into the walking dead, which is ironic now, of course.' Dawn shook her head. 'Nan was wrong, but I know she was acting for what she thought was Mum's good. I don't think she had any idea how…' she hesitates '… damaged Mum was.'

We fall asleep together on her narrow bed. She before me. I listen to her breathing and try to synchronise mine with hers, until at last I drift off.

Elaine sits in the armchair from her bedroom. It's been moved into the kitchen at The Old Vicarage. It is cold and damp and I am aware of noises coming from somewhere, maybe upstairs, maybe outside. Shouts from a man, who is trying to get me. But I feel safe because I sit in a small birdcage beside her, and she is feeding me single grains of corn through the bars. The skin around her mouth is stained orange with soup and her gums are receded and bleeding. When I finish the bowl of corn, she smiles indulgently, then covers the cage with the throw from the sofa. It's so dark suddenly, I feel myself beginning to panic. I try to call out but my mouth is sewn shut. I feel a hand on my shoulder. I jump. I think it's the man, the man who has no face and looms in the doorway. But then a dim light grows around me and I see the hand belongs to Tori, exactly as she was at the beginning, with curly blonde hair and clear brown eyes, wearing a white nightie and slippers. Seeing her makes me smile and as I do the stitches fall away from my lips. I tell her I need help, but she doesn't reply. She just watches me silently with unblinking eyes.

I wake with a start, my skin covered in sweat, fingers clenching the sheet. I feel for Dawn, but the bed is empty. I get up and look for her and find her sleeping in the bath. Her hands are clasped beneath her head and the damp towel we used to dry Alice is covering her. I walk back into the kitchen, the ever-present soupy smell sticking in my throat, and wonder if this is really what I want. As I stand there, I consider slipping away. Not returning. I could go and be Tori in a place where nobody knows me as anyone different. I could carve out a new life for myself. I could get a job in a florist or a travel agency. I could fabricate a mundane past that nobody would think to question. I sit down at the kitchen table and stretch my arms out in front of me, picturing Dawn waking up and realising I've gone, having to lose me all over again, having to deal with my rejection on top of everything else.

I must have fallen asleep because the next thing I know the cat is mewing and scratching at the back door and a hazy light is easing over the sky. I'm numb and uncomfortable from being awkwardly slumped over the table. I sit up, flex my stiffened shoulders, and check the clock on the wall. A quarter to five. The cat gives another faint mew and I open the back door. She trots in and begins purring, rubbing herself against my leg, so I feed her and as I do the longhaired grey cat skulks into my head; I must call Miss Young to check he's OK. I stroke the cat, who ignores me as she tucks hungrily into her early breakfast, and then I peer into the bathroom. Dawn is still asleep, curled uncomfortably in the bath and snoring softly. I hesitate for a second or two, debating whether to wake her and send her back to bed where she'll be more comfortable. I decide against it and instead take the covers from her bed and lay them gently on top of her. Then I walk down the corridor towards Alice's room. The silence is heavy, as if the flat is covered in a thick, insulating blanket. I reach for her door, my fingertips rest on the handle, but I don't open it. My hand drops away and I grab my jacket from one of the coat hooks and let myself quietly out of the flat.

THIRTY-THREE

As soon as I hear the tone in my solicitor's voice I know she has something serious to tell me.

'The situation with your parents' second house seems fairly straightforward. It's not rented out, but there are gas and electricity bills associated with the property, which your father paid. The utilities companies advise me that this usage is in keeping with a second home, people visiting – perhaps your parents – rather than continual residential use. Your father had a savings account, which until his death received two hundred pounds by standing order each week from his current account. The only money taken from the savings account was a weekly withdrawal from a Bristol cash point for the same amount, two hundred pounds. A few days before his death, Dr Campbell stopped the direct debit. Your father made no mention of any of this in his will. It therefore falls to you to decide if you want to sell the house or do something else with it. You can instruct us to sell it on your behalf, or perhaps you'd like to look at the property before you make your decision?'

I don't answer immediately. The temptation to tell her to sell it is huge, but there's a part of me that knows I have to go there. Henry Campbell had a secret house and there's the distinct likelihood that it holds clues to the whys and hows. And, of course, I'm scared that if it does have a link to what happened in France, then people will know. Things in St Ives are still delicate and none of us needs external influences making it harder.

'I'd like to see it first,' I say, trying hard to conceal my reticence.

'Right, I'll send the key and address by registered mail.' She pauses.

Paper rustles in the background and I presume she is looking back through her notes. 'It will be with you tomorrow. Will there be some-body at the address you gave me to sign for it?'

'Yes,' I say. 'You know, the house might have been used by a relative. They ... my parents ... were estranged on both sides, and I've no idea where any of my extended family lives. I know Henry has a brother and I think his mother is still alive.'

'That's definitely a possibility,' she says. 'Good luck and let me know how you get on. If you change your mind, I'll get someone to deal with things on your behalf.'

I walk into St Ives, my mind racing once again. I think about Henry disappearing to the house in Bristol. I try to remember how many nights he used to spend away. Had he a lover? Was Bristol his escape from The Old Vicarage and Elaine and what they'd done? God knows, that would make sense. This house might hold the answers. Things – anything – that might help explain what happened, and why.

I walk along to the very furthest point of the harbour wall. On one side of me still waters, on the other the open, surging ocean, which, with every crashing wave, throws up a briny spray that mists my face. I lower my eyelids and listen for the mermaid.

I am certain I can hear her.

She is singing to me. Her voice rising up from the watery depths.

'Morveren,' I whisper back. 'I can hear you.'

I think about her and Matthew beneath the waves, living, loving, adoring each other. She is smiling and happy as he caresses her rounded belly, runs his fingers over her skin, kisses her neck. I want to dive into the heaving swell to find them, to be a part of their secret world beneath the rhythmic breaking waves.

When Dawn opens the door she makes signs with her eyes, shakes her head, gestures with jabbing hand movements back down the street.

'What is it?'

But she shushes me with an urgent lifted finger, then starts frantically pointing again.

'What's wrong?' I whisper. But then I understand, as Craig's face appears from the dark hallway behind her.

'Oh, hi,' I say to him, trying to keep my voice light and relaxed.

Dawn glares at me.

'Hello, again. Can we help you?' he says. He rests a hand on Dawn's shoulder, but she shrugs it off.

'I ... was wondering ... well...'

Why am I there? Christ. Think. The article ... something to do with the article.

'Well ... if whether I might be able to take a photo. For the magazine?'

Dawn visibly relaxes and she smiles tightly.

'Dawn? What do you think?' Craig asks.

She still doesn't say anything, so I shake my head a little, hoping she'll understand she has to say no.

'OK then? If that's what you want. For the article.'

She didn't understand.

'Great!' I say as brightly as I can manage. 'I haven't actually got my camera with me so ... I'll have to come back. With my camera.'

'You came up to take a photo without a camera?'

I smile at him. 'Well, I was almost here when I realised I forgot it, so I thought I might as well ask first, and then if it was a yes, I'll ... you know ... come back.' My mouth has gone dry. 'I'm ... so forgetful.'

'You can use the camera on my phone if you want. It's pretty good.'

'Oh, OK. Yes, that would be great.'

Craig taps Dawn on the shoulder. 'Do you want to go and get it, Dawny? It's in my jacket pocket, the inside one.'

Dawn mumbles something and scurries down the corridor, seemingly relieved to escape.

He glances over his shoulder and then, happy she's gone, fixes his eyes on mine. 'You're her, aren't you?'

My heart stops.

'You're Dawn's sister. You're Morveren.'

'No. No, I'm—' My voice sticks in my throat. 'I'm Tori. I'm a ... journalist ... from London. I—'

His face breaks into a gentle smile. 'Of course,' he says, softly. 'I don't know why I said that. Wishful thinking, maybe. You've got the same eyes as Dawny, that's all. Not many with eyes as beautiful as hers. My mistake though.'

I want to laugh and say *No harm done*, that Dawn and I do have similar eyes, and exclaim *Isn't it a coincidence!* but I can't. I can't say anything. I can't make my mouth move or any words come out, all I can do is listen to the gulls high up in the sky laughing at how ridiculous I am.

Dawn arrives back with the phone and hands it to Craig.

'Actually,' I mumble. 'I have to go. I've got ... to be ... somewhere.'

'Don't rush off,' Craig says. 'You've come all the way up here. Why don't you come in? I'll put the kettle on, you can take a picture of Dawny, and then you can get back. Fifteen minutes won't hurt, will it? I can email you the photo. Or even get it printed at the chemist. They've got this clever machine I've always wanted to have a go on.'

Craig beckons me in and I glance at Dawn, who shrugs.

I go with them, walking in a semi-trance, lost in the inevitability that one day my truth will come out, and that when it does I'm not sure I'll be able to handle it. As we sit at the table he appears at ease; he doesn't look at me strangely or give any knowing glances. I watch him chat with Dawn. He touches her hand ever so lightly when she passes him a small plate of biscuits. There's a connection between them. They watch each other intently when the other speaks. Their eyes seek each other out. I feel as if I am intruding on them and cannot help but envy the way he is with her, the effect he has on her. Her tension has eased and there's a levity about her that warms me. He asks her opinion. He doesn't put words in her mouth. He lets her be. I realise now how controlling David is, and wish that every now and then he asked what I thought or wanted or felt.

Dawn and I sit and listen as Craig tells us about a lady he saw in the supermarket yesterday.

'She was having this right old paddy,' he says. 'Stormed in, can of beans in her hand, demanding to see the manager. Well...' He laughs now, and Dawn and I can't help but smile too. 'The bloke came out, looked about twelve years old, standing there in a suit two sizes too big, and each time he tried to speak, off she'd go again. He stood there like a mackerel, mouth opening, mouth shutting, desperate to get his words out.' Craig does an impression of the man, opening and closing his mouth, arms flapping with mock-frustration.

Dawn laughs.

It's a childish giggle, free as a soaring seabird, and I'm hit with another wave of envy.

'So, there she is, shouting at this mackerel in his baggy suit. "*These beans ... have sausages in them,*" she's shouting. "*I. Am. Appalled. I mean, a hair or a caterpillar or the end of some careless idiot's finger, maybe. But ... sausages? I mean, REALLY?*" Then she turns the can upside down and slurps the beans out on the floor.' Dawn laughs again. 'Then the mackerel points out it says baked beans *with sausages* on the label. She must have picked them up by accident. She looks at the label. Huffs loudly. And with that she's off out of the shop and the rest of us stand there not speaking, until...' And here he taps Dawn on the knee and beckons her closer. 'And this is the best bit, until this little kid, no more than three, sneaks out from behind his mum and starts picking out the sausages from the beans on the floor and pops them in his mouth!'

'No!' exclaims Dawn, shaking her head as tears of laughter gather in the corner of her eyes, her cheeks glowing with a flush of red. 'Mind you, sausages in baked beans? There's no call for that.' And now it's Craig's turn to laugh.

Dawn stands and as she does I catch her graze her hand against his shoulder.

I excuse myself and go to the bathroom. I lock the door and run the cold tap, splash my face, press the towel against my skin. The intimacy between them stings. It's something I have never had. I feel empty and more alone right now than I've ever felt, even as a lonely, only child behind the walls and locks of my home.

I walk back into the kitchen and find Dawn at the sink. Craig is beside her, but they split apart like naughty children when they realise I'm there.

'I'd better be going,' says Craig. 'I'll tell—'

He is interrupted by a loud crash and a shout from Dawn. She's dropped a plate, and shattered china litters the floor.

'Sorry,' she says. 'It slipped.'

She stares hard at Craig. He mouths something then looks at me and smiles, self-conscious suddenly. Dawn bends and starts to pick up the pieces of broken plate.

'He's lovely,' I say, soon after Craig leaves.

'Yes.'

'And you've been together all this time?'

She blushes. 'What? No! No, it's not like that.'

'I thought you—'

Her watch alarm interrupts me. She moves her chair and turns up the volume on the flickering television as her gossip show starts. I want to talk about Craig. I want to talk like sisters, ask her how they met, but she silences me yet again with a lifted hand as she leans closer to the television.

I hate that stupid television.

I go into Alice's room, kiss the top of her head, then pick up our book. 'I think I'll read a different story today.'

An hour later the theme tune that accompanies the credits of the programme drifts through from the kitchen. Then the sound stops as Dawn turns the volume to mute once again. I hear her footsteps in the hall and wait for her to appear at the door.

'Reading *again*?'

'We enjoy it.'

Dawn glances at Alice who sits motionless. 'I doubt she even knows you're here. But as long as you enjoy it...'

She lets her sentence hang unfinished, but I don't respond.

'Can I ask you a favour?' she asks. She goes to the bed and runs her hands over the covers to smooth away any evidence of me having sat there.

'Of course.'

'Do you think you might be able to look after Mum for a few hours on Friday? On your own? I normally don't leave her. Craig comes every now and then to sit with her, you know, so I can get money and that, but I never leave her more than an hour. But I'd like a bit longer, there's something I need to do. If you think you'll manage?'

'You can have as long as you need.'

'A few hours will be fine.'

'You should have longer. Go for a walk on the beach or something.'

A light smile crosses her face, replaced quickly with a wistful sadness. 'I can't remember the last time I went on the beach.' Then, as if justifying herself, adds, 'I only leave her for the necessaries. But...' She pauses, the half-smile still showing on her face. 'But if you think you'll be alright, I could remind myself what sand between my toes feels like.' Then she nods. 'Yes, that would be nice. I'll look forward to that. And you sure you can manage?'

'We'll be fine, I'm sure. Actually, I also have something I need to do. I won't be here tomorrow.'

'Oh?'

'I need to sort out something to do with Henry Campbell's will.'

'That bastard. How can you even say his name? They should be in bloody prison. It's not fair they got away with it.'

I have a sudden flash of Henry and Elaine. His body with the pool of blood beneath his chair. His empty, glazed eyes staring at nothing above him. Her triple-bolting the doors and checking behind the curtains a hundred times a day and tearing at her skin until her nails drew blood.

'They didn't get away with it,' I say then. 'They lived with it every single day.'

THIRTY-FOUR

'So what's the weather's going to do today?' I ask Phil, as I take my coffee from him.

'*Drok newl,*' he says, with a serious nod.

I stir in my sugar and think. 'Bad something or other?'

Phil grins. 'Fog,' he says. 'I reckon we've got fog as thick as semolina on the way. There's rain coming, too.' He takes my money and hands me the change. 'What are you up to today? Nothing that's going to be ruined by rain, I hope?'

'Going to Bristol.'

'What you doing there then?'

'Something I'd rather not be.'

'It's nice, Bristol. I went there once myself. It's a long way, mind. You staying the night?'

'Not if I can help it.'

He opens his mouth as if he might ask me something else, but I smile and turn to leave the shop before he can.

'See you tomorrow, Phil.'

'Looking forward to it already, love.'

I walk along the harbour in the direction of the taxi rank on the other side of town. A sudden gust of wind takes the corner of my jacket and whips it up against my lower lip. It stings and I instinctively touch my finger to my lip to check for blood, but there's none. I lick my lip and taste the salt from the air as I pull the zip up as far as it will go.

On the train I have a towering sense of déjà vu as I remember the journey down to Cornwall. Though I am travelling in the opposite direction, the feeling of going from somewhere familiar to somewhere unfamiliar is overwhelming, and the uneasiness in the pit of my stomach grows heavier the further I travel from St Ives. In St Ives I am hidden, cocooned and relatively safe, but sitting on this train I am exposed and vulnerable as I race closer to the world I left behind. I jump each time the electric doors at the end of the carriage push themselves apart. I imagine David or Jeffrey or Miss Young, or even worse, the ghosts of Elaine and Henry Campbell, walking through them at any minute.

When the train finally pulls into Bristol Temple Meads, a sense of relief spills over me; I'm desperate to escape the confines of the carriage, which has become unbearably claustrophobic. I step off the train and immediately miss the saltiness of Cornwall. The Bristol air seems tighter, darker somehow. Standing in the station taxi rank the feeling of ominous repetition deepens: another taxi to another address on another piece of paper. As I wait, my chest tightens and my breathing grows shallow.

I know I'm my own worst enemy. The anxieties I inherited from my life with the Campbells shouldn't merely be kept in check, they should be banished. They are based on lies and secrets; they aren't real. To allow them to run amok like they do is madness. I concentrate on calming my rising panic before it takes hold.

The taxi driver makes no attempt to converse. Instead he asks if I mind having the radio on. I don't, and as we drive we listen to horse racing. I watch him muttering under his breath, his knuckles whitening as he grips the steering wheel tighter and tighter and tighter, until he bangs the dashboard and turns off the radio with an aggressive punch and we sit for the remainder of the journey in tense silence.

He turns into a crescent and pulls up to the kerb.

'This is it,' he says gruffly, pressing a button to calculate the fair. 'Eight pounds forty.'

I give him ten and tell him to keep the change. He thanks me, a little friendlier now, and I climb out. The area is upmarket. There's no rubbish, no depression, just newly painted buildings and pavements that look like they've been vacuumed. The street curves in a graceful sweep of smart, terraced villas in varying shades of cream and white with window boxes and hanging baskets that would have made Elaine nod approvingly. Each house mirrors the last with shiny black railings marking tidy boundaries, broken at intervals to allow paths of black-and-white tiles to lead their way to pillared front doors. I turn my face into the gentle breeze that blows up the street, pushing my hair out of my face as it cools my nervous skin.

The house the Campbells own is different to the others. Rebellious weeds break through its chequerboard pathway, and leaves and rubbish scatter the small front garden. As I stand on the front doorstep I listen obediently to Tori's voice in my head as she tells me to be brave and reminds me I am here for information and I don't need to be scared. I'm not sure about opening the door and walking in. It feels wrong just walking into a house I don't know. I push my finger against the doorbell. My stomach pitches. There's a peephole in the centre of the door like a tiny bullet hole, and I imagine being scrutinised by an unseen stranger behind. I press the bell again. A gust of wind blows and lifts the fallen leaves at my feet, making them dance around me then fall back down. I lean across and cup my hands around my face to peer in the window. It's dusty and dark, a layer of grime and old cobwebs turning the glass murky. I can't see anything much, a chair, I think, and an old cushion or pile of clothes on the floor on the far side of the room. Other than that it looks empty. I step back from the window and open the zip pocket in my bag and retrieve the key. A single Yale carrying a red plastic tag with the word *Bristol* written in black block capitals.

It's your house, you know, says Tori indignantly. You are allowed inside.

I bend and peer through the letterbox. There's nothing; just a collection of pizza leaflets and junk mail, which litter the floor of the hall. I put the key into the lock and turn it, trying, irrationally, to be as quiet as possible. The door swings open with a loud creak. I stand on the doorstep and call into the house.

'Hello?' I call.

The hallway is filthy. Dirt and leaves coat the floorboards. There's an old coat in a heap and a bent bike wheel rests against the grubby white wall. This doesn't look like the sort of place where Henry would spend time. He had been clean and neat to a fault. I step inside and pull the door closed behind me. The noise of it closing makes me jump. I walk down the hallway into a large, dilapidated kitchen. I concentrate on keeping my footsteps as light as possible. The place stinks of rubbish bins and when I enter the kitchen it's obvious that the house has someone living there.

I fight the urge to turn and bolt.

Stay.

The state of the place is like nothing I've ever seen. It's a tip. The sink is rammed full of dishes, papers and packets litter the floor, and everything has a thick layer of grime. There's a large sash window with a line of pigeons on the sill outside. Their feathers are puffed out and they coo so loudly I can hear them through the glass. The wall beneath the window inside the room is smeared with bird droppings, fallen like drips of paint to the floor. There is a small, portable hob with two rings and a bottle of gas attached by an orange rubber pipe, and there are stubs of candle glued to surfaces by their own wax wherever I look.

I back out and then turn and walk back down the hallway. I don't think I've drawn breath yet. My hands are sweaty and every instinct inside me is screaming for me to run. There's a staircase with an ornate iron balustrade, the treads carpeted with yet more litter and grime. I peer up the stairwell, hesitating, but don't go up. Instead, I go into the room on my right, the one by the front door, the room I'd peered into from outside. A thick, sour smell hits me and makes me gag as soon as I step inside. It has high ceilings and an intricately carved cornice. There is no furniture other than the single wooden chair I've already seen. The chair has curved arms and a tattered upholstered seat. Beside it, on the floor, is a battered black radio with a coat hanger for an aerial. There are more candles and more rubbish – food containers, dirty plates, newspapers, empty bottles.

I don't want to be here when whoever has made this mess returns. I back out of the room but, as I do, there's a stirring. The sound of a person groaning. I jerk my head to look. It's coming from the pile of clothes in the corner. Except, now I'm in the room, I see it's not a pile of clothes. It's a figure, a man, his face to the floor, his arm outstretched. I scream involuntarily. My heart leaps into my mouth and I turn and make for the door, but as I do I trip and land on my hands and knees. I scream again. I look over my shoulder. The man has sat upright. He is mumbling. He wears a navy cardigan and fingerless gloves revealing dirty, calloused fingers. On his head is a woollen hat, greasy black hair streaked grey visible beneath.

He turns his head in my direction.

I scramble to my feet, ready to run, cast another look over my shoulder. And then I stop in my tracks. I take a sharp inhalation of breath and the smell in the room catches at the back of my throat. Fresh fear floods me instantly. I recognise him, but it takes a moment or two to place him.

When I do, my knees give way.

'Well, well, well,' his voice rasps, rusty and dry, his Cornish accent heavy. 'If it isn't Bella Campbell. I wasn't expecting to wake up to *you* today.' He laughs quietly, the noise incongruous against my shock and confusion.

The man is from Dawn's photograph.

The man is my father.

Mark Tremayne blinks blankly. His face registers no emotion. I can't move. I'm frozen to the spot as panic holds me in its vice-like grip.

I can't process this. Secrets and lies scream at me from the chaos. Can it be him? I only saw that one photograph. I could be mistaken. And he called me Bella. *Bella Campbell.* Not Morveren. I continue to fight my instinct to flee; I need answers. Even if I have got it wrong, if this man isn't the man from the photograph, he knows things.

He knows me.

'You're Mark Tremayne?' I breathe.

'Ah!' He laughs again, this time harder, and the laugh dissolves into a hacking cough. He bangs his chest with one of his gloved hands. 'So,' he says, grasping at the words. 'You're Morveren again.'

He stands up, unsteady on his feet and then he walks towards me. I shuffle backwards until I hit the wall. My hands feel for the doorframe. He continues to approach.

'Don't touch me,' I say weakly.

But he doesn't stop, he walks past me, through the door, and as he does I catch the smell of him, unwashed and foetid, like a tramp from the street. I lift the back of my hand to my nose to repel the stench. I am left there alone. I could run.

No, don't run. You have to follow him. You have to find out what the hell is going on.

So I walk after him into the kitchen. He is at the window, sliding the sash upwards. The pigeons jostle and grumble but don't fly away. He strokes one of them as he reaches into his cardigan pocket for a handful of seeds, which he scatters along the window ledge. The pigeons begin to peck frantically, as if they've not eaten in weeks. He turns back to me and then slaps his forehead and smiles.

'Where are my manners? I'm sorry. Forgive me. I'm not used to guests. Would you like a drink?'

He doesn't wait for my answer, but shuffles over to the sink and roughly shoves dirty plates and cups aside as he fishes for a glass.

'I want to know how you know Henry Campbell. Is it you taking money out of a savings account he set up? Why? Why are you here? Did you arrange for him to take me? Is that why you went to France? I don't ... understand ... I...'

I watch him fill a dirty, smeared glass with water, his eyes fixed on the tap.

'Answer me!' I shout then. 'Why!?'

But there's no reply. I shake my head to rid it of the sudden, vivid image of Elaine locking the top of bottom bolts of our front door while holding my hand so hard I think my bones will snap.

'I don't understand!'

The man straightens his back and faces me. I remain in the doorway, my arms wrapped around me, but I don't look at him. I should phone David. This is wrong. I shouldn't be here on my own. I'm unsafe. I have another flash of memory. A man, a monster, looming at the door, his hand reaching out for me. I feel as if I'm walking a tightrope suspended thousands of feet above a ravine.

'So he's dead then? The doctor?' Tremayne clears his throat and then spits something vile into the sink.

After a moment I nod.

'And her?'

I look at him again, and anger begins to well inside me as I look at his filthy, brutish face.

'How did you find out?'

'He wrote a note.' I'm surprised how steady my voice is. 'Shortly before he slit both his wrists.'

'Ah, yes. He likes notes.' He smiles with what appears to be genuine amusement. 'I knew he'd top himself. He was the type. No balls, see? Did the crime but never let go of it, let it brew, like an apple with rot – looks fine on the outside but inside it's black and festering. I walk up to the suspension bridge sometimes. Wait and watch for jumpers. I don't always get lucky, but you'd be surprised how many turn up to try it. You know there's this metal sign screwed to the bridge with the number of the Samaritans on it? Poor souls. Hardly any of them see it through. They spend hours dithering about on the railings then pack off home to bed. I've seen three jump over the years. Each of them had the same look about them. Different to the others. They hung low. The doc? He hung low.' He tips the glass of water up to his lips and then put the glass onto the pile of dishes in the sink. 'Why are you here?'

My skin bristles with sweat and my heart thumps. I can't read him. There are no signs. His body language gives nothing away, nor does the flat tone to his voice. There seems to be no remorse or guilt or grief or even a jot of happiness at seeing me alive. No relief.

I lift my shoulders, size up to him, feel myself growing taller and stronger, fuelled with an indignant rage. 'Why am I *here*? I'm here because this is my house and I want you out.'

'He left it to you?' He chuckles to himself and crosses his arms. 'Fancy that. My little girl done good.'

His little girl. This person's little girl? No. I'm nothing to do with him. This man is removed from me. A stranger. I am not his little girl.

'Did he know you lived here?'

'I have a key, don't I?'

'And he gave you money? Did you sell me? Your own flesh and blood? Is that what you did?'

I am hit by images of me as a wide-eyed toddler, scared and veiled in a dark French alley, my wrist is gripped in this man's large hands as Henry Campbell looks over his shoulder and counts out used fifty-pound notes.

'Sell you?' He looks taken aback, but instead of shaking his head or saying no, he nods. 'I wouldn't put it that way myself, but I suppose it's a way to see it.'

'Why would … you…? How…? You're my … father. It's—'

I can't finish my sentence. The thought that this man could have knowingly left me with my abductors then profited from that abandonment with no idea if I was being hurt or abused or just locked away from my mother and sister behind heavy bolted doors and curtained windows, leaves me hollowed out.

He rubs the side of his face and drops his head and for the first time shows some sort of contrition.

'Tell me,' I manage to say. 'Tell me why you helped him to abduct me.'

'I didn't give you to them, OK?'

I want to scream at him, *No, it's not OK. It's not OK at all*, but he continues to talk, his voice rolling out of his body as if he's on autopilot. I jam my mouth closed, bracing myself for whatever he's about to say.

'We searched everywhere. Searched every shitting nook and cranny of the caravan, that shithole of a campsite. The room with the table football and the drinks machine. The shower block. The swings. Under the slide. We checked the swimming pool, the woods around

– lots of us checking by then – but I knew you were gone. I was drunk, but I knew you were gone. And when I realised that, all I could think about was having a drink. Lots of them. I don't think I've had a day since then when I haven't woken up without my first thought being my next drink.' He stares at me, his eyes dead. 'That's the kind of man I am, Morveren. A drunk. You know they thought I'd took you? Those foreign police? They took me in and questioned me again and again, that sneering woman turning their foreign nonsense into English I could barely understand. Bloody frogs, bloody French frogs. They thought I killed you. Can you believe that?'

I shake my head. It's hard to take it all in. The pictures that are forming in my head. The chaos triggered by my taking. All the while I was oblivious.

He laughs. 'I didn't even want to go to bloody France! It was your mother's idea. She thought a fancy-pants holiday would help our marriage or some shit like that. Forgot people like us don't go to *France*. But no. She said we needed a holiday, that it was our last chance. She said it would be good for us to spend time together. Get me out of the pub, she said. I told her there was no problem. Things were fine. Jesus, I should've been allowed to relax without her harping on at me, don't you think? But she went on and on. Always nagging. Always wanting *more*.' His voice has grown tight. He pauses, screws up his face, and angrily jabs the air with a pointed finger and I ball my fists to make myself feel braver.

'The stupid cow went on and on all the bloody time. Said she was going to leave me. Said she'd made a mistake about France. That it was over, that *we* were over. ' He sighs and rubs his face. 'And then I gave her a slap. Nothing bad, mind, a light slap, but you should have seen the look she gave me.'

He whispers these last words. I swallow. Recall the fear in Dawn's voice when she spoke about this man. I don't want to be here anymore. Nobody knows where I am. I'm a dead girl going by a made-up name. I don't exist; if he hurts me I'll vanish.

I'll vanish again.

'How is she? How's Alice?' His voice is lighter, gentler, and the change in it sends a shiver through me. 'She was such a pretty little thing. All the boys wanted a go.'

I lean back on the wall, my palms flat against it. The solidity helps, as if I've anchored myself. 'Why did you take money from him?'

He pulls the cardigan tight across his body, wipes his nose with the back of his hand. 'After we buried you, your mum, well, she just stopped living. Sat there day after day, staring out of the window, waiting for you to come home. Moping, living inside that head of hers, blaming me, hating me. I started drinking more. Couldn't get work. And then one day, a few weeks after your funeral, I picked up the box of cards that people had left us that day. I was going to throw it away, hoped that might help. But I sat, poured a drink, and started to read them. I couldn't read some of them for crying.' He pauses and the corners of his mouth twitch in a soft smile and for the first time I detect the shadow of something that might pass for affection. 'And then there was this one. Written so neat. All fancy writing on fancy blue paper and it said, *She's here* and then there was an address.'

My hand shoots to my mouth. 'Did you go to the police?'

He snorted. 'Fucking pigs. Couldn't find their arse with a mirror. No, of course I didn't go to the police. They knew for certain you'd drowned, didn't they? Once they knew they couldn't pin it on me that said that over and over. They just wanted to get rid of us. They didn't give a shit about you. No, I would never have gone to them.'

Mark Tremayne leans back against the sink and folds his arms.

'So I took the van and drove up there. Took hours. And I parked outside and saw him drive through the gates. And I recognised him. He was on the campsite. He was one of them that had helped us look for you. It was dark, pitch black. And raining. The wall was high but I went over it. Didn't want to risk them not opening their fancy electric gates. Then I knocked on the door.'

And as he speaks I have a flash of the man I sometimes see looming out of the shadows in my nightmares. His features uncertain. His presence petrifying. I don't want to hear any more, yet at the same time I'm riveted.

'Campbell answered and I told him I wanted my daughter back. Fuck me, that mad bitch screamed like I'd ripped out her stomach with my bare hands. And then you were there and, God, it was like all the weight of the world left me. I smiled at you. Well, I think I smiled, maybe I didn't, because you hid behind her. I suppose I was jealous, but Jesus, that got me cross. How could you hide from me? Your own dad? I pushed past him. Went over to you, all the time that crazy woman screaming in my ear. I took hold of you and pulled you towards me, and then,' he says, with a loud and incredulous burst of laughter, 'you bit me. Like a mangy pit bull, you bit my bloody hand. I let go of you and you fell backwards into her.'

Again I search my mind and finally I can see it. It's him, this man, standing in the doorway. His hand reaches out to me. And I'm scared. So scared I hide. Elaine's skin is soft. She smells of Pears soap. She is warm and curls herself around me so I feel safe and protected.

'She picked you up. Held you close, whispered to you, held you like you were made of eggshell. Then she went for this poxy little knife on the table and started waving it around like it was a Samurai sword. She was mad as a rabid dog, that one. That house was nice, wasn't it? Smart. With that long driveway and those pictures on the walls.' His eyes drift to the window, to the hungry pigeons who still jostle and push for the last scraps of seed. 'And then she stopped screaming and the doctor offered me money.'

'You are an *animal*,' I say through gritted teeth. 'You should have taken me home. They would have gone to prison and you could have taken me home. How could you leave me? You knew it was wrong and you could have stopped it. Even if you didn't love me, she did, Alice did. You should have taken me home to her.'

His mouth twists into a foul grimace. '*Home*? There was no bloody *home*! Your mother was a ghost. Nothing in her eyes. And that silence, that God-awful quiet. The only thing that blocked it was the drink.'

He goes quiet for a moment and I catch a glimpse of the sadness, or perhaps loss, that thrives in the warm, damp darkness within him. He shakes his head.

'And anyway, you didn't want me. You wanted them, what they could give you. And it didn't take a genius to see what they had was better for you – fancy clothes, your hair brushed neat, in that big house, all warm and cosy with money. You were better off without me. You *were* all better off without me. I knew then that out of that Devil's mess, you'd fallen on your feet. Those people were your ticket to a better life.' He takes a deep breath, rubs his face, his movements those of someone weary of life. 'So I shook his hand.'

The air around me has grown thick as tar. I need to leave. I need to get out. I want to be back in St Ives. I want to be back where I belong. With my sister and mother in the flat that smells of soup.

'It wasn't right to do what you did,' I say. 'You should never have kept me from my mother.'

Tremayne begins to walk towards me.

'Stay away,' I whisper. But he keeps coming.

I press my body back against the wall. He is close to me now and leans in. His smell seeps into me, acrid and ripe, the stench of drink hangs on his breath. He reaches a hand out towards my face. I recoil. Turn my head to avoid his touch. Flinch as his fingertips graze my cheeks. I squeeze my eyes closed as my throat constricts.

'Look how beautiful you are,' he whispers, each word a poison feather brushing against my skin.

Leave. It's time for you to leave.

'Get off me.' The words sound so weak. My heart is beating faster, my palms are clammy, but I won't show him I'm scared. I won't. I sidestep towards the doorway. He doesn't move, but his eyes follow me. 'You're worse than the Campbells,' I breathe. 'I hate them and I hate you.' I move through the doorway and start to walk backwards, worried that if I turn away from him he'll come after me.

'Oh, no, don't *hate*, Morveren. *Hate* will eat you up and spit you out like gristle. Living with hate will be the end of you. And I should know.'

'And who exactly do you hate? The family you abandoned?' I have reached the front door. I'm nearly free. 'The Campbells who kept you in this house, who gave you money?'

'No, not any of them. Me. It's *me* I hate.'

Then he turns and walks back to the sash window, which he lifts open again. The pigeons aren't there but he leans out of it and whistles, as one hand reaches for a loaf of sliced bread on a small table beside him. He takes a few slices out and tears them into bits, which he scatters on the ledge. The pigeons are back within moments. Even though he is facing away from me I can hear his voice as he talks to the birds.

'There, there, you hungry little rats.'

'Don't you have any scrap of decency?' I shout. Everything I feel – the hurt, the confusion, the loss, the grief – erupts at once. 'You can't even say sorry? Don't you feel any shame or remorse at all?'

He bends forward for a moment or two and then turns and walks forward until he's standing in the kitchen doorway, no more than fifteen feet away from me. He holds out his hands, which are cupped around a pigeon.

'Know anything about pigeons, Morveren?' he asks. 'They flock together to protect themselves against cats and foxes. They keep each other warm, accept strangers into the flock, and pair for life. The parents both look after their young. They can even find their way home from thousands of miles away. But still folk don't like them.' He lifts the bird closer to his face, whispering under his breath as he does. The pigeon watches him warily. 'People think they spread disease.' He touches his lips to the bird's head, causing the creature to struggle. 'They don't though. You're more likely to be struck by lightning than get sick from a pigeon.'

'You ruined my life.'

He shakes his head. 'You're young. Not even thirty. You've got all your life to come. You got any kids yet?'

I don't answer.

'No? Well, when you do, look after them nicely. Tuck them into their beds, read them stories, feed them well. That way you can right all the wrong that was done to you.' He turns slowly and goes back to the window to release the pigeon. 'And,' he says with a laugh. 'Don't lose them.'

My stomach turns over, nausea rising inside me. 'You disgust me.'

'Dare say I do.'

I reach for the latch on the door.

'You think you had a bad deal,' he calls after me. 'But you did alright, you know.'

My hand falls from the door and I face him, my head spinning, drunk on the impossible ugliness of it all. 'You *stole* my childhood.'

'No, you had a childhood, a different childhood I'll grant you, but you had one.'

'You're going to hell.'

A haunting sadness settles over him like a mist. 'I'm there already.'

And then I tear open the door and fall out of the house, dragging deep lungfuls of fresh air into my body. The sun is strong and the golden streets of this part of Bristol shimmer all around me. I stare at the people walking the pavements, shiny as the sun, happily ignorant of the horrors that exist behind doors like the one I've just closed, the hidden world of child abductors and soulless men in empty houses with nothing for company but bitter memories and ravenous pigeons.

THIRTY-FIVE

Henry Campbell – 20th February 1991

Henry Campbell recognised the man as soon as he opened the door.

His face was emblazoned on his dreams. He looked ill. His eyes rimmed red, rheumy with drink, his black hair plastered to his face by the rain that fell heavily. The last time Henry had seen him was the funeral, and he'd changed, even since then. It was as if the world had been kicking him repeatedly, constant blows to the stomach, the head, and the heart.

'My daughter. I want my daughter.'

Henry didn't speak. He should have been expecting this, he'd left that note after all, but the shock of seeing the man floored him. He tried to form words, but none came. Then from behind him came a scream, the like of which he'd never heard. He watched Elaine run towards the man like someone possessed. She grabbed hold of the door and pushed it closed in Tremayne's face, but he was too quick and shoved himself forward with all his weight, jamming his foot between the door and the frame. The force of his counter knocked Elaine backwards. Henry turned to see her tearing at her hair, her body shaking, piercing the air with her screaming.

'Get out! Get out! Get out!'

'Where is she?' Tremayne's voice was an ominous rumble. 'Where's Morveren?'

Henry Campbell watched in horror as his wife's face twisted and snarled, but then, amid the chaos and noise, he felt a mantle of calm settle over him, relief that soon this nightmare would be over and the lying, the guilt and the fear would all finally stop.

Out of the corner of his eye he saw the girl.

'Mama?' she said softly. 'What's wrong?'

Henry swore under his breath, angry at himself for his inactivity. Why didn't he pick her up and hand her to her father? Or call the police? Why did he stand there? Impotent, ineffectual, useless.

Weak.

Tremayne dropped to his knees. A strangled sobbing noise escaped his dry, cracked lips. He dragged his hands through his hair, smoothing it back from his face as if smartening himself for royalty. 'Hello Morveren,' he said. The uncertainty in the man's voice surprised Henry. 'How are you?'

Henry watched as the little girl curled herself in behind Elaine's legs, her thumb wedged in her mouth, her head lowered to avoid this man's eyes.

Mark Tremayne held out his hand and beckoned to her. 'Come on, don't be like that. Come here. Come to your dad.'

The girl looked up at Elaine. Her thumb dropped from her mouth. 'Don't want to, Mama. Don't like him.'

Though she whispered it, they had all heard.

Elaine bent down and picked her up, wrapping her arms around her tightly, pulling her into her shoulder, a protective hand shielding her head.

Henry watched as a switch went off in Tremayne. The man jumped to his feet and ran towards Elaine. Henry reached out to try to pull him back, but Tremayne swatted his arm away like he was an irritating fly.

Tremayne lunged for the girl, his big, grimy hands grabbing at her.

Elaine gave out yet another guttural scream that came from the very centre of her being, as if he'd driven a blade into her stomach.

'Get away from her!' Elaine screeched. 'Get your filthy bastard hands off my daughter!'

'She's not your daughter! You took her. You fucking took her.'

Tremayne's fingers closed around the girl's arm, digging into her tightly, so hard that she shrieked too. 'Stop it, Morveren! You're getting me teasy. For God's sake come here. I'm taking you back.'

As he pulled again on the girl's arm, her eyes widened, exposing the whites around their brilliant green centres, and then in one swift movement she opened her mouth and sunk her teeth into his hand. Tremayne yowled and snapped his hand away, grasping it with his other.

'You little bitch,' Tremayne growled. Then he lifted his hand above his head and moved as if he was going to swipe at her. Henry knew he should stop him, but he was glued to the floor, horrified by what was unravelling, his voice vanished, limbs rigid.

'Don't you dare hit her!' Elaine turned the child away from the man's raised hand, whispered into her hair, soft, indecipherable words, stroking her, soothing her as she snivelled quietly into Elaine's shoulder. Henry saw his wife's eyes fall on the hall table, then one of her hands darted out to grab at an ornate, bone-handled paperknife. She locked eyes with Tremayne, brandished the knife in his direction, waved it about like a magic wand. 'You will take this child over my dead body!' she screamed.

Henry knew she meant it. She would fight this man to the death to keep this little girl – her Bella – with her. His death. Or hers. Whichever came first.

'Money.'

Henry Campbell wasn't sure if the strangled word had come from his mouth or someone else's, but judging by the way Tremayne snapped his head around to look at him, it must have been his.

'What?'

Unconstrained aggression had taken over Tremayne's demeanour, replacing the shock and anger of his daughter's rejection.

'Money,' Henry rasped again. 'I'll pay you. Anything you want. All you have to do is forget you've seen her.' He paused, tears welling; his weakness sickened him. What kind of man had he become?

No, not a man, he thought. *You are no longer a man.*

He braced himself for Tremayne's punch, imagined it would land in the centre of his face, maybe break his nose, perhaps his teeth, knock him flat. He imagined Tremayne would then beat Elaine until she finally gave up the child, and then he would snatch her into his arms, bundle her into his car and call the police. He was convinced it would all soon be over.

Elaine was crying in the background now. Long, agonised wails that cut into him. 'Don't take her. Bella stays here.' Then whispering through her tears. 'Bella lives here. With me. Everything's alright, my darling. Mama's here. Mama's here to keep you safe.'

Henry saw Tremayne glance over at them, saw his brow furrow, confusion flickering over the anger in his eyes.

Oh my God, thought Henry. *He's going to take the money.*

Then he watched Tremayne taking in the hallway, the distant sound of classical music drifting in from the radio in the kitchen. Then his body collapsed as if he was crumbling from within. Tremayne's hands unclenched and as they did, Elaine's crying ebbed.

'Go upstairs, Bella,' she said. Her body straightened in front of Henry's eyes. She pulled her shoulders up, lifted her chin. 'Quickly, angel. Mama will be up in a minute. Choose a story, yes?'

'Can Tori listen to the story, too, Mama?'

Elaine bent and planted a soft kiss on the head of the girl, who eyed Tremayne warily one last time. 'Of course she can, darling. Run up and I'll be there in a moment.'

Elaine waited until the girl had run up the stairs, her legs carrying her so quickly that she had to drop her hands in front of her to balance her as she climbed; she looked like a little dog scampering up.

'We can give her everything, Mark,' Elaine said, her voice low and strong.

Henry started to protest. No. No this had to end. He hadn't meant to offer the money. He hadn't expected Tremayne to say yes.

'Be *quiet*, Henry.'

Henry Campbell watched her step towards Tremayne with the air of an advancing predator.

'We can give her *everything*. She will have the best life and you will have money. We can give you enough money that you never need to worry about working again. You can drink what you want, smoke what you want, as much as you want, all day long. And you can reassure yourself that you gave her the best start in life. She won't want for anything. I will make sure she is safe forever.'

Henry Campbell looked between his wife and Tremayne. He could see the man's demons raging inside him, his confusion, his anger, his doubt.

Elaine must have seen it too.

'You hurt her, didn't you, Mark? She was injured when we found her, a wound that looked like a burn, circular and deep. A cigarette, maybe? It was nasty and it scarred. And she was terrified. Underfed. She ran away from you because you didn't treat her well, did you? Look how scared she was of you tonight. She didn't want to come with you, did she? She doesn't want to be with you because you aren't capable of looking after her, are you? *You* let her go, Mark. *You* are a bad father. *Unfit*. If you go to the police, I will show them her scars and you will be prosecuted. Are there scars on your other child? On your wife? The odd hit when you got a bit cross, had one drink too many, but you didn't mean it? You know, they don't let children stay with parents who hurt them. She'll be taken away from you and put in a home. Is that what you want for her? In care, alone, somewhere she might be hurt by strangers.'

He shook his head, as if trying to dislodge her words. 'No, you ... you are strangers,' he said. 'Stop saying all these things.' Tremayne put his hands to his temples and rubbed them hard. 'You took her.'

'No, Mark,' Elaine said softly. She stepped closer, like an assassin ready to finish off a dying victim with a last bullet to the brain. 'I am her *mother*. I am the mother she wants. You saw that, didn't you? Did she cry for Alice? Did she call out for her? No. She wants me. Do the only good thing you can do in your miserable life and let her stay where she's happy and safe. She needs to stay here. This is her home.'

Mark Tremayne stood for a moment, his hands pushing against the side of his head, turning circles as his face knotted with confusion. And then he fell to his knees like a puppet who'd had his strings cut. There was no fight left in him. Henry glanced at his wife and as he did so, he caught the victorious smile that flashed across her face.

THIRTY-SIX

I arrive back into Penzance station and see Craig.

The thick fog that had hugged the Cornish landscape like a shawl on the journey home turns into the heavy summer rain that Phil predicted almost as soon as I step off the train. It's getting late and getting dark, and there are no taxis lined up waiting, so I run to the bus shelter and wait for one to show up.

A car pulls up in the drop-off zone outside the station entrance. It's an old blue Peugeot, a small one, a 205, I think. Inside are two people who appear to be having some sort of heated discussion, though I'm not close enough and the rain is driving through the dusky light, so it's hard to be certain. The man looks familiar. I squint through the rain, and yes, it's Craig.

The other figure is a woman.

They are turned in the car facing each other and the woman has her back to me, so I can't see her face, but I know it's not Dawn because this person's hair is blonde. She appears to be gathering things into a bag, an air of irritation about her, before she opens the door and gets out. It's clear she is young, but I can't say for sure exactly how old she might be. Her hair is scraped into a ponytail and she has two pairs of gold hoop earrings in each ear, her skirt is hardly there and she is wearing impractical kitten heels with bare legs and a vest top that is growing transparent in the wet. I see her glance up at the sky, shake her head, then lift her bag to cover her hair ineffectively. She runs towards the station entrance. He must have called her back because she turns and after a moment's hesitation she goes back through the rain to his car window, then bends to kiss him, before turning again and disappearing through the station doors.

It's as if I've been punched in the stomach. As if it's me he's hurting, not Dawn. I remind myself that I don't know the whole story and that Dawn herself told me she and Craig weren't together. Am I being naïve? Am I latched onto the romance of Craig and Dawn for my own benefit? To reassure myself that sometimes life is beautiful? Does the hurt of seeing him with another woman come from my own need for Craig to love Dawn? I've only met him twice, so maybe I am imagining the way they are with each other. The way her face lights up and her body relaxes when he's with her. The way he looks at her when she speaks, the way they brush each other, thinking I won't notice, a finger over a hand, a hand on a knee, a foot against a foot.

I spend the taxi journey back thinking about Dawn and Craig and the girl with the double-hoop earrings.

THIRTY-SEVEN

That night I think about Mark Tremayne. Going over and over the horror of what he told me. Of what he did. I don't know whether to tell Dawn. I know I should but I can't predict her reaction. I don't want to upset her. Or make her angry.

I recall what he told me. The way he described me hiding behind Elaine. I have a flash of memory. His face materialising from the shadows, his hand reaching out, her skin so soft and safe. I remember how safe she made me feel. And as I'm drifting off, hovering in that space between wakefulness and sleep, it's as if somebody somewhere has turned on a switch. Like the woman in the green-and-white striped dress on the beach, a buried memory comes tumbling back. Or maybe it's a dream. It feels like a dream.

It's dark and I'm scared. I'm definitely scared. And cold. I can't feel my toes. I wiggle them, but nothing happens; it's like they're playing dead lions. There's a taste in my mouth. Dirt and grit and bits of leaf, which I try to spit away but can't. I have a graze on one knee. Crusted blood mixed with dirt. It stings. I look at my arm and see my skin is blotchy, that all the little hairs are standing tall on goose bumps. Tiny soldiers on tiny hills, I think. And then the next thing I know, I am blinking into the bright sunlight. There's a person looking down at me. It's a lady but her features aren't clear. She is fuzzy, just a shape, with a glowing ring of sunlight lighting her from behind, like a perfect golden halo.

The lady bends close and murmurs. She is smiling. She places a hand on my cheek and her touch feels velvety and familiar. She opens her arms wide and I climb into them, close my eyes, breathe her in. She smells lovely, all scrubbed and perfumed, with makeup, creams and soap. I lay my head on the lady's shoulder and push my face into the smooth curve of her neck. She stands and begins to walk away from the cold, dirty hollow at the foot of the tree. She is talking to me and there's a lightness to her voice that sounds like singing, and it's the most beautiful singing I have ever heard. Magical singing that makes me feel safe.

THIRTY-EIGHT

'You OK, love?' says Phil kindly, as he hands me my coffee.

'A bit distracted, that's all.' I smile and he smiles back. 'Actually, can I ask you a question?'

'Fire away.'

'If you have a friend, a good friend, someone you love, and you know the person they love is, well, you know, seeing someone else … would you tell them?'

'That's a tough one. I can tell you from experience there's nothing that hurts so much as knowing the person you love is mucking about. Personally, when it happened to me, I'd have given anything not to have found out, but I'm soft. I'm sure most folk would prefer to know.'

'I'm sorry it happened to you.'

Phil shrugs. 'One of those things. I'm over it now.'

But the look on his face says he's anything but.

By the time I arrive at the flat, whether or not I should mention the blonde with the hoop earrings is all I can think about.

'You're quiet,' Dawn says.

'A bit tired.'

'Did you have a good day yesterday?'

'It was fine.' I think of Mark Tremayne rotting in the house in Bristol.

You need to tell her.

I know, I reply silently. *But not now. I'll tell her soon, I promise.*

You're being a coward. You need to tell her about Mark Tremayne and the blonde girl with the ridiculous skirt.

While she busies around me, fixing soup, shutting out the cat, putting the kettle on, I sit at the table and pick at the edge of my nail, trying to find the right words.

Dawn stops wiping the table and stands looking at me, tightly balling the cloth in her hand. 'Are you sure you're OK?'

'Yes...' I hesitate. 'I'm fine.' And with that I put both things in a box to be opened another time.

'Right, well, I'm going to have a quick bath before I feed her. That OK?'

'Of course. I'll sit with her,' I say, but she's already left the kitchen.

I get up from the table and walk down the corridor to Alice's room, feeling the bite of my craven reluctance to be honest with Dawn. The stagnant depression that hangs around the bedroom hits me as soon as I open the door. It's no wonder Alice doesn't talk or interact when she's confined day and night to this dingy room decorated only by a wall of wretched memories. I walk over to the wall and look at the miserable montage with those headlines screaming out at me, and suddenly, violently, I hate it.

'You know, I think we should make this room a bit cheerier.' I pat Alice's hand. 'The past should be in the past and you need to stop fixating on this morbid rubbish.'

I begin to remove each article, carefully pulling the blu-tack off the wall so it doesn't take off the wallpaper, remembering Elaine's pathological hatred of the stuff. When I've cleared the area of newspaper cuttings, I look at the mermaids and hesitate.

'I don't know, what do you think? Leave them up or take them down?' I pause. 'There are so many of them. Too many. I think they have to go.'

The wall looks naked when I've finished, just empty rectangles of lightened wallpaper where each mermaid has sat for too long and I feel a little guilty. I glance at Alice, ready to reinstate the collage if I have to, but she shows no sign of distress.

'I'll get some picture frames for a few of the nicest pictures this afternoon. They'll look good when they're hung properly. And now you don't have to stare at the wall!'

I bend down and push my shoulder against the chair. It's not heavy and swivels easily to face into the room. With that done, I pat her hand again and then scan the room for the next thing to tackle. I am suddenly invigorated, filled with an energy I haven't felt for a long time. When I pull back the grimy net curtain that hangs over the window, the room instantly lightens and brings the outside in. Alice's bed needs to be swung out from the wall, I think, so I turn it, pushing the head end directly under the window. I expect to find years' worth of dust, grime and tumbleweeds of hair and the like beneath the bed, but there's nothing; like everything in this flat, it's spotless.

I stand back and assess the bed's new position. It eats into the room a bit and you have to walk around it to get from Alice's chair to the door, but I think it's worth it. I take the few things – the lamp, a box of tissues, a pointless alarm clock – off the cardboard box that makes do as a bedside table and collapse it. I shove the box under the bed then move the small table from beside the bookshelf. It needs a cloth to cover the chipped melamine so I go to the cupboard in the hall to where Dawn keeps the linen and root around. At the bottom, underneath the piles of rough towels and worn sheets is a navy blue blanket. The moths have had a go at it, but it will do. It needs to be folded in half, but once on the table with the lamp back on top it looks passable. I switch on the lamp to add some cosiness and then stand back and admire my handiwork.

'Look!' I say with a pleased smile. 'Isn't that better? You'll be happier in here now. I'm going to get you a few bits and pieces from town to decorate it and maybe I'll even paint it for you on the weekend.' I re-straighten the rug that lies over her lap. 'A lovely buttercup yellow. And you'll need a new curtain. That old thing's vile.'

I walk back down to Dawn's bedroom and find her roughly drying her hair with a towel.

'Nice bath?'

Dawn nods.

'When you're dressed I've got a surprise for you in Alice's room.'

Suspicion settles over Dawn's face. 'What is it?'

'You'll have to see,' I say. Then I go back down to the bedroom, shut the door behind me and smile at Alice. 'Don't say a word, OK? Let's surprise her.'

When I hear Dawn's footsteps, I run back to the door, open it a crack and peer at her.

'What is it then?'

Dawn couldn't look less excited, but I don't let that put me off. 'Well, you know how her room's a bit,' I pause. 'Dreary?'

A look of confusion replaces the mild irritation on Dawn's face.

'Well...' I smile then step aside and fling the door open. 'Ta dah!'

Dawn stands motionless.

'What have you done?'

'I've changed the room around. Made it nicer.'

'Nicer?' she says, making no attempt to hide her anger.

'I thought—'

'No, you didn't. You didn't *think*. If you'd thought then you'd have left it how it was. How it's always been.' Her lips draw tight. 'The bed's blocking the way to the door. It's going to be hard to get her out to go to the bathroom, isn't it? And why is the lamp on?'

'So there's more light in here.'

She walks over and turns it off.

'How can she get better in the dark?'

'There's light from the window.' She says as she draws the net across again.

'But the net cuts out the light.'

'It doesn't. It's designed to let in light but stop people from the street seeing in,' she says, through her teeth.

'She needs the light on then.'

'Don't tell me what to do in my home.'

'I'm not telling you what to do, I'm—'

'You are. You're telling me how things should be. What do you know? What do you know about looking after someone who's not well?'

I usually avoid confrontation, but the sight of the net falling back across the window, reignites the claustrophobia I used to feel at The Old Vicarage and the retrospective link to my captivity seems to make me braver. 'I know she needs light.'

'Not in the daytime.'

'But the room's gloomy.'

'How dare you?'

'I'm sorry, but—'

'We don't need the light!'

'Dawn, you're making a mistake.'

'Yeah, well, that's easy for you to say. I don't think I'm making a mistake when the bills fall on the doormat each month. All I bloody care about is being able to pay them and keep her warm and fed. So if it's alright with you, we'll keep them off, unless you think she needs a lamp on more than she needs food.'

'Let me pay the bills then!'

Dawn glares daggers at me, before spinning on her heel and storming out of the room.

I sit heavily on the edge of the bed and drop my head into my hands. A smell hits me, the dank putrid stench from the house in Bristol that has clung to my sweater like a stowaway. I wince as Mark Tremayne leers into my thoughts. I look up at Alice.

'He knew,' I tell her quietly. 'Can you believe that? He knew they had me and he said nothing. He took money from them and then he left you both.' I stand up and slowly drag the bed back to its original position.

I don't move Alice's chair back, however, and I don't reinstate the wall. Whatever Dawn says or thinks, that vile collage is history. I'm not stolen any more and there's no place for it.

Dawn is putting the cat through the back door as I walk into the kitchen and sit down. She moves the box across the cat flap to block it and the cat jumps up onto the window ledge and sits looking in at us.

'I don't know why you've got the cat if you don't like it,' I say quietly.

'I told you,' she says. 'It showed up uninvited.'

I pick at something underneath one of my fingernails.

'Change isn't good for her.'

'I've put the bed back to how it was.'

The cat mews at the window, clawing her paw against the glass, inexplicably desperate to get back to the oppressive atmosphere of the flat. I stare at the flickering television while Dawn silently fumes. The smell in the kitchen – dense and fusty – bears down on me until I can no longer breathe.

'I think I should go.'

'Are you still OK to come up for a few hours on Friday?' she shouts after me as I walk down the hallway.

'Yes,' I call back. 'I said I would, didn't I?'

The sun has managed to push yesterday's *drok newl* away and is driving through the pale-grey cloud. As I walk down the street toward the centre of town, I scan each face of those passing me, sucking up their smiles like a human leech. I sit on the wall and look out over the harbour, trying to clear my head, taking long slugs of sea air, filling my body with its freshness. I watch the tide coming in, the waves carrying dark lengths of seaweed, dredged up by whatever storm raged out towards the distant horizon.

'I don't know if I can do this,' I whisper into the oncoming wind.

You have to, says a voice. You have no choice.

The voice isn't Tori's and nor is it the mermaid's.

This time the voice is mine.

THIRTY-NINE

There's a knock on my bedroom door.

'Tori? You coming?'

It's Greg. I make a face and silently swear; it's Thursday and I've forgotten about the party. I glance at the clock on the bedside table. It's five past seven. Going out with a bunch of people I don't know no longer seems like a good idea at all.

'I'm not sure,' I call. 'Sorry.'

'No way,' he shouts though the door. 'You're coming. It's turned into a beautiful night, nice and warm. It'll be great. Get yourself out here now.'

I walk over to the door and hover behind it, my hand resting on the door handle, unsure what to say next.

'Come on. It'll be great.'

I chew on my lip as I consider it.

Go on. Say yes. It'll do you good.

So I open the door and when I do he smiles. He's wearing a faded grey sweatshirt, loose around his neck to reveal the slope of his shoulders, and light denim jeans with holes worn through the knees that show his tanned skin, dusted with sun-bleached hairs.

'Coming?'

'Can you give me five minutes?'

As I change into a clean pair of jeans and a shirt and drag a brush through my hair, I go over Tori in my head like I'm rehearsing lines from a play.

Tori lives in London and is a freelance journalist. She came down to research a story and while she was here, she realised how tired she was and how much she needed a break from London. She is staying at the hostel Greg runs. She loves Phil's cappuccinos. You know, Phil? The guy who runs the café on the harbour? She has one every morning, which she drinks while sitting on a groyne overlooking the sea. During the day she reads or writes. And she walks. Long walks along the cliffs. She loves the sea, especially when the waves are high. Her parents are teachers. She has a sister and a brother who both live in London. They get on so well. She can't wait to get a cat. Tori doesn't need anyone's pity. She wasn't stolen, didn't open the study door to find a dead man covered in blood and doesn't have a real-mother quietly festering away in a dark room in a once-was-lilac dressing gown. And she's not married. She's definitely not married.

I glance down at my wedding ring and then slip it off and put it in the drawer of the bedside table. I rub my finger where the gold band had been. It feels different. I feel different. As if my tethering ropes have been cut. I imagine David's look of horror at the thought of me taking it off. He refuses to wear a ring, but says seeing mine on my finger is the most beautiful thing, that *I* am his most beautiful thing.

Fi isn't coming, Greg tells me, so it's only him and me. We walk into St Ives exchanging small talk somewhat awkwardly. At least, I am awkward. Greg seems fine and not that put off by the way my voice sticks in my throat and my laughter sounds forced.

As we approach the throng of drinkers enjoying the evening sun outside the pub, a doe-eyed girl in a pair of shorts that skim her bottom and fur-lined boots on slender, smooth legs, bounces out of the group of people with oh-so-shiny hair and teeth, and rushes up to Greg to plant a kiss on his lips, prompting an illogical stab of jealousy.

'I thought you weren't coming,' she trills. 'Thank *God* you have. I don't know *what* I'd have done if you hadn't shown up.'

'As if I'd stand you up,' says Greg, to the lithesome creature. 'Have you got the drinks in?'

She giggles. 'We're having tequilas,' she says, sounding like a gleeful child. 'I've got a tab running. Daddy gave me fifty pounds so I could get the party started. He's such an angel!'

'Good girl,' says Greg. 'I'd like you to meet Tori. Tori, this is Finty.' She offers me a perfectly manicured hand, which I grasp and shake. 'Tori's from London, like you.'

My heart leaps into my mouth.

'Really? What part?'

'Bloomsbury,' I say, praying it's an area she's unfamiliar with.

'Oh, how very *hipster*.' She makes a face that informs me Tori lives in the wrong part of London. I'm about to ask which bit she's from, but she turns away from me and grabs hold of Greg's arm. 'Come on, darling. I need help getting more drinks.'

I consider turning around and heading back up the hill to the hostel. These aren't my kind of people. I'm not sure they're even Tori's kind of people. But Greg gestures for me to follow him, so instead of leaving I push through the crowded pub with them until we reach the bar.

'How many do we need?' Finty asks him.

'One each for Tori and I to catch up and then a round for the others outside.' Greg turns to me. 'You like tequila, right?'

I've never tried it, but I don't have time to answer before he's ordered the drinks and the girl behind the bar, who smiles at me in recognition, is laying a tray with lots of small glasses filled with clear liquid, a saucer of sliced lemons and a salt cellar.

'Coming through!' Greg calls as he carries the tray back through the pub.

The girl giggles and pushes herself between him and me as if I don't exist. My heart pounds with nerves as we approach the table. Everyone whoops at the arrival of Greg and the drinks, like he's a triumphant general returning from battle. I try not to blush and sit quietly next to Greg on the edge of the bench, watching as he salts the back of one hand, then picks up a glass and a wedge of lemon with the other.

'See you later!' he cries and everyone cheers.

I reach for my shot and peer at it. It smells vile. I glance at Greg who nods encouragingly. I take a breath, then copy what he did, licking the salt off my hand, swallowing back the liquid, and then sucking on the slice of lemon. It's the foulest thing I've ever tasted, but I smile because it actually feels great as it burns its way down my throat.

We have another shot and then someone stands and takes hold of the tray. I reach into my back pocket and thrust a twenty-pound note into his hand.

'Use this,' I say quietly, and he smiles at me.

This is what I'd missed out on growing up, friends, a group of people to have fun with, and the feeling of freedom, the adrenaline it sends coursing my veins, is exhilarating.

'We'll pay in the morning,' somebody says. 'Tequila's the mother of all hangovers.'

'That's not for hours,' I say. My heart pumps like a pneumatic drill as I half-expect them to turn and stare at me, to dismiss me as shy, anxious Bella, but they don't. They laugh.

For the next hour or so there is joking and drinking and flirting. The group all look similar, with their sun-bleached hair and wooden beads around their necks or wrists. When I tell a couple of them that I'm sick of London, that the sea has got under my skin, they nod with understanding. At least half of those who live here have relocated from some grim city or another, escaping previous existences that sapped their souls.

'Right,' says Greg suddenly, slapping both hands down on his thighs. 'How about we take this party to the beach?'

There's a rumble of agreement and we wander into the street in a laughing mass. It's a beautiful evening, the sun is low in the sky and yesterday's torrential rain has given the warm air a clear freshness. My head loops a lightheaded circle and I remind myself to take it easy with the alcohol. I'm not actually Tori and I don't really drink.

The girl in fur-trimmed boots, with the improbable name, falls in step with me. She is magazine-beautiful, with professionally whitened teeth and bovine lashes. Everything about her exudes confidence and walking beside her any bravado I might have had seems to fade as it's sucked into her black hole of self-assurance.

Don't crumble, for goodness' sake. You are this girl's equal.

Yes, I say silently. I am. So I straighten my shoulders and push my chin into the air and walk like a woman who knows where she's going.

Greg comes up behind Finty and drops an arm across her shoulders, but then he turns to wink at me so I don't mind so much. Greg's beaten-up van is parked in a side street and when we reach it we all bundle in. I reach for my seatbelt, but there isn't one. I am about to mention it to Greg, but then I notice nobody has strapped themselves in, not even Greg, who's driving. I try not to think about what David would say about a driver who not only fails to appreciate the importance of buckling up, but who's also drunk enough tequila to floor a Mexican rugby team.

I'm silent during the ride to the beach and while the others laugh and joke, crack open cans of lager and light cigarettes, I rest my nose against the glass and stare out of the window. The road begins to wind through bracken-covered hills on our left and fields on the right that stretch down towards the sea. Soon we turn onto an unmade track that seems to go on forever until eventually we slow and pass though a five-bar gate, which hangs off its top hinge and rests open against a granite block, with grass and brambles knotting through it. We park and Greg stills the engine beside two other cars; another seven or eight people are gathered in the field.

'Want a hand?' Greg asks, reaching towards me as he slides open the van door.

'No, thanks,' I say and jump down.

Laden with food, crates of lager and a battered CD player, we follow Greg like the children of Hamelin behind the Piper. He leads us through a farmyard, deserted apart from a barking black-and-white dog, who is thankfully tied to a tree. I'm wary of dogs. Like Elaine was, of course.

'Oh, I love dogs!' Predictably it's Finty, who walks over to the creature in her furry boots and too-short shorts, and bends to fuss it. 'Hello lovely boy,' she croons.

The dog quietens and licks her hand, obviously smitten, and she dissolves into peals of girlish laughter, before kissing its head.

We turn down a narrow footpath with tangled hedges reaching high above my head on both sides and rocks that appear from nowhere to trip me up. I watch Finty in front of me, laughing at whatever Greg says, skipping merrily along beside him like a mountain goat in designer boots.

I look away from them and breathe deeply, drawing in the smell of salty grass that hangs heavily in the warmth of the evening. The sea is spectacular, glinting as if it's on fire under the setting sun, which is half-submerged and the colour of blood orange. From nowhere David comes into my thoughts and steps out of my head. He is walking ahead of us down to the beach. He isn't alone. Tori – as she was as a child when we used to play together – is with him. She is perched on his shoulders. His hands clasp her ankles. Her blonde hair, curled at the ends, bounces as he strides confidently forwards. She strokes his hair out of his eyes with her small hands, her fingers passing over his forehead, and as she does I feel his skin, damp with sweat, his greyed hair soft to touch. I feel how firm his hold is. His hands clasped around her ankles, squeezing hard, too hard, to stop her falling.

You mean, to stop *you* falling, he says, so loud and clear it's as if he's beside me.

'I don't need you,' I say. 'I'm not going to fall.'

'Yes, be careful. It's quite slippery,' says a girl behind me. I turn and give her a small smile and, as I do, David vanishes.

The path starts to head downwards, with large rocks, washed-up fishing debris and the odd stagnant pool of stranded storm water peppering the way. The last bit of the walk is the hardest, but as we clamber down the steep cliff path, the crash of the waves grows louder in my ears and pulls me towards it.

We finally make it down and it's breathtaking. I stand still to absorb it all. The beach is spectacular, a crescent cove of soft white sand with not a soul or a footprint on it, flanked by high cliffs on all sides and the navy sea breaking into huge rolling waves.

A boy stops beside me. 'What do you think, then?'

'It's beautiful,' I breathe.

'One of the best fishing spots in England, though don't tell the emmets,' he says and taps his nose. 'This place we keep for ourselves.'

'Emmets?'

'The tourists. It means ants. It's what the upcountry folk look like, swarming Kernow in their thousands and buggering up the waves on rented body boards. Cockblankets,' the boy says with derision.

I shift uncomfortably, hoping he doesn't think I'm an ant.

He bends to pick up some driftwood. 'For the fire,' he says. 'Get as much as you can, it'll be dark soon.'

We join the others and I add the bits I've gathered to the growing pile. Greg shoves handfuls of wispy grass under the driftwood and branches then sets about lighting the fire, brow furrowed, mouth set firm. He looks like an overgrown boy scout and I have to stifle a laugh.

I step away from the group and watch the breaking waves. They are trying to speak to me and I concentrate hard, hoping to catch what they're saying, and for a split second I think I hear singing.

'Hey!' The call breaks my trance and I turn to see two of the men struggling with an enormous log. 'Can you give us a hand?'

'Sure,' I say, and head over to them.

'This'll keep us going,' says one of them, as we dump it triumphantly beside the fire.

We watch the sun set into the sea, gazing quietly as it fades to strips of apricot and then disappears. The soft sway of reggae dances around us in air thick with the smell of sausages and marijuana. I reach for a can of coke and lie back against a rock that is still warm from the day's sun. I smile as I think how different this party is from the ones I've been to before, formal gatherings at the university, peopled with men wearing cords and women in button-up dresses nursing orange juice and talking academia. But lying here, listening to the chatter around me, a few people singing along to the music, the sounds cocooning me, I realise how much I've missed.

My mind turns to Dawn. I wish she was here. She could do with getting out of the flat. It can't be good for her to shut herself away with only her silent mother and a cat she doesn't like for company.

Greg collapses on the sand beside me.

'Hey,' he says. 'Told you you'd have fun.'

'Yes, I'm glad I came.' I take a handful of sand and let it fall from my fingers, watching it flow like water. 'I like this music.'

'Yeah? What music do you normally listen to?'

I think for a moment, knowing I should make something up, that I am supposed to be pretending I'm cool, confident Tori, but any band names I might have known in the cold, tequila-less light of day have vanished. 'Jazz, I suppose.'

Greg snorts with laughter. 'Jazz?'

My cheeks flush with heat and I shrug.

'I can't stand jazz,' he says.

It takes me a moment or two and then I burst into laughter. 'Me neither,' I say, through my laughing.

He grins and reaches over to hook my hair over my ear and my stomach turns over. Pitch-blackness has settled around us and in the flickering glow of the fire I see him smile.

'You're very beautiful, Tori.'

I lean against his arm, but immediately feel stupid and sit back. I look up at him. The smile has fallen from his face and I have a feeling – of both dread and thrill – that he is going to kiss me. I look over my shoulder, but nobody is watching.

'What about Finty?' I whisper.

'Who?'

'The girl in the furry boots. Isn't she your girlfriend?'

'Christ, no,' he says. 'I kissed her when she was on holiday last year. It's good for business to flirt with the tourists a bit, you know, keeps them coming back, but I'm not interested in her now.' He smiles so I am able to pretend he's joking about kissing tourists for the good of his business. 'Anyway,' he continues. 'I don't think she's too hung up on me.' He gestures with his head.

I look in the direction he indicated. She is lying on the other side of the fire with one of the boys who I'd helped carry a log. They are locked in an uncomfortable clinch, her lean leg hooked over his, one of his hands thrust up her top. I look back at Greg. Without taking his eyes off me he reaches over and wedges his can of lager into the sand, then he takes my chin between his thumb and forefinger and leans closer.

My heart is racing.

He kisses me. Hands strong on my shoulders, he kisses me gently, as if kissing for my pleasure rather than his own. David has never kissed me like this. He kisses me likes it's a boring chore he has to do before he gets to unzip his fly, before he gets to claim his wife. I realise now that I was wrong not to have kissed other people before I said *yes* to him, and this realisation goes some way to helping alleviate the guilt I feel for my disloyalty.

Greg stops and leans away from me, his hand searching the sand beside him for a bottle of vodka. He twists off the lid, tips it to his mouth, and then he puts his lips to mine and as we kiss the neat liquid spills from his mouth into mine. He bends his head and kisses the skin on my chest. With one hand he undoes the buttons on my shirt, then runs the flat of his hand over my breasts, cupping each one as he does.

'Not here,' I whisper then. 'Let's go somewhere more private.'

His eyes are glazed with lust, his lips wet with saliva and vodka. He takes my hand and leads me away from the rest of them, some sleeping, some dancing, some kissing, and in the shadows, behind a rock, we drop to the floor. It's cold away from the heat of the fire and I shiver.

I'm scared.

But you want this.

I fumble with the buttons on his jeans, then undo my own. His shirt is off, and though I can't see his tiger in the darkness, I know it's there. I can hear it prowling. I run my hands over his back, pretending I can feel its soft, dense fur. Greg kisses me again, harder this time, and I kiss him back, pulling him down on top of me.

This is what you want.

And as he pushes into me, I bite down on my lip to stop myself from crying out and tears gather in my eyes.

FORTY

When I wake I am cold and damp, and I ache all over. I ease my stiff bones into a more upright position, then pull my shirt closed and do up the buttons. I look down at Greg sleeping next to me. In the half-light he resembles a Greek statue, all chiselled features and classical proportions, serenity blanketing his comatose face. I have flashbacks to last night and feel a mix of emotions. There are echoes of how thrilling it felt to have my body awakened in a way it hasn't been before. There is guilt as my wedding vows echo in my head, promises I made to David, promises I never thought I would break. And there is also a new sense of fortitude, the conviction that when I finally return to David things will be different, that I have changed a little, that I am somehow stronger.

I don't know what the time is, but I imagine it's getting near to five as a hazy light has begun to flood the sky. The colours around me are muted, painted from a palette of light greys and blues then covered with a layer of muslin. I walk back towards the fire. The large log still smoulders, flameless, a giant bite taken from it, then the whole sprayed black with charcoal. Bodies litter the sand, partly hidden beneath whatever rug or jacket was chosen as a bedcover.

My mouth feels dry and my head throbs and waves of nausea pass through me. Greg and I drank, had sex, and drank some more for most of the night. I can't have had more than an hour or two's sleep. I look around the carnage in the hope of finding a bottle of water, but there are only empty bottles, cans and plastic bags stuffed with food wrappings.

Shrouded in silence, I walk across the sand towards the sea. The dawn sky is streaked with slashes of light, like the marks of a rubber through pencil shading. Everything is so quite. Even the crashing waves seem noiseless, as if I'm watching them on Dawn's silent television. The sand becomes wet beneath me as I walk closer to the break and my feet sink into it. I walk on until the reach of the sea runs over my numbed feet and disappears into the sand in a mass of foamy bubbles. The water is an extraordinary colour, neither grey nor blue nor green, but at once all three. I imagine Morveren and Matthew watching me from somewhere out in the depths. I can feel them staring, their hands clasped so tightly it hurts their bones. I thought they might be disappointed by my infidelity, but I feel no judgement from them, which is a relief.

Something in the shallows catches my eye. A black rock perhaps, but it can't be because when I look again, it's no longer there. Moments later it reappears and my heart jumps with childish joy. It's a seal. She hangs suspended in the water, her head above the waves, her body below, and she watches me for a minute or two before ducking back into the sea.

No, don't go.

I scan the cove. Where is she? And then there she is, this time only metres from the shore. She dances back and forth in the breaking waves, a special show just for me. She lifts her head clear of the water, her black body rising and falling in the swell. But then something catches her attention and she pitches backwards into the water and is gone.

Greg comes to a halt beside me.

'Did you see her?' I whisper.

'See what?' His voice rasps against his parched throat.

'The seal.'

'They love this beach, it's nice and quiet.' He steps away from me. 'I'm taking the van back with whoever wants to go. I'm teaching at eight and fancy a couple of hours kip in a proper bed. You coming?'

'Yes, please. I don't feel that great.'

Greg leaves me but I don't follow him immediately. The tide must be coming in because the waves now run further up the beach. I take a few paces back and watch the sea claiming my footprints, erasing them as the waves break then pull back, leaving unblemished sand, as if I've never been there.

Those who have to work pull themselves into semi-wakefulness when Greg announces we are heading back.

'What about the mess?' I ask, surveying the debris-littered sand.

'The others will do it,' says Greg, as he starts towards the path. 'Don't worry, they won't leave it.'

Five of us trudge slowly back like weary camels in a train. By the time we reach the top of the hill, it's all I can do to stop myself curling up in the long grass on the verge and falling asleep right there. Greg and I say goodbye in the reception of the hostel. He doesn't kiss me but thanks me for a great time, which makes me feel slutty. I pull the room key from my pocket and struggle to unlock the door, battling cold fingers and a now pounding headache, the type that makes your vision blur. When the door opens, I fall inside and collapse on the bed, but as soon as I close my eyes, the Campbells appear, spinning around in my head as if on a fairground ride.

Elaine is angry.

Her arms are crossed, upset with me for behaving so badly, for putting myself at risk. How could I drink so much? Get into a van with a drunk driver? How could I have sex with a stranger?

'You're married *for God's sake!'*

'I'm sorry. I didn't mean—' I start to say, but she doesn't want to hear my excuses. She turns her back on me.

I glance at Henry, but he shakes his head and turns away too. I reach out to them, my fingers nearly touching them as they whip around and fly towards me, their faces bloodied and rotten, their tongues swollen, their skin falling from their bones.

I wake up with a jolt, terrified, and push myself off the bed. I trip over something. Then stumble and fall. I try to catch myself, but my hand misses and I hit my head on the corner of the bedside table. There's a sharp pain and when I touch my forehead and look at my fingers there's blood. I am going to be sick. My vision falters. I grab at the bedpost to steady myself and then everything goes blank.

FORTY-ONE

My head feels as if it has been sawn in half and my brain scooped out. I try to open my eyes but the sunlight streaming through the windows is blinding. The bedcovers are tucked around me and there's a glass of water beside me on the table. I reach for it and drink. For a second or two it helps, but at the last gulp everything begins pounding again.

I don't know how long I've been lying like this, trying to breathe slowly, hoping it will help the pain that has spread from my head throughout my body, but I am roused from my half-sleep by a knock on the door. Then the door creaks open a fraction.

'Tori? It's Fi. Are you OK?'

I want to cry out that I'm fine, that she can leave me, but don't manage it. Fi, her purple hair tied off her face with a brightly coloured scarf, arrives at the foot of the bed.

'I wanted to make sure you're alright,' she says. 'You were in a bit of a state a few hours ago.'

'I've felt better.'

'I heard a crash and came in. I found you on the floor. Do you remember?'

I shake my head, which doesn't help my headache.

'You hit your head. There was blood. You talked to me, well, I say talked, it was more a mumble. You don't remember?'

'No.'

'God, I should have called a doctor. I thought because you were talking you were OK. I put a plaster on the cut. It's not too bad, but I think you might be a bit concussed though. Maybe you should pop into the surgery? You shouted something out after I put you into bed. I came back but you were asleep or at least I thought you were.'

'I have nightmares.'

'I know you do,' she says. 'My room's above this one. I hear you.' She sits on my bed and rests her hand on mine. It feels intimate, but not uncomfortable, and I have to resist the urge to curl myself into her.

'Thank you for looking after me.'

'No problem. You'll see a doctor, won't you?'

'I'm sure all I need is a bit of sleep. I'll be fine tomorrow—' As I close my eyes I remember Dawn.

I sit bolt upright.

'What's the time, Fi?' Each word jabs at my temples.

'Just gone ten,' she says. 'Maybe nearer half past.'

'I have to get up.'

'You should stay in bed. That was quite a nasty knock. You need to look after yourself. I don't think you're looking that well. I—' She stops talking mid-sentence and looks downs at her hands. 'Sorry, it's probably none of my business.'

Ten minutes later I am walking as fast as my body will let me up the hill towards the flat. I have another flash of last night, Greg's hands on my waist, his stubble rough against my neck. David appears, his disapproval like a vice. I recall my wedding day when, in front of a handful of people, I'd sworn myself to him – and him alone – for the rest of my life.

'I was someone else back then.'

David's face clouds with anger; he doesn't understand.

'Don't look at me like that. It was Tori. Not me. Greg hasn't even met your wife. He had sex with Tori. Ask him.'

And his face fades.

I knock on the door and wait for Dawn to open it. When she does, she immediately runs back down the corridor without saying anything. I stroll after her, and find her repositioned on a kitchen chair watching her television programme. I sit at the table and rest my head on my hands and listen to the shrill voices of the television women as they discuss immigration and its effect on the products stocked in supermarkets. When the end credits roll, I lift my head.

'Hi,' I say.

Dawn stands, pushes in her chair, mutes the television, and then picks up a J-cloth and wipes the already clean table, pausing by my hands. I lift them so she can clean beneath them. 'Did you just get up?'

'No,' I say.

'You look like you just got up. And what did you do to your head?'

'It's nothing.'

She turns her back on me and runs the tap to rinse her cloth. 'I thought you'd forgotten.'

'Forgotten what?"

'That I need to go out.'

'No, I didn't forget. That's why I'm here.' My head feels like it's splitting open with the effort of speaking. 'You can go now.'

'Can't. It's the wrong time. Mum needs lunch.'

'I'll do it.'

Dawn shakes her head.

'Why? We'll be fine.'

'Really?' She begins to twist her fingers into her T-shirt.

'Yes. I'm nearly thirty, you know.' I stand to switch the kettle on. 'I can make soup.'

Dawn nods her head, slowly at first, then more certain. A smile spreads over her pale face. 'Yes,' she says, suddenly convinced. 'OK. I'll go. You'll be fine. Of course you will.' Then she disappears into her room.

By the time I've made a cup of tea she's back. She's wearing a stone-washed denim jacket and jeans of the same colour, with white trainers that look like they've never been worn.

'What time will you be back?' I ask, as I stir in my sugar, watching the whirlpool that forms around the spoon. I remove the spoon and the whirl fades to nothing.

She looks at the clock on the wall. 'It's gone eleven-thirty. I reckon no later than two?'

'Enjoy.'

'And you're sure?' Her face suddenly appears wracked with doubt again.

I manage to stop myself telling her not to fuss, and instead I nod. 'I'll see you at two.'

Dawn's smile returns, and she walks out of the kitchen. She says goodbye to Alice, the front door slams and the flat is plunged into quiet.

I let the cat in the back door then sit back down at the table and flick through a clothing catalogue that is lying on it, stroking the purring animal and drinking my tea. My body is aching more now, rather than less, and I can't keep my eyelids from closing. I look at the fluttering television in the hope that it might wake me up. There's some sort of craft programme on, though without the sound it's hard to be sure why they are covering perfectly good chairs with what look like black bin bags.

I push the catalogue across the table and stare into the distance. I think of Mark Tremayne alone with this kind of silence for days and weeks and years. The presence of this man in my thoughts, my father, a stranger who makes me feel sick to the pit of my stomach, feels like a violation, and I shake my head in the hope that it will rid me of him.

I wander through to my mother's room, leaving the cat watching me from the threshold. I turn back to look at her. 'You could come with me, you know. Curl up on the bed in Alice's room?' I bend down and making a clicking sound and reach out to her.

But the cat doesn't move.

'Fine,' I say. 'Suit yourself.'

In Alice's room I walk over to her chair and kneel beside it, resting my chin lightly on the back of her hand. 'How did they get me out of France, Alice? How come nobody noticed? Why did nobody think it was strange they went on holiday and came back with a child?' I pause and sigh heavily. 'Is that what you think about too? I imagine it is.' I draw in a deep breath. 'Would you like me to read to you?'

She doesn't say no, so I take our book off the shelf and begin to read. But the reading is soporific and soon my words being to slur.

I must have dozed off, because I wake with my head on her knee, and the book on the floor. I wince as I sit upright; my muscles feel like they've fused. I check my watch and realise with horror that it's twenty minutes past soup-time. I stand and am sent reeling by a now blinding headache. In battle with my aching body, I limp through to the kitchen like a wounded soldier. Without thinking, I empty the contents of the soup into the bowl rather than the pan, then realise what I've done.

'Doesn't matter,' I mumble to myself. 'There are worse things in the world than cold soup.'

Ten minutes later, we are done. I take the bowl back to the kitchen, then wander into Dawn's room and pick up the photograph of our grandparents. I lie back on her bed and hold the frame to my chest. Her bed is soft and comfortable and her pillow smells of Dawn, which is strangely comforting.

And the next thing I hear is the sound of Dawn's key in the lock.

I glance at her clock. It's just before two.

'Shit,' I mutter, as I leap off the bed.

'Hello!' she calls.

'Oh, hi!' I shout back as I straighten her covers, and run into the kitchen, rubbing under my eyes and pinching colour into my cheeks. She walks into the kitchen and smiles at me. She looks great, the fresh air has done her a power of good, and I smile.

'How was your day?' I ask.

'Good,' she says. 'Yours?'

She is carrying a large parcel and walks straight through to her bedroom, returning without it.

'No problems at all.'

Dawn switches the kettle on. 'Fancy a cup?'

'No, I'm fine.'

'I'll go and say hello to Mum. It's so odd being away from her like that. Can you believe I actually missed her!'

Dawn is gone only a few minutes before she reappears with a face like a storm. She shoves past me and drops to her knees to open the cleaning cupboard. She reaches in and pulls out some bottles, slamming each onto the floor then banging the door shut, which bounces back open defiantly. She flies out of the kitchen back to Alice's room.

'What's the matter?' As I follow her, my heart beats faster and faster; something is terribly wrong.

Dawn is kneeling beside the armchair, which is moved to one side. Alice stares straight ahead. Everything looks fine to me at first, nothing different, but then I see Dawn blotting a towel angrily over a dark patch of carpet.

'She's been sat in it for ages,' spits Dawn, biting back angry tears. 'It's drained all the way through to the floor. She must have been desperate.' She turns on me, her eyes burning. 'You didn't take her to the toilet? How could you leave her to wet herself and not even notice?'

'I ... I didn't... Oh God, I'm sorry. I was ... I was tired.'

Trembling with anger, she helps Alice to her feet and they walk slowly past me. I avert my eyes from the dark patch on her once-was-lilac dressing gown. I begin to walk after them, but Dawn turns and shoves me backwards hard. 'Leave us alone,' she says, her mouth twisted into a hateful snarl.

I turn and drop to my knees beside the dark circle of urine and reach for the towel that Dawn left next to it. I press it into the wetness. The smell is strong and I gag through my tears. The seat cushion needs washing, I realise. So I carry it, sopping wet, through to the kitchen to find Dawn scrubbing at the soup bowl and cup. Shame cuts through me. The pan is in the cupboard. What reason would I have had to wash, dry and put the pan away but leave the bowl, spoon, stained kitchen roll and empty soup can out?

I open my mouth to speak, but Dawn gets there first.

'Don't. Even. Bother,' she says spitting her words out as she rams the dishcloth into the sink. 'You couldn't even heat her soup?' She spins away from me, picks up the already clean bowl and starts scrubbing at it again. 'All these years and I've never not heated her food.'

'I don't know what happened. I—'

'Shut your mouth.'

She reaches for the bottle of bleach and undoes the cap. She pours the viscous green-tinged chemical liberally around the sink, then using her fingers she scrubs it around the stainless steel. I watch as the skin on her hand begins to turn pink. I want her to stop, but I can't speak. I am frozen, mute with horror as she grinds her fingers into the neat bleach.

I'm sorry, a voice inside me says. *I'm so sorry.*

Guilt and humiliation tighten their grip on me and, however hard I bite on my lower lip and dig my nails into my palms, I can't stop myself from crying. I lower my head in the hope she doesn't notice.

'Oh, yeah, that's right. That's *perfect*.' Dawn snorts bitterly as she thrusts her hand around the sink with such ferocity that I worry she might tear her skin. 'Turn the tears on.' She shakes her head and drags her hand across her outraged face, and I notice the shining snail-trail of bleach just millimetres from her eye.

'Dawn—'

'Shut up.' Her tone is low and ominous. 'Get out of this flat.'

'Please, I—'

'That's my mum you abused. I've cared for her all my shitty life. You've no idea what I had to give up to do it. I tore my soul in two to look after her. How could you do that? I wouldn't treat a dog on the street like you treated my mum. You go on about how much you want to help and then two and a half hours. That's all I asked for. Two and a half measly hours.'

I don't move, glued to the spot by remorse and fear. She walks over to me, leans into my face, so close I can feel her breath on my skin and smell the bleach on hers.

'Get out of this flat, you silly little cow.'

FORTY-TWO

The only noise in the room is my breathing. The image of my mother sitting in her own urine is impossible to push away. I lie on my bed and stare upwards. As I do, the walls of the room begin to creep in on me. Little by little the ceiling comes nearer, the walls encroach, until I am lying in a crypt, the sheets are my shroud. I remind myself I am in a bedroom in a guest house in a town by the sea called St Ives and I turn on my side, curl myself into a ball and wait for sleep to take me away.

A noise wakes me.

I sit bolt upright and listen for it again, but all I can hear is my heart pounding and my breathing loud against the dark stillness. I look at my clock; it's nearly three. *Someone in the room. Someone watching me.*

I clench my fists, as a figure moves into the shaft of moonlight that streaks through the window.

Tori.

She moves silently. Sits on the end of my bed. Her blonde hair curls into soft ringlets at her shoulders. Her eyes are wide. Her skin is pale, white tinged with yellow, not a freckle nor a blemish on it.

This isn't a dream. Or at least it doesn't feel like one. It's as if she's real, though I know she can't be. It's my mind playing tricks on me. It's stress or exhaustion. She is watching me, blinking slowly, her hands lightly clasped on her lap. A clammy sweat spreads over my body and I rub my eyes, squint hard at her, but she doesn't fade. There's a smell in the room. I try to place it but can't. It's familiar and pleasant; it calms me, wraps me in a comforting cocoon, eases away the fear.

Are you real or in my head?

'You know,' she says softly. 'I loved you coming to see me.' She lowers her gaze. 'I used to look forward to it.'

My skin prickles like nettle rash.

And then she disappears like the seal, there one moment and gone the next.

FORTY-THREE

I wake with a nervous energy fizzing through me. My first thought is of Tori, of how she came to me last night, but I dismiss it. How silly to think of her as anything other than a figment of my imagination. I used to see her as broad as daylight when I was a child. We would play for hours. Have conversations. It is ridiculous to think anything of it. She was a hallucination, a reaction to stress. Nothing more than that.

My main concern is Dawn. The thought of seeing her terrifies me. I can't face her raw disappointment and anger again.

Why didn't I heat the soup?

It would have taken a minute. Two minutes maximum. And not taking her to the toilet? It doesn't bear contemplating.

It's pouring with rain and by the time I arrived at Phil's café I'm soaked through. I take off my jacket and drops of water splatter the floor.

'What a summer, eh?' he says with a shake of his head.

'What's the word for rain?' I ask, shaking my hair out.

'*Glaw*,' says Phil. 'Morning, Tori.'

'*Myttin da*, Phil.'

'Aye, *myttin da*, nice one, love.' He hands me a coffee and passes three sachets of sugar across the counter. I regard them for a moment or two then shake my head. 'I won't, thanks. I'm giving up sugar.'

I sit in the window and repeat the word for rain over and over until it sticks.

Glaw. Glaw.

Glaw.

The glaw cloaks the harbour in grey. The sea is grey, too, a fabulous gunmetal grey. The beach holds a single stalwart family, the children seemingly oblivious to the downpour, playing happily, wheeling about in large circles. The parents are dressed as if it's January, clutching take-away tea and huddled under a golf umbrella.

I sip my coffee; if I could stay in town all day I would. The idea of facing the flat makes me feel queasy.

'Can you teach me another word?' I say to Phil as he clears the dead cups and crumbed plates from the table beside me.

Phil puts his tray down and rubs his chin. 'OK, try this one. *Dwy genes*.'

'Say it again?'

'Doo. Gen. Ez,' he repeats slowly.

'*Dwy genes*,' I say. 'Got it.' I blow across the top of my coffee. 'What does it mean?'

'That means goodbye, love. *Dwy genes*. Goodbye.'

'And one more.'

He laughs. 'You think you'll remember another?'

'Make it an easy one.'

'An easy one...' He pauses, thinking. 'Try *ov vy*. Ov. Vy. You'd say *Tori ov vy*.'

'What does it mean?'

'I am,' he says. 'I am Tori.'

I say the words over in my head.

Ov vy. Ov vy. I am.

Who am I?

Ov vy who?

'No. Not that. Something else,' I say. 'I won't remember that.'

He doesn't question me. 'What about *sewena*, then?'

'Meaning?'

'Cheers.'

'Yes, cheers is good,' I say as I raise my coffee cup. '*Sewena*.'

'*Sewena*, love.' And he lifts a pretend glass to me.

'Phil?'

'Yes?'

'What brought you down here?'

'To Cornwall?'

I nod.

'To be honest there's not much to say. My life took a turn and I ended up coming here.'

'Go on,' I say. 'If you don't mind. I'm interested.'

He hesitates. 'Where do I start? I had a good life. No, better than good, it was great. Gorgeous wife, clever, fun, she was everything to me and I loved her more than anything else in the world.' He smiles at distant memories. 'I had a nice house, great job, two kids who'd finished school and were starting out on their own. I was happy. I even had a job I loved. I was dead lucky.'

He turns away from me and peels the cling film off a metal tub of grated cheese.

'And?'

'Restructuring. I was *non-profitable*.'

'You lost your job?'

'I did. The boss told me I had two weeks. Eighteen years I'd given them and only one sick day in all my time.' He pauses and scratches his chin. 'I left that afternoon with a cardboard box and a pocket money pay-out.' He sighs. 'I'm not proud of it, but after that I sort of hit the rocks. Slumped on the sofa, didn't shave, watched telly day and night. My wife got me through it. She was incredible. She let me mope for a while, and then one day, out of the blue, she marches in, turns the box off, puts me in the tub, then drives me down to the job centre. Said she'd had enough of seeing me with a face as long as a horse. Said I'd find something, anything to get me out and about and smiling again.'

'And did you?'

'No, love.' He laughs. 'But the wife did. Three weeks later she left me for the bloke behind the desk at the job centre.'

'That's tough,' I breathe.

'I had nothing left, so I upped and left, and came down here to start over. Saw this place needed someone and here I am.' He unwraps another metal container.

'Why Cornwall?'

'Seemed the furthest place away. It was here or Scotland and I reckoned Scotland would be chillier.'

'Do you miss her?'

Phil nods. 'Every day. You can't turn off love, that's the tragedy.'

I am quiet while I finish my coffee.

'Did she marry him?'

'The guy in the job centre?'

I nod.

'No, they only lasted a month. Not even that.' He doesn't sound bitter or angry, more resigned. 'She reckons she wants to get back with me.'

'Why don't you? If you love her, surely that's all that matters.'

He shakes his head sadly. 'Too much water's passed under our bridge. It's difficult to fix a broken heart. You always see the scar. It wouldn't be the same.'

'Maybe it doesn't have to be the same?'

'I'm happy enough here. This is my home now. There's no going back. It no doubt sounds daft to you, but one day you'll understand.'

I understand him perfectly right now. I understand about not going back and about water and bridges and things not being the same.

I smile at him. 'I'll see you tomorrow, Phil. *Dyw genes.*'

'Aye, *dyw genes*, love. And you keep dry, eh?'

I peer through the window. 'I'll try,' I say, knowing full well there is no hope of that. I put my damp jacket on and ready myself for the rain and the flat and for Dawn.

FORTY-FOUR

A car drives past me, splashing through a puddle on the side of the road. The sound of the tyres in the rain triggers a memory. Just a flash. But it's vivid and it stops me in my tracks.

It's raining hard. I can hear windscreen wipers and the sound of the wheels is loud but muffled. There are voices. They are talking. Their voices are low and tight. I can't hear their words. It's Elaine and Henry. At least I think it is. I can't see anything. Something is covering me. Or is it? Maybe I have my eyes shut. No. No, there's something over me, a rug or a blanket, because I can't breathe easily. My breath is hot and damp. The rug smells musty, like old carpets. I want to take it off but I can't. She told me not to. Told me to stay put. Not to move. There was the same fire in her eyes as his. Like the other man's. Henry? No. The other man. So I stay under the cover, breathing in my own hot air, listening to the sound of the rain and the windscreen wipers and the two of them talking in strangled voices.

FORTY-FIVE

I don't move for a while. I stand in the rain, my hair plastered to my skin, water running down the back of my jacket, over my lips, soaking me to the skin. I don't know what to think. That was a memory. Clear as anything. Why now? Why has it only come to me now?

Dawn says nothing when she opens the door. Instead she fixes me with an expressionless look then turns and walks away. I hover on the doorstep, water from the cracked guttering falling on me in a trail of monotonous drops.

I go into Alice's room, but having closed the door behind me, I find it hard to look at her without seeing the pool of urine collected beneath her chair like Henry's pool of blood. I pick up the mermaid book and turn to *The Merrymaid of Zennor*, then I sit on the floor beside her, my back resting against her chair, and begin to read, allowing myself to be pulled into the story, the familiar words cosying around me.

My heart aches for Morveren and Matthew as they run from the braying villagers. What if they'd been caught? What if the people had held Matthew down as he kicked and cried to be with his lover, while she was forced back to the ocean to live without true love for eternity? I will them on to their blissful freedom, desperate to see them disappear into the watery blackness, their hands clasped, her muscular tail thrusting them forward to their peaceful forever.

I hear a noise and glance up; Dawn is standing in the now open doorway. I scramble to my feet and hurriedly put the book back on the shelf.

'About yesterday—' I begin.

'Let's get something straight,' she says, looking at something just above my head. 'There is nothing you can say that can excuse what happened. I know you didn't do it on purpose, but I don't want to talk about it because if we do, I can't promise I won't chuck you out for good.'

Her eyes, the colour of frosted grass, fix on me, and I nod. Then she pulls her ponytail tighter and I notice her hands are the colour of raw steak and on one there is a sore that looks wet with clear fluid where the skin has broken.

Dawn walks out of the room and a few moments later reappears with a large carrier bag under one arm and carrying a small tray with two mugs and a loaf cake in a plastic wrapper in the other. She places the tray on the bed then reaches into the bag and pulls out a package exquisitely wrapped in shiny striped paper. She hands it to me.

'Happy birthday.'

I don't understand at first. I watch her reach into the bag and take out a bottle.

'It's not champagne, but it's fizzy.' She takes out the cork, which pops weakly, and pours some into both of the mugs. 'Well,' she says, nodding at the present in my hands. 'Open it then.'

'But it's not my birthday.'

She doesn't say anything, instead she holds one of the mugs out towards me.

'My birthday's in September.' I persist. 'The second.'

Dawn takes a deep breath and shakes her head. 'No,' she says. 'Your birthday's today. June the eighteenth. You're twenty-eight.'

'I'm already twenty-eight. I'm going to be twenty-nine on the second of September.'

It can't be my birthday. I can't be a summer baby, I'm an autumn baby. I'm a Virgo, modest, shy and diligent. I read it in a zodiac book of Elaine's when I was younger. I can be a worrier, sometimes over-critical, observant. I'm a typical Virgo. June would make me a Gemini. How can I be a Gemini? I don't know anything about being a Gemini.

I feel disoriented. Hollowed out. I haven't even considered I'd have a different birthday to the one we marked without excitement each year. But of course, Elaine and Henry Campbell would have no idea when my real birthday was. I think back over all those birthdays past. Henry shut away in his study or away at a conference or in the garden up by the oak tree. Elaine always tired and unconvincingly blaming the passing of summer. Never any fuss. Just a cake with plain candles and a single present. I'd grown up thinking my parents just didn't *do* birthdays. We were Christmas people, like we were cat people and Cotswold holiday cottage people. But now I knew. They didn't celebrate it because it wasn't real. It was fabricated. An annual reminder of their duplicity.

'Morveren?' Dawn is beside me. Her face has softened and she puts her arms around me with such genuine warmth I can't help my tears.

'I'm so sorry about yesterday.'

'I know.'

I pull away from her and dry my eyes on my sleeve. 'If it's my birthday today, what's the second of September?'

Dawn shrugs.

'The day I went missing?'

'No. You went missing in August. August the fifteenth.' Dawn pulls a tatty piece of folded paper from her pocket and holds it out to me. 'Your birth certificate. I thought it might help.'

'But I've got a birth certificate. I used it for—' But of course, the one I used for my university application form isn't my real birth certificate, is it? How could it be? I feel so stupid.

'It had to be a fake.'

'Can you do that?'

'It's only a piece of paper. He was a doctor. Probably had a dodgy friend in the registry office.' Her lip curls with spite as she mentions the word doctor. 'Money can buy you anything, can't it?'

Standing beside my real mother, on the anniversary of the day she pushed me into this hideous world, I feel more wronged by the Campbells than ever before. I take the birth certificate and carefully unfold it. It's worn and fragile, with holes down the creases.

Date of birth: June 18th 1986.
Place of birth: Truro.
Sex: Female.
Father's name: Mark Robert Tremayne.
Mother's name: Alice Frances Tremayne.

I refold the birth certificate and lay it on the table beside Alice's bed. Then I pick up the mug of sparkling wine.

'*Sewena*,' I whisper.

We clink mugs. 'Happy birthday, Morveren.' She taps the present. 'Go on, open it. It's from me and Mum.'

'It's beautifully wrapped,' I say, leaning over and putting the mug down so I can open the gift.

'I love wrapping presents. I don't get much chance to, so I took my time. Not to mention it's the first present I've given you in a few years.' She smiles.

'Is that what you were doing yesterday? Shopping for this?' She nods and I lean over and rub her knee. 'Thank you.'

'You haven't seen it yet. You might hate it.'

'I won't.' I slide my fingers under the tape and ease the paper open.

Inside is a framed print. A mermaid. I recognise her; it's a print taken from a painting by one of the Pre-Raphaelites, though I can't recall which one. She sits amid the rocks on a pebbly beach, her tail wrapped around her, her milky body rising seamlessly from the silvery grey of her scales. The sea behind her is a deep blue and dark-grey cliffs rise vertically in the background. Her hair is long and brown and while she combs it she reflects on something distant, oblivious to those outside her world who spy on her.

'It's only a print. I found it in the shop at the Tate. I know how much you love that mermaid story you read her.'

'I love it. Thank you. I'm lost for words.'

She smiles, clearly pleased. 'It's from Mum as well.'

'Thank you,' I say and reach over to take hold of Alice's hand.

As I do something happens.

'Dawn,' I whisper, hardly able to get my voice out. 'She squeezed my hand.'

'My God,' Dawn says, under her breath. 'Look at her eyes.'

Alice's eyes are focused. The pupils have widened and there is a slight movement, a slight flicking back and forth.

'Mum?' Dawn moves quickly to Alice's side and rubs her hand. 'Mum? It's Morveren's birthday. She's twenty-eight. And she's here. Look Mum, she's here. She came back to us.'

And then our mother turns her head and looks at me.

Dawn draws in a sharp breath.

I drop to my knees and pull her hand into my chest.

Dawn bursts into tears, a mix of laughing and crying.

'It's Morveren,' I say and her hand squeezes mine for a second time.

Dawn and I don't leave her alone that day. We sit and talk to her, my misdeed of the day before a forgotten memory. When it gets to six o'clock, Dawn leaves us to make her supper, and I sit and carry on chatting to her, not wanting to stop for even a moment for fear of her returning to whatever dark recess of her mind has held her captive. I tell her about the hostel, my room, Fi's purple hair and how she looked after me when I hit my head. I tell her about Phil's coffee and the cat that lives in the flat but never ventures past the kitchen door. I don't tell her about the night I spent with Greg because even thinking about it makes me feel uncomfortable now.

We might be imagining it, but as we spend time with her, colour seems to bleed into our mother's face. Her hand clutches the side of her chair. It's like she's filling up with life again. By the time we put her to bed, the reality of what's happening is sinking in. We sit on the edge of her bed. She doesn't look at us, she looks at the ceiling, yet she is changed, she is with us.

In the kitchen, I pick up the cat and kiss her soft fur.

'They said she might just get better,' says Dawn. 'That without treatment, without them taking her away, they couldn't guarantee it, but that it might happen. I'm not sure they believed it though.'

'Who's they?'

'The doctors.' Her voice is veined with bitter sadness. 'They tried to take her away from me, you know. Put her in some filthy hospital. They said I should get on with my life.' She shakes her head. 'Stupid idiots. She *was* my life and they couldn't see it. I had to look after her. What type of person would I have been if I'd abandoned her? She'd have lost us both. I couldn't do that to her. I couldn't.'

'You could have stayed at school, I suppose, if she'd gone to a hospital. That's probably what they meant.'

'As if they care about school for the likes of me?' she snorts. 'Stuck-up arseholes. No, it wasn't school they were talking about.' She stops there, but I can see she has more to tell me and her face tightens with the strain of holding back whatever it is.

'You can tell me.'

She pauses, her mouth opens for a fraction of a minute, but then she shakes her head. 'Anyway, school doesn't matter, not in the real world. This is the real world, Morveren. The real world where my mother was sick and I was her carer, and without me there was nothing for her. Looking after her was the most important thing. The only thing.'

'Our mother,' I say, stroking the cat.

Dawn turns away from me.

'I remembered something today.'

She glances back at me.

'The Campbells drove me out of France in a car. They hid me under a blanket in the footwell. That's how they got me out.'

FORTY-SIX

'Do you remember anything else?'

Dawn and I have mugs of coffee and are sitting at the kitchen table.

'I don't know. Maybe. A car driving along the wet road jogged me. Maybe other things will dislodge other memories.' I pause. 'Is there anything you can remember from the day I went missing? Maybe that will help.'

Dawn's body visibly tenses.

'I hate thinking about it.'

'So you do remember?'

She doesn't answer me.

'You don't want to think about it because you think it's your fault?'

No reply.

'You were seven, right?'

Dawn nods.

'It wasn't your fault.'

Still she doesn't speak.

'Please tell me what you remember, Dawn.'

Dawn sighs. 'I can't remember much. There are so many holes.'

'It doesn't matter. Anything.'

She breathes in, looks at her hands, then picks at a flake of skin at the edge of the weeping sore. 'From what I can remember, it all started the day we were supposed to be going on holiday. The car was packed up and you and I were ready to go, and then they started shouting.' She looks at me for a moment and adds, 'They were always bloody shouting. But this time Mum was saying that she was wrong about the holiday. That it wouldn't help and that she wanted a divorce instead.

She said he was a bad father and we'd be better off without him. There was a boy at school with divorced parents and he was always crying, so I got upset and was begging to go on the holiday. Anyway, she looks at me and says, *Fine, we'll go on the holiday but it's make or break.* I didn't know what that meant, but I remember being excited again. We hadn't been on holiday before and I'd told everyone at school. They'd call me a liar if we didn't go.'

Dawn takes another breath and closes her eyes for a minute.

'I remember all this as if it was yesterday,' she says softly. 'It's odd because I can't remember anything that happened after we came back from France, but all this? Like crystal. We drove to the ferry place. It took ages and they were pretty much screaming the whole time. I put my hands over your ears for a bit so you couldn't hear it. We got on the boat and Dad went to the bar, and we did colouring. I got cross because you just scribbled over the pages and wouldn't keep between the lines. I even remember what we had, chips and sausage, but it was cold and there was this sticky stuff on the sausage I didn't like. Then I don't remember much until the campsite. We were staying in a caravan. It was dirty and smelt bad and there was a patch of black mould on the ceiling, and Mum said Dad was bloody useless for booking something so awful and then she sat in the corner in a mood, rolling her thumbs around each other for hours and hours. She wouldn't play with me or read any stories and you were crying a lot, which got on my nerves.' She looks at me earnestly. 'Only because I was a child and probably tired and annoyed with everyone being cross.'

'I know.'

She nods, then sighs. 'So we're in this caravan and suddenly he starts yelling again. Going on about how we're supposed to be on holiday and that we should be having fun. Every time he said *fun* he gave this awful grin and waved his arms around like a madman. He gets some clothes out of the case and chucks them at Mum and says, *We're going out.* And she says no, but he doesn't listen, shouts louder, says they're going to have a good time if it's the last thing they do. And then she said, *It's over* and … he hit her.'

Dawn winces at the memory. I think of that man, Mark Tremayne, sitting in his filth with the pigeons, and feel sick.

'There was blood on her face from a cut in her hair. It scared me so much. I screamed and then he starts walking towards me, pointing his finger and saying he wished I'd never been born.'

Dawn's eyes shine with a film of tears and for a moment she's quiet.

'Mum steps between us and holds me behind her legs and then he tells her that the three of us ruined his life, that the four of us were going to go out and have some goddamned fun.'

Dawn gives a bitter, incredulous snort.

'Can you believe he said that? Those two things in one sentence? And then he pushes Mum to one side. Grabs me around my neck and pushes me against the wall of the caravan. I can still feel his hand on my neck.'

And then I am there. He's holding my sister's neck. My mother is sobbing. She claws desperately at him. She wants him to let Dawn go. I am cowering on the seat beside the table. The fabric is rough against my cheek and smells of damp towels. I tuck myself into the corner as far as I can go, burying my face into my teddy. He smells nice. He's scared of Dad, too. Scared of how his eyes have gone big and staring with red veins popping in the whites of his eye. And he doesn't like how he's hurting my sister. How he's really hurting her.

'...and then he just sort of drops me. He was shaking. And Mum was crying, but quieter. She grabbed me and, as she did, he turned and went into the toilet and shut the door.'

Her voice cracks with emotion and I reach over and rub her shoulder.

'And then Mum grabs you by the hand and drags you over to me and kneels down and whispers that I have to get out of the caravan. She says we have to hide underneath it and wait for her. She said she would get us when he had calmed down and then she'd put us to bed. She was speaking quickly and I nodded. Then we heard the flush of the toilet, and she said, *Quick, under the caravan*, then she pushed me out of the door even though we were crying. Then she closed the door and said, *And don't let go of your sister's hand, Dawn*.'

I watch her face contort in pain as she battles her guilt.

I reach for her hand and hold it. I can smell the alcohol that hangs in the mouldy caravan. I remember my mother bending down, her hand on my arm as she tucks the hair behind my ear and tells me to go with my sister. She tells me she loves me. There's blood on her face.

'We wriggled under the caravan. I told you it was a game. That we were going to pretend we were playing hide and seek. You just kept on calling for Mum and trying to get out from under the caravan. I tried to sing to you, even told you a story, but you kept on crying.' Tears begin to course her cheeks now. 'I wanted Mum so badly. And I knew—' She has to stop for crying, then the words that follow are punctuated with sobs and snatched breaths. 'I knew I ... shouldn't let ... go ... but I couldn't hold on ... I couldn't stop you ... and ... and you pulled out of my grasp and even though I called and I called, you never ... You never came back. I let you go.'

She shakes her head and fresh tears tumble down her face.

And then I know that this is the dream I've had before. I am running. My heart thumps in my ears. My breath comes in short, painful gasps. It is dark. And cold. The trees reach out to grab at me as if they are alive. There are roots in the ground that are covered with leaves and I keep tripping over. My feet are so sore. Every step hurts. One foot more than the other and when I look down at my feet I see I have lost a slipper. Dad will be cross.

'I didn't go and look for you,' Dawn says quietly. 'I stayed beneath the caravan because I was scared. I was scared of the dark and scared of him so I just stayed where I was.'

'It wasn't your fault,' I say. 'It wasn't. You were just a child.'

Dawn's whole body shudders with sobs

'It was their responsibility to look after us.' I kiss the top of her head. 'Dawn. Look at me.'

She lifts her head slowly, her body still shivering, and looks at me.

'It wasn't your fault.' I say, holding her face between both my hands. 'It wasn't.'

'He told the ... police...' she says, grasping at each word. 'That it was my fault. I heard him ... he said ... I was supposed to be ... with you ... they stared at me, nodded when he said it. Wrote it down in their ... in their stupid ... notebooks.'

I wrap my arms around her and stroke her back. 'It's OK,' I whisper. 'It's going to be OK now.'

FORTY-SEVEN

That night I am plagued by an unrelenting insomnia that pokes and prods me like a bored child. I can't stop thinking about my father, the man responsible for half my genes, the man sitting in that cavernous, putrid house with his stinking clothes and his rotten heart.

And when at last I sleep, I find myself with Tori. She looks unwell. Her skin is tinged yellow and there are dark circles around her eyes. She is painfully thin and wears a faded dressing gown that once was lilac. We are swimming in the sea. Underwater. Deep down dark, near the ocean floor. She holds my hand as we glide through the icy cold. I wave my free arm through the water, enjoying the way it slips between my fingers. I smile at her and she smiles back weakly, as if every ounce of energy is taken up with that one gesture. The water is deep green and there are no fish, just grey hunks of rock and seaweed that reaches way above my head, swishing to and fro in the current. I look back at Tori, her golden hair is fanned out like a magnificent, golden peacock's tail. I pull on her arm to get her attention but she doesn't respond.

'Tori?'

She laughs and a train of bubbles spews from her nose and mouth and wiggle their way to the surface of the sea, miles and miles above us.

'I'm not called Tori, silly.'

'Yes, you are!'

'I'm not. I let you call me it, but it's not my name.'

'What is your name then?'

She laughs again. 'You know.'

'I've forgotten,' I say. 'Tell me once more.'

She shakes her head and disappears behind an explosion of giggling bubbles. 'Silly, silly, you,' she sings.

Then she lifts a single finger to her lips and hushes me. I am about to ask her why I need to be quiet, but I feel something touch my ankle. I look down to see a single frond of black seaweed curling around my leg like melted bitumen. Around and around it creeps, growing thicker and blacker as it goes. Another crawling frond grabs my arm. Then another my other leg. I am being cocooned, a helpless fly in a sea-spider's web.

I reach for the little girl, but she has gone. She is swimming away in the distance, too far to hear my call. The seaweed begins to inch up my neck, into my ears and eyes. When I scream, a frond crawls into my mouth and thrusts its way down my throat. I gag. It's impossible to breathe, but as I begin to lose consciousness, I feel a hand on mine. She has come back for me.

With one tug she breaks me free of the murderous weed and pulls me to safety through the velvety water.

'Thank you,' I say to her.

But she doesn't reply.

FORTY-EIGHT

When I see the wheelchair my heart sinks. I'm not sure if it would cope with a walk to the end of the street let alone a walk on the cliffs, which is where I was going to suggest we go. The frame is speckled with angry sores of rust, the grey plastic seat is torn in places, with worn yellowed foam peeking out, and there's a worrisome clicking from one of the wheels as Dawn pulls it out of the ramshackle shed in the front yard.

'It's fine,' she says, obviously noticing my doubt. 'We've not used it for years, but it's perfectly fine.'

'Maybe a touch of oil? The wheel looks a little stiff,' I suggest.

'We're not going far.'

Dawn leaves the chair outside and squeezes past me, disappearing into the flat towards the kitchen. I pull the wheelchair into the house and wheel it backwards into Alice's room.

'Guess what? I managed to get us a day release pass,' I say, as I give Alice's shoulder a quick rub.

An hour later, the taxi drops us outside the church in Zennor. The driver sits in his seat, picking at his teeth, watching us in his rear-view mirror as we manoeuvre Alice out of the car and into her chair with the sun beating down on us like we're ants beneath a magnifying glass. Dawn is silent. She's in a bad mood. She thinks all of this is 'more trouble than it's worth'.

When at last Alice is out of the car and in her chair, I leave Dawn to fuss with an unnecessary blanket on her lap, and pay the driver.

I untuck my vest top and flap it to dry the sweat that runs in rivulets down my front and back. 'She'll bake under that,' I say.

'Why are we here?' she says, eyeing the church warily.

'You told me she liked it.' I start to push Alice towards the church. I tilt her backwards and rest the front wheels on the first stone step.

'I thought you wanted to go for a walk.'

'I do,' I say, panting with the effort of getting the back wheels up and pushing the chair forward over the uneven cobbles.

'Walking in the church?'

I heave the chair up the next step; it might as well have been an articulated lorry. 'We're...' I pause and lean my weight on the back of the chair to balance it. 'Can you give me a hand?'

Dawn grabs the handles of the chair from me and eases Alice carefully back down the step I'd negotiated with great effort, then swings it around and expertly pulls her up the steps backwards. 'I just don't see why we have to go into the church.'

'I want to show her the mermaid's chair.' I nudge Dawn to one side and take the handles again. 'The Merrymaid. I thought she might like to see her.' I wipe my bare arm across my forehead. 'God, it's hot.'

Dawn is dragging her feet like a petulant teen.

'You don't have to come in if you don't want to. You can go and get a drink in the pub and wait for us if you truly can't bear it.'

She perks up at this idea. 'Really? Yes, I think I'll do that instead. Do you want me to get a drink for you, too?'

'Please come in with us.'

Her lips tighten and she looks away from me, over the trees behind the church.

'Look, Dawn, it's for Mum. You said she used to come here all the time to sit by that carved pew.' Dawn scuffs her toe against a pebble on the path. 'Maybe seeing the Merrymaid will help. What if she draws strength from her?' I remember how I felt when I had my own hand pressed against the carving.

'Draw strength from her?' Dawn scoffed.

'Or,' I say, as frustration overspills. 'We could get that grumpy taxi driver back, take her home, and shut her in that room for another twenty years.' I stare at the miserable face of my sister. 'In fact, why don't we stick up all those bits of newspaper again? We could even nail the window shut, I mean, trust me, I know how well that works if you want to keep someone inside.'

And then she turns on her heel and walks away from me, pulling the gate closed behind her. It doesn't shut properly, but clatters against the frame and swings back open.

'Suit yourself,' I whisper, and start to push the wheelchair towards the door of the church, the wheel clicking rhythmically as we go.

When I reach the church I pause before opening the heavy door with a prickling anticipation. The air inside is still cool, in spite of the heat outside, reason enough, in my mind, to go in. I allow my vision to adjust to the darkness, enjoying the stillness that cloaks us. I think back to the first time I stepped into this church, a time before Dawn and before my mother, before Bristol and Mark Tremayne.

I push Alice as close as I can to the pew.

'Look, Mum'

She slowly turns her head towards the carving. I watch her face for signs of recognition. I take her frail hand in mine and pull it towards the carving. Her fingers reach the polished wood and I guide them over the mermaid's face and hair, then downward to the tip of her tail.

'That's the Merrymaid. That's Morveren.'

She gives an imperceptible smile, just the corners of her mouth. But it neither blooms nor holds.

'Speak to me,' I whisper. 'Just one word.'

I want to be able to burst out into the heat and announce a victory, that the carving has brought back speech to our dumbstruck mother, that it was a miracle and Dawn the doubting Thomas.

'Please, Mum.' I lift her hand to my face and stroke it down the length of my cheek.

Outside, Dawn is leaning against the wall of the pub, huddled in the shade, hunched and sullen-looking.

'It was lovely in the church,' I announce. 'Cool. You should have come in.'

Dawn ignores me but shoves herself off the wall and walks with me down the lane towards the coastal path. Dawn's mood and my irritation make conversation impossible. This isn't how I imagined our first family trip out.

'Dawn, this is daft. We came here for a walk, not to be annoyed with each other. Let's forget all that, shall we?'

After a long pause she nods and smiles, only a slight smile, but a smile nonetheless. But despite our truce, we still don't speak as we push Alice onwards. The cows are still munching in their fields, surrounded by clouds of flies that don't seem to bother them. The air is salt and heat and silage. It's like the summer afternoons I remember as a child, sitting on the lawn at The Old Vicarage with the sun on my back as I picked blades of grass and tried to make a whistling sound by holding them taut between my thumbs and blowing.

'Look!' I say, forgetting any remnants of tension. 'Up there! Some sort of bird of prey.'

'Where?'

I pull Dawn over to me and point.

'There,' I whisper. 'Can you see?'

Dawn is quiet for a few seconds as she scans the sky. Then she nods. 'I can see it,' she says. 'It's a sparrowhawk.'

We shield our eyes from the sun and watch the bird, which hovers noiselessly, high above our heads, its wings outstretched as it hangs in the air, shunted upwards by the intermittent nudge of a thermal. Its gaze is fixed on something that no doubt scurries or scampers or hops on the ground below it.

'It's going to dive,' Dawn says.

The hawk locks onto its prey. I hold my breath as it tucks its wings tight into its body and falls like lead shot from the sky. We wait for it to emerge from the undergrowth but there's no sign.

'It's gone,' I say and begin to walk on.

'No, she's there.'

I follow Dawn's outstretched finger and see the bird flying upwards with what looks like a baby rabbit trapped in its talons. The bird wavers in the air as the desperate creature struggles for life. Its efforts are futile. The hawk has it. And I feel the razor claws digging deep into its velveteen body.

'Poor thing,' Dawn whispers.

'The hawk needs to eat.'

'Still,' she says.

We continue on and soon the sea comes gloriously into sight, sunlight spilled across it like melted butter on glass.

'I didn't want to go in the church because—' she says.

'It's fine; there's no need to explain.'

'No, I want to tell you. I hate that place. I hate it because ... last time I went there was your funeral. And even seeing that church brings it all flooding back.'

'Oh,' I say, thinking back to the path I'd just walked along with headstones either side. One of those stones was mine. A shiver runs through me and I take a few deep breaths as if proving to myself that I'm not dead.

'That was the day she began to shut down. She began spending more and more time sitting in a chair looking out of the window. Collecting mermaid pictures from magazines. She stopped talking. Even when I spoke to her, the best I got was a smile that was barely there. Anyway,' she says with a sniff. 'I didn't fancy going in to the church again. Too many bad memories.'

'I should have thought. I'm sorry.'

She shrugs.

We reach the point where the tarmac turns to footpath. The path is too narrow and stony to get the wheelchair down, but there's a small bench to the left-hand side with enough room to squeeze the wheelchair in beside. We sit for a while in comfortable silence, looking out over the cove below with its turquoise waters and slip of white sand revealed by the retreating tide.

Occasional walkers pass by and we nod and smile politely at each other, acknowledging the spectacular scenery we temporarily share. I tip my face upwards into the sun and listen to the soft breathing of the two people beside me.

When I open my eyes I see Alice is staring out to sea. There's something about her. Her gaze is focused, not blank, as if she's actually looking at the sea or maybe the seagulls that wheel noiselessly out towards the horizon.

I reach over and stroke her hand. 'Isn't it beautiful, Mum?'

And then she slowly turns her head and smiles.

FORTY-NINE

Over the next few weeks she seems to continue to improve. There is a closeness growing that I could never have predicted that first day I walked into her bedroom, with its stale atmosphere and eerie silence, and saw that wasted stranger in her faded dressing gown staring at cut-outs on the wall.

Dawn and I have settled into a comfortable routine. Mum is listening to things we say. We've both seen her mouth twitch into something akin to a smile since that time on the clifftop. The first time I saw it I screamed. I couldn't help myself. Dawn came running, thinking some sort of disaster had befallen, and when I told her what I'd seen, she shook her head in disbelief.

This week she has begun to walk almost without help, a hand resting on one of our arms, her slippered feet shuffling. I am now utterly convinced it's merely a matter of time, of strengthening her withered muscles, of continuing to talk to her, until she recovers more fully.

We take her out each day. A taxi picks us up and drives us out to the cliffs on the outskirts of St Ives or to the paths around the disused tin mines at Botallack, their sad, redundant chimneys rising out of the salty clumps of grass, a monument to a time when the area's industry flourished. Dawn worries about the expense of the taxis but I tell her not to think about it; it's the least the Campbells can do.

Two days ago we went to Marazion. The causeway out to St Michael's Mount – exposed at low tide to allow an army of selfie-obsessed tourists to swarm across for National Trust cake – was uneven and seaweed-slippery. It gave Dawn the jitters.

'No,' she said. 'No way.'

'We'll be either side of her; she won't fall.'

'Not worth it. And what are we going to do when we get over there anyway? Hike up the Mount with her on our backs?'

I am experimenting with Mum's diet. At first I tried her on soft stuff, like Bird's custard and yoghurt. Last night I attempted a Shepherd's Pie. It wasn't great but she seemed to like it. Dawn stood in the corner of the kitchen biting what's left of her nails and watching us.

'I don't think that type of food is good for her.'

'She looks great on it.'

'Her digestion's delicate, you know.'

I didn't reply. As far as I can see it, Alice needs as much variety as we can give her. And I have discovered that I love cooking. I haven't ever really cooked before. Elaine never let me near the oven. Occasionally she would hand me a wooden spoon with cake batter on it, but that was as close to cooking as she'd let me get. And since I married David he's done it all. He says I'm not allowed anywhere near 'his kitchen'.

'A chef's domain is his castle,' he likes to say. 'And as you can't even boil an egg, I suggest it's better for everyone if you leave the cooking to me.'

So I let him get on with it. I wish I hadn't. I didn't realise how much I enjoyed it.

And anyway it got to a point where I couldn't take the smell of soup any longer. One day, about ten days ago, it actually made me retch, so I popped into the lovely bookshop in St Ives and asked the woman if she could recommend a recipe book.

'What type of food?'

'Oh, I don't know. Home cooking, maybe? Something a person who can't even boil an egg can follow.'

She suggested two and I bought them both. I had this idea that I would read recipes out of the books to Mum, then cook what we'd read about. And this is what we do. I sit beside her, open one of the new books and run my finger down the index until something jumps out at me.

Today it's a recipe for risotto.

'Perfect. You'll love risotto, Mum.'

I begin to read, breaking off to talk to her, hoping to engage her, hoping she'll be interested enough to reply.

'...*So, making sure it's well mixed.* I have to remember to do that, Mum, to mix it well. *Leave the risotto for five minutes, by which time the eggs and crème fraîche will have thickened.* Oh, that sounds delicious. We'll definitely enjoy this. *Serve with some freshly grated Parmesan cheese and if you're feeling particularly decadent some garlic bread. And voilà!*'

I finish reading, close the book, and jump to my feet. 'I need to get a few ingredients from the shops. Risotto coming up.' I kiss her forehead and she tilts her face towards me a little. 'I'll be back soon.'

'That seems an awful lot of things to buy. It's a bit of a faff, isn't it?' says Dawn, peering over my shoulder at the list I'm writing.

'I don't mind,' I say. 'Do you need anything?'

Dawn shakes her head.

Ten minutes later I am at the Co-op.

'Say it again, dear,' says the lady on the checkout, putting a finger to her ear.

'Arborio?'

'No, dear, I've not got any of that.' She shakes her soft grey perm. 'You'd need to go to Penzance or most likely the big M&S on the Hayle roundabout. They do fancy things like that.'

I thank her and then go back to the rice and pasta section and grab a box of long grain.

'Will that do the job?' asks the lady doubtfully, as she picks it out of my basket to scan it.

'I can't get to Penzance or Hayle, so it will have to. I'm sure it'll be fine. Cooking's all about being flexible, isn't it?' She looks at me in a way that suggests she thinks not.

I tell Dawn to sit down while I make the supper.

'No, I'll help.'

I smile at her. 'I'm fine, I think. Thanks though. Why don't you have a bath or a read? This'll take,' I peer at the recipe, 'twenty minutes.'

The cat winds herself around my ankles, mewing for food. I open a tin for her and stroke her as she tucks in, purring loudly. The tang of cat food hits me and from nowhere my stomach turns over in a light wave of queasiness. I pull my head back from the smell and wince.

'I didn't realise that stuff smelt so bad,' I say to the cat. 'Sorry you have to eat it every day. I'll pick you up some chicken tomorrow.'

The cat lifts her head and regards me, blinks twice, then returns to her food.

When the risotto is cooked, I put a bowlful on the tray along with a glass of water, and carry it through to mum.

'Do you want me to do that?' Dawn says, appearing at the door as I start to feed her. 'As you've cooked it. I don't mind.'

'We're doing fine,' I say, as I help a forkful of rice into Mum. I grin as she opens her mouth like a well-behaved baby bird. 'Look how much she likes this!'

Dawn perches on the edge of the bed behind us. She is uptight, fidgeting and twitchy.

'She doesn't need that fancy food you know.'

I gather a forkful of rice.

'It's expensive. Money doesn't grow on trees.'

'I bought it so it didn't cost you anything.'

'That's not the point.'

'Please don't worry about it,' I say, trying to keep my voice light. 'I'm happy to spend it.'

I turn back to Mum and smile. Watching her change, feeling my love for her growing stronger as she does, fills me with pleasure. Her skin is plumping up, a layer of fat gathering under its translucent flimsiness, as if she's a balloon inflating. Her hair seems less brittle, her eyes clearer, her lips tinted a soft rose pink, though this maybe a figment of my imagination. I have never had to care for anyone in my life and it feels good.

'There we go, Mum. It's not quite right because they had the wrong rice at the shop, but it's OK, isn't it? I've left some for mine and Dawn's supper too.'

'You'll have to tell people who you are soon.'

Her words make my stomach turn over. I turn to look at Dawn, who is standing with her arms tightly crossed, her mouth a thin, tight line, then turn away. I consider her words and their implied collision of reality and fiction as I play the fork around the edge of the risotto on the plate. I don't want even to think about going public. I'd be stuck as Morveren for good. There would be no escaping back to Bella's life. No hiding out in Tori's. I'd be a victim of the nation's sympathy, a social-media pawn, my face splashed all over that tiny black-and-white screen that flickers in the corner of the kitchen. I imagine David's face as he reads about it. Phil, desperate to act normal, as he hands me my coffee and tries to talk about the weather. Then Greg and Fi and the girl behind the bar in the pub, all discovering I'm not the glamorous journalist but some mousy librarian with a tragic past.

'Not yet,' I say. 'It doesn't need to come out yet, does it? It won't make anything easier for any of us.' I gather the plate and fork and empty glass onto the tray.

'It will come out, you know.'

'Yes, but when we're ready. We're doing well, aren't we? Like this? Why does anyone need to know?'

'They don't. I'm just saying things like this get out.'

And then we hear it. Scarcely audible, thin, but there nonetheless.

You've grown so much.

'Oh my god,' I breathe.

I drop to my knees beside Alice and grab her hand. Dawn is beside me, crouched on the other side of the armchair.

Alice looks at me with her pale watery eyes. 'You've grown so much.'

'Oh, Mum,' I say, my voice cracking with emotion. 'It's been a few years.'

'I can't believe it,' Dawn whispers.

'You came back,' Mum says, rocking as if in a gentle breeze.

'So did you.' I lean forward and kiss her hand, letting my lips linger on her smooth, papery skin.

'They said you were dead,' she says, her eyes drifting to the rectangles of space where the mermaids and headlines used to be. 'I knew you weren't.'

I think Craig and I both know that he's guessed the truth. After all, I've let myself in with the spare key Dawn gave me, and I'm not sure there's any good reason for Tori-the-journalist to have free and easy access to the flat. Nevertheless we continue the charade.

'You here again?' he asks, as I put my bag on the table. There's a casual air about him as he opens and closes the sticking kitchen drawer that Dawn's asked him to fix. 'More questions for the magazine?'

'Dawn is the only friend I've made here. She probably doesn't want me popping in all the time,' I say with a smile.

He bends down and peers at the drawer, then gives it a gentle shake. 'A girl like you? You must make lots of friends.'

I laugh.

'Well, I'm glad,' he says. He smiles at me over his shoulder. 'It's good for her.'

'Is she here?'

'She's gone into town,' he says. He reaches into a leather tool bag for a red-handled screwdriver. 'She's goes to the bank each month to draw money.'

I see the cat sitting at the window and go to the back door to let her in.

'Not sure Dawn would want the cat in at this time of day.'

'Why has she got it if she doesn't want it?'

'She didn't get it, it—'

'I know,' I say. 'It just showed up. But she feeds it. If she doesn't want it, why does she feed it?'

Craig shrugs and busies himself with the screwdriver and the drawer.

'Craig,' I say, pulling out a chair and sitting down. 'Can I ask how you met Dawn?'

'For the article? No, I don't think I want to talk about anything like that without Dawn here.'

'No, off the record. I'm interested. You're the only person she sees, aren't you? I'm intrigued. I know how much you look after her, I'd just love to know a bit more.'

His mouth sets into place as he concentrates on tightening the screw. 'We were at school together.'

'So you've known her for ages.'

He sits back on his haunches and sighs. 'It was my mum who made me talk to her. She was worried about her, you know, after ... well, you know.'

He pulls the drawer out, then pushes it back in. It runs smoothly and he drops the screwdriver back into his bag. 'It was a few years after. We were so young. She was so quiet, didn't help herself really. Nobody gave a shit about what she was going though, not even the teachers, and she sort of separated herself off from everyone. But my mum said she could tell she was lonely and coping with stuff at home, and so she asked her round for tea. I'm not sure she wanted to come at first, but her grandparents made her, I think.' He laughs fondly but then stops himself. His face falls. 'I shouldn't be speaking to you like this.'

'I won't tell her we've talked.'

He doesn't look convinced.

'Honestly. I won't.'

He hesitates, but then sighs and takes a seat opposite me.

'When she came round we got on really well. She just needed someone to be with, bless her. She was dead shy, but once we got talking she warmed up. She used to joke that I was her head doctor. I was happy with that. I loved her from that first day.'

'So you are together, then?'

Craig suddenly looks guilty, like a naughty child about to be found out.

'It's just...' I hesitate. 'Well, I saw you ... with that other girl? The blonde one. I saw her ... with you.'

I watch his guilt develop like a Polaroid. His eyes open wide and his mouth twitches as his mind whirrs, no doubt trying to work out where he's been seen and what excuses he should give.

'Look, it's none of my business,' I say. 'I shouldn't have mentioned it.'

'It's not what you think. Me and that girl. We're just friends. And Dawn and I, you know, we're not even together. Don't get me wrong, I'd marry her tomorrow if she'd have me but, well, she won't.' He looks up at me. 'I'm not ... *doing* anything with that other girl. I'd never ... I'd never do anything to hurt Dawn.'

He looks down at his hands, which are resting, palms down, on the table. 'Did you tell her? Dawn, I mean? About seeing me with the girl?'

'No. I wanted to, but it didn't seem fair.' I pause. 'I hate the thought of her being hurt.'

'I wouldn't—'

Then we hear Dawn's key in the lock. Craig stops speaking and jumps up from the table; flustered, he goes back to fiddling with the drawer. As she comes into the kitchen he makes an obvious show of opening and closing it.

'All fixed and running smooth,' he says.

Dawn is pale and chewing on her fingernail. She walks straight over to the cat without saying anything to either of us and puts her out. Then she mumbles something about not feeling well and walks into her room.

Craig and I exchange looks.

'I think I should go and see what's up with her,' he says rather awkwardly.

'Yes, of course. I've got to get going anyway. Tell her I hope she's OK.'

✹

As I walk back into the hostel, Fi waves an envelope at me. 'Post for you.'

I walk over to the desk and she hands me the letter.

I don't open it until I'm safely in my room. There's a blank compliments slip from the solicitor and a second envelope inside. I recognise the handwriting immediately.

It's David's.

Seeing his writing – untidy, scrawled in black biro, spidery – knocks the air from my lungs. I rub my face and sit on the edge of the bed to read what he's written.

FIFTY-ONE

Dear Bella,

I cannot believe you have done this to me. How is this any way to behave? To walk out on your husband and not be in contact? I've run out of excuses with Jeffrey and have told him to find a replacement for you. You have embarrassed me enormously. Jeffrey is an old friend and he did me a huge favour employing you. I cannot look him in the eye now. Hopefully our friendship will recover from this, but I wouldn't be surprised if it doesn't. Not only this, but I see from the bank account that you have stolen my money. I trusted you when I allowed you access to this account and now I regret my decision. Hindsight is a wonderful thing, isn't it? I have closed the account. I hope that without access to further funds you will have to come home. Bella, I cannot fathom any of this. What has got into you? I believe you need to see a doctor as I worry you have inherited your parents' 'instabilities'.

I understand from the solicitor you said I should bury your father without you. How heartless can you be? This isn't you. You've always been so kind and gentle. You certainly kept this selfish side of you well hidden from me, didn't you? Where is the sweet Bella I love? I want her back.

The solicitor is refusing to tell me your whereabouts but the last time I spoke to her she seemed to waver and appears sympathetic to my position. I know she will tell me – I can be very persuasive – but it would be so much easier if you just came home. As you can probably tell from the tone of this letter, I am angry. I don't want to be, as I know you're upset and your grief is making you irrational, but you have made it impossible for me to be anything else. Of course I miss you, after all I love you, but like a parent with an errant child there is huge disappointment.

Please reconsider your silence. I can help you, but not like this. You cannot deal with this alone. We both know you aren't capable. We both know you don't have the strength. You need me.

Come home, my love.

David

FIFTY-TWO

The letter throws my head into confusion as my old world invades the new. I sit on the edge of my bed and clench my fists, fighting the urge to pack my bags and head back to him. I think of Jeffrey, his face wrought with barely concealed disappointment, as he wearily nods when David tells him to find a new librarian. David's face, his shame, bite into me.

And then I recall how he pushed himself into me the night of Elaine's funeral. The sting of him entering me, my body unready for him. The way he rolled off me with a sated grunt. I see a ribbon of blood trickling from my hand that held the shard of glass from the Campbells' photo. David's hand enclosing mine, as he squeezed and told me to stay calm.

I pick up the letter again and read every word with fresh eyes. In each of them I see a need to control me. His frustration at my unpredictable behaviour screams out at me. He says he loves me, but he doesn't really care. That's obvious, and admitting it leaves me feeling deflated and let down. In the letter he says how disappointed he is in me, but I'm disappointed in him too. Where does he express his concern for my wellbeing? Where is his understanding about what I must be going through to make me run from him? And then the money, closing the account, hoping he can drive me home to him like a starving dog. He wants Bella home but I am not Bella. I am not his Bella.

Not any more.

I clench my fists tighter. No. I won't go back to him. I won't crumble and let him take control of me again. I grab at the letter and screw it tightly into a ball, which I throw into the corner of the room. Its rests there, still, discarded, but still I feel the pull.

No.

I won't go back.

Then without pausing to think any more, I stand and walk over to the door. I don't stop to consider what I'm doing. I open the door and I walk. One step in front of the other.

One, two, three, four.

Step by step I walk down the corridor to Greg's room. I stand outside. Then I bang on the wood with the flat of my hand. I bang so hard it stings, but I don't care, the sting feels good. The sting makes me sure that I am here. That I exist. That I am not her.

I am not Bella.

I bang again and again and again.

'Alright! Alright!' comes the call from inside. 'I'm coming!' He opens the door and furrows his brow. 'You OK?'

I don't say anything.

He has a towel wrapped around his waist and his tanned skin glistens wetly. 'I was in the shower. What's up?'

I catch a glimpse of the tiger creeping its paw around his side where his arm rests upright against the doorframe, its claws are sharp and they seem to glint. I can hear him growling softly.

'I want you to fuck me.'

He laughs. 'What?! I don't see anything of you and then you walk in and demand sex?'

'Well?' I need to lose myself. I need to be present. I need Greg to fuck me. 'Are you going to or not?'

And then the smile falls from his face and he steps aside to let me in.

FIFTY-THREE

Dawn is pacing the kitchen. It's a small room, certainly not fit for pacing, but she's pacing anyway. Her hand is grabbing at the cuff of one sleeve, pulling at it, turning her fingers into it so the fabric twists tightly around her wrist.

I've asked her a couple of times what's wrong, but each time she answers with a distracted *I'm fine*. I can't watch her anymore. I block her way and take hold of her hands. They're clammy, and now I'm close to her I see there's sweat gathered on her pale brow.

'Dawn, Jesus, just tell me what's wrong. I'm not stupid. I can see you're anything but *fine*.'

She looks at me with tightly pursed lips. She is blinking faster than usual and then her face suddenly crumples. She pulls her hands from mine and covers her face. 'It's money.'

'Money?'

'Oh God, I don't know what to do.' She leans back against the kitchen worktop and pushes the heels of her hands against her eyes. 'It's stopped. The money has stopped.'

'Benefits? Why. Why have they stopped them?'

'Not benefits,' she says, spitting the word out as if it's poisonous. 'I don't want to take anything from them, but even if I did, I can't get job seeker's allowance because I'm not seeking work. And I don't need any of their help caring for Mum because I don't want those doctors coming to assess her, then taking her away from me. Those social workers that kept coming round with their poking noses and empty words. In the end, I didn't even open the door to them and they soon stopped bothering me. Craig is always bloody on at me to at least get housing but I haven't needed to, he's always just paid the money into my building society each month. But then last month's didn't go in, and, well, now another one hasn't and there's no sign of it, and without it...'

'Who pays the money in? Craig?'

She bites at her nails and looks at me. Then shakes her head.

'Who then?'

'Dad.'

I draw back in shock. 'Dad? But ... but I thought you haven't been in touch since he walked out?'

'I haven't. Just the payments. On the first of every month he pays six hundred pounds into my account. He's done it since he went. And, oh God...' She begins to chew at the side of her nail fiercely. 'What am I going to do? I can't pay the rent without his money, and that keeps going up and bloody up. And I can't work because full-time care for Mum will cost more than I can even earn. And I'm not leaving her anyway...'

I think of Mark Tremayne, unwashed, bitter, his darkness needling into me. Six hundred pounds a month? Henry paid him eight hundred and he gave nearly all of it to Dawn and Alice? I try to clear my mind, think calmly, work out is if this changes how I feel about him. I don't understand. Why didn't he tell me any of this when I met him?

I feel lightheaded. He was supporting Dawn and Alice? From the start? I think back to him telling me what happened the night he showed up at The Old Vicarage. How he told me he was no good. That he was doing what's best.

'He was being paid by Henry Campbell.'

She looks at me as if I'm talking in tongues.

'Every month. When he left you he moved into a house that was owned by the Campbells. They let him live there and paid him money.'

'They ... *paid* him? I ... don't...'

'I saw him, Dawn.' I sit heavily down at the table, clasp my hands.

She shakes her head. 'How could you have? You don't know where he is. Nobody does.'

'He lives in Bristol. I went there and I saw him.'

'What? I don't understand. When?'

'A while back. The day I didn't visit here. I went to Bristol, to an address my solicitor gave me.'

'Your solicitor?'

'She's dealing with the Campbells' will. There was – is – a second house. She told me to go and look at it to see if I want to keep it or sell it, and when I got there I found him living in it. Though I'm not sure you can call it living. Existing, more like.'

I can see by her face that she still doesn't get it.

'Dawn, Mark Tremayne knew the Campbells had taken me.'

'No, no that's not right,' she says quietly. 'You're telling me that he was involved with you being abducted?'

'No. He said there was a note. Henry went to the funeral and left it with some flowers. It had their address on. He drove up there. Confronted them. Then they offered to pay him to keep quiet and he accepted.'

Her face twists into horror as the impact and implications of what I'm saying sink in. 'And you're sure it's definitely him?'

'I'm sure.'

She grimaces. 'Why didn't you tell me before?'

'I wanted to, but it wasn't the right time. I know you hate talking about him and it was hard knowing when to bring it up without upsetting you.'

'But this changes everything. I mean ... he ... *knew*?'

I nod.

For a while neither of us speak, lost in our thoughts, battling to make sense of a nonsensical situation.

'What was he like?' she whispers then.

'He was awful. The whole thing was awful. The house was foul, full of rubbish and filth, and it stank. It's like he's rotting away in there. I couldn't get away quick enough.'

'Did you go to the police?'

I lean forward and rest my chin on the table. 'No,' I say with a sigh.

'I should have. Just like I should have told you. But I don't want to face the world with this yet.'

'We have to. We have—'

'Please, Dawn,' I say. The words in David's letter are ringing in my ears and making my stomach tumble with unease. I don't want him to find me. I don't want to go back to that. 'Not yet. We need more time just the three of us. The last thing we need is a load of attention. Please not yet.'

She doesn't look convinced but grudgingly nods.

'It explains why there's no money,' I say. 'The solicitor said Henry stopped payments into the account Mark used when he died.'

'God, what am I going to do?'

'You mustn't worry.'

'How can I do anything else? I need money, Morveren.'

'We have money. Those bastards left everything they had to me. We have more than enough money.'

'It's your money. I can't use it.'

'It's not my money. It's *our* money. It's blood money, no different to what you've been living off all these years.' I stand and go over to her, put my arms around her. 'They ruined our lives, Dawn. We can use their money.'

'I don't want to see him, Morveren.' Her voice is quiet. 'Do you think he'll come after us?'

I want to tell her he won't. I want to reassure her.

But I can't.

FIFTY-FOUR

Henry Campbell – 15th August 1989

The door to the hotel room opened and Elaine walked in.

She was carrying a child. A sleeping child. She was about two or three. She wore a pink nightie and clutched a teddy bear.

'Elaine? Where have you been?' Henry asked, as he walked over to her. His stomach knotted. There was an air about her that cut through him like razor-sharp knives. Something was wrong. Something was very, very wrong.

'I went for a walk. I felt Him calling me. He drew me to her.'

'Elaine,' he said, making every effort to keep his voice level. 'Who is this child?'

'This child is our miracle, Henry.' Her eyes shined bright. Her voice was light and joyful in a way he hadn't heard in years, and each syllable was like a silver bullet. 'We prayed for a miracle and we were given one.'

'I don't understand.' He was desperately trying to think, but the rising panic inside him was making it impossible to see anything clearly.

'Don't you? It's not hard to understand. He takes my babies, so many of them, and now He is giving me one. This one He will never take from me. This one is mine to keep safe and care for.'

Elaine gazed down at the little girl and smiled. Then she leant her head forward and softly kissed her forehead. The girl stirred but didn't wake.

'Elaine,' he said, still keeping his voice as level as he was able. 'Where are her parents?'

Elaine started softly singing and rocking the child like a newborn.

Then she walked past Henry, and gently, as if handling the finest bone china, she lowered her onto the bed.

'Elaine, I asked you a question,' Henry said, his voice firmer now, his heart hammering in his chest. 'Where is her mother?'

Elaine covered the little girl with the bedspread. She leant forward to stroke her hair. She smiled again. And then she stepped back, a look of utter bliss on her face as she gazed at the sleeping child.

Henry walked over to her and grabbed her arm, pulled her around to face him. 'Elaine! For God's sake. Where is her *mother*?'

Elaine looked up at him, her eyes glistening with a film of tears, a beatific glow lighting her face. 'Don't you see, Henry? It's me. *I* am her mother. She is my miracle. *I* am her mother.'

FIFTY-FIVE

'I won't have a coffee today, Phil.'

'Blimey, love, hope you're not thinking of giving up your morning stops here.'

'No, of course not. I'm not sure I could get through my day without our morning chat. I've been practising my numbers. I can't remember four, though.'

'*Peswar*.'

'Arghh,' I say with frustration. 'Why can't I remember that one?'

He laughs. 'So what do you want if it's not one of my legendary coffees?'

'I feel like a fruit juice or something. I've been feeling a bit rough these last few days. Maybe time to start looking after myself a bit more.'

'Have one of those orange and raspberry juices. They're spot on.'

'Perfect.' I grab one from the chiller. 'Come on then, tell me what's the weather's up to.'

'Sunny today.'

'Good, I'm going to the beach.'

'Watch out for the *howllosk*.'

I furrow my brow.

'Sunburn!' He chuckles and then says, 'Anyhow, you enjoy the sun while you can, love, because I hear there's *hager-awal* coming in.'

'*Hager-awal*?'

'Ugly weather. A monster storm, by all accounts.'

'When?'

'By the end of the week, they say.'

Dawn doesn't look convinced by the walk down to the beach where we'd had the party. We walk slowly, taking little steps down towards the sea, supporting our mother between us.

Although Mum has said a few things since she first spoke, her conversation is occasional and limited. The effort of talking, of heaving words down that dusty forgotten road from her brain to mouth, tires her quickly. She needs time. I know that, but I find myself impatient. My head pounds with questions I'm desperate to ask. Dawn says we have to be careful what we talk about though. She's worried about discussing my kidnapping in case reliving the trauma sends Mum straight back to that place inside where she's been hiding.

Mum copes well on the way down to the beach. Every now and then we stop to give us all a breather, and she lifts her head into the onshore wind and breathes in like a dog smelling for the scent of sheep. We make it on to the sand and I ignore Dawn as she worries about the return journey, chewing her nails, glancing nervously back up at the narrow path we've come down.

The beach is empty, but for a family who have tucked themselves into the rocks at the foot of the cliff on the far side of the cove. The parents are reading, leaning back to back, while their two children grub about in the rock pools not far from them. Only the father looks up at us as we step onto the beach. He stares for a moment, then checks the footpath, searching, I'm sure, for more arrivals who might threaten their seclusion.

I have a flash of the party, of having sex with Greg on the sand, him touching his lips to my chest, his face dimly lit by the fading fire.

I turn back to Dawn, who is standing beside our mother with a protective arm supporting her.

'Isn't this beach fabulous?'

'Yes, it's one of my favourites.'

'You've been here before?'

'Of course,' she says, rubbing Alice's hand. 'It's a locals' beach.' She looks out towards the sea. 'I've not been since Nan died though.'

I have to hide an unreasonable surge of jealousy. I hadn't considered she might know the beach. But she's grown up in St Ives, with the sea and the seals and the sparrowhawks. Of course she knew it, just as I would have known it if I'd never been taken by the Campbells.

We sit Mum on a picnic cushion on a rock and settle on the sand beside her. Dawn carefully unties her trainers and slips her socks off, then burrows her toes into the beach just like I do.

I pick up a handful of sand and let the dry grains trickle through my fingers. 'Do you think our father is bad?'

'What kind of question is that?'

'I know you don't like him. I know Mum was going to leave him and that he was taking the Campbells' money and didn't give me back to you. But he's an alcoholic, isn't he? And finding out he was supporting you, that the money he took was going to you, has confused me. I wonder if we should feel more sorry for him?'

'Sorry for him?' she laughs incredulously. 'You're joking, right?'

I shrug. I'm not joking, but I don't want to push it.

Then Dawn lifts the hair behind her ear to reveal a thick, jagged scar cut into her hairline like a carving in a chalk field.

'He did this,' she says. 'Because I knocked his beer over. I was carrying a blanket for Mum from my room into theirs because it was cold and the gas had been cut off because he hadn't paid the bills. I couldn't see where I was going and I caught his beer on the table. He was blind drunk and hit me so hard my feet left the ground. I was nine.'

I stare at the mark, transfixed, wanting to reach out and touch it, erase it with my fingertips. She lowers her hair and then points at my arm.

'And that scar? The round one. The one I knew you had?'

My stomach seizes and I touch my fingers to the rough, raised patch of skin.

'You were about a year old, maybe a bit older, and you were crying in your playpen. Mum was out somewhere and he wasn't stopping you cry. I told him you wanted to be picked up but he said babies need to learn to be good and that if we kept going to you every time you made a squeak you'd turn into a spoilt brat. But you didn't stop so I started singing a lullaby to you to try and calm you down, and then all of a sudden he shouted and slammed his bottle down, and stumbled over to you – he must have been drunk – and pushed the tip of his cigar into your arm. I ran to my room and hid beneath my bed.' She gently fingers the sand, then shakes her head. 'Do I think he's bad?' she continues. 'Yes, I do. But, you're right, he has problems. The drink made him do bad things. When he was sober he was nice. You never knew what mood he'd be in. He wrote to us when he first sent the money. Nan read the letter to me. He said this was the best way for him to help us and we were better off without him. He even said sorry. And that was the last we heard of him. Just the money into my building society account every month.' She kicks at the sand with her heel a few times.

'I always wanted a different father,' I say then. 'I used to wish Henry Campbell talked to me more, hugged me even. There was so much missing and I never understood why.'

'Is that why you married your teacher?'

'What?' I say, taken aback by her question.

'That's what they say, isn't it? That girls who marry old men are trying to get a father figure or whatever. I saw it on the television once. They talked to this girl who married a seventy-year-old when she was seventeen. In the end they all decided it was because her dad never paid her any attention because he really liked football and wanted a boy or something.'

I am quiet, wondering whether there might actually be some truth to her daytime television theory.

'Sorry. I didn't mean to annoy you.'

'No, I'm not annoyed. But not all people who have issues with their fathers marry old men and not all people who marry old men have issues with their fathers. Your dad left and Craig's not old.'

'Me and Craig aren't together so it's not the same thing.'

'You keep saying that but I know you feel something for him. I can see it.' I hesitate. 'And he told me he fell in love with you when you were children.'

'He shouldn't have said anything at all.'

I have a sudden recollection of Craig and the blonde at the train station. 'And you don't mind he's seeing that other woman?' As soon as the words are out I wish I could haul them back inside me.

Her face falls and her brow furrows. 'What do you mean?'

'It doesn't matter. It's none of my business. I saw him with someone ... he said you knew. I shouldn't have opened my mouth.'

But she doesn't look cross. Instead, she sighs and looks out to sea. 'It's complicated. I don't have space in my life for a boyfriend.'

'Of course you have space. And I bet he feels nothing for that other woman compared to what he feels for you. You've got a right to—'

'For God's sake. She's not a woman. She's a girl. And she's ... she's his daughter.' She fires the words like whispered bullets. 'The girl you saw is his daughter.'

'His daughter?'

'Blonde? Slim? Wears a ponytail. About sixteen? Does that sound like this *other woman*?' She kicks her heel into the sand again. 'You don't know anything about us. There isn't any other way. He can't be with me because he has her. And I can't be with him because I have Mum.'

'That doesn't seem fair on either of you.'

'I stopped worrying about what was fair a long time ago.'

'You deserve some happiness. And some fun.'

'Fun?' she snorts. 'I can't even spell the word.'

'Well, it starts with an *f*...'

She glances sideways at me and I smile, and she smiles back. 'Smart arse,' she says softly. She picks up another handful of sand and allows it to trail through her fingers like an hourglass.

'Come on,' I say then, batting her shoulder and jumping to my feet. 'Let's have some fun now. How about a swim? I've been dying to get in the sea. Shall we?'

She looks up at me, a hand shielding her eyes from the sun. 'But it's freezing.'

'I've seen children go in. If they can, we can.'

'I haven't got a costume.'

I start pulling off my clothes. 'Nor do I.'

'What about Mum?'

'You'll be fine, won't you, Mum?' She doesn't look at me; her eyes look out across the sea, to somewhere faraway beyond the horizon. 'We won't be long.'

I pull my T-shirt over my head and drop it onto the beach, then I unzip my jeans.

'It's too dangerous. There's a riptide here. Look, on the surface, that flat area, that's a current beneath the surface.'

'We won't go far. Come on.' I push my palms together, now feeling agonisingly self-conscious standing in front of her in my bra and pants. 'Please?'

Dawn hesitates for a second or two, which raises my hopes, but then shakes her head, so I spin around and begin to run towards the sea, rejected and embarrassed and now not sure I want to swim anymore. The waves look terrifying and the water, which had looked inviting from further up the beach, now appears cold and angry.

Go on. Just do it.

So I take a deep breath and dive into an oncoming wave. It's brain-achingly cold and I am immediately tumbled by the freezing water, no idea which way is up and which way is down. Rolling around like a ball, I thrash my arms, trying desperately to find the surface. When at last my feet touch sand. I push upwards as hard as I can, and when I break the surface I take an urgent breath. Before I know it, another wave is upon me, but this time I duck beneath it and emerge the other side. I look back at the beach. Dawn is on her feet and watching me with one hand shielding her eyes and the other on her hip. I flip onto my front and swim a couple of strong strokes of crawl. I'm not the world's best swimmer – Elaine reluctantly took me to private swimming lessons on Henry's insistence, but only until I got my twenty-five-metre badge – and the waves are choppy, splashing me in the face as I swim, making it hard to see. I decide to turn back and take a couple of strokes, but rather than gain on the shore, I am dragged further away by the current that scared Dawn. Trying not to panic, I dive below the waves and swim as hard as I can underwater. When I surface I am only a little closer, and I'm already getting tired. Keeping my panic at bay, I close my eyes against the salt water and swim as hard as I can, not stopping to look at the shore or catch my breath. My legs and arms ache like mad, but when at last I open my eyes I find I'm finally making ground, and thankfully there is now less pull on me.

And then I hear screaming.

Piercing, guttural shrieks split the air. Mum is standing, her arms flailing. Dawn is trying to calm her but Mum is fighting her off. Out of the clutches of the current I am free to swim and am soon carried in on a breaking wave. I stumble onto the sand, legs like jelly, and clamber up the beach towards them.

'What's happened? What wrong?'

Mum's arms are outstretched to me. Her mouth is stretched into a silent scream.

'She started screaming ... when you disappeared beneath the water,' Dawn says, her face drained of colour, her body shaking. 'I told ... her not to ... worry, that you'd be fine, but ... but ... she wouldn't stop screaming.'

I hold Mum tightly against my shoulder, stroke her hair, whisper gently that everything's OK. At last her body relaxes, just the odd shudder ripples through her.

'I thought I'd lost you,' Mum whispers.

'No, Mum. No, everything's fine. I went swimming, that's all.'

'I thought I'd let you go again. That you went back to the sea.'

'Just a swim, Mum. That's all.' I rub her shoulders, as if she were cold. 'Just a quick swim.'

Dawn doesn't utter a word all the way back. Her face stays taut, her green eyes distant. When we arrive back at the flat, she goes straight to her room and closes the door behind her.

I feed, bath and dress Mum for bed. She seems fine, all trace of her panic now gone. I don't put her to bed straightaway. Instead she sits in her armchair and I sit on the floor and lay my head in her lap.

'I didn't mean to upset you, Mum. I didn't mean to make you scared.'

And then I feel a soft caress on my hair. She is stroking me.

'I'm sorry,' she whispers. 'I'm sorry. I'm so sorry.'

'It's OK, Mum. I'm OK.'

I don't move, but lie still and listen to her mumbling. I think back over those years I'd been a stolen child, shut away inside that house with Elaine, when all along I should have been here, with my head in this lap, this hand on my hair. I will never know why the Campbells took me and it's agonising to think I will have to live without knowing.

I hear Dawn's footsteps in the hallway. They pause at the door. I close my eyes and hold my breath, and pretend I don't know she's there.

Nothing is said and the footsteps walk back towards the kitchen.

FIFTY-SEVEN

In the days that follow our trip to the beach my sister is quiet, even more so than usual.

I ask her over and over to tell me what's wrong, but she won't.

'Talk to me. Please?'

'I'm fine. Honestly.' She looks at me and tries to smile. '*Honestly*, I am.'

But I know she's not. She's spending more time in her room with her door closed, appearing only to watch her television programme, then traipsing morosely back when it finishes. She has stopped hovering nearby, looking anxious when I do things for Mum. I don't like it. I want to share the joy of our mother's improvement. And what an improvement it is. The staring, cadaverous woman I'd first encountered is a distant memory.

'Do you remember much about me?' I ask her tentatively.

'Every last thing.' Her voice is quiet but strong; it's lost its rasping edge and is fuller and plumper, like her body.

I pull the chair over and sit beside her, take hold of her hand in both of mine and stroke her.

'You loved talking. You'd talk to anyone you met.' A look of sadness comes across her face. 'That's probably why you went with those people. I should have warned you of people more. I should never have sent you out of the caravan.'

I lean forward and kiss her hand.

'I'm sorry. Sorry.'

'Shush,' I say. 'I'm back now.'

She is silent and I see that she's fallen into a doze.

I tidy around her while she sleeps, straighten the bedclothes, neaten the bookshelf, and then leave her room, closing the door quietly behind me. The cat is sitting on the threshold of the kitchen and hallway, her paws neatly together. She mews a greeting but doesn't move.

'Hello, sweetheart. You can come out of the kitchen, you know. She's shut away in her room and I don't mind you out here.'

She mews again. I sit on the floor with my back against the wall and my hand outstretched, and rub my fingers together and making kissing noises. The cat inches herself forward a step.

'Brave girl,' I cajole. 'A little closer and I'll tickle your chin.'

She takes another step towards me. Her tail twitches. Every now and then she pauses and flicks her ears.

'Why are you so scared? It's a bit dark, but it's not that bad.'

Step by step she makes it to me and I reward her with a stroke. She closes her eyes and stretches up her chin.

Just as the rumble of a purr begins, Dawn appears at the kitchen door. 'What the hell is that animal doing outside the kitchen?'

She doesn't give me time to reply, but runs at the cat, shouting and flapping her arms. The cat skitters away from her towards the front door, where she finds herself cornered. She cowers in the corner, her ears flat against her head. Dawn bends down and grabs her by the scruff of the neck.

'You're not allowed in the house!' she shouts, only inches away from the animal's face. Then she marches down the corridor and flings the cat into the kitchen.

I run to the door in time to see the cat scrambling to her feet, having landed against the leg of the table. She scoots out of the cat flap with her tail high and her fur standing proud.

Dawn kicks the box across the flap to block it.

'I guess that answers my question why the cat is so scared of the hall.'

'Shut up.'

'No. You shut up!' I am surprised by the strength in my voice. 'What was all that about? I was only stroking her, for goodness' sake.'

'Why are you so sure you know best all the bloody time?'

'It has nothing to do with knowing best. You just lost it with an innocent animal for stepping over a line that only you can see.'

'I didn't *lose it*.'

'Yes, you bloody did,' I mutter. 'You're insane.'

'What did you say?'

'Nothing.'

'If you must know – though why you should need every bloody thing explained to you isn't clear to me – it's because I don't want it near Mum. If she gets ill it takes her weeks to recover and though I'm sure the cat won't give her anything, I don't want to risk it. And actually, it's not just me that can see the line, the cat knows it's there too. The only time it has ever crossed it was when you stuck your nose in.'

We stare at each other.

'Well, you didn't need to throw her like that.'

'I wouldn't have if you hadn't made the thing come out here.'

I open my mouth, then shut it without reply.

'Stop trying to change everything.'

If only it were possible to change everything, I think.

'I'm sorry about the cat,' I say, and then I turn on my heel and leave. I don't want to get into a fight with Dawn. I don't want us to say things to each other that we might regret.

I walk back down to St Ives and up onto the cliffs overlooking the wide expanse of Porthmeor beach. There isn't even the faintest of breezes and the sea is dead calm, like glass. Families patchwork the beach with their areas of sand staked out with rainbow windbreaks. I envy them, these people at ease with each other, happy in their company. So different to the strange new group of people I am tied to in blood.

I allow myself to imagine a time in the future when all this is in the past. When we don't have to tiptoe around each other anymore. When everything is settled and the three of us can come to the beach and sit and chat, and eat a picnic we prepared together, giggling and laughing as we buttered bread, cut ham and chunks of cheese, and wrapped slices of fruitcake in tinfoil.

FIFTY-EIGHT

I don't want to go back to the flat straight away. The thought of the stale air soaked with Dawn's anger and the smell of bleach and soup turns my stomach. Anyway, we both need some time to cool down, so after my morning chat with Phil, I set off on a long walk along the cliffs. I take my time, breathe in the bracing air and search each of the secluded coves below me for seals or dolphins. I meet a twitcher, his binoculars hanging about his neck, his special twitcher's hat pulled low on his head.

'You just missed a kestrel,' he says. 'It was a beauty.'

'That's a shame,' I reply, and carry on walking.

It's the afternoon before I finally get to the flat. I let myself in and find Dawn, her hair scraped back in an unforgiving ponytail, peering anxiously out of the kitchen door.

'Did you see the cat on your way up?' she asks. 'I forgot to unblock the cat flap yesterday.'

'I didn't, but it's unblocked now?'

'Yes,' she says, turning to peer out of the kitchen window. 'I did it as soon as I realised.'

'I wouldn't look so worried. Cats often go walkabout and she hasn't been gone long.'

'She never misses her tea. Never.' Dawn opens the back door. 'Cat! It's tea! Come on. Cat!' There's a tangible fear in her voice that tugs at me.

'She'll be fine,' I say. 'It's only a night—'

'It's been nearly twenty-four hours.'

I bite my tongue to stop myself from pointing out that maybe if she hadn't slung it against a table and scared it half to death, it might not have gone. 'It's warm and dry out there,' I say instead. 'She's probably having a whale of a time, chasing mice and flirting with Toms.'

Dawn says nothing.

'Honestly, she'll be back in her own time. Our cat often went missing for a day or two and always came home.'

Our cat.

I swallow. The hairs on my arms prickle. I am caught unawares by Bella's life, her cat and her home, and her mother calling out of the back door for him to come in for his supper. I reach for the back of the chair to steady myself as my knees threaten to buckle.

'This is your fault, you know,' Dawn says quietly.

'Hmm?' I look at her, my hand gripping the chair hard as my head spins. 'Did you say it's my fault? What do you mean?'

'It doesn't matter.' She's hovering at the back door, craning her neck left and right, her hands wringing.

FIFTY-NINE

'Is the cat back?' I ask when I arrive the next morning.

'Yes,' Dawn says. She opens the fridge and gets out a carton of milk. 'I told you she'd be fine.'

'She's not that good, actually.' Dawn hands me a cup of tea and gestures to the box on the floor by the back door.

When I look inside, my stomach heaves.

'Oh my God.' I bend down, resting both hands on the box and gag twice.

The cat is on her side, eyes open only a fraction, her breathing shallow. There's a deep cut on her hindquarters that runs from her tail to what's left of her shin. The fur around the cut is soaked with old blood and new. And there are maggots, about twenty of them, no bigger than a grain of rice, writhing aggressively in and out of the torn fur and flesh. A waft of some foul smell hits my nose and I lift my hand to block it.

'She needs a vet.'

'I don't know any vets. She'll be fine though. She needs to rest, but she'll be better in a couple of days. I've been giving her little teaspoons of water and picking those things off her with tweezers. I didn't get all of them but I'll have another go after my tea.'

I stand up and face her, fighting to keep my tears of shock and anger at bay. 'If this animal doesn't see a vet she'll die.'

'I told you, I don't know where the vet is and I can't afford one anyway.'

'I'll pay for it! Jesus, I said you didn't need to worry about money anymore. There's no way she'll get better. She needs antibiotics or she'll get gangrene or blood poisoning or ... or ... I don't know, but she needs a vet.' I bend down again and watch the maggots burrowing themselves around her wound. I reach out and pick a few off and retch as I do. 'If money is that much of an issue, you should have asked.'

'I don't need your bloody charity.'

I snap round to face her. 'It's not charity! I don't understand what goes on in your head, Dawn. The cat needs a vet. If you can't afford to pay it then I will. It's not charity, it's your responsibility to look after your cat.'

'It's not my cat, it just—'

'I know!' I say through gritted teeth. 'It showed up out of nowhere. But you feed her, she thinks she lives here, you were calling for her all yesterday. You should have taken her to the vet as soon as you found her.'

'I wasn't sure how long it would take. And I can't leave Mum that long.' Dawn's face is strained, but the set of her mouth is stubborn. 'Mum is my priority. And anyway, the vet would probably put her down. That's what they do. The cat's best chance is to stay here where she can rest and sleep. That's what she needs.'

'*That's what she needs*? That's your answer to everything, isn't it? Everything will be alright as long as nobody leaves this flat. First Mum and now the cat?' I pick up the box. 'Look at her,' I say, pushing it towards Dawn. '*Look*. At. Her!'

Dawn turns her head away.

I breathe heavily, anger welling over. I put the box on the table. 'This is mad, Dawn. You know that?' I put my jacket back on, then grab hold of the box again. 'The cat needs the vet and I'm taking her.'

'Put the box down,' Dawn's green eyes are ablaze. 'Who the hell do you think you are?'

She walks over to me and places both hands on the box. 'The cat is mine. I don't want the vet to put her down. I haven't got the money to *give* to a vet and I didn't want to leave Mum to go and *find* a vet. So don't you waltz in here like some know-it-all princess and tell me what to do.'

Neither of us takes our hands off the box.

'You've got some front,' I say. 'I haven't *waltzed* in anywhere. I came here looking for my family. You act so bloody hard done-by all the time, but it's me that's done without. Me that had no mother—' Something catches me there, an image of Elaine Campbell, clear-skinned and smiling, warmth spreading out of her like rays from the sun. I pause, tears choking me. 'Actually,' I whisper. 'It's worse than that. I *did* have a mother. I had a woman who for all her insanities was my mother. And that was ripped away. It was a charade. Everything I thought I knew, the peculiar life I was happy with, all of it vanished in an instant.' Dawn glances up at the ceiling, her mouth pursed tightly. 'Every memory I have means nothing. It's all a lie. Do you have any concept of what that might be like?'

'I have more of a concept than you could ever know. I know exactly what it feels like to lose someone. To have your heart torn out. To give up something you love. It's you that doesn't have a clue. You and your buckets of cash and your never having had a worry in the bloody world. Drawn curtains and locked doors are the worst of it? Get over yourself. You know *nothing* about what it's like to be me. Nothing about living in the real world. You know nothing at all.'

'Well, you know nothing about me either and who's fault is that? You think you've taken any interest in finding out about me? About my life? And if I don't know anything about you there's only one person to blame. *You*. You haven't opened up to me once. You haven't told me anything about your life. How on earth could I possibly know about you? I wouldn't be surprised if you still don't believe me. If you're expecting me to suddenly announce I'm lying, because that's the only reason I can think of to explain why you're so closed off all the time. It's like you hate me.'

Tears are gathered in her eyes.

'And that's the real tragedy,' I continue. 'Because this family was ripped apart by the most God-awful happening, but we were given a second chance. I *found* you. I came home and you should have seen it as a miracle. But you didn't. You don't. To you we're just two strangers linked by circumstance; you've got no feelings for me at all. You'd be happier if I'd never shown up. Admit it! That way you could have kept Alice where you want her, shovelled soup into her three times a day, kept her mouldering in a box like this poor cat, dying and hopeless, but at least you'd have her all to yourself.'

I shake my head and give a bitter laugh as I let my hands fall from the box. 'God, how angry you must have been when I knocked on the door and ruined it all? I bet you never thought about me once, did you? You let me walk away on that campsite and never gave me a second thought. Maybe our father was right? Maybe it *was* your fault I went. Maybe you did it on purpose because you always hated me!'

My heart feels as if it's melted, dissolved by my acid-words. I turn and start to walk out of the kitchen.

'Don't you dare leave!' she screams from behind me. 'You're not running away like you always do, out of that front door at the first sign of trouble! You should listen to yourself. I'm sorry you were taken, I really am, but you weren't hurt or raped or abused. You were taken to a big house and had a comfortable life with people you still *miss*. I was left with nothing. You think I didn't want to go to university? I was clever at school. Got good marks and I could have gone. But I had to stay here.' Dawn swings her arms wildly around the kitchen. 'Living with the ghost of a sister I could hardly remember, a dad who drank a bottle of whisky before lunchtime then belted me from here to hell and back, and a mother who did nothing but cry until one day she shut up altogether.' She laughs through her tears. 'You know why she shut up? Because dad had me up against a wall with a broken beer bottle at my neck. She thought he was going to kill me. She was screaming and then went silent, like someone had switched her off, and after that she never said another word. And then when I was thirteen years old, Nan died and Granddad went six months later, so that was it. I was a carer. Looking after Mum day and night. No hours off, no weekend, no breaks. Bathing her, feeding her, doing all the housework. Worrying about everything, about having enough money to eat, about keeping her with me, and then ... and ...' Dawn was struggling to talk, her words coming now in breathless snatches. 'I had to ... give up the one person who could have...'

Her hands cover her face and she takes a couple of deep breaths and then looks at me again.

'And do I regret the things I did?' Her eyes bore into me. 'No, Morveren, I don't because looking after Mum is my job. My duty. It was my duty, my responsibility, to clear up the mess your blink-and-miss-it existence in my family left. And you know what makes it all worse?'

I stare numbly at her, as if I've been hit by a lorry, winded, damaged irreparably.

'That now you're back, she doesn't even need me. I have no purpose. I might as well be dead.'

'Don't say that.'

'Why not? It's the truth, isn't it? That day on the beach I couldn't help her. But you could.'

'No, Dawn, it's not—'

But I don't get to finish.

Her watch beeps. She turns off the alarm and stares at me for a moment or two.

I shake my head, but she reaches for the volume switch on the television.

I step forward and grab her wrist. 'Don't.'

'Get off me.' She yanks her arm free and turns on the sound.

'We need to talk.'

She pulls out her chair and sits down.

'Turn the television off.' She doesn't look at me, but leans forward and turns the volume up so high the sound becomes distorted.

'For goodness' sake, Dawn! We need to talk.'

She is silent. I look at the television. One of the five women, neat hairstyle, shiny lips, and singsong voice magnified to a ridiculous level, is introducing the show's guest.

'Turn it off!' I shout above the bellowing television.

No response.

I reach to switch it off myself but she throws her body over it, protecting it from me.

'Don't be ridiculous!' I grab her shoulder and pull her backwards, and as she moves, she brings the television with her. It falls and the deafening sound of the applauding audience is silenced in the shattering of glass.

We both look at the broken television lying on the floor between us.

'You're right,' she says then, her head lifting slowly, her voice scarily quiet. 'My life was fine before you came back. My whole life was looking after Mum and now she doesn't need me. I've looked after her for years and got nothing from her. You come back and within weeks she smiles and talks and eats fucking rice.' Her face is wracked with pain. 'So, tell me, what do you think I should do now, Morveren? Caring for her was all I had. Twenty-five years ago you took her from me when you went away, and now you've come back and taken her all over again.' Her hands clench at her sides. 'And that's what's screwed up, I should be happy that she's getting better, shouldn't I? But I'm not. Look at me, I'm not happy. I'm selfish and bad. Dad was right all along. I've got this life because I deserve it. And you're—' She breaks into tears again. '—you're right. I wish you'd never come back.'

And then I turn my back on her. I leave her standing in her spotless kitchen with the shattered television, and the dying cat in the box with the maggots, and our mother in her dingy bedroom. I leave her with her grief and her pain and her ruined, wretched life, and I slam the door on all of it.

SIXTY

The air is muggy, thick with the promise of Phil's *hager-awal*, the sky filled with deep-purple clouds. I walk out onto the sea wall that projects into the water, separating the harbour on one side from the ocean on the other. The waves are choppy within the harbour and angry beyond, crashing ferociously against the wall, bursting high into the air like briny fireworks. My vision blurs with tears of anger, self-pity and regret as Dawn's hateful, hurtful words echo around me.

You weren't hurt, or raped, or abused.

You took her from me when you went away, and now you've come back and taken her all over again.

I wish you'd never come back.

I bang my hands down hard on the wet railings. Scream as loud as I can into the oncoming weather, my words whipped away from me by the raging wind.

'Are you alright?' There is a man with silver-white hair standing beside me. He looks worried, his snowy eyebrows are hooded over soft brown eyes. His hand rests on the top of my arm, and his voice is gentle, like one of those policemen trained to coax jumpers from Mark Tremayne's bridge in Bristol.

I look at him but it's as if he isn't real, as if he is a character in a film, as if I am watching him but unable to interact. I pull my arm away from him and run along the harbour wall and back through the meandering tourists, back up to the hostel, the only place I have left to go. I fling open the door and run inside, crashing so hard into someone coming the other way, it knocks the wind out of me.

'Steady!'

It's Greg.

His face breaks into a wide smile. 'Hey, Tori.'

Hearing her name stings like iodine.

'What's up? You're crying?'

The sympathy in his voice breaks me in two and I fall into him, wracked with fresh tears.

'Shush,' he soothes. 'It can't be that bad.'

I curl into him, and his chest feels warm and strong. I let him steer me back to his room, where we sit on his unmade bed. The room smells of aftershave and hair gel and clothes that need washing. I pull my knees up to my chin. More tears come, rolling down my cheeks as my body heaves with silent sobs. His body presses against mine and he rests a hand on my knee.

'Do you want to talk about it?'

And then I tell him everything.

Once I start, once the barricade is breached, I can't stop, and he is perfect. He doesn't interrupt, he looks shocked then alarmed then sympathetic. He shakes his head in disbelief. He strokes my hair. There is no trace of blame or judgement. And at last, when the truth is out, I feel free, like one of the gulls on the thermals above the surging ocean. Not Bella, not Tori, not even Morveren, but a chaotic composite of all three strange and tragic parts.

He brushes my tears away with his hand. I look up at him and lie backwards, pulling him with me, fumbling for the buttons on his jeans, desperate to have him inside me, to feel connected to something real, something life-affirming. We make love and I give everything of myself to him. I give him the real me. I am charged with emotion and his every touch feels electric, as if we are the only two people on the planet, as if, outside his closed door there is nothing, just a white, empty void that holds this room and this bed and the two of us suspended.

I arch my body up to meet his lips, listen to his whispers in my ear, run my hands over the tiger that prowls his back, and think of nobody else but myself. Dawn, David, my mother, my father mouldering away in that dank house in Bristol, the loathsome effigies of Elaine and Henry, all of them are gone.

When I wake, I am alone. I look at my watch. It's nearly nine. I pull the duvet over my shoulder and turn on my side, smile as I remember the way he understood, the way his face was soft with kindness and compassion. But then I remember the awful fight I had with Dawn. I flinch at the things we said to each other. And then her television. That was unforgivable of me, however cross I was, however upset. She has had over two decades of caring for our mother and was only a child when she first had that responsibility thrust upon her. Of course she was going to have some quirks and habits.

I return to my own room and shower and dress in clean clothes and then grab my purse. As I come down into the reception area Fi calls to me.

'Hey, there was a girl here last night. She was in a bit of a state, crying and that, she could barely speak. She asked me to give you this.' Fi reached below the counter and retrieved the graffitied shoebox tied round with string from the shelf in Dawn's bedroom.

'Did she ask to see me?'

'No. Just wanted you to have the box.'

I return to my room and sit on the bed, then I open the box. Inside are letters, lots and lots of letters, and a note scrawled on a scrap of paper on top of them.

Dear Morveren

I want you to have these. You were always with me. I thought about you every day – for all sorts of reasons. The thought of you was sometimes the only thing that kept me going. Come back when you feel you can.

  We need to talk.

Dawn

I guess there are about a hundred letters. Each one is dated. Some are long and some are only a few lines.

I pick up the first one and I don't break until I've read them all.

SIXTY-ONE

AGED 8:

Dear Morveren,

Dad got cross today. He shouted so loud and he smelled nasty, like beer and I thort he will hit me again. He said I was bad because I lost you. Then mummy cried and we went to the church. It was boring but she got me crisps from the pub. I love crisps but I miss you lots.

Love Dory

AGED 9:

Dear Morveren,

Dad went mad today. proper mad. He held a broken bottle on my cheek and squeezed my neck so hard I thought all the breath would go out of me. mum was screaming and then she was hitting him and then he went out and banged the door. mum was just still and her eyes coudnt even see me even when I shouted at her. Then she just said I'm sorry and she hasnt said anything more. Not even one word. I dont like how she stares at nothing. Nan said she so sad the shock of dad hurting me has made her go depressed. I dont like it at all.

Love Dory

AGED II:

Dear Morveren,

Today we had a maths test! And I came top!!! I thought mum might be happy when I told her but she didn't seem that happy. All she does is stare out of the window, waiting for you. Well, that's what nan says. I really like Craig. He's my only friend actually. And his mum and dad are really nice too. His mum makes cakes and puts them in a tin with Lady Diana on it and we just help ourselves! I am so glad she asked me round for tea that day. How are you? I hope you are ok and I really am sorry I let you go. Not a very good big sister. I hope you don't hate me!!!! (I wouldn't be surprised if you did.)

Love Dory

AGED I5:

Dear Morveren,

It's two days after Christmas. I thought about ending it on Christmas Day. I keep thinking about when you went and that if I'd just looked after you right then none of this would be like it is. I was looking at Mum when we had our Christmas dinner. I'd put a paper hat on her head and pulled two crackers. I even found this turkey-flavoured soup. I gave her a new blanket (it was in Woolworths and was half price because the lady said there was a mark on it, though I looked and couldn't see any mark at all!) Anyway, when I saw Mum sitting there with this blank face on her, not even a flicker of happiness to be spending Christmas with me, I thought about taking a load of pills and just, well, going. But then I tried to think of who would look after Mum and there's nobody. She only has me. There isn't even anybody checking in who would find me and take her somewhere safe. She would just starve to death. I find it so hard looking after her all the time and not being able to go out and stuff. God, that sounds selfish, doesn't it? Sometimes I hate her. But writing that makes me feel bad because I love her so much. I just wish she'd speak to me.

Give my love to Granddad and Nan. I miss them ever so much.

Love Dawn

AGED 16:

Dear Morveren,

I need to tell you something. Something so awful I can barely write the words. I'm pregnant. You're the first person I've told. I'm scared and I don't know what to do. I feel so sick. I'm quite far gone, I think. There's a bump already. I don't know. I should go to the doctor, shouldn't I? And I should tell Craig, but I don't know how to. I wish you were alive so I could talk to you. I reckon you'd know just what to do.

Love Dawn

AGED 16:

Dear Morveren,

I had my baby yesterday! I called her Stacey Morveren Cardew-Trem-ayne. Stacey is my favourite name, and Morveren, well that's after you! The hyphen is funny, isn't it? Sounds so posh! But it's not though, it's just Craig's surname and ours pushed together. Stacey is so pretty and has loads of hair. I think her eyes will be green like ours, though the midwife said it's hard to tell for a few weeks. Right now they are a dark bluey colour, but I can definitely see green. Having her hurt like anything! (She's your niece. Isn't that weird?)

Tell Nan she's a great-nan!

Love Dawn

AGED 16:

Dear Morveren,

So the bastards at social services said I can't keep Stacey. She's only six days old and they're going to take her from me. They say I can't look after her. They came round on a surprise visit and said the flat was unhygienic. The bloody cheek! I told them it was none of their fucking business but they said it is their business if there's a baby and they think the baby might get sick. As if I'd let her get sick! They said I should put Mum in a home but there's no way. NO WAY. She's my mother. How can I leave her in some home being looked after by strangers? I told them that, so they said they'd take my baby. I didn't know people could do that. I hate them all. Stacey is the most beautiful thing in my life. I want to run away with her and Mum. But how can I?

Love Dawn

AGED 16:

Dear Morveren,

Craig and his mum and dad are going to look after Stacey. The social services says it's a good idea. I'm so sad she's leaving me but I'm relieved she's not going into care. I'm not sure if Craig is totally ok with it, but neither of us wants her in a kids' home. His mum and dad have been brilliant. His mum has sorted her shifts out so she can look after her while Craig works. He's going part time at the video shop, but hopefully he'll get a better job soon. He has all these plans! I've told him and his mum that soon as I can, I'll have her back. I need to sort myself out, get on top of it all. There is no way I would have let Stacey go anywhere with strangers, but these people love her and I know she'll be happy. Craig will be a good dad. Not like ours. Craig will be kind and will never, ever hurt her. I know that.

Love Dawn

AGED 16:

Dear Morveren,

Craig and his mum came and took her today. I'd packed her clothes in a plastic bag, and put in the nappies and the milk and her little teddy bear. I sat up with her all night long. I put my nose against her hair and just breathed her, and then I stroked her little cheek and told her how much I loved her and how sorry I was and that when she grows up I hope she forgives me. Last night I nearly changed my mind. Thought about putting Mum in a home and keeping Stacey with me. But who would love Mum if it's not me? Nobody would love her, nobody would care for her, and what kind of life is that? At least Stacey will be with her dad and her nan and granddad. And I can see her of course. Craig and his mum came with this lovely pram they bought from an ad in the back of the paper and his mum knitted her a pretty blanket. Seeing it made me cry buckets! When Craig held his hands out for Stacey, I couldn't hand her over. There was this voice in my head screaming 'Don't take my baby'. But Craig needed to get back to settle her before work, and he couldn't wait around all day so I gave her to him. It felt like he was pulling a bit of my body off. I sat in the kitchen asking myself over and over why I've given up the most important thing in the world? How can a mother live without her baby? I can see why Mum went quiet now. And then I looked around the kitchen and I saw the state of it. How many dirty pans there were, the bin overflowing so that rubbish and our clothes are in crumpled heaps everywhere. I went into the bathroom and saw the toilet dirty, the sink with this black grime all round it, more clothes and rubbish. Maybe if the cow from social services had seen it tidy and clean she might not have said she'd take Stacey. So I went and bought all this cleaning stuff. I bought a massive bottle of bleach and bin bags and I started cleaning. I worked all day and night and I scrubbed and scrubbed and cried all the time I did it, and my hands hurt with the chemicals and the scrubbing but it was a good hurt, like it was my punishment for letting go of your hand. If only I'd held on. I miss Stacey, Morveren. I miss my baby.

Love Dawn

AGED 19:

Dear Morveren,

I thought today you might not ever have existed. You could be made up. I can't remember your face and as far as I know you might just be a story everyone told me. I wish this was true, because if you never existed then you wouldn't be here with me all the time. You are though, Morveren. You're here with me all the time. Like a ghost.

Love Dawn

AGED 21:

Dear Morveren,

Craig asked me to marry him again today. I said no as usual. What else could I say? I can't do it. Everything I have – all my energy – goes to Mum. He said he loved me and then he cried. That was hard. I've never seen him cry before. That was really hard. Did I tell you Stacey starts school in September? Well, she does. I'm going to make sure she works as hard as she can so she can do something with her life. I tell her to live every day to its full because life is precious, isn't it? You and I both know that. Mum's OK, but God it's quiet. Even after all these years I still get a headache from the quiet.

I wish more than anything I had my sister to talk to.

Love always

Dawn

SIXTY-TWO

The sky above me is deep grey with heavy rainclouds and the wind sends leaves and dust scurrying around me in angry whirls. I stand on the doorstep for some minutes, wracked with nerves. We had set on each other like filthy pit bulls in a ring, poisoned the waters that ran between us. How can we face each other after all we said? And those letters. Those heartbreaking letters.

My heart thumps in my chest as footsteps approach the door. Then the latch. The handle turning. The door opens and there she is. Her eyes are puffy and red. Her hair bedraggled, her clothes are those she wore yesterday, now crumpled from sleeping. We look at each other for only a few seconds before we fall into a hug that feels like the first and last in the world.

There is no sign of the broken television or the box with the cat. I don't mention either. Mum is sitting at the kitchen table. She is dressed in a clean, pressed blue shirt and a pair of beige trousers. In place of her usual slippers she has a pair of brown slip-on shoes and her hair is brushed and styled neatly with two combs. She has a hint of lipstick on her lips and her eyes shine out of freshly powdered skin. When she sees me, she smiles.

'Mum,' I say. 'Don't you look beautiful?'

'Dawn did it.'

Dawn looks at me. 'You were right. About lots of things.'

'I read your letters. Every one.'

We both sit down with Mum at the table and Dawn and I talk. We speak about going forward, about giving all three of us time to adjust. We speak about how we shouldn't underestimate the enormity of the trauma we are dealing with, that this will take time and patience and understanding. I tell them that sometimes, often when I'm least expecting it, I find myself missing my old life and how confused this makes me.

'Why didn't you tell me about Stacey?'

Dawn looks down at her hands. 'I couldn't find a way. I kept wanting to and then I clammed up with guilt. I didn't want you to hate me or judge me. And every time I thought about telling you I imagined how awful it would sound, that I gave my baby up. I didn't think you'd understand. I should have been braver.'

'I can't imagine what it must have been like to give her up. Was there no way you could do both?'

The question sounds harsher once it's out of my mouth and I worry for a moment that she will become defensive, but she doesn't. She nods a little, the look on her face resigned and a touch regretful.

'Maybe. I was young, and ... I did try ... but I couldn't manage. Looking back I think I made a mistake, but at the time?' She shrugs. 'I don't know. I knew I could never have found anyone to care for Mum like I did, but Craig and his parents loved Stacey and would look after her perfectly. Better than me...' She trails off as the sadness of reliving what happened eclipses her ability to talk.

'What's she like?'

Dawn's face immediately lights up. 'Oh, she's incredible. Such an amazing girl. She's growing into the most confident, independent woman. And she's beautiful.' Dawn grins at me. 'Though obviously I'm biased. She's clever, too. Works hard and did brilliantly in her exams.'

'I'd love to meet her.'

'I'd love that too.'

Mum seems to follow our conversation as much as possible. I worry that talk of Stacey might confuse or upset her, but she remains passive, taking sips of tea and occasionally looking at one of us and nodding. At one point I hold her hand and she closes her fingers around me.

Dawn notices and smiles and then takes hold of her other hand.

'My sunrise and my mermaid,' whispers Mum. 'My two girls.'

Then she eases her hands from ours and stands.

Dawn stands too and takes her elbow. 'I'll help you, Mum.' Then she does a slight double take and looks at me. 'Unless you want to?'

I shake my head and Dawn leads Mum out of the kitchen. I go to the sink and rinse a cloth beneath the tap, squeeze it out and wipe the table down.

When Dawn returns, I say, 'We need to have a chat about our father, about Mark Tremayne. I need to work out what to do about the house in Bristol.'

Dawn is about to reply when a loud knock at the door interrupts her and makes me jump. 'Who could that be?' she asks, her face showing surprise.

'Not Craig?'

'No, he's taking Stacey up to college. She needs help taking her art display down.'

There's another loud knock.

'I'll get it.' I walk out of the kitchen and down the corridor. Mum is standing at the threshold of her room, staring at the front door. Her hands are playing with the hem of her shirt.

'Don't worry, Mum.'

I open the door and a strong gust of wind, wet with drops of rain, hits my face.

I gasp in shock.

A group of people, two of them holding long-lens cameras, hover on the doorstep. A woman in a tailored, ivory suit with a raincoat over the top that flaps in the wind at her sides, her dark hair secured in a tight pony tail, holds a microphone. There's a van behind them with the *The Cornish Herald* logo emblazoned across it.

'We are hoping to talk to Morveren Tremayne. Is she in?'

She lifts her eyebrows and smiles. A man starts fiddling with his camera and points the lens at me. I hear the heavy click of a picture being captured. I stare at the unfamiliar faces gathered in a pack. Dawn comes up behind me. I turn helplessly.

'What's going on?' she says.

My mouth opens, but no words come out. Panic takes hold of me, twists my stomach into a tight, uncomfortable ball as the outside world rushes into the flat like air into a vacuum. Why are they here? How did they find out?

Mum appears beside me.

The ivory-suit woman starts talking. Her microphone points at us like a weapon. She looks at Alice. 'Mrs Tremayne,' she says in a clipped voice that has none of the soft Cornish tones I'd become used to. 'How did you feel when you lost your daughter in France? Were you happy with the way the French police handled it? What are your feelings now she's back?'

Dawn tries to step between them and us. She ushers me and Mum behind her with protective arms. A flash of a camera goes off. Then another. There's a man fiddling with equipment in the parked van. Another van with a different logo pulls up on the kerb.

I snap my head round to look at Mum. Her eyes are wide. There's a distance in them, a glaze. Or is that my imagination? Her cheeks have lost their rosy tinge. Perhaps that's just the powder Dawn has put on her. Then she makes a quiet sound, a whimper, like a kicked puppy. Her head shakes back and forth as her hands clench and unclench repeatedly at her sides.

'We don't want to talk to you,' Dawn says, trying to shut the door.

One of the men with a camera puts his foot against the door to stop it closing.

'We have a few questions for the girl that went missing,' ivory-suit woman says, her voice lifting in its persistence. 'Morveren, what do you feel about the Campbells? Do you feel in any way responsible for Dr Campbell's suicide?'

Dawn kicks the man's foot away. 'Go away.'

She slams the door closed then falls back against it.

Another soft moan comes from our mother.

'Mum?' Fear shoots through me. 'Mum? Mum!'

Dawn grasps her shoulders but she doesn't respond.

'I don't understand. Only we knew,' says Dawn. 'You, me and Craig. Did you tell your husband anything? Could he have found out from that doctor's will? Maybe there was another letter?'

I turn away from them and pace a few steps down the hall.

Everyone knows now. Bella and Tori have gone like a vanished mirage. There's nothing I can do. I think about David. He'll hear the news. He'll see my picture. His students will post things on social media. I have nowhere to hide.

Dawn shepherds Mum back into her room. I follow and stand in the corner and watch as she strokes Mum's hand and sits her in her armchair. Alice is quivering, her lips move with silent, indecipherable words.

I see Greg's face, recall his understanding, and a wave of nausea rises up inside me.

You bastard.

'It doesn't matter, Morveren,' Dawn says gently. 'We couldn't keep it quiet forever. It had to come out.'

'But I wasn't ready. I'm ... not ready. And look ... look at her ... she's terrified. She's not with us. What if she doesn't come back again?'

Dawn turns to me and puts her arms around me. 'It's fine. She will come back. It's a shock, that's all. It's a shock for all of us. You too. Oh dear, you're white as a sheet.' She strokes my cheek with the back of her hand, but I pull away.

'I should never have come back.'

'How can you say that?'

I look at my mother's stricken face. Guilt sets like concrete in my stomach. All her worst memories exhumed as newsworthy gossip. My head aches. I'm not sure if I'm more worried about how I am going to deal with the fall-out, or how my poor mother will, being dragged from her grief-stricken silence only to be thrown back there. And all of it because of me.

No. Because of Greg.

How stupid you were. How stupid to trust a man like him.

'I ... trusted ... why would he tell...? I'm ... I'm not ready ... for this. Don't you understand?'

'It doesn't matter if you told someone. It doesn't. It's done. It's out now. In a way it's good because we couldn't have hidden forever.'

'But people...'

'People will tire of it in no time at all.'

Dawn's voice is soft and coaxing, but I want her to scream at me again. I want her to tell me it's all my fault. Tell me how spoilt I am. How selfish and disconnected from reality. I want her to shout at me for meddling. If she was angry it would give me something to rail against, something to fight, but her compassion leaves me feeling contemptible and hopeless.

'Hey,' she soothes. 'Sweetheart, it's not that bad.'

She blurs as my eyes well.

'People had to know. It couldn't stay a secret,' she reaches out and wipes away my tears, her damaged hand rasping my skin like sandpaper. But I turn my face from her. I don't want her sympathy.

You bastard.

SIXTY-THREE

I push through the braying journalists and tear down the hill. Dawn shouts after me, but I ignore her, ignore the air burning in my lungs, and I keep running.

I am wracked by the shock waves of my worlds colliding. Bella's heartbeat pulses in my chest, memories of her mother who died calling out her name, her father who slit his wrists, her husband waiting for her, waiting to make her decisions and cook her food and fetch her sweaters. Then this new person. Morveren. Who exists in a world of just three people and a terrible tragedy. A drowned girl who returned to the family left destroyed by her disappearance. And Tori. The imaginary friend who kept me company as a child, who held my hand and listened to me cry, who helped me find those moments of rebellion in an otherwise controlled existence. Tori, who provided me a mask when I needed one.

How do I become one person?

I am an amalgamation of us all. There's no common ground. What am I expected to do? Erase Bella and become Morveren? Remove any last traces of Elaine and replace her with Alice? David with Dawn? Forget my reliance on Tori? I can't do it. As I run, anger and fear battle inside me. Anger at life and fear of life.

I turn towards Porthmeor beach, then pause briefly at the top of the concrete steps to scan the shoreline. There are a couple of children on body boards and a crowd of surfers making the most of the large waves that herald the approaching storm.

I leap down the steps two at a time, then jump onto the soft sand. I weave in and out of stalwart holiday-makers, determined to enjoy their summer break, in warm clothes with thermos flasks and raincoats packed in their beach bags.

I reach the beach hut and fling open the door.

Greg is naked from the waist down. He stands between the legs of a girl. Her skirt is hitched up, her soft, brown thighs encircle his moon-white buttocks. His weathered, untrustworthy hands rest on the wall either side of her head. That cruel, inked tiger slinks across his back, snarling nastily at me, saliva dripping from his sharpened teeth.

'You utter bastard.'

'Jesus!' He pulls back from the girl who flushes red as she desperately tries to pull down her skirt. Her long blonde hair partly covers her face, but not enough that I can't see she is barely out of her teens.

'How could you?' I spit.

'I never told you I wouldn't see other girls, Tori. It's part of the job—'

'Fuck the job, you prick. I couldn't give a stuff who you screw. And it's not Tori. Remember? I told you something. In confidence. Something more serious than you could ever dream up in that vacuous head of yours. How could you tell the press? Why would you? Why the hell would you go to a newspaper when what I told you was private?'

He pulls up his shorts and ties the drawstring. Runs a hand through his hair. The girl behind him starts snivelling. 'It's not that big a deal, is it?' he says. 'People would've found out sooner or later.'

The contempt I feel for him burns my insides. 'You have no idea of the harm you've done.'

He steps closer to me, reaches a hand out. 'Look, Tori, I didn't mean—'

'How much did you get?' I slap his hand away. 'How much did my story get you?'

'I don't know what—'

'Can't have been much, not nowadays, not when stories get out for free. Maybe enough for a couple of drinks, yeah? A few shots of tequila with the next piece of London skirt stupid enough to fall for your bullshit? You're nothing. Enjoy your pathetic life while you can,

Greg, because one thing I've learnt is that tomorrow it might all be gone.'

The man in the off-licence gives me a meaningful stare when I hand him my credit card. Concern for the woman with tear-swollen cheeks who stands shaking in front of him clutching a half-litre bottle of vodka is etched into his face. He opens his mouth to speak.

'No need for a bag,' I say, before he gets the chance.

The wind has whipped the sea into cross tufts of white on charcoal. I walk with my back straight, as erect as I can. My hair knots around my face, the sea air encasing each strand in a stiff, salty wrapping as I place one foot in front of the other and count my steps.

One, two three, four.

SIXTY-FOUR

I pass walkers who hurry through the dark beauty of their surroundings, their hoods flapping, zips pulled up as far as they will go, people so desperate to get home before the storm that they hardly notice the green-eyed woman striding the cliffs in the opposite direction. There are no more tears. I'm past crying. I wish for the thousandth time I'd never found out. I wish Elaine had stayed alive to keep Henry strong, to stop him from revealing the truth to me. I walk and drink and mourn my life before his letter.

It's dusk when I reach the church in Zennor. The heavy clouds hang low and black. The wind lashes the trees so their branches dance a frenzied jig, reaching down as if to pull me in to join them. I heave the heavy door open and peer in. There's nobody inside. I step in and close the door, which shuts the storm out and plunges me into still, dark quietness.

I go straight to her side. Crouch down next to her. Graze the fingers of one hand against the polished smoothness of her rounded belly.

Why did you abandon me?

I see my mother's shaking body, the fear in her eyes mirroring my own. I close my eyes tightly to shut it out, but all I get is a barrage of more. Dawn's hurt face, her bitter words, the cat in her box with the writhing maggots, the journalists, Greg between the legs of that girl, Henry's gaping wrists.

I drink from the bottle and lean my forehead against the Merrymaid, pushing it hard against the wood so it begins to hurt. And then from the back of the church comes a noise.

Someone is in the church.

My heart misses a beat and I scuttle backwards into the shadows, clasp my folded legs tight to my chest and hold still. I try not to breathe. Every hair on my body stands proud. I don't want them to find me. I don't want sympathy or pity or questions.

There are footsteps but they are light, barely perceptible, tiptoeing perhaps. I tuck more tightly into the shadows and bury my head in my arms. The person turns into the mermaid's chapel and stops.

I catch a scent. It's a comforting fragrance that I've smelt before but can't place.

I tense every muscle, squeezing myself into the smallest space possible, hoping I can stay hidden, hoping whoever it is will take a look at the pew and then leave. But there is no sound of footsteps leaving and no surprised voice asking me what on earth I am doing huddled up in a dark corner of church. I lift my head a fraction and see a girl standing no more than three metres away. She stares down at me. Her face is placid, expressionless. She says nothing. She is thin, her skin yellowed, tinged purple in places. Her eyes are sunken and she wears a white nightdress.

I know her.

I place the bottle on the floor, lean forward onto my hands and knees, and crawl closer to her, then I sit back down and cross my legs, my movements hindered by the vodka I've drunk, the church tipping around me in loose loops. I squint in an effort to focus.

'Tori?'

There is a peel of gentle laughter. 'No, I'm not Tori.' Her voice is faint and thin. I recognise it. It's not Tori's voice, not the voice I hear in my thoughts, but I have heard this voice before. And this voice is real.

But what is real?

I push my hands into my eye-sockets. When I take them away I expect to see her gone, but she's still there, not moving, contemplating me, her demeanour restful and knowing.

'Are you here to see the mermaid?' I ask. I gesture behind me in the direction of the pew so she knows what I mean.

The little girl shakes her head.

I look at the carving then back at her. 'She's lovely.' I pause, waiting for her to say something, but she stays quiet. 'Where's your mummy?'

Still she doesn't move. Her silence is beginning to unsettle me and my anxiety heightens. With my weight on one hand, I reach back for the bottle of vodka. There's a little over a third of the bottle left. I hesitate for a moment, wondering if it's bad to drink neat spirits in front of a young child. I tip the bottle to my lips, keeping my eyes on her. The little girl stares back at me and then slowly sits down. She crosses her legs and folds her hands neatly in her lap. I breathe in and catch her smell again.

What *is* that smell?

We sit on the cold floor and I drink as she watches.

'I enjoyed our swim,' she says.

A chill shivers its way down my spine. 'What swim?'

She laughs, a soft giggle, as loud as organ music against the silence. 'The swim where I saved you from that nasty black seaweed. You remember.' She giggles again but the giggles are lost beneath the noise of my hammering heart.

I tip the bottle to my lips. It's the vodka. She is an alcoholic hallucination. Perhaps I am asleep beneath a tree by the river and she is my white rabbit.

'I'm properly here, you know. I'm not made up or anything. You kind of call me.'

'Call you?'

'I can hear your voice calling me. You sounded very sad today.'

'I haven't called you.' I am beginning to feel scared, the unease that's building inside me tumbles around like a burgeoning snowball. 'I don't even know your name.'

'You do.'

I want her to leave. I had come to the mermaid for peace and reassurance, not to be freaked out by some peculiar child, real or otherwise. 'Can you go back to wherever you came from now?'

'But I want to talk to you.' She scratches one arm and I notice there is a white plaster in the crook of her arm, with a tiny dot of brown blood at its centre.

'Do you have a mother?'

'Of course. Everyone has a mother!'

'Won't she be wondering where you are?'

'She died.'

'Oh, that's awful. I'm sorry.'

'And my dad,' she says. 'He died too. Everyone's dead. Will you swim with me again?'

I don't reply.

'We could pretend to be mermaids?'

I tip the bottle to my lips. My head swims drunkenly. She smiles at me and, as she does, my trembling unease begins to fade.

I look at her and then at the carving. I beckon her nearer and lean in close. She does the same. 'Do you want to know a secret?' I whisper.

Her eyes light up and she claps her hands together three times in quick succession.

I put my finger to my lips and raise my eyebrows, and she nods again, this time with more solemnity. 'You mustn't tell anyone, but I am a mermaid.'

She sits back, a disappointed look on her face. 'That's not true.'

'It is actually.'

I tip the bottle to my lips. I can hardly taste the vodka now; it slips down my throat like silk over satin.

The girl looks at my legs, her forehead wrinkles and her mouth curls in doubt. 'You've got no tail.'

'Don't you know anything? Mermaids can change their tails into human legs if they want to come on dry land. It's very painful to walk on their new feet though. Every step is like a thousand needles stabbing into our soles.'

'If it hurts so much, why do you come on land?'

'We all have our reasons.' I gesture at the carved mermaid behind me. 'She came to find her one true love. She heard him singing and knew she couldn't live without him.'

The little girl considers the carving with wonder and admiration. 'And you?'

'Me?' I think for a bit. 'It's complicated.'

'Tell me.'

'Tell you why I came here? Well—' I pause, buying myself time to dream up a story for her. 'I came looking for my mother. She's a human, you see, but nobody told me she was. I was taken by mermaids when I was just a baby, and I always thought I was pure mermaid. All my life I lived in the sea in the most beautiful underwater palace that had golden walls and a seaweed garden in a rainbow of colours. I played with the fish and hunted for pearls in the oyster beds, but all that time my real mother was up on the land crying for me. She sung lullabies all the time but I couldn't hear them.'

'Poor her!'

'Absolutely. Poor me too!' I smile. 'So when I found out I had a human mother—'

'How did you find out?' she interrupts.

'It doesn't matter,' I say, waving her question away.

'I want to know.'

I pause to think. 'I started having dreams about humans, especially this one human. A beautiful lady with soft, clear skin who sat on the cliffs all day and all night and wept so many tears they made a stream down to the sea.'

The girl inches closer to me.

'So I went to my father, the king of the Mermaidland.'

'Mermaidland?' She frowns at me. 'Are you *sure*?'

'Fantasia Miracula, then.'

She grins. 'Yes, I knew it was something like that.'

'I asked him if he knew who the lady in my dreams was. He didn't want to tell me, but I begged and begged and begged. And then he told me how he'd fallen in love with a mortal—'

'A mortal?'

'That's another word for a human being. Anyway, they had a daughter. And that was me. I'd been born with a tail, so my mother couldn't keep me, and my father took me to live in the sea with him. If I'd been born with legs, I'd have stayed with her on dry land. My father told me how she cried every day for me and every day it broke his heart to listen to her sobbing.'

'How could he hear her?'

'Her crying came in on the wind.'

'That's sad.'

'Anyway, I pleaded for him to change my tail for legs so I could go and find her. Well, now it was his turn to cry.'

'Too sad to see you go?'

I nod. 'But he could see it was what I really wanted, so he gave me a special magic potion to make my beautiful tail vanish and a pair of legs appear in its place.'

'Is that what you're drinking now, the potion. Does it keep your tail from popping back?'

I laugh. 'It does. It keeps the pain away too, because even though he warned me it would be like a hundred needles stabbing—'

'A thousand.'

'What?'

'You said it was a thousand needles stabbing.'

'Did I? Well, it's lots anyway and it hurts, but the potion helps, because you can't imagine what all those needles stabbing at you all the time feels like. It's *really* sore.'

She grimaces and looks warily at my legs.

'So here I am. On land. A real mermaid.' I smile at her and take another drink.

'Did you find your mother?'

The smile falls from my face. 'Yes, I did.'

'Was she very happy to see you?'

'She was almost dead from sadness.'

The little girl gasps with shock. 'Will you stay with her or will you go back to the sea?'

I shrug and shake my head. 'That's what I'm trying to work out.'

The little girl inches forward and uncurls my fingers from the bottle. Her touch is cold, like ice, and I shiver.

'Take me swimming,' she says as she places the bottle on the floor.

'I want to see your beautiful tail.' She pulls at my arm. 'Come, it'll be fun.'

I hesitate, but she tugs a couple more times, and eventually I stand, struggling to keep my vision focused. I bend shakily for the vodka bottle. 'I have to keep this with me. For the needles,' I say, and she looks at me in sympathy.

Outside my eyes take a while to adjust to the darkness. There are no stars and the black, racing clouds hide and reveal the moon in snatches. The wind is raging and heavy raindrops are driven hard by the rising gale so they sting my face. I follow the girl down the lane towards the sea, every now and then I catch the familiar scent of her. She walks quickly on white-slippered feet and occasionally I lose sight of her and have to hurry my steps. By the time we reach the cliff edge my bottle is drained. I lurch from side to side, tripping over the half-buried rocks. Once I fall and graze my hand. We continue for some time, me stumbling, her trotting beside me like a faithful dog as the wind swirls around us.

'Stop here!' She has to shout to be heard. 'We can get down to the sea from here.'

'Are you sure you want to go in?'

'Yes!' she says. 'I really do! It'll be *wonderful*!'

'I don't think we should, you know.' I am cold now and the darkness makes the thought of the water terrifying. As drunk as I am, I have sense enough to realise that swimming in wind-whipped waves that crash against jagged rocks in near-pitch black is no activity for a small child.

Then the clouds part and the cliff is lit by dappled silver moonlight.

'Look, look!' she squeals, as she kicks off her slippers. 'You can see all the way down. It's fine.'

And then she skips away from me down the sloping grassland that leads to the cliff edge. I call out for her but either my words are taken by the wind or she ignores me.

'Hey!' I call. 'I was joking about being a mermaid! It was a story. We shouldn't go. It's too dangerous!' I watch her deftly skipping over tufts of grass and rocks and around gorse bushes. 'Stop!'

The clouds close in overhead and the cliffs are plunged into blackness once again. And then the heavens open and the rainfall comes fast and heavy and angry. There is a rumble of thunder in the distance.

Hager-awal.

I start to run after her. Calling for her to stop. Please stop. Please. The sea's too dangerous. It was a story. It isn't real.

You mustn't go into the sea.

I reach the edge of the cliff. The land drops away beneath me now, steeper, more severe. Desperate to see through the dark, I squint and scan the cliff. Panic begins to grab hold of me, restricting my breathing, setting my heart racing yet again.

Where are you?

The clouds unveil the moon again and in the light I see her. She is far below me, dancing like a pixie down towards the cliff edge. I run, slipping on the wet grass, my skin tearing as it catches on gorse and brambles. I reach the edge and the rocks make a treacherous stairway down to the sea. I crouch low and using my hands and bottom I clamber down. I reach the rocks at the foot of the cliff. She is standing on the one furthest from me, a flat rock, like an island amid the crashing waves. I call out, but she doesn't turn. I begin to climb out towards her, cutting and grazing my shins and ankles as I slip and stumble on the rocks. A wave breaks, spraying me with freezing saltwater, rolling smaller rocks like marbles at my feet. The spray stings my eyes and the scratches on my legs. There is a flash of lightning. The wind roars in my ears. The sky closes in above me and I can't see a thing.

Another roll of thunder.

I call out for her again, but am hit and nearly bowled into the sea by another breaking wave.

'Stop,' I gasp as I reach her. 'Stop, you can't go in. You'll be killed.'

I breathe deeply, trying to catch my breath and smell her again. I finally place the smell.

Pears Glycerine.

It's the soap Elaine used. The soap we both used when I was growing up. How she loved the smell.

'Don't do it.'

'You're a mermaid remember? We'll be fine. Come on. Can't you hear that beautiful singing?'

When she jumps, I scream.

No, Bella!

My hand reaches blindly for her, desperate to grab a part of her, desperate to stop her. But she is gone. I call out for her.

I search the white, foaming water, boiling like Hell at my feet, but there is nothing, only crashing waves that soak me with every break. And then, quiet as anything, the singing. An exquisite noise carried softly up from beneath the water. The singing calms me enough that I have a moment of clarity.

I have to save her.

I draw in a breath and then jump and I am instantly surrounded by an implausible stillness.

The sea is neither cold nor warm. There are no rocks and no pain and I am surprised to find I am no longer scared. I hold my breath and search for her. And there she is, up ahead, her blonde hair fanned out in the water like a shimmering halo. She reaches out to me, smiling, tiny bubbles escape from her mouth. Then she takes my hand and we swim out, and as we swim the darkness begins to lift. Fabulous-coloured shafts of light cut through the water, showing iridescent fish, and seaweed that glows with neon brightness. It is magnificent.

'See?' she says, pointing at my legs. 'You *are* a mermaid. I knew you were.'

I look down at where she points and see that instead of a pair of jeaned legs there is a tail. I stare at it. It is the most fantastic thing I could have imagined, plastered with a multitude of mother-of-pearl scales that shimmer in an array of greens, purples, reds and blues. Beads of brilliant light flare across its surface as if it were on fire. I move my tail back and forth, feel its strong, muscular pull, and then we're off, cutting through the silken water like a hot iron through ice.

Everything is so beautiful, so tranquil. So safe. I laugh. Of course. This was what Henry Campbell had meant in his letter.

He wished me peace and at last I've found it.

SIXTY-FIVE

Voices lure me like distant fairground music. Snatches of conversation, no discernible words, mumblings that make no sense. I am floating, though not in water. My hair flutters softly, my arms are stretched out like wings. There is sunlight, though I can't tell from where it comes. The voices drift away from me and I fall back into the dark, as if listing on a gentle swell.

Then there is a hand on my forehead.

'Morveren.' The voice is a siren's call. I recognise it.

I struggle to open my eyes and manage a crack. White light blinds me. I see her, but only a glimpse of her, her face bathed in a raft of light.

Then I hear her call urgently. There are more voices, this time nearer. I try to reach out to them, hoping someone will catch me before I float too far away.

'Morveren.' It is a man's voice. 'Can you hear me? Morveren?'

There's a hand on mine. Try to focus.

'Sweetheart.'

I turn my head in the direction of Dawn's voice.

'How are you feeling?'

'The little...' My throat hurts like I've swallowed razorblades. 'A little girl.'

'Shush,' whispers Dawn.

'Try not to speak,' says the man.

'No,' I rasp. 'The girl. Did you find her?'

Dawn shakes her head.

'Who's she talking about?' the man asks Dawn.

Dawn shrugs and rubs my hand.

'She was in the water. I tried to save her.' My head pulses painfully with each word.

'Don't speak,' says Dawn, who strokes my forehead.

'I'll check out the girl with the police and the lifeguards. It could be the morphine.'

I close my eyes.

'She was there. She was in the sea.'

'Get some rest.'

SIXTY-SIX

Craig and Dawn found me in the early hours of the morning.

'I'd hoped you'd come back to the flat, you know, after you'd calmed down, but when you didn't I got worried. I called Craig and he came with me to the hostel, but that girl with the purple hair hadn't seen you. It was Mum who put the idea of the church in my head. That was where she always used to escape. Craig said it was worth a shot, so he borrowed his dad's car and we drove out there. Your bag was by the bench with the mermaid on it.'

They say it was fifty-fifty which way they went, up onto the road that led back to St Ives or down towards the sea on the coastal path. The storm had quelled by then and Dawn was thankful that it was starting to get light.

'I don't think we'd have gone onto the cliffs in the dark. I think we'd have chosen to search the roads.'

They followed the footpath along the coast and just as they were about to give up, questioning why anybody would wander out this way in a storm at night, they found the empty vodka bottle lying next to my trainers.

'Did you see a pair of slippers? Small. White?'

'No,' she says. 'There were no slippers.'

My shoes were near the shallowest part of the cliff, where the grass and heather rolls down to the sea, and she guessed with growing dread that I'd gone down to the water.

'We got nearer and nearer the edge and I was sure I'd find you drowned.' She kisses my hand and tears roll down her cheeks. 'And there you were, sprawled at the foot of the cliff, your skin as white as snow against the black rocks, your hair all matted around your face with seaweed knotted into it so I couldn't tell what was hair and what was weed.' She swallows and kisses my hand again. 'I thought you were dead and I knew at that exact moment that I loved you more than I could ever love anyone.'

She describes how grains of sand and grit were stuck to my bluish lips. How I was bent, contorted, my shoulder cut badly, one arm half-skinned, and how the sea lapped at my feet as if it were kissing me.

'I've never seen the sea that flat. It was like a mirror.' She smoothes the bedcovers that lie across me. 'I told Craig not to move you. For all we knew you'd broken your back or your neck or whatever. So he took off his jacket and put it over you, and then I laid down next to you on the rocks, hoping my body would keep you warm. Of course, there's no bloody mobile reception anywhere around Zennor, so Craig ran back to the pub and hammered on the door until they woke and he could use their phone to call in the coast guard. The helicopter was there within fifteen minutes.'

Dawn tells how she shielded me from the wind caused by the helicopter blades and cupped her hands over my ears to block out the sound. They hovered above us, let down a stretcher, then flew me away from her.

'We were lucky,' she says. 'Half an hour more, they said, and the tide would have risen over us and we'd have drowned.' She strokes my forehead. 'I'd never have left you. I'd have stayed with you until the end, until the sea took us both.'

Later that afternoon a doctor appears and sits on the edge of my bed.

'How are you feeling?' he asks.

'My arm is sore, and my ribs are a bit tender, but otherwise, I feel fine.'

'You've had quite a day or two.'

'Actually, it's been quite a month or two.'

'So I gather. The papers have been camped outside the hospital since you arrived.'

'I'm sorry about that.'

He smiles. 'Oh, don't worry. I quite like it. I pretended I was a celebrity yesterday and went out with my sunglasses on. And,' he says somewhat triumphantly, 'you're trending on Twitter.'

My stomach turns over. 'How long will I have to stay in?"

His face falls serious as he remembers he's a doctor and not a film star. 'A few days. We need to keep you in for observation. And you have to finish the intravenous antibiotics. You were lucky you didn't break anything. Something or someone must have been looking out for you. Not that I believe in that kind of thing.' He laughs. 'And there's something else.'

'Yes?'

'Are you aware that you're pregnant?'

'That's not possible.' I shake my head. 'I can't be.'

'It's early, only two or three weeks.'

'But I can't be pregnant. We've been trying. The doctors said it was unspecific infertility.'

'Infertility is a difficult call.'

My disbelief is replaced with a vivid recollection of the vodka I'd drunk. 'But the other night. I drank so much.'

'Your baby should be fine. You'd be surprised how good the body is at protecting the foetus. Most alcohol-related complications during pregnancy occur when the mother gets drunk and falls over.' He laughs, which seems inappropriate, so I don't smile. 'Don't worry, Morveren. A binge or two in the early days of pregnancy is unlikely to do any harm.'

He stands, checks the chart that hangs over the foot of the bed, then leaves.

How can I be pregnant?

I rest my hands against my stomach. I remember feeling tired, faint even, but put it down to stress and the nightmares that plagued me. I remember occasional sweeps of nausea. The baby is Greg's, of course. We'd not used protection. I told him it was fine because I couldn't get pregnant. Why Greg? I hate Greg.

When I tell Dawn, she beams. 'That's wonderful.'

'It is?'

'How could it not be? It's a baby.'

'But I don't want to be with Greg.'

'Well, you're married to David, so first you have to decide whether you still want to be with him, I think.'

My stomach twists at the thought of David, of my infidelity, of his desperation to have a child, and I close my hand around the healed cut from the photo frame and wonder briefly if he'd accept the baby as his.

'I'm scared, Dawn. Scared of telling David and scared of being a mum.'

'You just have to be honest with David. And as for being a mum? You'll be brilliant.'

Later that afternoon, a nurse appears at the door. 'Morveren, dear, you've another visitor.' She sets a fresh jug of water on the table beside me and clears away my lunch plate. 'It's your husband.'

'David?'

'Have you got more than one?' she says with a laugh.

I feel myself panic as I remember that my wedding ring is in the drawer of the bedside table at the hostel. I swear silently. Maybe I could pretend it came off in the sea. He couldn't be cross with me about that, surely?

'The doctor said I can take the drip out now. Let's get it out before he comes in. You'll feel more comfy then.'

I hold out my arm and she removes the cannula, wipes my arm with a piece of cotton wool, then sticks a small white plaster on it. I watch a pinprick of blood bloom on the white and have a flash of the little girl's arm that night in the church. She had the same plaster on the inside of her elbow. The same prick of blood. This flash triggers a second memory, like a row of falling dominoes, a subliminal memory I can't recall having had before. There's a bed with clean white sheets, the smell of cleaning fluids and disinfectant. Henry Campbell is there. He's stroking my head. My mind fuzzes. Or is it me? I try everything I can to grasp the memory but it slips away before I can grab hold.

My heart begins to beat faster. I recall my voice calling into the raging wind and rain just before I swam in the sea.

No, Bella!

My head throbs. There are things I can't remember. Snatches and flashes like pieces of a scattered jigsaw. Why can't I remember? I push my fingers into my temples until it hurts.

The nurse bustles out and takes the old water jug with her.

'Can't you stay with me?' I call after her without thinking.

She turns to me. 'Won't your husband want to talk to you alone?'

'Please stay.'

I see a knowing look spread over her face, and her eyes look at me kindly. 'I'll be outside. You need me – for anything – you call me, OK? You can press the button or shout. Or,' she says, 'I can tell him you don't want to see him.'

She looks at me for a moment or two and I know she understands, but then I shake my head. 'No, I have to talk to him.' I try to smile, but can't manage it.

When she leaves, I turn my head to look out of the window. It overlooks the hospital courtyard and out to the wards on the other side. The brick between the windows is grey and grimy, the glass puncturing it like dull, black mirrors. Behind each I imagine people lying in beds in rooms that look like mine. Why were they there? Appendicitis. Cancer. Undiagnosable diseases with poor prognoses? Every window held a different story. Was any as strange as mine?

David coughs as he comes into the ward. I try to smile at him but I am filled with an anxiety so thick that it makes it impossible. I'm aware of not having brushed my hair, of looking pale, and having lost some weight and I wish I'd checked my appearance in the mirror. He carries a bag, which he drops onto the floor when he sees me. He doesn't say anything but takes a few moments to draw the curtains around the bed and I feel immediately hemmed in.

'Don't draw them,' I say, but it's only a whisper.

'Good God, I could kill you for what you've put me through,' he says as he bends to kiss my forehead. 'I've been so worried.'

He kisses my lips. He smells familiar but not comforting.

'Tell me you will never, ever do something like this again. Do you hear me?'

'I'm ... sorry.'

He doesn't reply. I want him to tell me I have nothing to be sorry about and that he only cares that I'm safe. But, of course, he won't.

'How did you find me?' I ask. The atmosphere is getting more and more claustrophobic. The air tighter. I want him to pull back the curtains that seal us off from the ward.

He strokes his fingers down my cheek, studies my face, his eyes scanning me as if checking for damage.

'The newspapers. Your story is all over the place. The Campbells, I can't believe what they did. I knew they were strange, not normal, and I even had my suspicions about them. But, God, I never thought they were capable of something like that.'

He seems disappointed in himself for not spotting it, as if he has somehow failed, as if it were his mistake that they got away with it.

The lady in the bed nearest mine coughs, a thick rasping cough, which ends with a hollow whimper as she deals with her pain.

'You can't stay here. I need to get you home.'

I have to tell him about the baby.

He sighs heavily. 'I haven't been able to think with you gone. My work has suffered dreadfully. I assume you got my letter? That you know about Jeffrey. He has struggled to find someone to take over, but I think he has someone at last, thank God.'

The baby.

'We need to talk,' I say.

'Yes, we have plenty of time, first of all I need to get you home, back in our own bed. You need looking after.'

I don't say any more. I am happy not to have to do it now. He will be devastated. All those times I'd waited for a suitable moment to break the news that there was no pregnancy yet again, preparing for his face to cloud and his scant attempt to cover his disappointment, jollying himself along with a tight *I'm sure it will happen next month,* when all I'd wanted to hear was that it didn't matter and that we could stop trying.

The night before Elaine died he suggested IVF. I told him I didn't want IVF. That the injections, the complications, the pressure of carrying the child to term, scared me. But I could see the resolution in his eyes, the determination, the single-mindedness. And then the next day she died and the subject didn't come up again. But it is lurking there like a predator ready to ambush. Maybe I should tell him the baby is his. The dates wouldn't work, but would he care? Maybe it could be unspoken, we would just not address it, pretend the child is his. I'll never tell and he'll never ask. We will explain the early birth with a dismissive shake of our heads, and he will have what he wants and I'll have a husband to look after me. To tell me what to do. To make my decisions.

But then, as this thought drifts into my head, I begin to feel faint.

'You've gone quite green, my darling,' he says. 'You need to rest.'

'Yes,' I whisper.

'I'll stay with you.'

'I'll only be asleep.'

He looks doubtful.

'I'll call when I wake. Where are you staying?'

'A hotel in Penzance. It's seen better days, but then, Christ, the whole town has. Thankfully we won't be here long.' He takes my hand in his. 'And I've found a doctor, a therapist, who can see you. You'll like her and she has a very good reputation of dealing with all sorts of depression.'

'I don't need a therapist.'

'For God's sake, you tried to kill yourself. Of course you need a therapist.'

'Kill myself? No ... that's not what—'

'You threw yourself into the damned sea in the middle of the night! What else do you call that, Bella?'

The name washes over me like a wave. There are no flashbacks, no panic, no recollections of Elaine or The Old Vicarage.

I shake my head and set my mouth. 'My name isn't Bella. It's Morveren Tremayne.'

SIXTY-SEVEN

'The trust fund you mentioned when you explained Henry Campbell's will to me, are you able to investigate it?'

'Investigate it?'

'You said it was dormant, that nothing had been paid into it or out of it for over twenty years, yet there was a sum of money in it.'

'The money has been absorbed into the estate, so no longer resides in the fund.'

'But is there any way of knowing what it was used for? What the payments were for?'

'Yes, of course. It will mean a little bit of work. Going back that far, looking at accounts that old isn't as straightforward as it would be using recent accounts. But I can definitely do it.'

'Thank you. I'd appreciate that.'

'Can I ask why?'

I hesitate. 'There's no reason really. Well, possibly. I suppose with the complications that we've spoken about, given my identity and the abduction, it would be helpful.'

'Yes. To be honest, I imagine the police would ask to see the information in due course anyway. We might as well be ahead of the game. I'll get back to you as soon as I have any further details.'

'Thank you, I appreciate that.'

'Did you go to the house in Bristol?'

'I did,' I say, trying not to hesitate. 'Nothing of interest there. It looked like Henry might have been meeting a woman there. It might not be that, of course, I can't say for sure.'

I don't say any more. I haven't told anyone other than Dawn that

Mark Tremayne was living there and that he knew the Campbells had taken me. I am sure there's a chance he will go to prison when people find out, and I don't find the thought of this easy to stomach. There's no doubting that in the past, maybe even still today, he was, or is, a violent alcoholic and a liar, but he is also a broken man, a man with no hope and no self-worth, and he used Henry Campbell's money to support Dawn and my mother from afar. He'd lived in squalor and, however misguided, had done what he felt best to make amends for his failings. This, perhaps combined with a perverse loyalty to my blood-father, makes me reluctant to hand him over to the police.

My solicitor clears her throat as if dislodging something uncomfortable. 'Now, regarding the complication in terms of your identity, there is no contest to your claim on the will. The clause he added – which makes sense now, of course – leaves no doubt that Dr Campbell fully intended you to be sole beneficiary of the estate.'

I don't say anything.

'Are you selling both houses?'

'Yes. Both.'

'In which case, you will need to go to The Old Vicarage and go through their personal belongings and effects.'

'Do I have to?' I think about walking back through those gates, across the driveway, and then approaching the house with its clambering roses and its Virginia creeper and lurking ghosts, and fear soaks me.

'No, you don't. There are people who do it for you. I can recommend a couple of firms. Perhaps have a think about it and get back to me.'

'No. I'll go.' As I say the words I shiver. 'I need to.'

SIXTY-EIGHT

The last memory I have of Alice Tremayne is seeing her shivering with fear and shock while those hideous journalists pushed at the door.

'She's alright, isn't she?'

Dawn smiles. 'She's fine.' She puts her hand on my knee. 'She can't wait to see you.'

Dawn gets out of the taxi and then takes my hand as I climb out carefully. My ribs are very bruised and hurt with even the slightest movement. I told David I didn't want him there. Predictably he didn't want me to go, not without him, but I managed to stand up to him, which made me feel stronger. He doesn't understand that I need to see Dawn and Alice on my own, that I don't want the added pressure of him there, of worrying about what he thinks of them, knowing he'd be judging them, the flat, the way they talk. I don't want him to take over or try to mediate or offer us his sensible advice. It's not his situation to solve.

I stand for a few minutes and enjoy the warm breeze on my face. I breathe in Cornwall, the salty air, the gorse on the hills, the call of the gulls, the hum of traffic ferrying the visitors in and out of St Ives. I allow my eyes time to take in the front door of the flat with its green peeling paint, remembering what it felt like to stand on the same spot in the rain, adrenaline coursing my veins as I willed myself to knock for the first time, to step through that portal.

'Come on,' says Dawn, unlocking the door. 'She's desperate to see you.'

I take a deep breath to prepare myself for the thick, heavy air, but as I step into the hall, I gasp in surprise. I look at Dawn and she grins.

'It needed doing.'

She has painted the hall a light cream. The brown, wiry carpet has gone and at the end of the hall spans a foil banner in rainbow colours saying: *Welcome home!*

'There are floorboards,' I say.

'The carpet was awful, wasn't it? When I pulled it up these boards were underneath. Craig sanded them for me and gave them a coat of floor varnish. They need another really, but we didn't have time.'

'I can't believe how much lighter it looks. And you painted it yourself?'

Dawn holds up her hands by way of explanation. They are covered in cream splodges and I notice the skin between the paint marks is pink, not red and raw.

'I only had time to do the hall before today. Craig said he'd help with the rest. I think he enjoys it.'

I smile.

'And I was wrong, by the way,' she says. I stare at her face and I'm warmed by how lit up she is from within.

'About?'

'Change. Mum loves the hall. And thank you for the new television, it was delivered a few days ago. That was kind. You didn't have to.'

In the kitchen there are flowers and I notice a new tea towel folded over the edge of the sink, fresh and white with little flowers running along the edge. Alice stands beside the table, hands clasped stiffly in front of her, her cheeks rosy, eyes shining.

'You know something, Morveren Tremayne?' she says. 'I've spent nearly my entire life worrying about you.'

I walk over to her and wrap my arms around her. Even though she is unrecognisable as the skeletal person in the faded dressing gown, there is still nothing to her, and I hold her gently for fear of crushing her.

'Oh, my darling,' she whispers through her tears. 'Oh my dearest darling.'

'Morveren?' calls Dawn from her bedroom.

I drop my arms and step back from Mum, pushing the sleeve of my shirt against my eyes to dry the tears. 'Yes?'

'I've something else to show you.'

Mum smiles knowingly as Dawn appears carrying a large cardboard box.

'What is it?' I ask.

She rests the box on the table and gestures for me to open it. I lift a flap and peer inside. With a small mew, the cat pops both her front paws up on the side of the box and reaches up to touch her nose to my fingers.

'You were right about her, too,' Dawn says. 'I took her to the vet after you left that evening we broke the television. He said it was touch and go. But she made it. They had to take her leg, but otherwise she's fine.'

I pick her out of the box, careful not to catch the stitches that tie a large line of shaved fur where her leg used to be. I stroke beneath her chin and she starts purring immediately.

'Poor you,' I whisper. 'Three legs, that's going to take some getting used to, isn't it?'

'I wasn't able to pay the bill immediately, so I was hoping you might be able to help out. Just a loan, though. I'll pay it back. She is my cat after all. And she can't go on being called Cat.'

Mum shakes her head sadly. 'Yes, poor mite needs a better name than that.'

'Have you chosen one?'

'I wanted to run it past you,' she says. 'I thought Nino. It's the nickname of John William Waterhouse, the painter who did that mermaid picture I gave you. That or maybe Tripod, which is the only other name that sprung to mind.'

I laugh. 'Nino suits her.' I touch my lips to her soft head. 'Eh, Nino? Do you like your new name? Don't worry, you'll get used to it.'

We make tea, eat custard creams and chat easily. We don't talk about the past or about our relationships with each other. There is no talk of regret or missing out. All the time, I hold Mum's hand, stroking my thumb over hers.

'I've been thinking about what to do with myself,' Dawn says. 'Mum and I have talked and she'll be fine for a few hours a day.'

'That's great,' I say. 'And I can help, too. Just as soon as I've sorted my head out a bit.'

'I know, but you'll have other things to think about. You've got the baby to deal with. Mum and I aren't going anywhere.'

'I keep forgetting about the baby,' I say. 'I suppose I'll get used to the idea soon. So what is it you want to do?'

'There's a course, an NVQ in Health and Social Care, in Truro. It's not long; I mostly learn on the job. When I spoke to them on the phone they were really positive about me having been a carer already.'

I don't say anything.

'Don't look at me like that. It's what I want to do. I enjoy it. I'm good at it too.'

'But—'

'It's flexible, I can work it round Mum and the money's better than you'd imagine.' She looks at Alice and smiles. 'I want to do something that's going to follow on from how I've spent my life, not be a full stop to it.'

I look at my sister, overwhelmed by admiration for her. A person so resolute, so sure of herself. From the moment Elaine Campbell carried me unresisting away from my life, other people had controlled me. I was envious of Dawn.

'The course sounds great. You'll be brilliant.'

'You think so?'

'I know so.'

Later, I am with Mum in her room. 'You know Dawn thinks it's her fault I was taken don't you.'

Alice is quiet.

'That's what our dad told her. At least that's what she said to me. You don't blame her too, do you?'

'Of course I don't,' she says, shaking her head. 'How could I?'

'That's what I told her,' I say. 'She was too young to have been left in charge of me.'

'She was too young to have been left in charge of herself. I was lucky I didn't lose her too. But I was so scared he was going to hurt one of you. He was so angry that night. Had such a rage inside him, had the devil eyes. I panicked. I just wanted you away from him until I'd calmed him down or he'd passed out. I was going to leave him. I had this plan that the three of us would move away, live happily some-where. I wanted a vegetable patch and a dog. I had it all worked out. Best-laid plans, I suppose.'

I touch my fingers to the scar on my arm, the scar Dawn said he'd given me with a lit cigar.

'I should have been stronger from the start. I let him run roughshod over me. I did everything wrong, never stood up to him properly. And then, after you went, when I should have been there for Dawn, I let my grief destroy me. I should never have put Dawn through what I did. I should have cherished her, every bone, every hair, but I took her child-hood. Depression is a dangerous beast, once it gets hold of you, gets its claws into you, it's a devil to escape.'

'Dawn said you never believed I was dead.'

'Not for one moment. I used to see you everywhere. Walking down the street, on the television, in the shops, on the ferry. My heart would leap for a moment and then I'd realise it wasn't you and I'd feel dead again.' She smiles at me faintly. 'I could hear your heartbeat. If I con-centrated hard. I'd spend hours in those early days being still and quiet so I could hear it. I knew someone had you. I knew you were alive. I can only thank God it was her that took you and not a murderer.'

'I wish I knew why they took me. And how. How did they go to France and come back with a child and nobody notice? I have so many questions but I'll never know, will I? Not when the only two people who have the answers are dead.' I pause for a moment or two. 'Do you hate them?' I ask then.

'The "them" who snatched you?' She raises her eyebrows a little.

I don't reply.

'I'm supposed to hate them, aren't I?' she says. 'I'm supposed to hate them with every breath in my body. And in a way, I do. But it was my fault you went. Me that sent you out of that caravan. They found you – God, knows where – and even though they took you they kept you safe. You're here. Alive. Maybe if they hadn't taken you, you would have wandered into the sea and drowned? Maybe it's not as easy as just hating them. Maybe it's not that simple.'

SIXTY-NINE

'**D**o you mind waiting for me?' I ask David. 'I won't be long.'

He nods, though I can tell he's not happy at being excluded, and then leans forward to turn on the radio. JazzFM blurts out as I climb out of the car and walk up to Craig's front door and knock.

'Hello, Morveren,' he says, in a way that instantly rids my tummy of the fluttering butterflies. 'It's good to see you up and about.'

'Thank you so much.'

'What for?'

'For saving my life.'

He shrugs as if it was nothing. 'I'm not sure any of us could have coped with losing you again.'

I smile at him.

'Would you like to meet Stacey?'

His place is small and lived in; it feels like a home, with school work piled on the table in the corner of the living room and DVDs scattered on the floor by the television. Something is bubbling away on the hob in the kitchen. The girl I'd seen with him that day is sitting on the sofa, watching television, eating a packet of crisps.

'Stacey,' says Craig. 'This is Morveren.'

The girl looks up and smiles. She puts her bag of crisps on the sofa beside her then wipes her hands on her leggings. 'Hi,' she says, a little shyly, and I can see Dawn in her immediately. 'Are you feeling better?' she asks, as she turns off the television with the remote.

'Much better, thank you.' I sit next to her on the sofa and become intensely aware of the baby inside me. 'It's good to meet you.'

'You look like my mum.'

A lump catches in my throat.

'Do you want a drink?' Craig says from behind me. 'Tea or juice?'

'No, thank you,' I say.

'Stace?'

'I'll do it, Dad.' She stands up. 'Juice?'

'Lovely,' he says.

'She's a pretty girl,' I say, when Stacey leaves the room.

'Beautiful,' he says. 'And clever, too. A real hard worker.'

'You must be very proud.'

'Couldn't be prouder of anything.' He laughed. 'And I'm flattered you thought any girl so young and beautiful would fancy someone like me.'

I feel myself blushing and look down at my hands. 'I'm sorry about—'

'It's fine,' he says. 'No harm done. How were you supposed to know?'

Stacey comes back with two glasses. She hands one to Craig, then sits back down.

'Mum says you're going to have a baby.'

'I am.'

'That'll be so cool,' she says, her eyes shining. 'It'll be like having my very own little brother or sister and I've always wanted one.'

I resist taking her hands in mine and dancing around the room. 'Yes,' I say. 'It will be just like that.'

I don't stay long. I am aware of David in the car and don't want him getting impatient. In any case, Craig and Stacey and I have plenty of time to catch up and get to know each other.

'You can come over any time,' Craig says. 'You're family, after all.'

'Thanks, I'd like that.' I turn to Stacey. 'And how about we go for a coffee together soon?'

'Sounds great.'

I get back into the car and David drives us into St Ives. The silence in the car is oppressive. I can hear him breathing. Can feel his irritation growing in the way he beats his fingers on the top of the steering wheel. He parks in one of the car parks towards the back of the town and we walk down towards the harbour. He tries to hold my hand but I cross my arms so he can't.

'I knew you'd find it too hard to cope on your own.'

'I didn't do badly.' I tighten my arms around myself.

'Drinking a bottle of vodka and then throwing yourself into the sea?' he says with a disparaging laugh.

I stop and he turns to see why. I am about to question him, ask him why he feels the need to say that, but then he smiles, like he always does, to show me he means it with affection, and so I start walking again and let his comment slide, and as I do I begin to feel my old life creeping back.

We reach the harbour and Phil's café. Drizzle begins to spritz my face. I look up at the sky; it's the same dirty white it was on the day I first stepped off the train in Penzance.

'What do you feel like?' I ask him. 'Phil does a great cappuccino.'

But it isn't Phil behind the counter.

'Is Phil here?' I ask the new man.

'No, mate, he's gone.' The man has an earring in his right ear, spiked grey hair and an accent from the east end of London.

'Gone? Gone where? I only saw him a week ago.'

'He left pretty quick. He's gone back up north.'

'He's coming back though?'

'Don't think so, not to live anyway. I'm looking after this place until they find someone permanently.'

'Oh. I see.' I can't hide my disappointment.

'Now, what can I get you?'

'Two cappuccinos, please.'

'Ah, you're not Tori are you?' he asks, wiping his hands on his apron.

I glance at David who raises his eyebrows.

'Yes, that's me. Sort of.'

'He asked me to give you something when you came in.' The man disappears and returns with a letter. 'Here you go.' I take hold of it and thank him. 'I'm Ed, by the way. I'm glad you showed up. I was a bit worried I wouldn't know who you were and he was quite keen you got the letter. He said you had green eyes and liked your cappuccinos.' He winks and I smile. 'Right, now, two of the same coming up.'

He certainly doesn't have Phil's craftsmanship, but when I take the coffees he smiles brightly.

'It's good to meet you, Tori.'

'Actually, my name is Morveren.'

Ed looks confused.

'It's complicated,' I say. 'Phil knew me as Tori, but it's not my real name.'

I join David on one of the tables outside, protected from the drizzle by a stripy sun-awning 'You know, I still have no idea who I am,' I say to him. 'Am I Bella or Morveren? An only child or a sister? Phil thinks I'm Tori. Miss Young thinks I'm Bella. You do too. Dawn and Mum only know me as Morveren.'

'Well, as Shakespeare said, a rose is still a rose.'

'I'm not sure this is quite what he had in mind.'

While David checks his mobile phone, tutting under his breath as he reads an email, I open the letter.

Tori,

I wanted to say goodbye face to face, but you've not been in for a bit. I'm off to see if I can make a go of it with my wife. You got me thinking. I still love her and if we can get back together I'd be the happiest man alive. Life is short and we only get one shot. Might as well be heudh (that means 'happy', love).

Hope the weather stays good.

Phil

I fold the letter and slip it into my back pocket. 'Phil has gone back to his old life,' I say, looking out across the harbour. The breeze buffets my hair and strokes my face with rain that's barely there.

David makes a grunting noise, but doesn't look up from his phone.

'Can I ask you something?' I say.

He lays his phone on the table and looks at me.

'Do you remember what you said that day in Norfolk?'

'Norfolk? Well, I certainly remember Norfolk. I don't remember everything I said. I said lots of things, didn't I?'

'When you gave me the ring.'

David looks puzzled. 'I asked you to marry me.'

'You didn't ask me to marry you, David. You told me to marry you. You said, *Marry me*. There was no question mark.'

He laughs at me and furrows his brow. 'I don't think it needs to be a question. It can be statement of intent or even a plea.'

'You tell me what to do all the time. You do everything for me. You overpower me.'

'That's not true.'

'You make sure I'm warm enough. You tell me when to get out of bed. You found me my job. You check to see if I've fastened my seatbelt properly. Even if I've checked myself.'

'That's habit. I love you and I want to keep you safe. All of those are things people do for those they love.'

'You won't let me cook.'

'You don't like cooking.'

'But that's just it, David. I do like cooking.'

'You should have said then.'

'I didn't know I did. I'd never had an opportunity to find out.'

'And you think this is my fault? Is that what you're suggesting? Surely, if you tell me you don't cook and then you *don't* cook, unless we're to starve, what am I to do?'

'I'm not saying it's your fault. I know it's mine, too. Elaine used to tell me what to do all the time. She wouldn't even let me breathe on my own. When I left her, I headed off into the world totally unprepared. I was lost without her and I needed you to take over from her. I needed someone in control of me because I wasn't strong enough. I'd never been allowed to be. I married you because you told me to and I was happy to be told.'

'You're being ridiculous and all this pseudo-analysing is rather upsetting. We have a marriage that works. You want to be looked after and I want to look after you. What's so wrong with that?'

'I'm different now. I have been alone and I had to cope and I did. Maybe not like you would have done, but I did. You told me I wouldn't cope alone so often I believed it. I might cope hopelessly, but I'm getting there. I don't want to be scared of being in control of my own life anymore. If I fall flat on my face, if I make mistakes, it doesn't matter, because I tried.' I put my hand on his. 'Does any of this make sense?'

'Not really. I think everything that's happened to you has got you confused. I understand that, but I don't think you do.'

'If I ask you something will you answer me honestly?'

'If I can.'

'Was I the first of your students you slept with?'

He looks shocked. 'Why are you asking me that?'

'I want to know if I was the first.'

Silence.

'Was I?'

'No,' he says, his voice suddenly defiant. 'You weren't.'

'Was I the second?'

He doesn't answer.

I look out across the sea. The gulls are circling in large, screeching groups behind a fishing boat that chugs slowly back through the opening in the harbour wall.

'You were the last, though.' He lifts my hand to his mouth and kisses it. 'And the only one I married. You are my precious girl.'

We sit within feet of each other but are a million miles away. Our marriage is finished. It was finished when I chose not to rely on him. When I slipped Henry Campbell's letter into my pocket and told him I'd burnt it. When I realised there was more to me than just being someone's possession, that being controlled isn't the same as being loved and that to find out who I really am I need to fly free.

'It's over, David.'

He shakes his head and grabs at my hand. I pull away from him and stand up. I cross the road and step onto the sand of the harbour beach.

'You don't know what you're saying,' he says, following me. 'I told you, you're confused. You've only just got out of hospital for God's sake.'

'I don't love you anymore,' I say, turning to face him. The drizzle is heavier now and strands of hair around my face stick wetly to my skin.

'Because of the other girls? They meant nothing. Nothing at all.'

'No. Not because of them.'

'Then what's put this idiocy into your head? Because you're wrong, I know you love me.'

'You see? That's the problem. What you just said. Telling me. All the time. That's what's put this in my head. I don't want this anymore. I'm a different person, David. More than just by name. These last few months have changed me, and I'm sorry, I really am, but our marriage is over.'

He puts his hands on my shoulders and his eyes lock onto mine so intensely I have to look away. His fingers dig into my shoulders. They squeeze tighter and begin to hurt me.

'Don't do this,' he says. His eyes are hooded, not with love or even desperation, but anger and affront.

A gull cries overhead.

'I won't let you do—'

'I'm pregnant.'

David's fingers release their grip and his hands fall to his sides. His eyes search my face, but I look away from him, listen to the gulls and the waves and the children playing.

'Pregnant?'

'It's not yours.'

'Whose? Whose baby is it?'

'It doesn't matter.'

'How long have you been seeing him?'

'I'm not seeing him. We had sex three times.'

'But how could you? While I was worrying about you? Day and

night. I didn't stop thinking about you. I couldn't sleep or eat. I couldn't work. How could you?'

I don't reply.

'Do you love him?'

'No, I don't love him.'

'Why are you doing this to me? I was there for you always. I cared for you and loved you and now you do this to me?'

'I'm sorry, David.' I reach out to touch him, but he shakes his head and steps backwards.

His desperate eyes flick back and forth over my face. 'Is this why you said all those things? Because of this baby?'

'I don't—'

'You thought I wouldn't want anything to do with you so you were pushing me away.' He puts his hands over his face and is silent for a few minutes. I don't say anything. I let him process what he's feeling. Soon he lowers his hands and looks at me. 'I think we can still make it work. Get rid of this baby. We will forget all about this. It'll be like it never happened. Get rid of it and we'll start again.'

'No, David,' I say gently, my body flooding with strength and conviction. 'I'm keeping my baby.'

'Then it's over.'

'Yes,' I say. 'It's over.'

And then he turns and stumbles away from me across the sand like a broken soldier.

SEVENTY

My mobile phone rings and I recognise my solicitor's number so I excuse myself from the kitchen and slip outside the door to stand on the patch of crumbling concrete that constitutes the tiny back yard.

'So,' she says, after we exchange perfunctory pleasantries. 'I'm actually calling about Dr Campbell's estate and, specifically, the dormant trust fund in your name that I've been looking into.'

'Oh,' I say. 'I'd forgotten about that.' I'm not sure I'm that bothered about raking over the details of the will, but I don't tell her this, instead I stay quiet and let her talk as I pick at the paint on the rotting door frame with my fingernail.

'So, it transpires that...' She pauses, perhaps to find her place in her notes. 'The payments into this fund came from a variety of different sources. Some were family members of the Campbells.'

My ears prick up at this. 'But they were estranged from their families.'

'There are several payments made from Fraser Campbell, who is Henry Campbell's brother, and also from their father's account. There are other payments too, from a variety of sources in varying amounts. A nursery in Bristol and a Christian association amongst others.'

'But why would all these people pay into an account with my name on it? What was the money used for?'

'Well, the payments out of the fund, which were administered – as I told you previously – by Dr Campbell, were paid to a number of institutions and individual professionals. And all of them were located,' the solicitor hesitates again, 'in France.'

'In France?'

'Yes. One recipient was a hospital. Another a hospice called L'Hospice de Fragonat, in Les Sages des Montes, not far from Lourdes and about six miles from Vaiches.'

'Vaiches?' My heart skips a beat. 'But isn't that where the campsite is? The one I went missing from?'

'Exactly. And the dates coincide with your disappearance.'

'But ... I don't understand.' My head grapples with what she's telling me, but none of it makes sense.

'The payments were covering treatment.'

'I was in hospital?' I press my fingers against my temple and squeeze my eyes shut. 'So the Campbells admitted me to hospital? How come the police didn't find me?'

'No, the monies were transferred before you were taken from the campsite. The last payment out of the fund was to the hospice. It was made the day after your parents reported you missing. I hope you don't mind, but I telephoned the hospice. Given your circumstances and the coincidences, I wanted to dig a little deeper.'

'And?'

'Remarkably they had records, sketchy handwritten notes, but they were there. The lady I spoke to was very helpful. She said that Bella Campbell was discharged from L'Hospice de Fragonat on August the sixteenth 1989. Two days after Morveren Tremayne was reported missing.'

'But there isn't a Bella Campbell. I'm Bella Campbell.'

'There was another child.'

My stomach turns over. 'What? Bella is real? They had a real daughter?'

'They did. Again, her medical records are fairly limited – nothing like what we would find today – but what notes there are show that Bella Campbell was a very sick child. She was suffering with an inoperable brain tumour, and receiving treatment at a specialist neurosurgery not far from Paris for several months before being discharged. She was then transferred to Fragonat at the end of July for palliative care; she was never going to survive.'

'They knew she was dying?'
'Yes. They knew.'
They knew she was dying.
And so they replaced her.

SEVENTY-ONE

Henry Campbell – 15th August 1989

'You have to take her to the police.'

'No, she's staying with me.'

'What on earth are you saying? I don't believe what I'm hearing.'

Their voices were strained, low, angry whispers designed not to wake the little girl who lay sleeping in the bed.

'I'm saying this child is a miracle. I am supposed to save this child. We will lose Bella, but I'm supposed to be a mother. I'm supposed to be this child's mother.'

'But she has parents who are looking for her.'

'They are monsters, not parents! Henry, look, she's covered in bruises. She's thin and terrified. She called to me.'

'For crying out loud. Are you listening to yourself, Elaine?'

'Bella will die. The child I longed for all those years. You really think I'm not supposed to be a mother? Well, in the next few days or weeks she will die. When we were told there was nothing more they could do and we went to Lourdes, and I begged Her, mother to mother, for a miracle. I felt Her love. I felt it, Henry. And then the very next day I find this child? It's no coincidence. It's a miracle. This is why I'm here. I was supposed to find this child and I am supposed to save her.'

'No,' he said. 'We won't do this.'

'So you'll send me to prison? Because if you go to the police I will run with her. I won't be here when you get back. I'll disappear and you won't see me again, and they'll hunt for me. If I'm caught they will send me to prison. Is that what you want?'

'What I *want*? Of course that isn't what I want! But you're talking about abduction, taking a child from her parents. Her mother. A mother who loves her like you love Bella.'

'Her mother doesn't deserve her. She is beaten and scared. Did you not listen? Do you want to send her back to that abuse and cruelty or do you want to do something good? I can save her, Henry. *We* can save her.'

'This is insane,' he breathed. 'I can't listen to this a moment longer. I'm going to the police. I have to.' Henry Campbell turned and walked towards the door.

'Do you love me, Henry?'

He stopped in his tracks and faced her. He took in her honey-coloured hair tied messily up on her head, her sunken cheekbones hollowed out by misery, her eyes emptied of tears. He had loved her with a depth and passion that had made his heart race and his breathing shallow since the moment he saw her sitting across a crowded bar in her red silk dress. Though his parents didn't take to her, thinking her somewhat hysterical and tarred with personality tics that made her company difficult, he hadn't cared. The intense love at first sight had endured, through glorious courtship, an oftentimes turbulent marriage, and even – against the odds – the agony of watching their vibrant, beautiful daughter waste away to non-existence.

He glanced at the little girl curled up in the bed. 'Yes, I love you. More than you will ever understand.'

'And you'd do anything for me?'

He closed his eyes and shook his head. 'But Elaine. This?'

'If you take this child away from me I will kill myself. I will do it and it will be on your head.'

'Elaine—'

'I mean it; I'll kill myself.'

Her eyes blazed, the raised vein on her neck pulsed quickly, like an animal twitching beneath her translucent skin. She wasn't lying. He knew she was telling him the truth, that she would kill herself, and then he would have a dead daughter and a dead wife. He would be left with nothing but searing grief. He collapsed onto his knees, broken by his own weakness.

The next day Henry Campbell carried his daughter from the hospice. Her head rested against his shoulder. She was light in his arms. Such a tiny thing, so thin, nothing to her. She smelt of medicines and painkillers, of disinfectant and a hint of the lavender oil designed to mask it. Her breathing was steady but shallow, warm on his neck. He stroked her hair, soft silken curls, fine as strands of spider's web; somewhere beneath them was the tumour that slowly claimed her.

'There you go, my darling,' he whispered, as he opened the car door and laid her gently on the back seat.

He covered her with the heavy, warm blanket he had taken from the tiny cupboard in their hotel room. She didn't need it; it was a hot and sticky night, but he didn't like the thought of her uncovered.

'I love you, Bella.'

'Yes, Daddy,' she murmured.

Henry closed the car door and put his hand on his forehead. He looked up at the sky, black and studded with glinting stars, a million of them visible in the clear night.

'Monsieur,' came a voice behind him.

Henry turned to face the nurse who was in charge of the night shift.

'*Attendez de parler au médecin.* Do not take her. Doctor Albert, he will want to talk with you. *Je vous en prie. Bella n'est pas en état de voyager.*'

Henry straightened his shoulders and spoke calmly to this kind woman who had helped care for Bella for the last few weeks.

'Please don't worry, Sylvie. It's fine. We would like Bella at home with us. She will be well cared for. Don't forget I am a doctor myself. Please. Don't worry. *Ne vous inquiétez pas. Merci. Merci beaucoup.*'

Then he turned away from her concern.

He climbed into the car, ignoring her continuing protestations.

Don't you see? he wanted to say to the nurse. It doesn't matter. It doesn't matter where she is or what else is happening. Nothing matters anymore because she is going to die.

My daughter is going to die.

SEVENTY-TWO

My head spins. I feel lightheaded and close my eyes.

And she is there. In bed. There are crisp white sheets and her blonde curls fan the pillow. The window is open and white curtains billow in the breeze like a pair of tethered ghosts. She has a plaster on her arm, a tiny dot of dried blood in its centre. Thin, her skin pale and tinged yellowed, she has dark circles around her eyes that look as if they are melting deep into her head.

I creep closer. At first I think she might be dead, but then her eyes half open and she turns her head towards me. A weak smile brushes across her face.

I gently put my hand in hers.

'Hello.' Her voice is almost inaudible. Breathless.

'Hello.' I hear my voice whisper.

I climb onto the bed and lie beside her, curl my body into her hot, sweaty heat, and slip my fingers into hers. I will pretend she's my sister because I miss her so much. I miss her to play with and to laugh with and I miss her to look after me. I miss her so much my heart aches.

'I love you, Dory,' I say softly. 'I love you so much.'

SEVENTY-THREE

Henry Campbell — 16th August 1989

They drove through the night so both children would sleep. It rained so heavily he could hardly see through the windscreen. They stopped only to throw the teddy bear and the child's nightie into the sea, which heaved in the darkness like an ocean of oil. He picked his way through the wet darkness to the water's edge and hurled the items as far as he could.

Climbing back into the car he felt as if he'd been shot in the stomach, his blood draining from his body, leaving nothing but a useless husk. As he drove he listened to them. Bella's snatched breaths coming as if each might be her last, as if her body was running out of battery. The other one muttering quietly to herself, almost under her breath. They had made a bed for her on the floor between the front and rear seats. Hidden her with coats. Elaine had a blanket at hand to cover her fully if the need arose.

He had no idea what he was doing. All he knew was he loved his daughter and he loved his wife, and the thought of losing both of them was threat enough to drive his exhausted mind and body along in this madness. He was a criminal. A monster. This is what he had become. He had allowed Elaine to show him the scar on the girl's little arm – deep and red, he suspected it was indeed a burn, perhaps from a cigarette but more likely a cigar – her dirty fingernails, her pallid skin. He listened as Elaine told him how the child had reached up to her, grabbed hold of her, held on, when she'd found her abandoned in a small copse of trees. Henry had gone himself to the campsite. He pretended to help in the search so he could get close to the parents, search for evidence to either support what Elaine insisted, that the parents weren't fit to care for her, or dismiss it. And he'd seen him, her father, drunk and dishevelled, shouting and swearing, picking a fight with a journalist who asked him a simple and well-meaning question. His wife with fingerprint-bruising encircling her upper arms. Their other child cowering behind her mother's legs, eyeing her father with wary caution. He found himself starting to inveigle the idea into his mind. He began to wonder if Elaine was right. Perhaps it *was* in the child's best interests to stay with them. He began to believe the fairy tale.

For the duration of the journey he expected to see flashing lights in his rear view mirror. Before they passed through customs to board the ferry, they covered the child on the floor with the blanket.

His heart hammered.

Please find her, the voice in his head begged. *Please let her stir or cry out. Let them find her.*

But the girl didn't stir and Elaine bade the *douane* a cheery *bonsoir,* flashed him that smile of hers, flicked her hair and thanked him in creamy tones. Henry caught the man's longing. He'd seen it before in so many men, but for the first time he felt no jealousy. That part of him was dead.

When they pulled up outside their elegant house in the middle of a smart Bristol crescent, Elaine opened the back door of the car and scooped up the other child. She held her tightly and cooed softly in her ear.

'My miracle,' he heard her whisper. 'My God-given miracle.'

Bella sat in the back seat, propped up, a pillow against the window. She was sleeping, her face serene and peaceful. He didn't want to wake her. A small part of him hoped she had passed away, so she could be free of it all, but then she stirred. She tried to smile at him, but her wan little body wouldn't work for her. The effort was too great and he saw a wave of pain pass over her eyes.

He made up the bed in the spare room. The other child was in Bella's bed, in Bella's pyjamas, being read Bella's books by Bella's mother.

The next day they rang letting agents in towns across Oxfordshire, Berkshire, Buckinghamshire and Hampshire.

'We need a house with immediate occupancy. Furnished if possible. A house with a large garden and preferably fenced with gates. My wife,' he hesitated, 'likes to feel secure.'

They left Bristol, severing all ties with their old life, with their friends and with their family, and moved to The Old Vicarage before the week was out. Fraser didn't understand. Henry told him he'd had enough of trying to make things run smoothly between his family and his wife.

'But not seeing us again?' Fraser had asked. Henry knew this was devastating his brother. He would have been devasted, too, if he wasn't already past the point of utter devastation. 'Don't make that call now, Hen. It's a stressful time for you. Have a break. Get some space to sort yourselves out. You need to process everything you're dealing with. Maybe a few months. Then we'll have lunch together. Somewhere neutral. We won't step out of line. Mum is desperate to see Bella.'

'No,' Henry said, too strongly. 'No, it always ends in a fight. I'm not putting up with it anymore. Elaine and I need to concentrate on our family. It's too stressful to deal with your crap on top of everything else.'

'What crap? It's not *our* crap! It's *her*—'

'Enough, Fraser!' Henry pinched the bridge of his nose and bit back his tears. 'I just ... we just can't ... see you again. Any of you.' He took a deep breath. 'Elaine is my wife and she comes first. Life is too short to try to make something work that will never work.' He glanced at Elaine, who narrowed her eyes and nodded. 'You had your chance with us. It's done with.'

The rectory in Oxfordshire was ideal. The elderly owner was in two minds about whether to sell. She had grown up in the house and it was dear to her heart. She was happy for them to start renting immediately, then discuss the purchase at a later date if they liked it enough and she decided she could part with it. They had savings, plus Elaine's inheritance from her father's death a few years earlier. Money, thankfully, wasn't a concern, and a few weeks later they offered the lady a price well above the market rate and it was accepted without hesitation. The Old Vicarage was theirs.

SEVENTY-FOUR

I knock on the door of the house in Bristol, but there's no answer. I peer in the front-room window, attempting to see through the cobwebs, dirt and grime that coat it. There's no sign of him so I return to the door and knock again. When he still doesn't come, I unlock the door and push it open, but I don't go inside immediately.

'Hello?'

My voice echoes in the hallway. The house smells musty, the air thick with the putrid-sweet of unemptied bins and stale alcohol.

'Hello?' I call again.

But nobody's here. Mark Tremayne has gone. At first I assume he might just be out, but when I go into the kitchen the stench of rotting food hits me hard. I gag and lift the back of my hand to my nose to block the smell as best I can.

There are no pigeons on the window ledge. Just feathers and droppings in piles. I shudder as I walk through the rooms, taking in my father's wasted life. This was his penance. Living alone in this squalid filth with only his sins and pigeons for company.

This time I brave the stairs. On a half-landing is a bathroom. More grot. More vile smells. I close the door on it and ascend the next set of stairs. The room I reach first has a sign on it that makes my stomach clench. A wooden plaque, painted pink, stained with age and dirt, the word *Bella* painted in curling green letters. I open the door. A stained mattress and a discoloured pillow with no pillowcase lie on the floor, which is stripped of any carpet, the bare floorboards ringed by strips of carpet-gripper. The walls have wallpaper on them, sky-blue and pink stripes, with coordinating rabbits skipping merrily around a border at waist height. There is more mess, food containers, rubbish, dirty clothes. Beer cans and empty bottles of drink. Ashtrays that overflow with cigarette ends. At the edge of the room, beneath the window, I notice mouse or rat droppings and my stomach heaves. I don't bother to look in the other two rooms up there. The doors are open. There is nothing in them. Just emptiness.

I walk back down the stairs and into the living room, if you can call it that. On the floor by the chair is a newspaper. On the front page is my picture and a headline. His battered radio has gone.

I don't know what I was expecting. I know he has gone, but it doesn't make me happy or sad, angry or relieved. Instead I am numb. It suits me that he's gone. I don't want to trawl through all of this mess in the courts. I want to get on with my life. In Cornwall – with Dawn and our mother and my unborn child – I have a fresh beginning. It's as if everything up until this moment has been a prelude to the main show. With him gone there is one less obstacle with which to contend.

I have no idea what will become of Mark Tremayne. My father. As far as I know he has no money, no home, no possessions other than those foetid items he could carry, the old radio and perhaps a few clothes. I don't want to think of him out there. I have no affection for the man, but the idea of him out on the streets with nobody to love and nowhere to call home is unsettling.

I hope he finds somewhere warm to sleep, somewhere he can find help, maybe even salvation. I hope somewhere he finds peace.

SEVENTY-FIVE

'Are you sure I can't make you a sandwich?' Miss Young has been offering to feed me for over an hour. She scratches her left breast and readjusts herself.

'It's very kind of you, Miss Young, but—'

'Do call me Suzie, dear.'

'I'm really not that hungry.'

'No wonder you didn't tell me what was in his letter,' she says. 'What a shock that must have been?'

'It was.' I ignore the question in her voice and don't expand further. 'It really was so kind of you to take the cat.'

'Bless him,' she says. 'He does have a tendency to wander home. I had to find a bit of wood to block up the cat flap to stop him getting back inside the house, and now he spends a lot of time sitting on the doorstep waiting for your—' She stops herself and shifts awkwardly. 'I mean, Mrs Campbell.'

'Well, he'll find it hard to get back to The Old Vicarage from Cornwall.'

Her face contorts in horror.

'Or you can keep him?' I say quickly, resting my hand on her arm. 'You know, if you've grown attached.'

'I have rather.'

I smile. I'm happy for her to have him; I'm not sure I really wanted to take him back to Cornwall to slink about in my new life. I gesture towards Henry Campbell's filing cabinet. 'Would you mind if I got on with this, Miss Young. There's an awful lot to get through.' I bend down and press an orange sticker to a cardboard box so the rubbish clearance team know to skip it and the discarded papers it contains.

It is a massive job, sorting through the Campbells' effects. The solicitor asked if I was sure I wanted to sell the house. I hadn't hesitated and being back here I have no doubt at all. The place makes me on edge and anxious. The brick walls seem higher than I remember, and even with the curtains and doors open, I feel totally hemmed in. There's a malignancy about the place, a deep-rooted evilness. The house represents the Campbells, the place they'd kept me veiled from my family, yet at the same time, those happy childhood memories I have are glued to every brick and blade of grass. I hate it here and I want to get away as quickly as possible.

I open Henry's filing cabinet. There's nothing much in the drawers, just his fountain pen and two bottles of ink – one blue, one black – a small box of paper clips and a blotter, receipts and miscellaneous papers. I check every sheet for anything that might offer information about Bella Campbell. When I happen across something handwritten I try not to think of his hopeless body and the slick of blood beneath. So far I've found nothing and I tip the contents of the drawers into orange-stickered boxes.

Green stickers go on the furniture I am selling, his desk, the brass lamp, the leather armchair, anything that looks like it might have value. I avoid looking at the portrait of Elaine, as I stick an orange sticker on its corner. The chair and rug have already gone. Miss Young made sure anything with Henry's blood on it was removed immediately, which was kind of her.

I break to eat the ham sandwich I made this morning, and then the slice of fruitcake that Miss Young thrust on me. It is delicious. I sit on the overgrown lawn. It's close, the air heavy, and the flies buzz around me. The grass is yellowed with thirst, and weeds and greenfly have overrun the roses.

Feeling recharged I head back inside. Most of the rooms are done, the items within are decorated with dots that portend their fate. There is one room left to do, however.

The attic.

By now I have convinced myself that the boxes that must be in the attic will contain answers: papers, hospital records, bank accounts.

Nothing that can hurt you.

I pause at the bottom of the narrow stairs and look up. It's as dark and eerie as it always was. I step onto the lowest tread and hear Elaine's voice telling me not to.

'It's dangerous,' her voice says. 'Dangerous! Don't you ever, *ever* go up there.'

I force myself to continue up. I tell myself not to be ridiculous, that it's just an attic, but I hold the screwdriver I'm carrying in front of me like a sword, nonetheless. When I get to the top of the stairs, I take out the key from my pocket, neatly labelled with a tag and Henry's handwriting, and unlock the door. There is no handle, and I hope the screwdriver will do the job. I push it into the square thread that would usually hold the handle and turn it. The latch clicks and, with my heart pounding, I swing open the door.

I gasp in shock. My knees buckle and I have to catch myself on the door frame.

Pushed up against the left wall, its head tucked into the sloping eaves, is a bed.

It's the same bed I've dreamt about so many times. I step into the room and walk slowly over to it. As well as the bed there's a familiar bedside table and two white curtains that hang limply at the dusty window, cased in cobwebs. A pair of child's slippers rest neatly on the floor. A white cotton nightie is folded at the foot of the bed.

I've seen this all before.

I have a flash of what the bed feels like to lie on. I close my eyes and push my fingers against my temples. I walk over and touch my fingers to the bedspread. I catch a smell of cleaning fluids and disinfectant long since gone, but there in the back of my memory. The sheets are thick with dust and the bedspread has moth holes eaten into it. I lie on the bed and curl myself into a ball. It feels familiar. Did I sleep here? Was this my room? Fear creeps over me. I close my eyes. Hear the thunderous sound of feet on the stairs. Shouting. I mustn't be in this room. She can't find me. I want to hide, but it's too late. She's there in the doorway. Her face is dark and angry. As frightening as the monster man who haunted my dreams.

'You are *never* to come up here! Do you hear me?' She is puce with rage. Grabs my wrist. Yanks me out of the room. 'I have told you time and again! This room is out of bounds. Do you not understand!'

'I'm sorry, Mama.'

'Get downstairs.'

I sit up and swing my legs around so I'm sitting on the edge of the bed. Beside me, on the bedside table, is a painted wooden box and a brown leather photo album like the ones Henry kept in his study. I reach for the box and open it. Inside is a plastic ballerina held in a frozen pirouette, a small oval mirror behind her on a pink satin background. I turn it over to find the small metal key that winds it and turn it a couple of times. Then I open the lid again and the music starts and I recognise it. Tears spring in my eyes, though I'm not exactly sure why. I draw my sleeve across my face to dry them and reach for the leather album. Unlike the other albums, which now sit in a box with orange stickers attached to them, this has no gold lettering on the spine. I open the cover and there is a photograph under the protective film. It shows a group of men. Five in the front, seated on chairs, the others stood proudly behind them, their chins lifted, hands behind their backs. It's a sports photograph, a hockey team. The photo is grainy and the hairstyles dated. Written on the mount is a list of names and *King's College, London. First XI.* Henry Campbell sits in the middle and wears the captain's cap. His face and shoulders are strong and lifted, his muscles well-defined, his pose commanding, so very different to the bookish, withdrawn man with whom I grew up. I turn the pages and see more photographs from Henry's university days. Then Henry and Elaine. Henry is wearing graduation gowns and holding a scroll tied with red ribbon. Elaine is beaming up at him, her honey-coloured hair for once set free, loose and fanning her shoulders. And then their wedding day. A long white dress. Wide smiles. Family and friends surrounding them. I don't want to see this. I don't want to see how they were before.

I turn to the next page and stare at the facing photo.

I rock back my head, take a few deep breaths of air, then look again at the picture. It's Elaine. She is in her hospital bed holding a newborn baby and smiling for the camera. She is years older than the wedding photo, but her skin is radiant. Her new dressing gown, crisp and white, is buttoned up to her chin. Her hair shines. Flowers surround her, mostly roses, in an array of colours. There are hundreds of cards and a large, pink teddy bear holding a red heart in its paws. A baby sleeps in her arms. Serene and peaceful, her light blonde hair glistening as if she's been dusted with gold. Beneath the photo, in Henry Campbell's nauseating writing:

> *Bella Grace Campbell, our beloved and longed-*
> *for child, 2nd September 1984*

The second of September.

My stomach flips. Their child's birthday. I sit on the bed and think back over all those sullen, disappointing September-the-seconds. They had never belonged to me and it was no wonder the Campbells didn't celebrate. All they could think of was her. Each year it was her present they wrapped, her name on the card. It was the one day they couldn't pretend that she had never existed.

The rest of the album is filled with family snaps of the three of them. Each is lovingly labelled. Bella's first footsteps. Bella on a swing in the park with Elaine. Bella and Henry on the beach in Dorset. I touch my fingers to the picture. The sand Elaine told me she hated. Henry is smiling, tanned and muscular, the proud dad showing off his sandcastle, as Bella grins at his feet in a flowery swimsuit with a frilly skirt. The photograph is dated two years before I was taken.

I turn the next page.

It's her.

It's the girl from my dreams and my room at the hostel and the church. In this picture she is dressed in a tartan pinafore and red shoes, her hair a mass of blonde curls.

I look down at the bed and see her. She is lying there, pale and weak. Her curls dress the pillow. She was in this room. *In this bed.* I met her. I have played with the music box. I talked to her. Heard her thin, sick voice. I called her Dory. The name I used to call Dawn. Then, when she went, she became Tori. In my muddled child's mind, confused, unrooted, displaced, Tori, the amalgamation of the sister I loved and lost and the child who lay in this bed, shut away and dying.

I look around the room, a shrine to Bella Campbell, to their child who died.

I dry the tears that have begun to fall unchecked down my cheeks and then turn to the last page. There's no photo, but instead, trapped beneath the film, is a single sheet of blue Smythson notepaper with Henry's copperplate handwriting curled across it.

SEVENTY-SIX

Henry Campbell – 27th August 1989

Henry made a bedroom for Bella in the attic room. He made it look nice, as cosy as he could. He bought white bed linen with an embroidered trim and off-the-peg white curtains. He crept into her old room and took her music box, the wind-up one to which she loved to listen, while staring mesmerised at the tiny dancer who slowly revolved as the tinny notes played. He sat with her day and night, nursed her, changed her drip, stroked her forehead and administered morphine. Elaine came in occasionally, but she never interacted. She wouldn't look at her, wouldn't touch her. In her mind she was already gone.

One day he had left her to make a small bowl of soup in the hope that she might eat and when he returned he found the other child sitting on the edge of her bed. She was holding Bella's hand and chattering away, more animated than he had ever seen her. He stood in the doorway and watched as she touched Bella's face. Bella turned her head. The other girl smiled, marched her fingers up and down Bella's arm like a drunken soldier. He watched Bella's hand flex open and closed, as a smile crossed her face like a glimpse of sunlight from behind a passing cloud. He walked over to them and took hold of the girl and gently led her away from his daughter and out of the room.

At the door she stopped walking and looked up at him with those remarkable green eyes. 'Can I stay with Dory?'

He didn't answer her, merely moved her out of the door, then closed it and collapsed on the floor and cried, sobbing for his daughter, for his wife, and for the green-eyed girl.

Elaine found her in the attic again a few days later. Henry had slipped out to bathe while Bella slept. He heard a crash and a scream and then Elaine erupting. There had been so much shouting he'd jumped out of the bath and run, dripping wet, into the hallway to see her dragging the child down the stairs. Then she marched back up, muttering expletives, and locked the door, removing the handle. He returned to their bedroom and listened to Elaine shouting at the child in the next-door room.

'It's dangerous, do you hear me? I told you that, Bella! I told you. If you go up to that room, very, *very* bad things will happen to you. The monsters will get you. The monsters will eat you up. Promise me. Promise me you won't ever go up there again!'

'I won't,' the girl said, over and over. 'I promise, I won't.'

Bella died three days later. He held her close to him as she took her last torturous breath. His sickening guilt and the physical pain he felt rendered him immobile. He sat with her cradled in his arms, kissing her forehead, whispering his love for her until dusk. When he told Elaine, her face registered no emotion. Impassively she turned and walked away from him. As she reached the bottom of the stairs her knees crumpled and she threw a hand up against the banister to catch her fall.

SEVENTY-SEVEN

Henry Campbell – 10th September 1989

My darling Bella,

Today, my love, I lost you. I held you in my arms as you drew your very last breath. I carried you down the stairs and outside. It was dark, not even the moon was in the sky. The air was cool on my skin, fresh with the earlier rain, for which I was grateful. I wrapped you in a blanket so you would be warm. My tears fell on your hair and on your skin but I didn't wipe them off. They stay with you. I carried you up to the large oak tree and laid you gently on the grass. I told you I'd build a swing in that tree when you got better. Do you remember? Even though I knew it was impossible, I never stopped hoping. But I was wrong to hope. As I dug, my sweat mixed with my tears as the spade's dull thud beat into the ground. She wanted you somewhere else, somewhere isolated and far away, scrubland she said. But I need you near me. I need you in a place where I can visit you, sit with you, remember you. I need to be able to feel you.

She loved you too, my darling. I promise you. It might not have seemed that way at the end, but she loved you so much, the thought of not having you drove her mad. You were all she ever wanted. For years it was only the promise of you that kept her going. And then the cruel twist of fate. Nothing we could do to save you. Her world was ended. The thought of living without you changed her. Twisted her. She lost her mind. I wish I could have done something to help her, but her devastation pushed her past the point of help. The deep love she had for you warped her beyond repair.

My darling, I love you so very much.

Forgive me.
I wish you peace,

Your father

SEVENTY-EIGHT

I go downstairs and open the back door. The longhaired grey cat is waiting outside. He loops around my ankles, purring to be picked up. I bend to stroke him and he closes his eyes and lifts himself off his front feet to meet my hand.

The sky has closed in.

Perhaps it will rain. I walk across the lawn and listen to the birds calling to each other from the canopies. I remember again how she taught me about the trees, holding my hand, picking up leaves and describing their structures. I glance down at the weeping willow, which dips into the pond, the still, brown water reflecting the tree in perfect symmetry. The grass crackles under my feet, insects flit over it, grass-hoppers bounce out of the yellowed shafts. I think of her watching her child die, a child loved to the point of madness, and for the first time I feel sympathy for her. And Henry. A broken man. Lost and grieving for all those years.

The oak tree rises out of the garden and I am drawn towards it. I see him digging. That small body lying still beside him. Blonde curls inching out of her blankety shroud. I see him crying, tears falling unchecked on the freshly turned earth. He places her gently into the hole he has dug, covering her over with his bare hands, caressing the earth with the same love with which he will craft the bench that encircles the trunk of the magnificent tree.

The bench is covered with broken twigs and leaves. I brush a few away and sit, then look up through the branches, grey sky and clouds visible in the gaps between.

It would be easy to collapse. Easy to give in, to curl up and lick my wounds beneath the weight of the past, like my father, like Henry Campbell. I could allow history to overshadow any chance of a future. I rub my hands over the rough wood of the bench and tell myself that from this point onwards I have a choice. There are two paths I can follow. I can either be the child who was taken from her family, who was locked away by desperate, damaged people who made her dependent, who allowed her to love them. Or I can be someone else, thankful for what I have now, a product of my past but not defined by it. Bella Campbell didn't have a chance at a life.

But I do.

I do have a choice. For me and for my unborn child.

I place my hands on my stomach and feel for the life, the pulsing beat of the baby within me. I would die for this child. I know that already.

I think of Bella. 'I hope you are at peace, because,' I say, my voice loud against the stillness, 'I am now. I wasn't sure I could be, but I am. I've found peace.'

There's a flurry of leaves, a murmuring through the branches like a whispered voice. Something catches my eye. Down by the pond. A flash of golden curls. Bare feet running through the grass...

Then nothing.

I scan the trees, searching for her, but she's gone.

The first spots of rain begin to fall. I turn my face up into them and smile. A clean slate. Rain to rinse the world of its sins. I head back down towards the house. The cat is nowhere to be seen, no doubt headed back to Miss Young's to escape the weather. I walk into the kitchen and lock the back door behind me. Then I go into each room and close the curtains. In the hallway, I run a hand over the console table, leaving two finger tracks in the dust.

I hope whoever moves in will have a happy life here. I close my eyes and hear myself playing somewhere upstairs, catch the smell of beef stew drifting in from the kitchen where a radio plays softly in the background. Memories.

All just memories.

I am closing early today. I put a sign in the window apologising for it. I wouldn't usually close on a Saturday afternoon, but it's a special day.

I walk home and make sure Mum is ready in time for the taxi. We live in a small fisherman's cottage overlooking the sea in the centre of St Ives. It has a narrow staircase and low ceilings, and the sitting room has an open fire and dark beams. It was bought with the Campbells' money and to begin with I worried that their presence would hang in the bricks and mortar, but it doesn't. It's a happy home. They would have wanted me to be happy, I'm sure of that. Dawn moved in with Craig and Stacey about six months ago. She wasn't sure it would work, but all three of them are so happy now, especially Stacey. Mum and I have Nino. Mum is besotted with her, and spends most evenings sitting in our living room with the cat curled up on her lap.

I still think about the Campbells. I try not to, but it's impossible to keep them away sometimes. The police found the remains of Bella's body near the oak tree. Even though I knew they would, it was a shock. When the police telephoned me I collapsed and sobbed. Dawn did too.

Mum helps look after my son, Matthew, my beautiful boy. She says it's a way to make up for not having looked after me. She still talks about her guilt, guilt about losing me, guilt for allowing Mark to hurt Dawn and me. The therapist she sees says it's understandable. Guilt and fear caused her to close herself off, to split her inner world from the external and, as she recovers, the feelings that prompted her elective disconnect will still be there. Mum sees herself as complicit in both the Campbells' crime and my father's abuse. Being with Matthew helps her and from my point of view it means I can concentrate on making the café work. I contacted the owner and offered to buy it not long after I accepted an offer on the house in Bristol. It was a rash decision, given I have no experience of running a business, and signing the contracts was terrifying. But Fi has been a great help. She practically ran the hostel singlehandedly, kept all the books in immaculate order and is showing me how to do it. I don't know what I'd do without her, her friendship as well as her expertise.

I've called the café *The Merrymaid*. I love it and can't imagine doing anything else. I cook everyday, make my own bread and cakes, quiches, homemade cottage pies and lasagnes, and Jenny, the girl who works for me on the days I don't go in, makes a coffee that beats even Phil's.

The taxi drops us outside the pub in Zennor and we cross the road to the church. As I climb the three steps and open the gate I pause briefly. The churchwarden has removed the headstone with my name on it and where it stood is a mound of bare soil like a scar in the grass. Looking at it doesn't make me feel sad or morbid or even regretful, instead I feel uplifted. I see it as a physical sign of my rebirth. It's a powerful thing to come back from the dead, and I love who I am now. I am becoming more self-assured, more confident, and I have friends in St Ives. Many of them are other mothers. We meet up and talk about baby stuff, banal things to do with feeding, routines and exhaustion that don't seem important but really are.

There's my support group too. It took me ages to stand up and talk about what happened to me. It does help, although I fought tooth and nail against going at the beginning. I kept trying to tell everybody I hadn't tried to kill myself, but it fell on deaf ears. It was Dawn who persuaded me to try it, and I'm glad; it helps to hear other people talk about their stories, their issues, the bleak times when they felt they just couldn't go on. I understand it.

Greg and I still see each other, not romantically, but for our son. When I told him about the baby, I expected him to run for the hills, but he surprised me. He wants to be involved in his son's life and he tries hard to be a good dad. He doesn't always manage it, but he loves

Matthew, and Matthew loves him back. Of course, I have reservations. There's a chance that one day I will have to pick up the pieces, comfort my son if his dad disappoints him, but at the moment Greg is stepping up to the mark and it's important he and Matthew are allowed a relationship. We live close to each other, so he pops in often, and officially they spend one day and a night together each week. Greg picks him up at ten and drops him back the following morning, always mucky and tired, but with a smile on his face. Greg is excited about teaching him to surf. He thinks he's got a world champion on his hands ... something about his balance.

I go to the front of the church, my son clasped in my arms. He's so beautiful. He has blond hair like his dad, not very much but enough, and his eyes have turned a deep, dark brown. He's as good as gold. I cannot believe how much one person can love another. We had a difficult birth. He was quick. Too quick, and we only just made it to the hospital. Dawn was with me. Matthew had the cord wrapped around his neck. The midwife told me I had to push him out quickly; there was an urgency in her voice that scared me witless. Dawn held my hand and was amazing. She has this calm about her, an inner strength that I envy. It was she who told me, while sobbing with joy, that he was a boy. I would lay my life down for this child. Since having him, I have been able to forgive Elaine a little more. Until he was born I had no idea what loving a child with all your body, heart and soul would feel like, how encompassing it is, how you subsequently regard everything else in relation to that child. I can't imagine the pain of losing him, of what that might do to me. Losing their children sent my mother and Elaine to the far reaches of their minds, and now I can understand that a little more.

Mum looks amazing today. She turns to me and smiles when I sit down. Her skin glows and her hair has been curled specially. She's wearing a wide-brimmed hat. We shopped for it in Truro last week.

'Ready?' I say to her.

'I am, my darling, and how's my best boy?' She kisses Matthew's forehead.

Matthew Trystan Tremayne. Our best boy.

I hand him to her and she cradles him like he is made of eggshell. 'I can't think when I've been happier,' she whispers.

I rub her shoulder.

The music starts and we turn to look at the back of the church. My stomach is a knot of butterflies.

Dawn walks with tentative steps along the aisle of the church. I can see how scared she is. Her lips are quivering in the smile on which I told her to concentrate. She has goose bumps, even though it's June. Her dress is a simple ivory shift, her bouquet a single white amaryllis. Her mousy hair is loosely pinned and a lick of mascara outlines her green eyes. She looks exquisite. I turn to Mum, who's crying now, and give her a reassuring squeeze.

The music stops and Craig shifts uncomfortably. His suit doesn't quite fit properly and I know he can't wait to get out of it and into jeans and a sweater. He smiles at Dawn and she smiles back. They both look at Stacey, who reaches out to take her mother's flower. She kisses them and sits down next to me. I take her hand.

The vicar addresses the small but intimate gathering and Craig reaches for Dawn's hands. As they begin their vows, Matthew starts fussing.

'Oh dear, I think he's hungry, Mum,' I whisper. 'Do you think I can feed him in here or shall I take him outside?'

'I don't think the Merrymaid will mind.' She strokes my son's head.

Matthew quietens as soon as he finds my breast. He reaches up and slips his fingers between my lips.

'You know,' whispers my mother. 'You used to do that when I fed you.'

We hold the reception back in the café. There are about thirty of us. I unwrap trays of sandwiches and cakes, and we open champagne and hand it around. Mum stands at the front and chinks her glass with a teaspoon until everyone quietens.

'Dawn asked me to do the speech today. I think she quite likes hearing my voice.' Mum smiles as everybody laughs, and then she lifts a piece of paper and reads with no stumbling or stuttering and a soporific lilt that seems to sing the words.

'*Something happened to our family, the kind of tragic thing that people pray never happens to them. I won't talk about that, not on this happiest of days, but to understand Dawn and how precious she is, we need to be aware of it. When I was lost, Dawn put her life aside to care for me. It's something I can't ever forgive myself for, but sadly I wasn't strong enough to fight the darkness that took hold of me. I will always be grateful for her deep love and selfless devotion. To know such a person is the greatest of honours. To call her my daughter, the greatest of pleasures. Today marks the start of her future. Hers and her Craig's. This day is the beginning of their lives as a family. It's time for her to live for herself, with the man she loves, and their amazing daughter.*' The love she feels towards my sister shines out of her like the beam from a lighthouse. '*Every now and then the world is graced with an angel. One of these angels stands in our midst. This child came to me as the morning sun rose over the sea and the birds broke into song. My Dawn. My angel. May every day from now be blessed with the love and happiness you deserve.*'

My mother joins me a little later on the low wall overlooking the harbour, where I am sitting with Matthew, who is fiddling intently with my necklace.

'They're so happy, aren't they?'

'Yes. They are. And you?' I say turning to her. 'Are you happy?'

'The happiest I could be.'

She reaches over and takes my hand and we both turn our heads and look out across the sea, past the harbour wall and out beyond, to where the waves swell and crash.

We sit quietly. I don't tell my mother that I can still feel her – Bella, Tori, the Merrymaid, whoever she is – but I can. She watches me. Deep beneath the heaving grey sea, she is always there, always watching. And sometimes, when the world feels heavy, when its walls begin to inch in on me and my tainted past threatens to eat away at my new life, I walk up on to the cliffs and there, alone with the wind and the gulls, I close my eyes and listen to her singing.

Acknowledgements

I am grateful to all those who surround me with friendship and laughter, and I appreciate every one of you, but there are a few people I'd like to mention for having been particularly important while writing this book. Broo Doherty. My agent. Dearest friend. This book belongs to both of us. Karen Sullivan, I am so proud to be part of 'Team Orenda'. You are a force of nature with a genuine passion for books and authors. Thank you for loving this story, for your invaluable input, and for producing this book so very beautifully. Mark Swan, you have perfectly captured the spirit of my story in your stunning cover and I still get tingles when I see it. West Camel, your eagle eyes are second to none. Thank you for your enthusiasm for this book. David Headley, giver of legendary hugs, thank you for lending me the best bookshop in the world, Goldsboro Books, to launch these books of mine. I am privileged to have the support of many incredible writers. I'd particularly like to thank Iona Grey, Hannah Beckerman, Tammy Cohen, Clare Mackintosh, Lucy Atkins, Cesca Major, Kerry Fisher, Jenny Ashcroft, Susi Holliday, Claire Dyer and Louise Douglas. Thank you to Mari Hannah for sage advice at just the right moment. To Amanda Keats for some super editorial suggestions. Sian, you've read this far too many times! Thank you for your input, and also your unwavering support in everything I do, always. I'd like to thank the generous-hearted blogging community, a group of people with a remarkable love of reading who share their passion so keenly. Thank you for getting behind me, and my books. You're all awesome. Particular mention goes to Anne Cater, Liz Barnsley, Dawn Crooks, Cami Cameron and Sophie Hedley for their almost constant cheerleading. And writer Edward Ian Kendrick for the same. There are a special group of crime writers, a group that must stay nameless, who have made me laugh every day for the last year without fail. Your (mostly filthy) wit, advice and camaraderie has been unbeatable and never lacking. You're a wonderful group of people, dear to me, and you know who you are. I'm constantly touched by the generous support of my gorgeous friends. A special mention to Sarah Bell, Nell Williams, Anette Crick, Lucy Jacobs, Sara Crane, Sophie Pentecost, Nacera Guerin, Vanessa Fisher and Polly Kemp. You literally rock and one day you'll cotton on and ask for a percentage! Thank you for recommending my books and for always asking when my next one is coming. To Dieter Newell, who very generously supported CLIC Sargent by bidding for a character name in this book as part of the 'Get In Character' fundraising auction. CLIC Sargent is a fabulous charity with which I am delighted to be involved. Thank you to my family. My rock. My parents, my sister, and my three daughters who take my breath away. My love for you all knows no bounds and is the foundation for my obsession with the delicacy and importance of family bonds. And lastly, to Chris, my soul mate. Thank you for challenging me, for reading every word I write, for your encouragement, and for your love. And, baby, I love you right back.